DEMAND OF DESIRE

His mouth left her lips, moving to her ear, whispering hoarsely, "Let me love you."

There was no need to ask. In the shadows of the candlelight, her closed eyes were shrouded beneath bluish lids, but the intensity of her expression betrayed her desire. This time, she did not stiffen, but gave herself up to the strange sensation of his palm brushing her nipples lightly. She tried to bring his head back to hers, but instead he bent lower, to tease her aroused nipples with his tongue. His hands seemed to be everywhere, urging her on, sliding down over her flat stomach, stroking along her hips and thighs. And still his mouth and tongue moved over her breasts until she thought she could stand no more.

"Please," she whispered.

"Love me, Sarah," he urged, covering her hungry body with his own. "Love me now. . . ."

Follow the Heart

Anita Mills

AN ONYX BOOK

ONYX
Published by the Penguin Group
Penguin Books USA Inc., 375 Hudson Street,
New York, New York, 10014 U.S.A.
Penguin Books Ltd, 27 Wrights Lane,
London W8 5TZ, England
Penguin Books Australia Ltd, Ringwood,
Victoria, Australia
Penguin Books Canada Ltd, 2801 John Street,
Markham, Ontario, Canada L3R 1B4
Penguin Books (N.Z.) Ltd, 182–190 Wairau Road,
Auckland 10, New Zealand
Penguin Books Ltd, Registered Offices:
Harmondsworth, Middlesex, England

First published by Onyx, an imprint of Penguin Books USA Inc.

First Printing, August, 1990
10 9 8 7 6 5 4 3 2 1

Foreword

From the beginning of European colonization in America, it was inevitable that France and Great Britain should clash over territorial claims. While initial French settlement was along the St. Lawrence River and the Great Lakes, it gradually extended into outposts in the Ohio and Champlain Valleys. The British colonies, although they were situated along the Atlantic coast, claimed all territories stretching westward, including the areas targeted for French expansion. A series of wars, called King William's War, Queen Anne's War, and King George's War were fought between 1689 and 1748.

The final and decisive struggle, termed the French and Indian War, took place between 1754 and 1763, and was actually the American phase of the Seven Years War in Europe. For the first two years, it was an undeclared war, prompted by the Iroquois' allowing British settlers into the Ohio Valley for the first time. The French, fearing to be shut off from the lucrative fur trade there, struck back, first in the Ohio Valley, then in upper New York.

By 1755, both France and Great Britain had committed regular troops to the struggle, and it looked as though Britain had the upper hand after victories in Nova Scotia and at Lake George. The French, however, retaliated by defeating the British at Fort Duquesne, giving rise to the career of an officer named George Washington, who managed to organize the colonial retreat.

On May 8, 1756, war was officially declared between the two nations, and the North American continent and India became the primary areas where Britain was determined to win. As William Pitt the Elder determined, when he came to power in 1757, France was to be driven out of America once and for all. But the first two years were beset by reverses, and France's colonial power was at its zenith.

My story opens during this time, when there was little to cheer the British. They'd lost Duquesne in the Ohio Valley, Oswego on Lake Ontario, and the French and their Indian allies were raiding deep into English colonial territory. Moreover, the French tactics, making use of the Indians' uncivilized methods of fighting, required a rethinking of how the war ought to be fought by the British. A partial answer lay in an alliance with the Iroquois League, also called the Six Nations, and in the formation of ranger units, beginning with Robert Rogers' Rangers.

Using Robert Rogers' journals, first published in 1765, and other sources far too numerous to list, I have portrayed actual events of that fateful winter and summer of 1757. While there were few pitched battles, the conflict was bitter, brutal, and bloody for those living in the frontier between New France and the British colonies. Massacres were common, and both sides were known to either tacitly condone or openly encourage the atrocities committed by their Indian allies.

Ultimately, New France was no match for the colonial and British armies. Their population, which numbered 80,000 or less, simply lacked the resources of colonies whose combined citizenry numbered 1,200,000 by 1750. But perhaps the conclusion of the war is best left to another book.

The Hastings family, Sarah Spender, Joanna, Kanendeyah, Etienne Reynaud, and Adam's rangers are wholly fictitious characters. The political and military events and the chronology in which they occurred are as accurately portrayed as possible. The Indians are shown as they appeared in contemporary accounts—savage and sadistic, yet often blindly loyal allies, too willing to fight in causes that ultimately would cost them their existence. In most cases, they were no worse than those who exploited them.

I give you a story of two people who face separation, betrayal, and the rigors of this war in their quest for happiness and love.

1

Spender's Hill: March 20, 1756

Still shaking with suppressed rage, Sarah Spender noticed the black felt ramillie lying where Lord Audley had left it. Furious, she picked up the offending article and marched to open the door, hoping he'd not yet mounted his horse.

"Wait!"

The viscount turned around expectantly, a broad, self-satisfied grin spreading across his handsome face. His eyes mocking her, he nodded. "I knew you were a sensible female, Sarah," he told her smugly, starting back toward her with a certain eagerness to his step.

Oh, how she wished to wipe that look from his face, to scratch those eyes, to humiliate him as he'd humiliated her. But he was the rich and powerful son of the Earl of Westerfield, and she but poor Sarah Spender, daughter to the late and quite disgraced Baron Spender. And she'd not dignify further his low opinion of her. Seething, she waited until he got closer, then sent his hat sailing over his head.

"I believe you forgot your ramillie, sir," she told him stiffly. "And I should not want you to return for it. Indeed, but if I should ever see you again, 'twill be far too soon to suit me."

The grin faded swiftly, replaced by chagrin, then cold anger. Telling herself that there was no further insult he could offer her, she turned, her back straight, her head high, and walked back up the front steps. His jaw worked as he stared after her with those cold blue eyes of his. At the top step, she paused quite briefly.

"Good day, Lord Audley."

Mastering his temper with an effort, Devin Hastings bent to retrieve the tricornered hat, then stood to jam it onto his carefully powdered locks. Telling himself that she was in no way more exceptional than any other female he'd ever wanted, he spoke in a harsh, clipped tone. "One day, Miss Spender, you will come to regret such rashness. There will be a time when you are heartily sick of drudging in someone else's house."

"At least I shall know my bread comes from honest labor, my lord," she retorted.

Before he could answer again, she retreated into the house, shutting the door and latching it. She started up the stairs, only to stop to lean against the newel post at the landing. She had to control her impotent fury—she had to—it would never do for Silas or Mrs. Findley to know what had happened. They'd be angry for her, and that would never serve—not when they'd been fortunate enough to gain positions in his father's house.

Forcing herself to look around her, to see the cracked plaster and the worn wood, she tried to take a more rational view of her circumstances. She did, after all, have other, more pressing business than Audley to consider. And she had to pack what little she could keep before her papa's creditors descended in a pack on the morrow. With that lowering thought, she made her way up the rest of the stairs to the chamber she'd called her own as long as she could remember. Mrs. Findley was already busy at the task of folding and sorting Sarah's things one last time. Wordlessly the girl moved to help her.

A clap of thunder, followed by a sudden wind against the panes of the old house, signaled the beginning of a storm. Well, at least his elegant lordship would get a sound soaking, she reflected with a small measure of satisfaction. Aye, and it would serve him more than right if he contracted the ague from the chill rain. At the very least, he ought to ruin his expensive clothes.

As the storm built in intensity, water seeped in around the edges of the windows, streaking the wall and forming small puddles on the floor. It was all of a piece, Sarah mused soberly as she turned her thoughts away from the odious Lord Audley. Folding her much-mended petti-coats and placing them neatly in the scarred leather-covered trunk, she had to admit the dreary weather reflected the state of her mind. Tomorrow, after the funeral, she'd be bound for a life of drudgery in York.

"It don't seem right, it don't," the old woman muttered behind her. "Them as got gets, and them as falls on bad times, well there's none t' give 'em anything." She held up Sarah's faded blue muslin and shook her head. "How yer to be a-mourning wi' naught but one black gown, and it not a-fittin' ye, well, 'tis beyond me understandin', it is."

Sarah looked down at the ugly black crepe that hung on her body and tried hard not to feel sorry for herself. "As 'tis York and there are none to know me there, I thought perhaps I should just wear what I have."

"In a reverend's house?" the housekeeper sniffed. "Aye, and he'll think ye ain't got proper feelin'."

"There's no help for it," the girl reminded her.

"It ain't right—yer but past a babe yerself, and here ye are, a-thinking yer a governess. Me 'n' Silas was talkin' on it this mornin', we was, and a-wondering if ye couldn't speak to the earl—"

"No."

"Humph! S'pose not, what with 'im a-bein' such a pinch-farthin', but it ain't as though he don't know ye. Besides, the pickle yer in is of 'is makin', ain't it?"

"No, the blame was Papa's—he was run off his legs ere Westerfield foreclosed." Sarah sighed and reached for the last of her nightrails. "Besides, the earl did not hold the gun to Papa's head, after all—that was Papa's doing."

"Might as well 'ave, don't ye know? But I s'pose you 'ave the right o' it—the alms plate'd be empty if it was a-waitin' for a Hastings to fill it. Still—"

"I don't want to hear it," Sarah cut in tiredly. "What's done is done, and I shall merely be glad when 'tis all over. I am glad enough that the Reverend Mr. Tompkins considered me sufficiently accomplished to teach his boys."

''Well, he ain't seen ye—he don't know as yer but nineteen and a green'un, I'll wager.''

That was the truth, but Sarah had been afraid to put that in her letter. It wasn't as though he'd be likely to turn her away, not when he'd not even asked for a character beyond a recommendation from Miss Wallace, the Friday-faced woman who'd been her own governess. And, judging from what he was willing to pay, he could not be excessively particular. Thirty pounds per year and a roof over one's head was scarce the sort of wage to make many apply, after all.

''Aye, and if Westerfield wouldn't aid ye, ye'd think p'raps Lord Audley . . . or the captain mayhap . . .''

''Captain Hastings does not know it, and as for Audley . . . well, it does not signify.''

Sarah's temper rose anew at the thought of Devin Hastings, and she had to bite back the scathing assessment of his character that came to mind. It would do no good to say it; she had to hold her tongue, she reminded herself again. But she still seethed every time she let herself think of him—the way he'd come over to offer his condolences and a slip of the shoulder at the same time. Did he think her father's suicide had deprived her of reason? Did he think her straitened circumstances made her any less a lady? Obviously, he did.

At first, she'd not been able to credit her ears—she *was* so green that she did not quite fathom his meaning when he said she ought to have fine silks and jewelry to call her own. At first she'd stared, thinking that he was somehow making her an offer of marriage. She flushed anew, recalling how he'd spelled it out for her then, telling her that these little arrangements were nothing out of the ordinary—his money for her favors. Maybe not for him, but to her such a thing was inconceivable.

And he'd been so arrogant when she'd refused him, saying that she'd think better of it when she was faced with struggling for her bread. And when she did, he'd still be waiting, he'd said. It was as though he thought her a plum ready to pick! Her fists clenched, bunching the thin lawn and creasing it. The insult was beyond bearing, and on reflection she wished she *had* scratched his eyes out. And now she could think of a dozen things she wished she'd said but hadn't. At least she'd had the satisfaction of throwing his hat in his face, and that was something. Beyond that, she had to admit that there wasn't much she could do about his insulting, insufferable manner.

"Now the captain—he ain't as bad as the rest of 'em, I'll be bound," the old woman went on. "I allus thought 'im a friend o' yers, ye know, what with 'im a-runnin' tame 'ere when yer mama was a-livin'."

"That was a very long time ago."

Sarah shook her head, trying not to think on Adam Hastings. Audley's younger brother was as different from the viscount as night unto day—there'd be none to ever hear of *him* offering a *carte blanche* to a girl whose father was scarce cold, or to any other unfortunate female, she was certain. No, she'd not dwell on Adam, not when she'd foolishly cherished a *tendre* for him for years. It would not serve now, and she knew it. Even younger sons of earls did not throw themselves away on penniless females.

"Don't s'pose ye could think again on young Mr. Wicklund, eh?" the old woman hinted. "It ain't as if he don't 'ave a care fer ye."

It was no secret to anyone at Spender's Hill that the vicar's son had offered for her—or that she'd turned him down. It had been hard to do it, terribly hard when she considered what she faced. But she had had to—she could not take advantage of a boy's youthful passion. To have married him would have caused a breach between him and his parents, not to mention the scandal of it. As he was not yet of age, they'd have had to make a run for Gretna, and then faced the possibility that Reverend Wicklund would have applied to annul the marriage. She'd have been branded a scheming adventuress, she was quite certain. And, besides, she did not love Roland quite like that. He was her dear friend, nothing more.

The fact of the matter was that she believed she loved Adam Hastings, and had for as long as she could remember. Against her resolve not to think on him, her thoughts turned yet again to him. He was dashing, he was hand-

some, and he was a daring soldier. At twenty-four, he'd
served his king well enough that there was talk that he
might make major without buying the promotion or without the influence of his wealthy family. But beyond that,
he was more than rich—he was kind.

Even now she could remember how he'd indulged her
when she was but a small girl, letting her follow him
about until Miss Wallace had put a stop to it. His brother,
on the other hand, had scarce noticed her until they'd met
again at Squire Lynch's Christmas party last year. Then
he was all attention, raising her papa's desperate hopes,
but now she knew his interest was anything but honorable. If only Adam had heard and come home . . . if only
Adam had returned her regard.

"Well, if 'twas meself, I'd just a taken Master Wicklund and let 'em try to interfere, don't ye know? I mean,
with the scandal and all, it ain't likely that that mama o'
his woulda turned on ye."

Reluctantly Sarah forced her thoughts away from Adam
once more. "Mrs. Findley, I'd as lief not discuss Roland
Wicklund or his mother. Suffice it to say that whatever
she might do publicly, she would most certainly make
the both of us pay quite dearly privately."

"Still—"

"No. There is no use wasting our time wishing things
were different, because they are not. Papa will be buried
on the morrow and then the creditors will come to take
whatever is left, you know."

"Oh, Miss Sarah!" The old woman's face contorted
piteously and her lower lip quivered. "But it ain't right!"

In an instant Sarah caught her in her arms and hugged
her. "Now, Findley, we are agreed—there are to be no
tears for what cannot be helped." Her own throat ached
and she had to swallow hard. "We must try to be glad
that we both shall have roofs over our heads."

"But your home!" the old woman wailed.

Sarah managed to look over the housekeeper's shoulder, forcing herself to see the shabby bedchamber for
what it was. " 'Tis but a poor place now, for all that I
shall miss it," she whispered, choking.

For a time they stood there, servant and mistress,

clinging to each other for comfort. Finally Sarah released the woman and stepped back. "What watering pots we are, to be sure, Finny," she murmured, reverting to the name she'd called her years before. A crooked smile twisted her mouth. "We shall survive, you know. We shall."

The old woman sniffed and wiped her face with a seamed hand. "It fair breaks m' heart, it does, 't see ye alone before the world."

"Now, Finny, you must not think such things." Sarah squared her shoulders resolutely. "I assure you that I consider 'twill be an adventure. Besides, I do not mean to be a governess forever." But even as she spoke, the words rang hollow, for in her heart she knew there was nothing else she could honorably do.

2

Smartly attired in his scarlet dress regimentals, Adam Hastings mounted the steps of the great house at Milbrook Park and flashed a smile at his father's butler. Stubbs, usually the epitome of all that was formal and correct, unbent enough to beam at his master's younger son.

"Captain. So very good to see you home, sir."

"Good to see you also, old fellow." Adam blinked to adjust his eyes to the dimness of the marble-tiled foyer. "M' father in?"

"In his bookroom, sir." The elderly retainer hesitated, clearing his throat, and then murmured, "But if you would not take it amiss of me to say so, sir, he's in a rare taking today."

"Gout?"

"That and other things, sir."

"I see. Is it anything I ought to know before I beard him?"

"As to that, I doubt you could mend it, Captain." The old man leaned closer to confide, "Thing is, he was like the cat over cream until the countess's bills arrived from London by early post yesterday."

Adam shook his head, knowing full well there was little like the spending of a few pounds from the enormous Hastings fortune to put the earl into the devil's own temper. It was as though he begrudged his countess the clothes on her back. "Poor Mama," he murmured sympathetically, certain that she must be in bed from the row.

"I believe her ladyship has the headache just now," Stubbs admitted with a straight face.

It was to be expected, for the once lovely and vivacious Lady Emma, daughter to an earl herself, had long since learned to protect herself from her husband's bullying tirades by withdrawing into a chronic invalidism. And so it had been as long as Adam could remember. And now she appeared to be little more than a weak, timid creature whose principal means of rebellion was spending her husband's money. But he suspected his mother of shamming it, for she never seemed to remain ill any longer than it took for his father's anger to abate.

Adam frowned. "Surrounded herself with the salts and Margaret again, eh? Poor Meg."

"Lady Margaret is away."

So his sister had escaped briefly. Now, that did surprise him, but he was glad of it. At twenty-three, poor Margaret was too often the victim of her father's scorn, constantly reminded of how she'd failed in her duty to her family by not snaring a wealthy lord. What the old man could not see was that his determined oppression of the girl had made her timid and colorless. And, having observed the married state as it applied to her parents, she could not be altogether faulted for wishing to avoid it.

"Where did she go?"

"To your Aunt Trowbridge's, I believe."

"And Papa allowed it?"

"Actually, when Lady Westerfield insisted that she could not spare the company of Lady Margaret, his lordship was most adamant that she should go." The butler coughed again to hide his amusement at the countess's wiles. "Lady Margaret left yesterday."

"I see." So it had been a matter of spite, then. How very like his father to even the scales in his mind. "Devil of a row, eh? Well, in that case, I'd play least in sight just now, Stubbs, and let me announce myself. He and I never rub together well at all, and there's no need for him to curse at you when he sees me, is there?"

"Oh, I should not wish to be remiss in my duty, sir," Stubbs murmured, hesitating.

"His temper's not like to improve when he discovers what I have come to say. I hear he's taken the Spender property," Adam added significantly.

The butler understood immediately. So that was the lay of the land. Adam had come home to aid Miss Sarah, and Stubbs was glad of it. There was not a servant at Milbrook Park who thought the earl had done the right thing there. "Perhaps 'twould be best, sir," he agreed, standing back to let Adam pass.

He watched as the captain crossed the tiled floor, the heels of his highly polished military boots clicking against the marble. There was a set to the young gentleman's shoulders that did not bode well for the meeting with his sire. Not that things had ever gone well between them, not since the boy'd been born, and it had occasioned more than a little gossip amongst the servants, with some going so far as to speculate on his paternity. Privately, Stubbs did not think the countess had played her lord false, for the rumored recipient of her favors had been as overbearing as her husband, and he did not believe Lady Emma a total ninnyhammer. No, whether he was rightfully a Hastings or not, Adam would have clashed with the old man in any event. He did, after all, have an inborn decency that the earl seemed to lack.

The elderly retainer shook his head regretfully, laying blame where it was due. He understood the problem better than any of them: the earl did not like that which he could not rule, and Adam, chafing under his attempts at control, had rebelled against the diplomatic career his father had chosen for him. There'd been a terrible row over it, so much so that the boy'd had to buy his own commission, and for a time, the earl had threatened to cut his allowance. But Adam had inherited a goodly sum from his maternal grandfather, allowing him to thumb his nose at the old man's threats. The end result had been that, although billeted but twenty-three miles from the Park, the young man rarely came home, choosing instead to take his leaves with Lord Audley in London.

The trouble with the younger son, Stubbs reflected soberly, was that he lacked the slyness of his brother. Aye, now, that one had learned to dissemble early, gaining him both the earl's goodwill *and* his money. Humph. There were those as thought Lord Audley the better man, but if Stubbs had to choose between Westerfield's sons, he'd take the captain anytime.

Wrenching the door open, Adam stood still, letting his eyes adjust even further to the darkness of the library, and then he walked inside, leaving the door ajar to admit light from the much brighter hallway. He could barely make out the figure of his father slumped in a chair.

"Sir."

"So you deigned to come home finally, did you?" the familiar raspy voice observed sourly from the wing chair's shadowy depths. "Not that you have got any more sense, as I can tell it, for I see you are still playing at soldier. You mean to favor your mama and me with your presence more'n a day?"

"I have a fortnight's leave."

The old man's bushy eyebrow climbed upward in disbelief. "And you ain't got a high flyer to spend it with? Or are your pockets to let? Though as warm as Winfield cut up, I shouldn't think you could have run through the bloody fortune already," he grumbled. "Know demned well you ain't come to do the pretty by me."

"Actually, I thought someone should attend Spender's funeral and look to his daughter," Adam responded quietly. "And I knew you'd think to do neither." He moved to spark a flint to the brace of candles nearest him.

"Damme, boy!" The old man exploded. "You still

think I've got all the money in the world, don't you?
Them's wax! Get the tallow ones if you are of a mind to
light 'em.''

With a sigh, Adam pocketed the flint and reached to
draw the heavy draperies that shrouded one of the windows. ''You haven't changed any either, have you, sir?''
Ignoring his father's reddening face, he lifted the heavy
brocade and tied it back. The morning sunlight filtered
in from the terraced garden outside, a welcome respite
from a week's worth of chilly rain. ''At least it does not
storm just now,'' he observed with satisfaction.

''You'll let in the light and fade the furniture,'' the earl
grumbled, unwilling to give up his pique long enough to
welcome his son.

''How are Mama, Margaret, and Dev?'' Adam countered.

That brought a snort of disgust from the old man.
''Your mama's a foolish simpleton, and so I told her!
Thinks I mean to pay the tradesmen for a bundle of nonsense! One hundred thirty pounds to a demned dress-
maker—fifty pounds for ten pairs of shoes! Damme if *I*
have ten pairs of shoes myself! And a gross of wax candles for the London house—and new peas—why the devil
would she order new peas for there when I am here, I
ask you?'' he demanded. ''Extravagant female!''

Despite his own irritation with his father, Adam had to
suppress a smile. ''I'd heard she was indisposed,'' he
admitted.

''Indisposed! Aye, she is indisposed! When I would
call her to book for it, she said she had the headache!
The headache!'' The earl's voice fairly dripped with sar-
casm. ''Well, I was not to be put off this time, I can tell
you—I told her I wouldn't have such extravagance!
Demned hard on the leg, but I went anyways.''

He shifted uncomfortably, easing his swollen leg onto
a cushion in front of him, then warmed to his subject.
''Females! They're all in league, if you was to ask me,
boy! No sooner than I had sat myself down, the foolish
dragon she keeps was a-wavin' salts in your mama's face
and tellin' me to get out—me as pays her wages!'' he
recalled, his indignation rising. ''And then the maid came

in and set fire to a bowl of feathers—for the headache, she said! It smoked so foully I could not stay in the room! And there was the stench of camphor all throughout the place, I tell you! How any of 'em can bear it—well, 'tis beyond description!''

It was an old scene oft repeated with variation, but Adam let him play it out again. Finally he interrupted impatiently. ''And the others?''

''Humph! The silly widgeon as is your sister has taken herself off to m' sister Trowbridge. Liza says she thinks she can find the gel a husband, and if you can believe that, you are a bigger simpleton than your mother,'' his father answered. ''Girl's daft, and so I told Liza—takes after your mother—but damme if I won't give her three months to manage the trick. Though how she's to do it, I am sure I don't know—fortune or no—for your sister's bent on discouraging them as would come up to scratch for her, and so I have told the silly chit.''

''Is Dev well?'' Adam changed the subject, unwilling to listen to yet another tirade about Margaret's supposed failure as a Hastings.

The earl's frown softened at the mention of his elder son. Leaning back in his chair now, he nodded. ''Audley does well for himself—I admit it, damme if I don't—got Pitt's eye, you know, and that's where I'd have him. Newcastle's on his last legs, I am certain of that. The Whigs and Tories both don't like the way this thing with France is going, and there's bound to be war anytime. I say it ain't going to be many more months ere the king asks Pitt to make the next government, and I'd expect your brother to be part of it.''

''So I have surmised from his last letter.'' Adam shrugged, hiding the slight he felt whenever his father spoke of Devin. ''At least then you can say one of your sons does well for himself, I suppose.''

''Aye.'' The old man eyed him with sudden wariness. ''But you ain't here to ask how we go on, and I daresay the Spender thing is but a hum,'' he decided shrewdly. Clasping his hands across his portly stomach, he cocked his head for a better view of his tall son. ''Might as well open the budget and come out with it—you ain't home for nothing, are you? Stands to reason there's business afoot, else you'd not be here. And it ain't money, is it? Don't need mine—got Winfield's, after all." He shifted his body again, this time easing the leg down. "So it cannot be a promotion, though I'd think you'd want to buy one if you wasn't wantin' to sell out."

"No. Strange as it must sound to you, Papa, I should prefer to earn it. The army abounds with officers whose only claim to position is that they can afford to buy the gold braid that goes with it."

"Ought to use old Winfield's money for it," his father advised testily. "He ain't here to see what you are become, though I am sure there ain't no soldiers on that side neither."

"You will be happy to note I have invested that in the funds, sir. My wages are sufficient for me and my batman, and what else does a soldier need?" Adam countered. Then, seeing his father clearly did not believe him, he came to the point. "I want to know what you mean to do about Sarah Spender."

"Ain't going to do nothing about her! Why the devil would you ask that?" the earl demanded testily.

"I heard you foreclosed on Baron Spender, that you sent him to ruin—you might as well have fired the ball yourself."

"Lies! Utter rubbish! Fellow ruined himself by playing too deep when he couldn't pay, and that's the truth of it." He leaned forward in his chair. "But I don't like the sound of what you are saying," he muttered, scowling up at Adam. "Spender couldn't come about, you know—told me so—and I didn't want my blunt squandered with his. Well, no reason to throw good money after bad, is there? And if I hadn't foreclosed, there'd a been nothing left worth having. There—that's the God's truth, and don't you be believing otherwise, you hear? 'Tis a pack of lies, if you have heard aught else, I tell you."

He eyed his son defensively, and when Adam did not respond, he added, "As 'tis, I waited so long that the house is naught but a ruin. No, you cannot lay Spender's death at my door, sirrah!"

"You've left his daughter destitute, Papa."

"I didn't leave her anything!" the old man retorted, stung by the accusatory tone of his younger son's voice. " 'Twas Spender as was run off his legs, and too fool to know it until 'twas too late. If he did not see fit to provide for the chit, 'tis none of my affair." He looked away, grumbling. "Besides, she'll right her ship, you mark my words. Deuced pretty little thing, if I remember her. Won't be a day before she gets herself a protector."

"Is that what you want?" Adam asked incredulously. "You'd let a gently bred female join the demimonde out of desperation? Papa, have you *no* conscience at all?"

"Don't want anything of the sort! Don't care what happens to the gel, if you must know. Damme, boy, but it ain't like she was a relation—'cause she ain't," he finished dampeningly. Looking up again, the earl regarded his younger son with acute disfavor. "Trouble with you, Adam, is you favor your bird-witted mother rather than me."

But Adam had ceased to attend, thinking instead of Sarah Spender as last he'd seen her, a lovely country-bred innocent, a girl far too good for what his father suggested. He changed tactics, appealing to the earl's sense of the social order.

"Papa, she is one of us—her family has been landed and titled these three hundred years past. You would not have it said you abandoned one of your own class, would you?" he coaxed. "Surely you must—"

"Humph! It ain't like she was a Hastings, after all. And I cannot think what I am to do for her anyways—I mean, she's too demned old to send away to school, ain't she?" Seeing the open condemnation in his son's eyes, Charles Hastings grew more defensive. "Sit down. I'll be bound if I'm going to break my neck looking up at you. I cannot aid the girl, and that's that."

Shaking his head, Adam remained standing. "Would you have the world call you for what you are, sir—a clutch-fisted old man who would rob an orphan?"

"I don't give a farthing what anyone thinks." The earl moved again in his chair, his gout suddenly seeming even more painful. The boy had scored a flush hit, but it would never do to let him know it. Besides, Devin's political

ambitions were the paramount thing. Aye, it would not
be useful to have the neighborhood grumbling that the
Hastings family had profited unduly from the chit's misery, the old man reflected silently. "All right," he decided reluctantly, sighing at the thought of the expense.
"I don't own as I owe her anything, mind you, but 'twill
be judged as we are uncharitable if we do nothing, I
suppose." His eyes met his son's sullenly. "You may ride
over and tell the gel I will see she has a character and
passage money to wherever she would seek employ-
ment."

"Paltry."

His father stared at him as though he'd taken complete
leave of his senses, and then he found his voice again.
"The devil you say! Well, I won't, sirrah, and there's the
end to that! If it pricks your conscience, *you* do something for the chit then!"

It was useless to argue further, and Adam knew it. For
stubbornness, Charles Hastings had no peer, and once he
took a stand, right or wrong, he could be expected to
cling to his position with a tenacity that would have done
Caesar proud. "Maybe I will, sir—maybe I will. If you
cannot recall your duty to your own kind, I assure you
that I can." Exhaling slowly, he backed away from his
father. "I should have known better than to hope for decent feeling from you, shouldn't I?" he gibed bitterly.
"But I own it surprises me that Dev has done nothing
for Sarah. I thought he had more than a passing interest
in her."

"Spender's brat? Nay, afore God he did not! Audley
knows his worth—unlike one as is in this room, sirrah."

The gulf was as wide as it had ever been between them,
and both were painfully conscious of it. The earl's words
hung in the air, yet another reminder of how much he
favored his elder son. Finally Adam inclined his head
slightly.

"Good day, Papa."

"Wait—"

Adam hesitated, but his father apparently thought better of whatever he'd started to say. The thin lips clamped
together, cutting off the words, and he looked away. The

strained silence was more deafening than the earlier
shouting. "I'd not be late for Baron Spender's funeral,
Papa. Should any inquire, I shall say your gout prevents
your attendance."

His piece said, he turned and walked from the room,
leaving the earl to stare balefully into the gloom. It was
beyond the old man's comprehension that he could have
sired the young fool, and yet he knew now that he had.
But all the regret in the world would not change the boy's
hatred now, he supposed.

As the echo from his son's bootsteps receded, the earl
straightened within the chair and reached for the wine
decanter on the table beside him. His hand stopped in
midair. Damn the bloody young fool! Could he not see
that Charles Hastings had no wish for a conscience?

He lurched from his chair and hobbled to the door,
shouting after his son, "Tell her I'll put fifty pounds in
her purse! Aye, and I'll give her one of Emma's day
gowns to take with her! Your mama's got plenty to
spare!"

But he was too late. The hall was empty and he could
hear the horse and rider turn into the lane.

3

Pondering Sarah's fate most of the way to the village
church, Adam felt a certain helplessness. The girl's
penury rested in part on his father's greed, and that troubled his conscience. Ever since Roland Wicklund had
written to urge his intercession with the old man, Adam
had been unable to rid himself of thoughts of Sarah
Spender. Memories of times past, times when the earl

and the baron were on friendlier terms, seemed to flood over him, bringing images of the hoydenish girl riding astride when she was a child, ignoring Miss Wallace's dire warnings of permanent injury. Even now he could see her tangled hair flying in the wind, a wild, glorious auburn mane.

A slow smile spread over his face as he remembered her. Aye, she was different from the milksop misses who sat primly along drawing-room walls, but who could fault her for it? And who would want to? That she lacked a mother to teach her the simpering coyness required of her sex was as much a boon as a lack, as far as he was concerned. And thankfully the sour Miss Wallace had had little effect beyond the schoolroom, for the last time he'd seen Sarah, she'd been running across the lawn to save a rabbit from one of her father's hounds. He and Devin had sat watching her from the carriage when Dev had insisted they pay a call.

But there was more to Sarah Spender than that. Only two days before that little scene, they'd both gasped when she'd come to the Lynches' country party. Neither of them had actually seen her for a couple of years after Devin left for London and he'd bought his commission. The transformation from gangling female child to lovely girl had left them nearly speechless. Dressed in a plain, faded, sadly outdated gown that must have been made over from one of her dead mother's, she'd outshone every other female in the room.

At the time, Devin said it was her hair, but Adam rather thought otherwise. Aye, he knew fine ladies in London who would have spent weeks trying to emulate the soft huskiness of her voice. And then there were those light brown eyes that warmed to the color of hot spiced cider, eyes ringed with gold flecks that gave them a fire and expressiveness beyond description—amber eyes, he'd called them. They were the sort poets wrote of. In the year since last he'd seen her, he'd not forgotten those eyes. And Devin, as sophisticated as he fancied himself, had murmured under his breath that "Sarah Spender is a veritable flower among cabbages."

Adam reined in, his thoughts coming to a halt with the

awareness that he'd reached the lane to the church. Judging by the assemblage of conveyances and horses in front of the place, it would seem that Baron Spender was far more popular dead than alive. He nudged his horse down the lane, stopping just short of the gathering crowd. Dropping his reins, he dismounted. His horse drifted to the shade of a large tree and began to graze on the dead grass.

Ignoring the curious stares of those who probably wondered how a Hastings could dare show his face at Spender's funeral, he murmured brief greetings to several people before going inside. As he took a seat in the back rather than moving forward to the Hastings' pew, his eyes searched the small chapel for her, finding her. From where he sat, he could see little more than the back of her heavily veiled head, but he knew instinctively it was she.

The chapel filled quickly, obscuring his line of vision. He retrieved a prayer book from the seat beside him and tried to think good of the dead, but it was difficult. Spender had left his daughter a legacy of poverty through his folly, and Adam, who counted himself her friend, could not forgive the baron for it. The pity of the matter was that the fellow had not popped off sooner.

Sarah had heard a disapproving murmur uttered by someone behind her, and ducked her head, twisting surreptitiously to see. There, in the back, she caught a glimpse of scarlet, and her breath caught in her chest. Then a sidewise glance at the empty Hastings pew at the front disappointed her. He had not, after all, come home.

She sank back onto the hard bench and prepared to hear Reverend Mr. Wicklund's ambiguous eulogy of her father. It would not be an easy task for the vicar, for Thomas Spender had not tended to the spiritual side of his life at all. But as the words came, her mind wandered. It wasn't fair to have expected Adam Hastings to return, she chided herself. It was not as though she meant anything to him.

But her rebellious thoughts turned once again to that night he'd stood up with her at Squire Lynch's. His kindness had made her forget the dowdiness of her gown and the pity of her neighbors. Teasing that she'd grown up overnight and that he must surely be the envy of every buck there, he'd made her feel far more beautiful than she was. She'd always regretted being a trifle short and small-boned, but next to Adam Hastings' height, she had felt protected from the sneers of the more favored females present.

Even now, she could see again the scarlet of his military frock coat, with its bright blue lapels buttoned back and trimmed with the gold braid of an officer, the snowy white lace that frilled his stock above the gold gorget and crimson silk sash. No, from the gold epaulet on his shoulder to the tan kerseymere of his knee breeches, he'd been as finely dressed as any of the country gentry in their silks and brocades. But as handsome as he was, he'd not been nearly so self-absorbed as the rest of them. She'd laughed when he'd called himself a macaroni and complained of the powder on his wig, saying he much preferred simplicity. He'd said it to put her at ease, she was certain, and he had. No, if only for that night, she'd been the envy of every female in the room. Just this once, she allowed herself the luxury of remembering the faint, clean smell of Hungary water warmed by his skin. It was a memory she would cherish forever. For one warm summer night she'd dare to pretend he could love her.

Resolutely she put him from her mind and turned her attention instead to the very real problems that faced her. For all her brave words to the contrary, she did not relish the thought of being a governess, not at all, and every fiber of her being seemed to cry out against such a fate. Her only consolation was that she would finally escape the doubtful charity of neighbors who insisted on giving her the unusable and the unwearable.

Ahead of her lay her father's black-draped coffin. She stared briefly at it and felt nothing beyond bitterness. In life, he'd robbed her of her mother's portion and of her future; in death, he was robbing her of her home. If she could have cried, it would have been for herself rather than him. She closed her eyes and prayed to erase the resentment that overwhelmed her.

Mercifully, they finally stood for the last prayer, signaling the end of the service. In the chill closeness of the closed church, Sarah leaned forward to hold the pew in front of her. Her petticoats, weighted by the heavy full skirt, twisted about her legs. Beside her, Miss Wallace mouthed the words. The last "Amen" brought forth an audible collective sigh of relief.

Outside, the air was even chillier than the stagnant air in the church. She drew in a deep breath and let it out slowly before she allowed her eyes to search the yard. And then she heard the still-familiar voice call out, "Miss Spender!" and for once she was grateful that the veil hid the rush of blood to her face. She tried to keep her voice from betraying the excitement she felt as she turned to face him.

She'd never seen a handsomer sight than the captain in his smart scarlet regimental uniform, and she hoped she would always remember him just as he was. He smiled and held out his hand to her.

"Sarah."

"Captain Hastings . . . 'tis so very kind of you to come," she managed to murmur. She felt suddenly quite self-conscious, afraid that she might give away her thoughts of him.

"Alas, I feared you must have forgotten me by now."

He bent over her hand, possessing it in his strong fingers. And as he spoke, his blue eyes were far more sober than she remembered them.

"As if I should." Then, fearful that she must sound too eager, she added hastily, "As we have been neighbors all my life, sir, 'tis not a likely circumstance, is it?"

"No, I suppose not." His fingers squeezed hers comfortingly. "I cannot tell you how shocked I was to hear of your father's death, Sarah, and I want you to know you have my sympathy." It sounded hollow even as he said it, and he hastened to add, "I am terribly sorry for what happened, my dear."

"Thank you, sir."

He peered closely at her, trying to see again those unusual eyes and that fire-sparked hair of hers, but the hideous thick black veil concealed them almost completely.

He wanted to know if she were as lovely as he and Devin had thought her.

Behind Sarah, Miss Wallace cleared her throat as though to remind the girl that others waited to speak with her. To Adam she nodded a frosty acknowledgment. "We were of the opinion that you were garrisoned outside London, Captain—Sussex, isn't it?"

"I am," he answered politely. "But whether I shall remain there is unknown until this thing with France is resolved. But for the time being, I have secured a short leave and mean to stay at the Park. Sussex is, after all, not so terribly far from here," he reminded her.

"Ah, yes—we have heard the rumors of war here also," Miss Wallace unbent enough to say to him.

Sarah lifted her veil again to study him covertly as he spoke to the older woman. He'd not changed much in the space of a year, except maybe that he was even more handsome than she'd remembered him, if such a thing could be possible. She dropped her eyes, suddenly very conscious of the quiz she must appear in the awful, ill-fitting black dress. Miss Wallace nudged her impatiently, hissing for her ears only, "There are others who would pay their respects also."

"What will you do now?" Adam asked as he backed up to let the pallbearers pass bearing the wooden coffin.

Not wanting to answer him, not wanting his pity, she countered with a question of her own. "Did your father send you?"

"No. I but heard of Baron Spender's death in a letter from Ro, else I should have been here sooner."

"Adam!"

To Sarah's dismay, Roland Wicklund was bearing down on Adam, his hand outstretched in greeting. Disappointed as the captain's attention transferred to the younger man, Sarah wished Roland at Jericho just this once. And then she felt the restraining hand of an elderly woman who had stopped to tell her how much she resembled her late father. But she barely attended, listening instead to Roland and Adam.

The corners of Roland's eyes crinkled as he squinted from the sun. In an aside to Adam he murmured low,

" 'Tis difficult to tell how many came to see if Spender were really dead—it surprises me that Chawleigh did not pry up the lid for a look, you know. Spender left owing him a bloody fortune.''

"Ro—'' Adam nudged him significantly. " 'Tis scarcely the place," he hissed in a low underbreath.

"Daresay you are right, but she'd say so herself. Oh, bought a new horse, Adam—going to race him if Papa don't cut up too great a dust over it. Been waiting to show it to you.''

Adam's eyes met Sarah's over Roland's shoulder. "May I call on you this afternoon, Miss Spender?''

Any joy she'd felt in seeing him was dashed on the rocks of reality then. She colored uncomfortably at the thought of his discovering just how far things had sunk with her. Torn between a desire to be with him for even a few minutes and the fear that he would pity her, she shook her head. "Uh . . . oh, no . . . really, but I shall be packing and . . . please do not think me uncivil, but—''

"Tomorrow, then?''

Behind the heavy veil, her eyes widened. Surely he must have heard from his father that she would be gone by then—that her house belonged to the earl now. Her voice faltered slightly as she shook her head again.

"Alas, but I shall be going to York.''

For some reason, she was making it deuced hard for him, but he pursued manfully. "Miss Spender . . . Sarah . . .''

She wanted so much to speak with him in private, but her pride stopped her yet again. "I fear there is too little time, sir.''

He could not very well force her to see him, so he drew back, oddly disappointed. "Then I shall wish you well now, Sarah.''

"And I you, Captain Hastings. May God keep you safe wherever you are sent.'' There seemed to be nothing more to say between them. All of the fine words she'd practiced in her heart for years seemed inappropriate now. After a moment's hesitation, she moved past him to greet

Mrs. Brightwell, hoping she'd managed to hide what she felt for him.

There was so much she wanted to say to him, so much she had wanted to hear from him. She'd know how he got on, how the army suited him, where he was going, but there was no time. Her heart felt terribly heavy now, but at least she'd seen him—at least he had come.

Adam frowned, perplexed that she'd not been more pleased to see him. Perhaps she blamed him for what his father had done to hers. Reluctantly he went back to Roland. "I should like to see this paragon of horseflesh you have picked out, Ro."

"Think you I do not know a prime one, Adam? You are not the only judge in the neighborhood, you know," Roland retorted.

"I know you do not, my dear fellow—you forget that I've seen the nags you've had."

"This one's a sweet goer, I swear. Come on, you can ride him and judge for yourself," Roland coaxed with the enthusiasm of showing off for an old rival.

Adam glanced briefly to where Sarah stood, still speaking with the older woman. "Show me, then—I've naught else to do, after all."

He followed the younger man to where a bay stood tied beneath a shade tree. Intrigued, he studied the animal with a practiced eye, taking in the deepness of the chest, the curve of the powerful shoulders. And then he knelt to feel along the bony ridge of the foreleg and around the hock. Standing again, he ran his palm along the horse's back and down over its flanks. The horse's tail swished, but otherwise the animal was calm.

"He looks sound," Adam murmured approvingly. "For once, I think you may have discovered a good one. The bloodline?"

"Straight from the Barbary Turk."

"But can he run?"

"Can he run?" Roland fairly howled. "He'd leave that nag of yours standing, I tell you! Come on, and I'll show you what Mercury can do."

"Well, I had thought to see Miss Spender, but—"

Roland's expression sobered. "Aye, a bad business that

is, Adam—the old man dead and the creditors come to take everything from her. M'father says she won't have a bedsheet left by nightfall.''

"You mean they are coming even before she is allowed to leave?''

Roland nodded. "Disgraceful, ain't it? My heart goes out to Sarah in the matter, but there's naught to be done. Oh, I offered for her,'' he added importantly, "but she wouldn't have me—said we should not suit, or some fustian such as that. And I'd have been good to her, don't you know?''

"Who allows this?'' Adam demanded.

"Thought of it myself—'course, m'father don't know it, but—''

"No, no. I mean, who's seeing to Spender's business?''

"Why, 'twas the earl himself who gave the permission—I'd thought you knew it. It won't be pleasant for her, I'll be bound—she should have taken me. I'd have seen she didn't starve.'' Roland's face creased unhappily as he stared after her for a moment. "But she didn't want me.''

But Adam had ceased listening to him. Instead, he stared at Sarah with new understanding. How very like her not to want anyone to know how things stood with her. But then, he supposed that pride was all she had left. Well, she ought to be told of what he'd been able to wring from his father—she ought to know he'd tried.

"I say, Adam—what say you to the race?'' Roland persisted.

"Not today. I find I have some business, after all.''

"Sarah? I wish there was something you could do in that quarter. She's too good for what's going to happen to her, don't you know? Maybe your father—''

"Maybe.''

"Bad business,'' Roland repeated, shaking his head. "There was some people as thought maybe your brother'd try to do something for her. But I guess we mistook his interest.''

"Dev? He's too busy advancing himself, or so Papa tells me.'' Adam's expression lightened as he watched

Sarah move toward Reverend Wicklund's carriage. "I'll see you later, Ro, and we'll race your nag. Right now, I am for Spender's Hill."

4

His mind still seething from Roland's revelation, Adam didn't know precisely how he could help Sarah, but he meant to try. At least he could tell her what he'd wrung from his father—she ought to know that the earl would pay her passage wherever she chose to go, and with a little luck, he might be able to shame the old man into doing more. If only he had more time.

Ahead of him, a steady procession of carts and carriages clogged the road and slowed passage. As he followed them up the last bend in the narrow drive, he could see men swarming over the place, carrying all manner of things from the house itself. Laden with furniture, plate, candlesticks, portraits, and linens, many of them were engaged in heated quarrels over what others had discovered. Their angry voices carried as solicitors vociferously defended their clients' claims.

He stared, his fury rising at the sight of human vultures come to pick over Spender's meager leavings. And he knew why Sarah had not wanted him to come—Roland had the right of it, he knew now. By nightfall she would be left with nothing beyond the clothes she wore.

Spurring his horse, he rode into their midst, brandishing his saber and shouting, "Thieves! Bloody blackguards!" The crowd scattered, running before him. Their flight disgusting him even more, he reined in and dismounted as they turned back toward him. "Who the devil gave permission for this outrage?'' he demanded, waving the saber at them menacingly. ''You are naught but robbers, come to haggle over a dead man's leavings! You—'' He gestured to a man who still clung to a pair of candlesticks. ''Put those back on the instant—d'you hear? Aye, all of you—you'll carry everything you have taken back inside!''

They faced him, collective indignation written on their faces, and made no move to obey him. As he prodded the fellow with the candlesticks impatiently, a murmur of disbelief spread through the mob. For a moment they hesitated, as though to decide if he were sane. He jabbed a little harder, and the man yelped, dropping his booty.

''Here, now, he ain't but one—he cannot stand us all!'' someone shouted from the safety of the crowd.

''And wot's he got t' do wi' the business, I ask ye?'' one of his fellows demanded.

''Unless you mean to see your fat friend stuck like a hog, you'll put Miss Spender's things where you found them,'' Adam repeated, gesturing again with his weapon. The sunlight glared off the blade. ''Now.'' His voice had dropped, but there was no mistaking that he meant what he said.

''Here, there ain't but one of 'im!'' someone yelled again.

''Aye,'' Adam agreed almost softly, ''so you will have to decide which of you wishes to take me. I am certain to get at least one, and perhaps more.''

Nonplussed by this unwelcome turn of events, they milled uneasily, none wishing to be the first. Then a red-faced fellow's chin jutted forward belligerently as he took the lead and swaggered toward Adam, stopping just short of the blade's range. ''And who might you be, me pretty fellow?'' he asked sarcastically. His black eyes took in the bright scarlet uniform. '' 'Tis captain, is it not? If you are come for your share, you are too late—the bill said claims were to be presented by two o'clock.''

Adam ignored his insolence, turning instead to the others. ''And you dare call yourselves Englishmen? You who would rob a girl ere her father is even buried? Shame on the lot of you!''

" 'Ere, 'ere now, fellow!'' one of them blustered, his face flushing. "Ain't like that at all! I got a claim of five 'undred, and Miss Spender knows 'tis right. Now, I mean to get m' money or something for it—'tis as plain a matter as that. Besides,'' he added defensively, "the earl's man knows I'm 'ere—said I was to come if I was t' get paid.''

"Then he was mistaken,'' Adam cut in sharply, "for I am Westerfield's son, and I refuse permission in his name. Aye, if all is not returned to the house, I shall have you charged with theft!'' Taking in their mutinous expressions, he shook his head brusquely. "Nay, if your claim is just, lay it before the courts ere you rob a girl. I've no patience with your greed.''

"Now, see here—'' A low rumble of dissent rippled through the crowd, bolstered by the curious who'd come to join them. "It ain't—''

"Then I collect you are the sacrifice,'' he told the burly man who'd spoken. As the mob started forward, he pressed the saber point against the soiled waistcoat. "Well?''

The fellow went pale and backed away. "It ain't like that—it ain't at all,'' he protested. "Don't want to rob nobody, but—''

A well-dressed man, obviously a solicitor, spoke up. "Be reasonable, sir—aye, 'tis unfortunate about the girl, but these people have lost much also. To ask some of them to wait years for the courts to settle claims would be ruinous—even a man of your honor's worth must surely see it so. The end will be the same anyway, and I—''

"You be reasonable!'' Adam snapped. "Would you feel the same if 'twas your daughter? How in the devil do you expect Miss Spender to live with what you would leave her? Go on—else I am prepared to spill blood!''

"But the earl's man said—''

"I do not care what he said! Aye, and—''

Suddenly there was an uncomfortable silence as everyone stared past Adam. Several of the men shifted uncomfortably and stared at the ground, ashamed now to face the girl who stepped from a neighbor's carriage.

"What is the meaning of this?'' Sarah demanded clearly as Adam swung around to face her, and then her

face flamed in embarrassment at the sympathy she saw
in his eyes. She felt utterly mortified to discover that he
knew just how desperate her circumstance was. She
fought back tears that he should see her thus.

"'Tis but a misunderstanding, Miss Spender," Adam
reassured her. "They were a trifle overeager, and now
have agreed to wait for a formal settlement."

Her eyes traveled from the weapon in his hand to the
silent, sullen men and then to the piles of furniture and
goods on the lawn. "I see," she managed heavily. Turning back, she met his gaze soberly. "No." For a moment
she bit her lip to still its trembling, and she feared she
would lose her composure in front of him. "No. 'Twill
be no easier next week—or next month even. Gentlemen,
do what you must—and be done. Papa owed the money,
after all."

There was a fatalism in her voice that struck at the
hearts of most of the men. Adam stepped toward her, but
she backed away. "No, I am determined, sir. I . . . I
have feared this day too long, you know, and now 'tis
come. While . . . while I appreciate your kind concern,
I . . . I'd rather you did not," she finished quickly. Her
eyes were swimming now, awash with tears of humiliation. Pressing her hand over her mouth, she turned and
fled toward the house.

It was several seconds before anyone spoke. Finally
the solicitor cleared his throat, "Well, sir?" he addressed Adam. "None of us wants to hurt the lady, you
understand, but Baron Spender owed the money."

"If you say wait, I'll wait," someone conceded grudgingly behind him. "But I'd ask every man here to do the
same."

Taking a deep breath and exhaling it slowly, Adam
stared after her. He looked down at the saber in his hand,
feeling suddenly helpless. "No. Go on—take what you
will, but be quick about it," he muttered, jamming the
blade back into his dress scabbard.

"It ain't like the earl will not see to her, is it?" someone else asked. "I mean, he will, won't he?"

"Aye—damn him! Aye, he will!" His temper flared
anew at the thought of what his father had done to her.

He brushed past them, determined to go after her, to find her, to tell her not to despair. Pushing the door so hard that it banged noisily against the jamb, he thrust it aside and strode in, shouting for her, "Miss Spender . . . Sarah! Dammit, Sarah, come back!"

He kicked open doors, discovering each room to be the same, empty to the walls. Two men on ladders shrank against the windows where they removed the hangings when he passed them. "Vultures!" he spat contemptuously. "Sarah! Where the devil are you, Sarah?" he called out again as he strode angrily up and down the halls. His shouts echoed eerily through the naked house.

Flinging open the back door, he found her in the garden, kneeling on the ground to pluck at a dead weed between the flagstones of the walk. Where the black veil had fallen away, he could see that her face was tear-stained, but she was not openly weeping. When she saw him, she looked away. His anger faded at the sight of her, replaced by a deep need to comfort the girl he'd known most of his life. He walked to stand over her, his shadow falling across the stones in front of her.

"Sarah . . ." He spoke gently.

"Please . . ." Her voice was little more than a whisper. "Your pardon, sir, but I . . . I am not prepared for company just now." Looking at the decay around her, she shook her head. " 'Tis scarce the Park, is it? But it is, after all, my home, and I shall miss it."

"I know." Fishing in the coat of his scarlet tunic, he found a handkerchief and knelt down beside her. Knotting the cloth over his fingers, he dabbed at the wet streaks on her face. "Why did you not write to me of this?"

"I had not your direction beyond the Royal Sussex—and 'twas not your affair, after all, Captain Hastings." She sniffed, trying to control her running nose, hoping he would not note it.

"Captain Hastings? Is that how you would greet one who has been your friend for an age, Sarah?" he asked, trying to keep his voice light. "You must have considered that I would have tried to aid you—Sarah, I have known you since I was in short coats and you were naught but a babe in arms." Moving the handkerchief over her nose, he ordered, "Blow."

"What could you have done?" she asked tiredly, taking the handkerchief away from him and blowing loudly. "What could anyone have done?" She rocked back on her heels and looked around her at the crocus tips amid the dormant plants. "This is what I shall miss most," she murmured, her voice husky. " 'Tis all I have left of Mama, and I cannot take it with me."

"There must be someone to help—a distant relation, perhaps? Or one of your father's friends? I mean, dash it, Sarah, but someone's got to care!"

"Do you really think so?" Her voice turned suddenly bitter and her mouth twisted. "There is no one—and even if there were, do you think 'tis what I should want?" Her fingers clutched the folds of the heavy black crepe, pulling it up for his attention. "Look at this gown—look at it! 'Tis what charity is, Captain Hastings—the poor are given what the almsgiver would not wear! But do not be feeling sad for me—I . . . I shall be taking a position in York!"

"Doing what?"

Her chin lifted at the tone in his voice. "I shall be governess to five dear little boys—or so they have been painted to me."

"No, by God—" He choked, trying not to laugh at the way she said it. "Sarah—"

"And though I shall despise it excessively, I am sure, I shall at least have the satisfaction of earning my bread."

"Somehow I cannot see you with a houseful of boisterous children, my dear, when you are scarce more than a child yourself."

"I am nineteen, sir," she retorted.

"And as green a girl as I have ever seen! Egad, Sarah, but what will you teach them—watercolors?"

Stung by what she perceived as a reflection on the same abilities she herself doubted, she crumpled the handkerchief and threw it onto the ground beside her. "My watercolors are dismal, if you must know, but my knowledge of Latin and sums is more than adequate, sir. I am not a simpleton, no matter what anyone thinks."

"My dear girl, York is the length of the country."

"So it is."

It was so very far from her home, so very far from all she had known. And whether she admitted it or not, she *was* a green girl who'd never been more than twenty miles from Spender's Hill. He looked into those strange, beautiful eyes of hers and knew why he had come. She was the Sarah whose hair flamed in the sun, whose eyes sparkled like polished amber, and he wanted her. Even as he watched, those eyes seemed to change, with the gold flecks spreading from the black pupils, fascinating him, drawing something from deep within him. Without hesitation, he decided.

"No, Sarah." He reached with one hand to pull the veil the rest of the way off her head, and with the other he smoothed her shining hair. "You can come with me."

She stared, bereft of speech, unable to find her voice for a time. It was an illusion, a dream, she told herself, afraid to hear the rest. For if after all her girlish fantasies of him, he should prove to be no better than his brother, she could not bear it.

"Sarah, I would stand your friend."

She shook her head dumbly, unable to look away from the brilliance of his blue eyes. Tears welled, threatening her composure again. "I . . . I cannot," she whispered finally.

"Sarah . . . Sarah . . ." He leaned closer, pulling her halfway onto his lap, cradling her as though she were a child against his chest. "I am a soldier, you know, and a younger son, but I am not a poor man. And while the army is not much of a life for a female, it cannot be worse than what you would find in York." His arms closed around her shoulders, enveloping her, holding her close. "I'd take care of you, if you would let me."

She stiffened in his arms and tried to push away. "Do not—I pray you will not say it, Adam. Please."

"What the devil . . . ? Sarah, I am asking you to marry me," he told her as his hands caught her shoulders. "I know I am not a catch like Dev, but if you tell me that you prefer York to me, I'll know it for a hoax."

"Marry?" She sucked in her breath sharply, gasping.

"Marry! But . . . Oh!" Unable to express the intense flood of happiness that overwhelmed her, she threw herself against his shoulder and clung to him.

His hands slid down over her back, smoothing the awful gown against her spine. She seemed so small, so vulnerable in his arms. "How else am I to take care of you, Sarah?" he asked softly. "If I didn't wed you, there'd be the devil to pay with the gossips." Her shoulders shook beneath his hands. "Shhh, don't cry, Sarah—'tis all right now. 'Tis sudden, I know, but we'll muddle through." He shifted her in his arms and lifted her chin. " 'Tis Adam, Sarah—come to save you from five little boys in York." His smile twisted wryly. "Though I must admit 'tis not very flattering to have you turn into a watering pot just as I have declared myself, you wretched creature."

Her eyes flooded and her chin quivered, but she managed to shake her head. "I am not crying, Adam—t-truly I am not. I'm happy!" she wailed, turning her head into his chest again.

"Here . . ." He shifted her onto his other leg and tried to see her face. "Well, is it to be York or me?"

She had no illusions that he'd spoken for any reason other than pity, but she'd take him any way she could get him. And somehow, some way, she'd make him love her as much as she loved him in that moment. Yet some imp prompted her to hesitate.

"Welllll . . ."

"Dash it, Sarah! If you are not careful, I'll cry off," he threatened.

Her eyes searched his face, seeing again the incredible handsomeness, and she felt she must surely be the most fortunate of women. The lump in her throat grew, making speech nearly impossible as she nodded. "Remember when we playacted knights and ladies in the priory ruins?" she whispered finally.

"Aye."

She smiled tremulously, meeting his puzzled eyes. "I choose you for my champion, Sir Adam. Go forth and slay dragons for me, will you?"

"Every one I can find."

He looked deep into her amber eyes and felt a surge of tenderness mingled with desire. In the ordinary way of things, he knew it would not be considered a good match for him, that his father and Devin would call it a *mésalliance* even, but somehow he knew also that she would lighten his life. And that would be worth far more than any gold she could bring him. As she looked away finally, he leaned forward to nuzzle the shining, fragrant crown of her hair, thinking how very lovely she was.

"Choose your first dragon, Sarah," he murmured softly.

The gold buttons and braid pressed against her cheek, and the red wool was rough beneath her skin as she savored the warmth of his body against hers. "The first is already vanquished, sir."

"That unruly crowd?"

"No. York—I did not truly wish to go there."

His arms tightened about her shoulders, holding her closer. "I pray you will not dislike being a soldier's wife," he mused aloud. " 'Tis not an easy life for a gentle lady."

The gate swung open behind them, and they heard someone utter in disgust, "There's naught of value here, save those benches, and they'd not fetch five pounds between the lot of 'em."

Sarah jerked upright self-consciously, brought back to reality all too soon. Adam muttered a curse under his breath as she slid off his lap and stood. Catching a low-hanging branch, he pulled himself up. The intruders, two of them, stopped short when they saw him.

"I say, sir, but—"

" 'Tis of no moment," he interrupted brusquely. "Do what you will." To Sarah he ordered, "Gather what you have need of—I'd not stay amongst the scavengers any longer than necessary."

"Now?" She looked about her in consternation. "But where . . . ? And I have nothing of worth—that is—"

"Then bring nothing but what you have on." He smoothed the auburn tangles back from her face. Smiling at her confusion, he explained, "I am taking you to Milbrook Park with me. I expect Papa will be in a taking, but it need not concern you.'' His gaze met those amber eyes again and softened, as did his voice. ''No matter what he will say, the matter is settled between us, Sarah.''

The thought of the earl's censure was a daunting one. She drew back, suddenly afraid of what she might cost him. ''Oh, but—''

''I am of an age to make my own marriage, my dear.''

Overwhelmed, she forgot the presence of the others and flung herself into his arms again. ''I'll give you no cause to regret it, I swear, Adam,'' she choked out.

''Silly goose,'' he murmured fondly, stroking her thick hair with his palm.

''Disgraceful,'' muttered one of the men.

Adam released her then and stepped back, draping one arm around her shoulders as he faced them. Grinning boyishly, he announced, ''Miss Spender has consented to be my wife.'' As they stared in shock, he dropped his arm and took her hand. ''I hope you do not mind riding before me on my horse, my dear, but I'd not leave without you.''

''Just now I should walk the whole way if you asked me,'' she admitted candidly. ''No, of *course* I shall not mind it in the least.''

5

They rode some quarter of a mile with Sarah perched precariously, her voluminous petticoats rising over her displaced panniers like hoops on end, the whole of which was covered by the awful black fabric like a rather bizarre tent. And to make matters worse, the wind came under the canvas-covered wire cage, lifting it and catch-

ing the petticoats over it, billowing them like sails. Held
on by Adam, Sarah fought valiantly to maintain her balance. To him, the unwieldy garment made her more than
an armful. Almost as soon as they were beyond the first
bend in the road, she twisted around to tell him, "You'll
have to let me down in the copse—I cannot ride further
like this."

For answer, he guided his horse to a thicket of trees
and reined in. Before he knew what she meant to do, she
ducked beneath his arm and slid to the ground in a
whoosh of billowing black. The panniers lifted as she
brushed against the horse, giving him a view of her legs
before the wire cage settled again.

"The Frenchman who created these things ought to be
hanged for it," he muttered, dismounting to join her.
"Why fashion dictates that a female must encase herself
in wire and whalebone is beyond me."

"Well," she countered, " 'tis a mystery to me as to
why men wear wigs when God gave them hair. Besides,
I have never seen bees swarm a hooped skirt, you know."
A throaty chuckle escaped her and her eyes crinkled
against the sun. "I have not forgotten when Ro dressed
his peruke with a concoction of vinegar and honey to
hold the curl. The bees followed him to church, and we
all had to depart the place."

"Egad."

"Aye. When it comes to vanity, I suspect we females
cannot hold a candle to the gentlemen." Then, recalling
poor Roland's plight, she could not suppress a smile.
"And the sad case of the matter was that the powder
stuck to the mess, rendering the thing unusable after
that."

"Well, I promise I shall never dress my wig with
honey—'tis bad enough that some use lard."

"As though you would."

One corner of his mouth twitched as he nodded with
mock gravity. "Alas, but 'tis not truly a dress uniform
without the thing," he reminded her. "But you will never
see me scratching my head beneath it with a needle in
church, I assure you. Personally, I think perukes an
abomination—like panniers, in fact."

"Well, they are not made for riding, I own, and I've got to get out of this ere I am blown away." She looked down at the offending hoops and sighed. "Do you think your mama will forgive me if I arrive without wearing it? Or will she think me the veriest trollop?"

"Mama is abed today with the headache, so that need not be a consideration. And I have always known you to be a hopeless hoyden, anyway."

"Adam!"

"But my tastes have never run to milksop misses, I assure you."

" 'Tis a very good thing, then, for I could never be one," she retorted, lifting her wide full skirts above her well-turned ankles and starting for the thicket.

Amused, he watched her almost disappear behind two large oak trees. She was truly an Original, and he certainly was not repining over having offered for her. As she bent over, her hair caught sunlight and shadows, gleaming red and brown. No, she was not in the ordinary way at all. In fact, Dev had been right: Sarah was quite lovely. Even as he watched her turn away, her wide skirts visible on either side of the tree, he realized with surprise that he'd probably always wanted her more than he'd admitted. His mouth went dry as she lifted the ugly gown to fumble at the tapes beneath.

"Do not be looking at me!" she called out.

"I'm not!" he shouted back.

"Word of a gentleman?"

"Aye." Reluctantly he turned his back on the thicket and fixed his gaze on his horse. "Word of an officer and a gentleman."

It did not take her long. He could hear the twigs and dead leaves crunch beneath her slippers as she came up behind him. "You must promise me not to laugh, you wretch. Now I am more unfashionable than ever."

He swung around, seeing her standing there almost diffidently, now totally swallowed up in the awful black crepe. She looked smaller, more vulnerable. His eyes traveled to the discarded petticoats and panniers, left lying on the ground like large barrel hoops, surrounded by white cambric flounces, and he could not help grinning.

She pulled at her skirt where it lay in limp folds about her ankles. "I need to be a full foot taller now, don't I?" she asked ruefully.

" 'Twould be a pity if you were." His shoulders began to shake. " 'Gad, Sarah, but if Miss Wallace could see you now."

"Let us hope no one discovers they are mine."

"One female's unmentionables are very like another, my dear, and aside from the fact that you had hoops, yours are definitely unremarkable." He caught her hand and pulled her toward the horse. "But if we tarry, there'll be those to say I had quite another reason to wed you."

She held back. "And just how many unmentionables have you seen, Adam?"

"Enough. Come on."

This time, the ride was considerably more pleasant. She leaned back, resting against him, feeling the hard, cold gold buttons of his dress coat through her gown. He seemed bigger, stronger than the boy she'd known for so many years. His arms, where they circled her holding the reins, were hard, and his hands quite unlike the fashionably limp white ones of the neighborhood dandies.

"Adam—"

"Huh?" Jolted back from his own reverie, where he'd been speculating on what Dev would say when he saw Sarah, he squared his shoulders behind her. "Your pardon—I was not attending."

"Adam, just how many females . . . ? That is, well, I mean . . ." She colored and hoped he could not see her face. "Od's bod, Adam—I know not how to ask it!"

"You want to know how many females I've known in the biblical sense? Or are you asking how many I've had a care for?" he countered.

"Aye—but 'tis the same thing, is it not?"

"Alas, 'tis not. Besides, 'tis not the sort of thing a gentleman ought to discuss with a lady, my dear."

She had the feeling that it must have been rather a lot, and that perhaps she really had no wish to know, but she pursued the matter gamely. "Fustian! If I am to be your wife, I should expect you to discuss anything with me," she maintained stoutly.

"Most females pretend not to know of such things, Sarah."

"I think I should rather know than worry."

"That I shall be an inconstant husband?" He leaned forward, bringing his arms closer about her, and rested his chin against the crown of her hair. "You flatter me, Sarah—and nay, though the sea shall separate us, you'll have naught to worry of me. There—does that satisfy you?"

"The sea? Adam—"

"And there's not an Indian female as could hold a candle to Sarah Spender," he added gallantly.

"I don't think you have answered me."

"And I don't mean to. Dearest Sarah, my wild oats are already sown, and you find me ready to be a faithful husband forever." Despite the lightness of his tone, he felt her stiffen in his arms. "Speaking quite seriously, however, the nameless ladies of my past acquaintance are gone from heart and memory."

"But did you love any of them?"

"Not that I recall."

He'd already said more than most men would, she supposed, and his answers, however vague they seemed to her, would have to suffice. She sighed and held her tongue.

The chill breeze ruffled her hair, loosening tendrils and whipping them at her temples. He looked down on her head, seeing again the brightness where the sun caught, and he was glad that she'd left the awful veil on the ground at Spender's Hill. Despite the spirit he'd always admired in her, she felt so very small and slender. A strong desire to protect her nearly overwhelmed him. And then she leaned forward, brushing a firm breast against his arm, and a very different desire coursed through his veins. In some ways, she was not slight at all. He moved his arm, letting it touch her again, then reminded himself she was an artless innocent, that she probably had not the least notion of what he was about. His hand dropped, holding the reins and riding crop almost impersonally across her lap.

She shivered from the cold, reminding him that she'd

brought no cloak. "Lean back, and I'll try to warm you," he murmured, folding her once again in his arms. She was seated at an angle, her legs off to one side, her body twisted forward, and the wind was cold through the woolen dress. She nodded, turning to face the arm that braced her, and let him shelter her with his body.

His father would say he'd contracted himself a *mésalliance,* and Dev would probably agree, but he had no lofty political aspirations. And he had no great need of an heiress, no desire to further his fortunes with a dynastic marriage.

But there would be talk, and a great deal of it. Aye, they'd set the neighborhood gossips talking of how he'd thrown himself away on her, of how he'd forgotten what he owed his name. Well, he didn't care a fig for that— his name was less important to him now. It gave him a sense of satisfaction that he'd been there to aid her, to see the gratitude on her face. Now, instead of struggling with five little boys in York, she could rear her own—and his.

In front of him, Sarah sat quite still, unused to the closeness of a man. Despite her friendship with Adam and Ro, she'd not so much as been touched by either of them before her papa died. And then Ro had spoiled everything by kissing her and making her an offer she could not accept. But now it would all be different, she supposed. She would be a wife. And her life would be inalterably and forever changed. And with that jarring thought, she had to wonder if Adam would expect that intimacy Miss Wallace had mentioned so darkly.

Her knowledge of the other sex was sketchy at best, and colored by Miss Wallace's sour condemnation of men. A brief review of that woman's terse and dire warnings came to mind, unsettling her. She had not the least notion of what to expect other than that it would be unpleasant if he should choose to claim his marital rights of her.

"You are quieter than I have ever known you to be," he said suddenly.

"I could say as much about you."

"Aye."

Unable to tell him of what was on her mind, she blurted out instead, "Will your papa . . . ? I mean, that is, I know he will not be pleased, but . . ."

"Is that what troubles you? You must not think it matters to me."

"Adam, I'd not cause a breach between you—I should rather go to York than that."

"What—you would cry off already?" he teased, trying to lighten her mood.

"Lord Audley may be set against me," she ventured with uncharacteristic timidity.

"If he is, 'tis jealousy—nothing more than that."

"But if he is?" she persisted.

"He'll recover, I promise you," he reassured her. "When all is said and done, Sarah, Devin puts a good face before the world—and he has no reason to throw a spoke in my wheel. If he'd thought to have you, he'd have offered for you himself."

It was her opening to tell him, but she couldn't. "Will the countess be terribly displeased, do you think?" she asked instead.

"Mama?" he snorted. "She'll love you, if for no other reason than to vex Papa. Theirs was the *mésalliance*, Sarah—not ours."

"How awful for her to live like that."

"What a dreary pair we are today, Sarah," he said finally. "I can quite understand about you, of course, but I have not an excuse, have I?" His arms tightened around her, pulling her even closer. "I should count myself fortunate, don't you think? 'Tis not every day that a man contracts himself to wed Sarah Spender, is it?"

"I do not require Spanish lies, Adam—really I do not."

He looked up at the sky, inquiring soulfully, "Spanish lies, she says—did you ever hear the like of that? A female unmoved by compliment is a rare treasure indeed."

"Adam—"

"At least I shall know what I am getting, don't you think?" he continued. "I have seen you chase Old Beau across the lawn, shouting insults at the poor creature. And I've not forgotten your devilish temper when you landed in the creek either."

"I was a child then."

"My point, dear Sarah, is that I shall not be surprised when you turn termagant on me. Besides, you will make me the envy of half the officers' corps, so your temper's a small price to pay." He raised a hand to smooth her auburn hair. "You are quite pretty, you know."

" 'Tis fustian, sir, but I give you leave to say it," she answered, smiling.

They'd turned down the narrow drive into the Park, and the great house loomed ahead. Lord Audley, who'd been about to mount the steps of his shiny, lacquered carriage, stopped when he saw them, and Sarah's heart thudded uncomfortably.

Oblivious of her distress, Adam raised his hand to greet his brother, murmuring, "By the looks of it, 'tis Dev we beard first, my dear."

Lord Audley's finely chiseled face was marred by a deep frown as he started toward them. He was not nearly so perfectly dressed as when he'd called on her, having forgone the fashionable peruke for his own black hair, which he now wore like Adam's. That he was the catch of the neighborhood, if not of the kingdom, meant nothing to her. Any girlish notions she'd had about him had been dispelled when he'd come to the Hill. She tensed as he came to stand beside the horse.

"Sarah would have it that you do not mean to welcome her," Adam told him. "But I knew that for a hum. Here, help her down, will you?" So saying, he eased his body back from hers and waited.

Audley's mouth opened, then snapped shut. He'd speak to Adam later, when they were alone. Concealing his feelings admirably, his frown fading, he reached up to her.

"Miss Spender."

There was no help for it, then—she could not very well spurn him without drawing attention to it. She leaned forward into the arms of the man she now despised. His hands closed on her waist, tensing; then he lifted her easily and set her on the ground. As Adam dismounted, his brother released her.

"Papa is in uneven temper—I do not know that I'd have

brought her here,'' Devin murmured. '' 'Tis scarce the time for company.''

"Sarah's not company, Dev.'' Adam draped an easy arm about her shoulders and faced him, grinning broadly. "Wish me happy, brother—Miss Spender and I are to be married.''

Lord Audley's face froze in disbelief; then his eyes narrowed as his jaw worked to conceal the surge of anger that rushed through him. He exhaled sharply, then drew in a deep breath before he trusted himself to speak. "Well, 'tis rather sudden, is it not? You cannot have mentioned this to Papa,'' he said finally.

"Not yet. But I'd have your felicitations, brother.''

"No.'' The viscount's eyes raked over her and he lost the temper he'd been trying to hold in check. One eyebrow lifted, his gaze lingered deliberately on the awful black crepe that trailed on the ground. "My compliments, Miss Spender—you appear to have done quite well for yourself,'' he said sarcastically. To Adam, he shook his head. "I did not know you for such a fool.''

"Time was when I thought you had an interest in that quarter also,'' Adam retorted, stung. His fingers closed on Sarah's arm, holding it. "And I'll brook no such insult to my betrothed, Dev. You will, of course, apologize,'' he added stiffly.

"I don't think so.'' Lord Audley inclined his head slightly toward Sarah, then turned and strode away, obviously angry.

Adam's face reddened as he called after him. "Dev! Dash it, but you've no cause! And I'll not stand for the insult!'' When his brother did not stop, he threw down the riding crop he carried and started after him. "You may be the elder here, but you'll be civil to Sarah!''

Alarmed, Sarah hastened to catch him, nearly tripping over the folds of her skirt. She grabbed his elbow, pulling him back, and held on as he tried to shake her off. "Please . . . I'd not be the cause of trouble betwixt you. Maybe we should not have come here, Adam. Please,'' she implored huskily. "I'd not have you quarrel for me.''

He stopped and looked down at her, seeing again those

amber eyes, and forced himself to master his anger. "No. He had no right—"

"I'd go back to the Hill."

"And do what?" he asked furiously. "We Hastingses have left you without so much as a bedsheet." He shook his head. "No. I've as much a right to be here as he has, and I'll be *damned* if I am leaving this time. I've a right to bring my bride home."

"But if—"

His hand covered hers where it still held his sleeve, and his expression lightened. "Besides, he'll come round—and so will Papa. They have but to know you." He glanced to where Devin swung up into his carriage, and his frown returned. "He'll not speak thus to you again, I promise you."

She stood there clutching his arm, hoping desperately that he was right. But she had little hope of it. In her heart, she knew Audley would not easily forgive her for taking his brother's more honorable offer.

"Come on." Adam squeezed her hand briefly before releasing it. "Let us discover what Mama's maid can find you to wear before I present you to Papa."

"Will he be in a terrible taking, do you think?" she asked, once again feeling very unsure of herself.

"Papa? The thing to remember about my father, Sarah, is that nothing I do pleases him. And he is seldom civil to anyone." His mouth twisted wryly as his eyes met hers. "Had I anywhere else to take you, I should have done so, but there is so little time."

"I don't understand why—"

"The war, Sarah. I expect to hear any day that we are called to fight this thing with the French. If it happens ere I return, my orders will be sent here."

She glanced around her, seeing the immense gray stone house and the wide parklands, and felt a sense of foreboding. "Adam, I'd go with you," she whispered almost desperately. "I'd not stay here."

But he was staring after Audley's carriage and did not answer her.

6

Sarah's first supper at the Park was a decidedly strained affair, with the earl appearing even more testy than she had remembered him, while his countess took it upon herself to chatter incessantly, as though by doing so she could somehow cover his bad manners. No mention was made of the betrothal, and Sarah wondered if Adam had even broached the matter to his father yet. From time to time she looked up from her plate to covertly study the Hastings family, and discovered that Lord Audley watched her openly. Surely he did not mean to be so bold, not in the face of her betrothal to his own brother.

As the plates were removed in preparation for dessert, Lady Emma turned to her husband, murmuring, "I really do not have mourning gowns proper for a young lady, you know." Ignoring his darkening scowl, she pursued the matter gamely. "Indeed, there's been no need—'tis three years since poor Bertram passed on, you know, and then 'twas only black gloves, because he was but a distant connection on my Aunt Graybill's side. 'Twas most fortunate that I discovered the black taffeta she is wearing, although I cannot think it really suitable. But I daresay we shall contrive . . . A visit to Mrs. Craven in the village, perhaps," she ventured doubtfully. "Alas, her work is only a shade above passable, but—"

It was enough to stop his wineglass halfway to his mouth. His face darkened ominously; then he shook his head forcefully. "No! Emma, I forbid it! And while I do not cavil at your giving her one of yours, I see no need to squander m' blunt on a bunch of gowns for one as isn't a Hastings, and damme if I will. Black's black, anyway,'' he finished, scowling at his wife.

The last bite of bread seemed to swell in Sarah's mouth until she could not swallow it, and her face grew hot with embarrassment. Across the table from her, Devin Hastings smirked as though to tell her she'd never be acceptable to his father.

"She cannot stay here in rags," Lady Emma protested. "Surely two or three dresses—"

"Humph! But you ain't never bought two dresses in your life, have you? Within the space of a week, you'll have commissioned a dozen of 'em. Well, 'tis time to nip the bud ere it blooms, Emma, and I find meself paying for ball gowns for the chit! She ain't mine, and I ain't going to do it! There—I've said m'piece and that's the end to it!''

Surprisingly, Adam's mother did not let the matter drop. "She cannot stay here in rags, Charles," she repeated. "I'd not have it said we are remiss, and now that she is here, 'twill be remarked that we are cheese-parers if we do nothing."

"The responsibility is mine," Adam said quietly.

For once, he had the satisfaction of seeing his father stare, too stunned for speech. "Aye," he continued, "I thought Mama would wish to see me wed from this house, seeing as Sarah has none."

The countess's hands flew to her face in consternation, and she looked as though she meant to cry. "Married . . . Oh! Oh, Adam, no!" she choked, her voice little more than a whisper.

"What would you have had me do? Leave her to face the world alone?" He rounded on her. "If Spender is dead, we as much as put the ball in his brain, and you know it as well as I do, Mama."

"But—"

Stunned, the earl looked from his son to Sarah, then back again. His color, which had drained at Adam's news, returned with full choler. He raised his cane from beside the table, and for a moment Sarah was afraid he meant to strike his son. She rose hastily to lay a restraining hand on Adam's shoulder.

"Please—I'd best go, I think."

" '*Please—please,*' she says," the old man mimicked her. "Well, I ain't pleased, missy—not at all, I ain't! Spender's brat! Bah!" Words failed him again as he looked up at his son. "Nay, I forbid it, I tell you!" he sputtered finally.

"I am of an age, Papa," Adam reminded him coldly. "And this time, once I am gone, I do not mean to return."

The earl blanched, but did not give ground. "Sit down!" he roared. "Damme if I'm going to look up at the pair of you! Aye, you too, missy—I brook no insolence in this house!" Then to his son he added, "I ain't dead yet, you know, and if you want—"

"No, I don't 'want,' Papa," Adam cut him short. "You can give the whole of the Hastings fortune to Dev, for all I care. Indeed, I should expect it," he said bitterly, "for he is not such a disappointment to you." Slipping a hand beneath Sarah's elbow, he murmured, "I ask your pardon, my dear—I should not have brought you here." His mouth twisted wryly as his blue eyes met hers. "We'll be wed over the anvil."

"Not Gretna!" the countess wailed. " 'Twill be a scandal! Devin, tell him . . . Oh . . ."

Devin, who'd watched the scene played out almost as a bystander, stood suddenly to face his brother, his own feelings obviously mixed. "Adam, there is no need—can we not reason this out as men? I'd not have you go, and neither would Papa, if the truth be told, would you, sir?" he added, appealing to his father. " 'Tis so sudden. Perhaps a marriage is not necessary. Perhaps arrangements can be made whereby—"

"Such as you yourself would like?" Sarah demanded accusingly. Angered, humiliated, she turned on his father, her face flushed. "None of you has spared a thought to what I would wish, have you? How dare you sit there and speak as though I am nothing? Can you not address me? Do you think that because I am penniless now, I have no sensibility left?" she asked furiously. "Well, I am Sarah Spender, sir—neither a tart nor an urchin dependent on your charity! I am Sarah Spender, and my family has held lands in this kingdom longer than yours!"

"Sit down, gel!" he shouted at her.

"No!" Pushing back an errant strand of hair that had strayed from the curls on her crown, she took a deep breath, exhaling slowly; then she dared to stare directly into his pale eyes. "You may be able to bullock your wife, and you may attempt to bullock your sons, my lord, but I'll not stand for it," she told him evenly.

"Sit down, gel! Damme if I'm to tell you again!"

"I should rather go to York than trespass on your doubtful charity," she retorted. "But then, I should have expected this, shouldn't I? Your parsimony is the gossip of the county, after all."

As she turned her back on the old man, Adam grinned at her. "Good girl! Serve him soup from the same spoon!" He slid his hand down to clasp hers. "We'll go to the Red Stag, then press on to Scotland in the morning—unless, of course, I can persuade the bishop to forgo the banns."

Devin crossed the room behind them to stand in the doorway, barring it, as his mother pleaded with his father. "Charles, please—do not let him go. Oh, what if this dreadful war should come to pass? What if—".

"Dash it, Emma, be still!"

"Stand aside, Dev."

"No. 'Tis dark and cold and late, Adam, and Miss Spender is fagged to death." Audley's handsome face was grave, his blue eyes sober as he looked at them. "There is no saying that everything must be resolved one way or another tonight, is there? I suggest that Mama take Miss Spender up to her chamber whilst you and I and Papa reason together like men."

"Don't make me lay hands on you, Dev."

As Devin's gaze flicked over Sarah, Adam stepped in front of her protectively, a gesture that was not lost on him. And from the coldness in her eyes, he knew he was defeated anyway. Nonetheless, he appealed to her.

"Go on up with Mama. 'Tis not the first time the Hastingses have quarreled, and I daresay 'twill not be the last, but none of us would have him leave like this."

The countess, seeing Sarah hesitate, moved forward also. "Please, my dear. What difference can it make whether you are gone tonight or in the morning? Indeed, but 'twill cause unpleasant gossip when 'tis known you stayed at an inn unchaperoned, and I—"

"Not once we are wed," Adam retorted. "Dev—"

"Papa, tell him we can speak reasonably together," Audley prompted his father. "Tell him that there is no need for this."

"Still the peacemaker, Dev?" Adam gibed. " 'Tis not fractious Whigs you address, brother. Save your diplomacy for Parliament, where there are fewer deaf ears."

"Sit down, boy—aye, and you also, gel." This time when he spoke, the old man sighed heavily. "Take your death in the night air, anyways."

"There are matters to be discussed between us whether you stay or go," Devin continued. "Unless you mean to sell out, you will have to consider what to do with her if you are sent abroad, you know. And what if you do not come back—what then? She will be dependent on us whether she wills it or not."

He spoke almost softly now, but his words chilled Sarah to the core. Her fingers tightened almost convulsively in Adam's. "No," she whispered hollowly.

"If you are of a like mind in the morning, you may have the loan of my carriage to take you to Gretna—or wherever you choose to go." He looked to Sarah. "All I ask is for Adam to sit down with Papa this once."

She hadn't wanted to come to the Park, and she didn't want to stay, but he had reason on his side this time. She looked up to see the anguish mirrored in Adam's mother's face, and thought she could not bear it.

"Adam?"

"Do you really think 'twould be any different this time, Dev?" he asked bitterly. "I'd not listen to him slander Sarah further."

The earl did not know what deep game his heir played, but he sensed the advantage in delay. And he knew he'd pushed his younger son too far. Rising with an effort from his chair, he leaned heavily on his cane and hobbled slowly toward them. Obviously in great pain, he seemed as pale as the old-fashioned periwig he wore. When he reached his wife, he stopped and lifted the cane toward Sarah, gesturing with it.

"Go on with you, now. You let Emma see you to bed, gel, you hear? Suffice it to say that I ain't turning any female out into the night." Even as he spoke, he swayed and balanced himself once again with the cane as beads of perspiration broke out on his forehead. "Got to have the laudanum," he gasped, gripping the silver handle until his knuckles whitened.

"One of these days, Papa, you are going to overdose yourself with the opium," Adam warned. Nonetheless, he dropped Sarah's hand and moved to support the old man, catching him strongly beneath an arm. Devin shouldered him on the other side. " 'Tis you who should be in bed."

"Nay, I cannot—get down, cannot get up. Need to sit, that's all."

"Where's his laudanum?" Devin asked tersely.

For answer, Lady Emma hurried to a cabinet and drew out a stoppered bottle, returning with it in hand.

"Take it with m' brandy—oh, lud lumme, got to sit down."

The countess handed Adam the opiate, then turned apologetically to Sarah, explaining, " 'Tis his gout that makes him cross, you know, for he was not always like this." Then, reaching a hand to Sarah, she urged her, "Come, let us leave them. If you are to be my daughter, 'tis time we had a comfortable coze. Or if you are too tired, at least let me see you to your chamber."

"You don't have to stay, Sarah," Adam told her. "I'll see him to his bookroom, and we can go."

The hollow planes in his mother's face seemed to sag further and her eyes filled with tears. With an effort, Sarah forced herself to shake her head. "No. I'd not say I caused a breach between you and your family. You'd best hear them out."

" 'Twill change nothing—the breach is not of your making, Sarah."

Devin breathed a sigh of relief. "Then 'tis settled, is it not? Mama will see to Miss Spender whilst you and I make Papa comfortable. Then we will talk, the three of us.''

''Perhaps you would wish to look at the latest fashion plates from Paris ere you retire?'' Lady Emma suggested to Sarah hopefully. ''Though with the current contretemps between us and the French, 'tis to be supposed we shall have to copy them ourselves. Oh, but then, you are in mourning,'' she recalled regretfully. '' 'Tis a pity, for you would show to advantage, I am sure.''

There was no help for it then. Sarah dutifully followed the countess out, brushing past Devin Hastings without looking at him. Behind her, she could hear the old man concede, ''Passable-looking chit, but she's got too much tongue to her. Can't abide high-tempered females.''

Then Lord Audley's next words chilled her, for he said, ''I know you did what you think best, Adam, but I'd counsel you to wait until the war is over. Twenty-four is overyoung to wed anyway.''

''Oh, my dear, but how I wish Meg were here,'' the countess continued, drawing her attention back. ''She'd be glad of your company, I am certain of it, for there's so little to do here at the Park. She and Charles do not deal together, I fear, but my poor Meg holds her tongue.''

Privately Sarah did not see how anyone dealt with the earl, but she was not afraid of him. It was Lord Audley she feared. It was Lord Audley who would stand between her and Adam if he could.

'' 'Tis such a shock—Adam's offering for you, I mean. There was not the least hint of an attachment between you, was there? All those years our lands marched with your father's, and yet we scarce knew you,'' Lady Emma rattled on. ''But then, there was a time before your dear mama died when your papa was not nearly so rackety . . . Oh, dear, I ought not to put it precisely that way, I suppose. And Adam did so like to ride over to the Hill back then, but I cannot think . . . No, of course he could not have developed a *tendre* that early—and he has been gone these three years past.''

''I saw him last year at Squire Lynch's.''

The countess's frown cleared abruptly. ''Then that was it, of course—I knew there had to be some attachment there. I could not think Adam would offer where his heart was not, not when he has seen the result of that folly. 'Tis strange, though, that Devin did not mention it, for they are quite close.''

"I was of the opinion that they were rivals, my lady," Sarah murmured, still straining to hear the conversation in the bookroom.

"Well, they quarrel, of course, but what brothers do not? When all is said and done, Adam can be expected to listen to Audley, my dear—Devin carries far more weight than Charles with him.''

It was not a very comforting thought to take to bed, Sarah reflected, wishing she'd gone to the Red Stag instead. But she hadn't, and now three men argued her fate without her.

7

They quarreled far into the night, with Sarah listening apprehensively from a chair pulled close to her chamber door. But she could not hear more than a few angry words at a time, only enough to worry her. The old man baited and shouted, and Adam answered him in kind, until she wondered how anyone could sleep in the house. From time to time, Lord Audley raised his voice also, pleading for peace between them.

A host of conflicting emotions warred in her breast as she tried to listen. It was clear that if he wedded her, his family would not support him in his marriage—or at least neither the earl nor Lord Audley would, and she doubted the countess would set herself against her husband and elder son. And the longer she listened, the more she realized that Adam would be whistling his share of the enormous Hastings fortune down the wind for her. She'd been foolish to think it could be otherwise, she chided herself.

For a long time she sat very still as the fact that he could not wed her sank in. All the railing against the earl's temper or the viscount's perfidy could not change that: Adam Hastings could not wed the penniless Miss Sarah Spender. He owed more to his blood than that, and she knew it.

But she could not quite let go of her dreams of him. She let herself remember how it had been in her mother's garden, how he had looked standing over her, tall and splendidly handsome in his scarlet uniform. Nor would she ever forget his kindness to her. *I know I'm not a catch like Dev, but if you tell me that you prefer York to me, I'll know it for a hoax.* He was a better catch than Audley, if he only knew it. *'Tis Adam, Sarah, come to save you from five little boys in York.* How very like him to have said it just that way. *Choose your first dragon, Sarah.* She'd been wrong; that first dragon wasn't York—it was his family.

She hugged her knees, reluctant to let go of the memory, yet knowing she had to do so, that she could not go on dreaming the impossible dream. Finally, when she could stand it no longer, she let go and stood up. He would be too much the gentleman to cry off, even if he regretted the rashness of his offer. No, she was going to have to tell him it was all right, that she understood. But if he were relieved, she knew she could not bear it.

Her spirits plummeted at that thought, and a knot formed in her stomach. She knew he'd offered in haste and out of pity, but she hoped he would at least appear saddened when she let him off the tenterhook. It did not matter—there could be no recrimination on her part. He had to know that she understood he could not wed her.

Her decision made, she dared not wait until morning lest she waver. Still clothed in Lady Emma's black taffeta, she slipped out of the chamber and crept down the servants' stairs to wait for him. But even as she reached the back hall, the angry voices stopped her. She listened for a time, but could make out nothing beyond the cutting tone of the earl's remarks. And Adam's answers were muffled by the heavy door.

Whatever he'd said, it did not mollify the earl, for the old man continued to rant. Her face reddened at what the servants must think.

The door opened abruptly, sending a slice of light into the dim hallway; then it slammed shut behind Adam. She could hear the anger in his footsteps as he passed not fifteen feet from her. She hesitated but a moment, then went after him. It was time to make it easier for him.

He walked fast, so fast that she had to break into a trot just to keep him in sight as he crossed the darkened yard toward the stables. Had it not been for the light from a nearly full moon, she'd have lost him. Shivering from the cold night air, she watched as he reached the long building and slammed his fist into the wooden door with such force that the frame splintered and the hinges broke. The sound shattered the stillness like a musket shot; then the door shuddered as it came to rest at an angle. For a moment he stood, a long shadow in the open doorway, leaning his head against the wooden facing. She walked up behind him.

"Adam—"

"What are you doing here?" he asked harshly. "You should be in bed."

"I . . . I heard. And I am sorry."

"Sorry—for what? 'Tis I who should apologize to you for what was said at supper. I should not have brought you here."

She knew real fear then. Despite all her brave thoughts to the contrary, she knew she could not bear it if he should change his mind. But she had to release him—she had to.

"Adam—"

"Go to bed. You've had a tiring day, Sarah."

"Please—"

"I'll be all right—go on."

She could tell by the tightness of his voice and the rigidity of his back that he was still very angry, and she sought the only means she knew to ease that anger. Moving closer, she reached out to touch his shoulder. "Adam, I would not have come if I'd known." When he didn't respond, she forced herself to whisper, "Adam, you do not have to marry me. I . . . I quite understand 'tis impossible, and . . . well, I do not expect it. 'Tisn't as though I cannot take care of myself—I'll go to York. I don't belong here, and I know it."

She bit her lip and waited, but he just stood there, his body stiff and unyielding beneath her hand. "Please, do not think you have to . . ." She swallowed hard. "I'm going to York, Adam."

"No, 'tis no life for a young girl, Sarah. I'd not have you a drudge in someone's house."

"Adam, listen to me! I . . . . I know about the money—I heard! Please turn around and look at me—please!" She tugged at his coat insistently. "Do not make this any harder, I beg of you! Adam, I am saying you do not have to marry me. I know you offered from pity, and . . . and I'd not have you do it," she finished quickly. "I . . . I don't want your money, and I never have."

He turned around at that, and his eyes caught the moonlight eerily as his hands grasped her shoulders roughly. "I don't pity you, Sarah—'tis friendship and more that I'd have from you."

"Adam, I know I am not what you require in a wife," she tried desperately. "I'm telling you that I understand."

He sucked in his breath and let it out slowly, shaking his head. "No matter what he says, or what anyone says, I want to wed with you—do you understand that? I think I could learn to love you, Sarah." And even as he said the words, he knew them for the truth. He searched her face warily, afraid that she would cry off out of a mistaken sense of honor. "I want to wed with you, Sarah," he repeated softly.

"On, Adam!" Relief flooded over her, making her almost giddy with happiness.

"But the devil of it is that I do not know how I am to care for you—Dev's right in that," he admitted, sobering. "An army's no place for a green girl, not when we may be called to fight in America. And yet you have not the experience for an establishment of your own.''

Her resolve forgotten, she could only whisper huskily, "I'll try, Adam—indeed, but I should not mind following the drum.''

His fingers loosened and slid down her arms lightly, sending a shiver through her. "No. But we'll contrive something, Sarah.''

"I don't care where I am.'' Her amber eyes misted and her chin quivered from the emotion that threatened to overwhelm her. "As long as I am your wife, 'twill be enough.''

"Do you mean that, Sarah—do you? You will not tear at me for leaving you when I must? Dev would have it wrong of me to wed you now.''

"No.''

" 'Tis hard for those who stay at home and wait.''

"It doesn't matter.''

"For now.''

"Forever. Adam, you speak with one who has never had anything—not for years, anyway,'' she amended truthfully. She leaned into his chest, resting her head against him. "All I want is for you to have a care for me. Can you understand that?''

With a groan, he pulled her closer, wrapping his arms around her, warming her. "Aye, 'tis what I want also,'' he whispered softly into the crown of her hair. "I want someone to have a care for me also, Sarah.'' His hand stroked her hair where loose strands had escaped over her neck. His voice dropped low. "Now's all the time there may be for us, you know.''

She shuddered involuntarily against him and slid her own arms tightly around his waist. "Adam Hastings, I very nobly tried to cry off once—you'll not get me to do it again,'' she told him forcefully.

"I might be as like to make you a widow as a wife.''

"I pray you will not speak foolishness. If you persist in such thoughts, I'll insist on going with you—if only to see that your stockings are dry, you wretch.''

He rubbed his cheek against her hair, savoring the clean smell of it, and teased her. "I'd not want you to mourn overlong for me—all I'd ask is that you choose a better second husband."

"As if there could be one!" she scoffed.

"Sarah . . ."

She twisted her neck to smile up at him. "I should be more afraid never to have loved you than to lose you."

He studied those strangely beautiful amber eyes of hers, thinking she surely must be the loveliest girl in the world, and he felt a sudden rush of tenderness for her. The taffeta crackled under his palms as his hands moved upward toward her shoulders. "Sarah . . . Sarah . . . if you want to marry me half as much as I want to marry you right now, we'll both be content in each other." His fingers found the pins that held her hair, and loosed them. The thick, luxuriant mass tumbled over his hands like silk as he gently pulled her head back and gave her the second kiss of her life.

Unlike Roland's tentative, inexperienced kiss, Adam's lips sent a shiver of anticipation through her from the moment they touched hers. She clung to him wholeheartedly, giving herself over to the feel of him, drawing security from his strength and from the heat of his body. Instinctively she twined her arms about his neck as her lips parted under pressure from his. And despite the layers of petticoats between them, her skin turned to gooseflesh. If this, then, was love, she wanted more of it.

Suddenly he let her go and stepped back. She stumbled slightly and clutched at the rough boards for support, wondering if somehow she'd done something wrong. His breathing was uneven and his eyes glittered. His voice sounded strangely hoarse when he finally spoke.

"I didn't mean to do that—I'm sorry, Sarah. 'Tis not right for me to take advantage of your innocence."

She blinked back tears of humiliation, and tried to understand why. "But, Adam, didn't you *want* me to kiss you?"

"Of course I did." One of his hands steadied her elbow as the other smoothed her hair. "But you have so little experience before the world, Sarah—you do not know what you can do to a man. You make me want to rush my fences, you know.'' His hands dropped. '' 'Tis just that there is so little time.''

''Adam, I don't care if you rush your fences.''

The huskiness in her voice sent a thrill through him, renewing desire. He stared into those eyes, then crushed her roughly against him, kissing her hungrily, tasting, taking, and all the while his hands explored her back, feeling the whaleboning beneath the taffeta. Her firm breasts pressed against the buttons of his vest as heat diffused through his body. And her hair, where it fell over his hands, nearly burned him, so completely aware of her he was.

She answered him kiss for kiss, savoring the newness, the power of the desire between them, until she felt as though she could not breathe. His hands moved to her waist, slipping between them to the lacings over her stomacher, then stopped abruptly. His body froze against hers.

''What . . . Oh!'' she gasped as blood rushed to her face.

Over his shoulder, she could see the lantern light flooding the doorway, and Devin Hastings' black hair gleamed above the yellow glow. His frown deepened when he saw her, making him appear almost evil.

Adam stepped back, but did not release her. His arm circled her shoulder reassuringly as he turned to face his brother. ''You waste your breath if Papa has sent you,'' he said coldly.

Lord Audley met Adam's eyes soberly. ''No. But I thought you were alone. I have calmed Papa.''

''It makes no difference, Dev. After we are wed tomorrow, I mean to take Sarah away from here.''

''Tomorrow?'' Devin's face betrayed his surprise, but still he attempted reason. Shaking his head regretfully, he sighed. ''Adam, consider. 'Twill cause gossip, you know. And we are agreed now, Papa and I, that she may stay here. I have got him to agree that if you are of the same mind when her mourning is done, then he'll not oppose you.''

''Do you think I do not know what he does?'' Adam

asked scornfully. "Do you think I am so great a fool that I'd believe that?"

"Mama will give her some town bronze whilst you are gone."

"No!" Sarah choked in dismay.

"While she is in mourning? Cut line, Dev—we both know that for a hoax. No, I don't have a year to wait."

Devin Hastings' eyes raked over her coldly, taking in her streaming hair and the loosened ties at her waist. " 'Tis chill—she ought not to be out here."

So he had come to push the quarrel in the guise of making peace. Adam nodded. Dropping his arm from her shoulders, he removed his scarlet frock coat, then carefully settled it onto her, pulling it close in the front. "Go on inside, Sarah—I'd speak to Dev alone." The back of his hand brushed lightly against her cheek for a brief moment before he stepped away. "Please."

She shivered despite the body warmth of the coat, looking from one brother to the other. Despite the quietness, the air seemed to hang heavy with the tension between them. "Adam—"

"No—I'll be in directly. You go on to bed—it has been a trying day for you."

She didn't want to go, to leave him to quarrel on her behalf yet again, but she had no wish to defy him. Instead, she dropped her gaze and walked silently past Devin Hastings. The taffeta gown swished as it brushed against the broken door facing. Outside, she gathered the scarlet wool closer and hurried toward the house.

"Papa's right, you know: you are throwing yourself away for nothing," Devin murmured as he hung the lantern from a peg. "Oh, I'll grant you she's a pretty creature."

"Dev—"

"But you don't have to wed her," he continued, turning back. " 'Tis as plain as a pikestaff she's naught but an adventuress, you know." His lip curled scornfully as he took in Adam's shirtsleeves. "I saw enough tonight to tell me that she can be bedded without the parson." Ignoring the perceptible tightening of his brother's jaw, he gibed, "For a few pounds, you could—"

His head snapped back from the impact, and he reeled, staggering to right himself against the broken door. For a moment he could only stare into Adam's angry eyes. He rubbed his jaw. "Fool!" he spat. "She's not worth—"

The second blow sent him sprawling to the dew-drenched ground outside. Furious, Devin lurched to his feet and ran at his brother, who stood poised with fists clenched. "She's a nobody, I tell you," he panted, swinging wide. "And I'll be damned if anyone strikes me with impunity—even you."

Adam ducked, and the blow glanced off his shoulder as he punched hard below Devin's rib cage. The viscount sagged as the wind left his lungs in a great gasp. He rolled to the ground and lay there to catch his breath. Adam stood over him, his hands still tightly curled.

"She's going to be my wife, Dev!"

Devin rolled, pushing into Adam's legs, bringing him down; then, grunting, he managed to get up at the same time. This time he crouched, waiting. "Bit of fluff," he snorted derisively.

"Think I cannot beat you? Think you can say anything?" Adam asked silkily, circling him. "I am not a green'un anymore, you know."

It was as though the years rolled away and they were boys locked in yet another quarrel. Devin rushed his fences, landing a barrage of quick blows to his brother's body, only to take a sharp right to the ear that staggered him. But he came back to deliver a sound right to Adam's chin, followed by a belly blow.

They fought hard, oblivious of the cold or the wet grass, rolling and punching until both were breathless. Finally Adam pushed Devin against the stable, gasping, "Had enough yet? Afore God, I am ready to beat your manners into you!" But his obvious fatigue gave the lie to his words as he leaned over to balance himself against the building. "Take her for a sister or lose a brother, Dev."

Exhausted, Devin nodded grudgingly. "Aye."

"Support me against Papa, Dev."

It was obvious that Adam's attachment for Sarah

Spender went far deeper than Devin had supposed. He stared into his younger brother's glittering eyes until he could meet them no longer. Finally he nodded. "Aye."

"I'd have you witness for me. There'll be less gossip if at least one of my family is there." Adam's breath still came in great gulps. He inhaled deeply, then expelled the air slowly. "I need you, Dev—I'd not see Sarah harmed further."

She was lost to him, no matter what happened, and he knew it. Telling himself that there were other ladybirds far more beautiful than the Spender chit, Devin forced himself to accept the inevitable. "You ought to give me time to prepare Papa."

Adam shook his head. "I'd give him something he cannot change—'tis all he understands."

"I can make—"

"No. Tomorrow."

"So soon?" But he recognized the determination in those glittering eyes, and knew it was useless to argue further. And maybe seeing Sarah Spender wed his brother would break his own foolish passion for her. "All right." His hand crept to his jaw, feeling the soreness there, and he grinned ruefully. "I suppose you expect me to wish you happy."

"I'd hoped you would."

Devin straightened his coat and tried to retie his stock with his swollen hands. "But what the deuce are you going to do with her when you are sent abroad?"

"Much depends on you—and Papa. If I can, I mean to take her."

"And if you cannot?"

"I'll look to you. Come on, I'm cold now myself." Adam started back toward the house, leaving Devin to stare after him. Finally, as Adam's meaning sank in, he hastened to catch up.

"The devil you will!"

"'Tis why I mean to wed her first." Adam stopped, turning to wait, and his face broke into a broad grin. "I know you, Dev—you'd cut me out with Miss Spender, but you are not such a rum one that you'd dally with my wife."

It was a painful truth, one that did not bear acknowledging. Instead, Devin fell in beside his brother, walking
slowly toward the shadowed portico. Suddenly he
stopped, recalling the lantern.

"I've got to go back—there'd be the devil to pay if
Papa's horses burned up. You go on in." When Adam
hesitated, he added, "Besides, I ought to look to Lucie—
one of the ostlers says he thinks she's ready to foal."

Adam went around to the back of the house, letting
himself in through the servants' door, then climbed the
back stairs. Below, he could see the sliver of light from
below the bookroom door, but he was in no mood to fight
further with his father. He was tired and sore, but
strangely exhilarated.

As he walked down the silent hall above, he paused
outside Sarah's door, stopping to rap it lightly, hoping
she was not asleep. Inside, he could hear faint movement; then she whispered through the closed door, "Who
goes there?"

" 'Tis Adam."

She started to open it, but he stopped her, holding on
to the doorknob. He'd not have the servants spread it
about that he trysted with her in his parents' house before
they were wedded. And yet every fiber of his being
seemed aware that she was there, and he closed his eyes
in the semidarkness, imagining her in her nightshift. His
mouth went dry.

"Until the morrow, Sarah," he murmured softly.

"What . . . ?"

But she could hear his footsteps as he went on down
the hall, and then a door creaked shut at the end. Puzzled, she went back to bed, where she sat propped
amongst the pillows, hugging her knees, too excited for
sleep. Tomorrow. Actually, it *was* already the morrow.
This day, she would wed Adam Hastings, and her life
would change forever.

8

Despite her lack of sleep, Sarah rose early on her wedding day, washed her hair, and left it to dry enough for the curling tongs. A quick search of the house revealed that Adam had already gone somewhere, so she escaped to the private garden behind the house to hide her disappointment, much as she would have at the Hill.

That it was chilly and the flowers still dormant made no difference—it was the fresh, clean air that drew her. Settling on a stone bench to collect her thoughts, she told herself that she was the most fortunate of females. Unlike so many girls of her class, she was not only making a grand marriage but also wedding someone she loved.

She leaned back, resting her head against the damp wall, remembering again how it had felt to be kissed by him. Even though she'd relived every moment of it a dozen times and more in her bed, she could not help blushing again. Was this, then, what Miss Wallace had spoken so darkly about? If it were, then she must surely be wanton, for she'd quite thoroughly enjoyed herself. Or was kissing merely a prelude to more? That gave her pause. Despite the relative freedom of her youth, she'd not the least notion of such things, and certainly Miss Wallace had been disinclined to discuss them. Not that she could, Sarah supposed, for she was an unmarried female herself.

Her friends, when she had them, had all been boys, so there was not much to learn there, for one could scarce gossip about such things with them. No, she and Roland and Adam had merely been grubby together until Adam, who'd been the oldest and therefore the leader, had been sent away to school. Then Miss Wallace had come, putting an end to such easy discourse anyway, saying it was not meet for a female to be in even a young boy's company unattended. Boys, she'd pronounced, were wicked creatures bent on ruining girls. And Sarah was not even precisely certain how they managed the task. As far as she knew, none of them had attempted to ruin her—except Lord Audley.

Neither Roland, who'd kissed her, planting wet lips on hers, nor Adam, who'd shown her the experience could be exceedingly pleasant, had ever suggested anything but marriage. Only Audley would have ruined her. And the ludicrous thing about being ruined was that it was all determined by a few words spoken by a churchman—without them, one was a hussy and a harlot, and with them, one was a respectable wife.

Scattered twigs cracked and crunched beneath booted footsteps, and for a moment she thought it was Adam come back. But when she looked up, it was his brother. She recoiled visibly, then dropped her head warily and smoothed her skirt over her lap. To her horror, he stopped in front of her. She looked up cautiously, seeing the purplish bruise along his jaw.

"My, but we are out early, are we not?" he commented.

"I have never been a slugabed."

"The paragon," he murmured, dropping to sit on the bench beside her. His long legs stretched out before him as he leaned his head back. "Lovely—and industrious."

She started to rise, only to have him lay a restraining hand on her arm. "No, don't go—please. 'Twas not my intent to offend."

"You startled me—I thought wealthy lords stayed abed late," she managed through clenched teeth. "And I'd not have you touch me."

He dropped his hand immediately, but not before she thought she saw a hint of amusement in his eyes. "In the ordinary way of things, we do, but as I have not been there yet, it can be debated whether 'tis early or late."

"Yes, well, I daresay 'tis no concern of mine what hours you keep, my lord."

"Let us not quarrel between us, Miss Spender . . . Sarah. I am come to make amends with you ere you wed my brother."

She eyed him suspiciously, noting again the bruise, and the fact that his usually impeccable clothes were rumpled and stained with mud and grass. Her eyes widened as they traveled over his open shirt and untied stock, then to the black hair that streamed over his shoulders. As she watched, he passed his hand over the dark stubble of a day's growth of beard and smiled ruefully.

"I suppose I am a shocking fright, am I not?"

"Actually, I was thinking you looked as though you'd been in a mill."

"How very observant you are, dear Sarah. My just deserts, don't you think?"

"My congratulations to the victor."

"I am come to cry friends with you, my dear, but you make the task deuced difficult, you know," he complained. "You give no quarter to the vanquished."

"My lord—"

"No, my dear, 'tis time for plain speaking, I think." Briefly he closed his eyes and then opened them as though doing so could somehow clear his mind. "Got a devil of a head today, I can tell you."

"Perhaps you ought not to drink quite so much," she murmured unsympathetically. "Really, but I must go, and—"

One black eyebrow rose as he cocked his head to look at her. "Still up in the boughs, eh? That you are right does little to ease my head or my conscience, Sarah."

"I did not give you leave to use my name, sir."

"No, you did not, did you? But 'Miss Spender' seems rather formal if we are to be related, does it not? Tsk. Here I am attempting to apologize for my utterly shameful behavior, and you refuse to let me humble myself at your feet."

"Alas, but you seem to be beside me, my lord," she pointed out. "And I should like to see you grovel, if you must know."

"Yes, well, I am not a particularly good groveler, you see, but I am attempting to secure your forgiveness. I know now that I quite misread the entire situation, and am prepared to wish you and Adam well, my dear."

"How very kind of you."

" 'Tis not an easy task to see one's own hopes quite cut up, but I cannot fault you for taking my brother's far-more-honorable offer."

"There was no question of accepting you, sir. I should have declined any offer, honorable or not, where I have not the least regard."

"Sarah, I am heartily sorry for the offense. I just wish we could begin again without rancor between us."

It was her turn to blink. "The blow to your jaw has, I think, addled your brain," she decided firmly. "I cannot forget what you thought me."

He sighed and stretched his weary frame again. "You will have to, I am afraid."

"I don't—" She stopped, aware now that he was quite serious.

"He's my brother, Sarah, and I am his. Don't attempt to estrange us before he goes abroad, I beg of you. We are not many, we Hastingses, and when all is done, blood rules."

"Do you threaten me, Lord Audley?"

"Lud, no! My dear, I am *begging* you to forgive and forget what I said to you yesterday. Nay, I am *bribing* you to do it."

He wasn't making sense. "Bribing me, sir?" She stiffened indignantly. "If you think you can keep me from marrying Adam, you are very wide of the mark! Indeed, but—"

"Sheathe your claws, Sarah," he cut in tiredly. "The wedding is all but done, and I am not so much a fool that I don't know when to withdraw from the field. I'm asking you not to tell Adam of my offer, that's all." When she did not respond, he sighed. "Despite our quarrels, he has always thought me better than I am—I'd like to keep his regard, Sarah."

"That is between the two of you, I think."

"You will not ease this for me, will you? Sarah, for

Adam's sake, I am asking you to cry friends with me—can you understand that? I'd not have a breach between us, particularly not when he goes to war. Whether you choose to believe it or not, my brother is very dear to me.''

The appeal in his eyes seemed genuine, softening the coldness of his handsome face, making her want to believe him. He was, after all, Adam's only brother, and no doubt much of what he was could be laid to his father. Looking away, she nodded. "I suppose I must," she conceded finally.

"Then we are friends?"

She was not certain she could ever feel any warmth for him, but for Adam's sake she would try. "Not friends perhaps, but neither enemies."

He appeared relieved. "Then I collect you will say nothing of this to Adam?"

" 'Twould serve little purpose now, would it?"

"No." A slow, wry smile twisted his mouth downward. "Adam's a lucky devil, I'll give him that."

Despite her dislike of him, she could not help chuckling. "I'll wager you were shocked beyond bearing when Adam brought me home, weren't you?"

There was that husky quality in her voice that had drawn him before. A pang of regret stabbed at him, but he managed to stifle it. "To state the matter mildly," he admitted dryly. "But as you see, I have recovered from the disappointment. Now, are you not going to ask me just why I have not yet got to bed?"

"All right. Then why are you still up, my lord?"

"Lucie."

Her body went rigid and her face betrayed shock that he would be so bold again with her. "Really, sir, but this is highly improper," she protested stiffly.

"I suppose I deserved that also, didn't I? Lucie, my dear, is a mare."

"Well, I couldn't know that, sir," she retorted acidly, perceiving that he was funning with her.

"Devin. Aye, I stayed awake until her foal was born about two hours past, and then I celebrated. Would you like to see the filly, my dear?"

"I should rather wait for Adam, I think."

"Oh, I expect him back shortly after noon, so you need not fear he has abandoned you amongst the ogres, Sarah. But you have not answered me—would you see Lucie's filly or not? If you are afraid," he added disarmingly, "I assure you I have never molested a female in the stables—not even a deuced pretty one."

She rose quickly at that, afraid that he meant to break the still fragile truce between them, and straightened her skirt over her petticoats.

"I pray you will save the false coin for someone else, my lord."

But he leaned back lazily and watched her with open amusement. His dark hair fell forward over his forehead in sharp contrast to his blue eyes, and for a moment she could see the resemblance to Adam. But he was darker, colder, she reminded herself, and therefore not quite as handsome to her.

"My, what a sheltered goose you are, my dear. When you are out in society, you will discover that it would be much more remarked if I did *not* compliment you." Abruptly he lurched to his feet to face her. "But you are as skittish as a filly yourself just now, aren't you? Well, 'tis not a bad thing that you are, I suppose, for your artlessness will be remarked as refreshing. So, do you see my prize or not?"

"Well, I . . . ."

"Still wary, my dear?"

"Yes."

"Adam is my brother, Sarah. There is not a female living who could come between us for very long." He held out his hand like one would to a small child. "Come, I'd show you Lucie's filly," he coaxed.

She still hesitated, uncertain whether to believe him at all. Finally she nodded. "But my hand is my own, sir, and I'd not share it."

Shrugging, he dropped his and stood back to wait for her. "After you, then."

Trudging beside him, she blurted out, "Did Adam say where he went?"

"No, but I do not expect him to tarry." Seeing that

this was not a satisfactory answer, he grinned. "Buck up, Sarah—you are getting an honorable man—he'll not leave you waiting at the church door, I promise you."

"I did not think he would."

"I brought him out to see the filly also," he added conversationally. "Since the mare is daughter to one we both claimed as children, I thought he might want this foal."

"Did he?"

"No, but he had an idea as to what I could do with it." He leaned past her to open the stable door, and she was gratified to see an ostler cleaning tack at the back. "But you have to see her first."

The musty scent of dust and hay assailed her nose, reminding her of the night before. It had been just within the door that Adam had kissed her. Blinking to adjust her eyes to the dimness, she stepped inside, grateful she'd forgone the whalebone half-petticoat the countess's maid had wanted her to wear. Otherwise, she'd not have been able to maneuver her skirt within the stable. The ostler looked up and smiled broadly at Devin, revealing gaps between rotted teeth.

"Come to see 'er again, milord? 'Er's a good 'un, I'll be bound, 'er is."

"I have brought Miss Spender this time."

Devin's hand moved up to grasp her elbow, and he propelled her between the stalls until he reached the last one. A very pretty bay mare stood, her neck stretched over the half-door, her sleek body blocking a view of her stall. The viscount reached out with his free hand to rub along the bony nose. "Steady, girl." Turning his head back to the ostler, he nodded approvingly. "I see you have already rubbed her down."

"Wouldn't a known 'er'd foaled," the fellow acknowledged proudly.

"Good. See to the ordering of the carriage for Lady Westerfield, will you, Jem? I believe she means to go into the village about eleven to see Mrs. Craven." Turning back to Sarah, he gestured to the mare, asking, "Well, what do you think of my Lucie, my dear?"

"She's beautiful, my lord," Sarah admitted. "Truly beautiful."

"Wait until you see the foal." He released her elbow and reached to open the half-door. Slipping inside, he managed to nudge the mare aside so that Sarah could see the spindly-legged filly behind her. It shied and wobbled when he touched it, moving forward to rub against the mare. Like its mother, it was a bay, but it had a star-shaped white spot centered on its forehead. When Devin looked back at Sarah, there was an intense pride in his eyes. "Well? We had hoped for a colt, but she's a pretty thing, isn't she? I helped her come into the world."

And in that moment, Sarah almost liked him. "She's as pretty as her mother," she answered sincerely.

"A filly out of Santa Lucia's Misty Morning by Daybreak. Here, would you like to touch her? Lucie won't mind, I assure you."

"Is that the mare's name? 'Tis no wonder you call her Lucie."

"Aye, 'tis a mouthful, isn't it? Actually, Daybreak is more to my liking for his name, but Papa christened Lucie himself. Her mother was Santa Lucia's Summer Lady, which Adam and I called merely Summer." He moved the bay aside and motioned her in. "Come on in." She looked down at the borrowed gown and hesitated. "If you are worried about Mama's dress, you needn't be— she quite counts it on the rag heap already."

"Nonetheless, 'twas quite kind of her to lend it to me. And I am heartily glad for it, I can tell you. Though I wish it did not have to be black," she admitted wistfully. "I shall look like the blackbird next to the peacock at my wedding." She stepped inside gingerly, taking care to keep the hem above the straw, and then she forgot about the dress.

The foal, nudged forward by Devin, nuzzled the gown, almost burying its head. Sarah sank into the clean straw, her full skirt billowing around her, and began petting it. " 'Tis so lovely and so fully formed that one cannot quite realize it came—" She stopped, coloring in embarrassment.

"That it came from the mare?" he finished for her.

"Do not be afraid to speak your mind to me, Sarah—'tis what I find so refreshing about you." He cocked his head to appraise the size of the filly. "Aye, 'tis difficult to believe, but I can attest that it did."

For Devin Hastings, the greater difficulty was seeing Sarah on her knees in the horse stall, utterly devoid of those false niceties usually associated with her sex. Sunlight from an open door above filtered through strands of straw to brighten her hair, and he looked away, knowing the time had passed for him.

"Would you like to have her?"

At first, she didn't think she'd heard him correctly. "What? Oh, but I—"

"Behold my bribe, my dear. Say nothing to Adam about my offer to you, and I am repaid."

"But—"

"Oh, aye, you can. I have already told Adam I mean to give her to you. 'Twill give you something to do whilst he is gone."

The smile of pleasure that formed on her lips froze. So that was the way the land lay—his apology had been but a hoax to delay her wedding. No doubt he and his father thought separation the best means to break the betrothal.

"No. I shall, of course, travel with my husband."

"Do not be a fool, my dear. You are too gentle a lady to follow the drum."

"You did not think me a gentle lady yesterday, as I recall."

He chose to ignore the barb. "You are scarce above a child yourself."

"I am nineteen, and I fail to see—"

"You have not been out in the world at all, Sarah."

"And you think polite society will prepare me to be a soldier's wife?" she demanded incredulously. "No, I mean to go with him." Her amber eyes defied him as she snapped, "If you think his absence will make me think better of you, I assure you it will not."

"If it comes to war, I shall not be here either—you'll not see me either."

"I am going with him," she repeated stubbornly.

"Sarah, I do not know what you think war is, but I

can tell you that it is not gowns and ladies' maids and pretty parties. If you want my opinion of it, I think 'tis selfish to wed ere he comes back. But I have withdrawn my objection in the face of his determination.''

"I said I'd not stay.''

He moved closer, affording her a view of little more than his stained buff breeches and his white silk hose. She pulled herself up by the half-door, ready to run if he came closer.

"What if he is wounded—or worse? Would you be across the sea alone?''

She backed against the door, reaching behind her to unlatch it. "This is your doing, isn't it?'' she asked bitterly as she slipped out of the stall. "Well, my lord, I do not know what scheme you and Westerfield have devised between you, but 'twill not serve. Trust you? I would be a fool to do so!''

"Don't be a peagoose, Sarah! Papa will let you stay here whilst Adam is gone.''

"I'd as lief live in a nest of vipers!''

Despite his intent not to do so, he lost his temper in the face of her stubbornness. "Don't let your dislike of me blind you, you empty-headed little ninny! Think of Adam, if you will! My wishes have nothing to do with this!''

The stable door creaked open at the other end, and both thought it was the ostler returning. As neither wished to quarrel in front of him, they fell silent, glaring at each other across the stall door.

"Sarah! Dev!'' Adam hailed them as he walked in. He stopped, taking in their red faces. "Is anything amiss between you?''

"No,'' Devin lied.

Relieved to see her betrothed, she ran to him, throwing herself into his arms. Adam's hands closed on her elbows as he looked over her shoulder at his brother. "What the devil goes here?''

Devin shrugged. "I told her that she should stay in England, where 'tis safe, and obviously I overset her.''

"We'll talk about it later,'' Adam promised her, setting her back from him and turning toward the stall. "Oh,

I collect Dev has shown you our surprise. Well, what do you think—do you want her?''

"Adam, I don't want to stay without you.''

"Then you won't,'' he reassured her, reaching into his coat to draw out a folded paper. Smiling, he held it out to her. "I am just come from the bishop, and 'tis all settled, right and tight. Dispensation of the banns— Wicklund expects us this morning.''

"Oh, but my hair . . . Adam! This morning? I mean . . .'' Her hand flew to her hair, feeling the dampness that lingered underneath. "I thought—''

"Wear it like a country maid—unless you are wishful of crying off,'' he teased her. "Dev changed your mind, my dear?''

"No!'' she retorted crossly. "But . . .'' Suddenly she noted his swollen and bruised hands. "Adam, whatever . . . ?''

" 'Tis nothing, I hit the door last night, that's all.''

His brother's bruised jaw took on new meaning for her. "I see.''

Devin looked away for a moment, wishing that somehow it had been he that Sarah Spender wanted so much. But he'd not climbed high in Pitt's esteem by being a fool. Aye, it was probably best that Adam take her away before he regretted it too much. But then his brother's next words shook him.

"If naught else, should you not be able to go, you can perhaps stay at Westerfield House with Dev. He's scarce home anyway.''

"No! That is . . .'' Sarah choked. "Please, I'd not . . .''

Devin started, then recovered. "If she has to stay, 'twould look better if she were to remain with Mama.''

"I'd not do that either!'' she snapped. "Adam—''

"But 'tis early times to worry over that on your wedding day, isn't it?'' Devin added hastily. Forcing himself to sound cheerful, he changed the subject. "And if you would have me witness the words, you will give me time to make myself presentable, Adam—though I warn you I am scarce fit company until I've slept.'' He eased out from behind the half-door and closed it again. "Give me at least an hour to bathe and be shaved, will you?"

As he left, Sarah fell silent. Adam had never said he'd take her with him—quite the opposite, in fact. And he'd made it quite plain that she might be left waiting for him. But in her happiness, she'd not considered where.

Unwilling to further overset her, Adam caught her hand, pulling her after him. "Come on—Mama has discovered another gown she thinks might fit you, and there's not much time. And when we are returned, she'll have Mrs. Craven here to fit you for new gowns. Between us, Mama and I mean to see you dressed as befits a Hastings, my dear."

His mother was not even going to his wedding. Sarah shouldn't have expected it, she supposed, trying to hide her disappointment. She had to tell herself that it didn't matter—when all was said and done, she'd still be Mrs. Adam Hastings.

"Sarah, he would punish her if she came," he told her quietly.

"I see. But he will not punish Audley?"

"He always forgives Dev." His fingers massaged hers as he held them. "But there is one thing to remember about Papa: once you are a Hastings, 'tis everything to him." He leaned over to brush a kiss against her cheek. "Come on—buck up, Sarah. 'Tis our wedding day, and I mean to make it memorable."

9

Sarah's wedding was so unlike any of her childhood dreams. Rather than having the elegant gown, the flower-bedecked church, and the throng of well-wishers, she had only the countess's black taffeta dress, the Reverend Mr. Wicklund's formal parlor, and Devin, Roland, and Mrs. Wicklund in attendance. And before the day was out, she had not a doubt that Roland's mother would have it told throughout the neighborhood how the earl and countess showed their displeasure at their son's marriage to that encroaching nobody, Sarah Spender, by not deigning to attend. That Viscount Audley had come for witness in their absence would be the source of a month's speculation, most likely, signifying a rift of sorts within the family at the Park. And the bruise on his jaw, not entirely covered by powder applied with the haresfoot, was certain to have been noted with a great deal of interest. No, they were going to be discussed at length, with Sarah roundly condemned as a scheming adventuress who'd caught the young captain in her coils.

But the dearth of company did not truly bother Sarah. Casting a sideways glance at her handsome bridegroom while he repeated the customary vows, she had to count herself the most fortunate of females. He was splendid—his tall, well-favored frame correctly covered in the striking red-and-blue-and-gold uniform, his hair hidden this time beneath the formal officer's wig he disliked, making him seem older and far more serious than the lighthearted Adam Hastings she loved. As she studied him, his finely sculptured face betrayed not a hint of doubt at what he did. And his blue eyes, as brilliant as a summer sky, reassured her with their warmth every time he looked at her. His voice strong, he repeated the words after the vicar, and then, as he finished, he squeezed her fingers in reassurance.

Then it was her turn to pledge her life and her person into his care. Despite the sharp intake of Roland's breath, she smiled into her bridegroom's face and spoke the words. On this day, she would have defied the king himself to wed the man beside her. Her heart was filled with gratitude and love every time she looked at him.

It was over in such a short time, and instead of well-wishers, she turned to face her childhood friend's bitterness and Lord Audley's rather subdued mien. After Adam's brother had correctly kissed her hand, she turned to Roland, who stood sullenly watching her.

"Please, Ro—I should like your approval above all things." Groping for words to explain her unexpected marriage to Adam, she tried to conciliate the younger man. "I know 'tis sudden, but—"

"My eyes are opened, Sarah," he spat at her. " 'Tis plain that a mere vicar's son was not good enough for you, was he? I suppose *he* did not come up to scratch," he added bitterly, nodding significantly to where Lord Audley stood, "else you'd have fancied yourself a viscountess rather than a mere Mrs."

"I own I *am* surprised, Sarah," Mrs. Wicklund said, lifting a thin eyebrow. " 'Sudden' is scarce the word for it, I should think. And with your dear papa put to rest but yesterday—tut, but I am sure I do not know what is to be said of this." Clearly she could have said a great deal more, but her husband was frowning his disapproval at her.

" 'Twill be said that we wished to wed ere the war begins," Adam responded easily. Addressing Roland, he added apologetically, "I am sorry you feel that I have stolen a march on you, old fellow. 'Tis just that I found I could let her go even less than you could."

"I thought you were my friend, Adam—I thought you meant to help her. You knew how it was with me—you knew it!" the younger man accused hotly. "Aye, if I'd ever suspected, I'd not even have told you about Spender!'' Roland's reddened eyes brimmed brightly and his jaw worked for a moment as he fought for control. ''But do not waste your pity on me—either of you— Roland Wicklund will come about!'' Abruptly he turned on his heel and fled the room, slamming the door.

''Oh dear, I should go after him . . .'' Sarah hesitated, then started for the door. ''Ro! Please, Ro . . . you do not understand!''

Adam laid a restraining hand on her shoulder. ''No. 'Twould serve no purpose now, Sarah. 'Tis time he needs—that's all.''

''His calf love will fade, I promise you,'' Devin agreed rather tersely. ''It always does.''

''Ahem.'' The vicar, embarrassed by his son's outburst, cleared his throat to gain their attention. ''There is the matter of signing the lines, I believe.'' He laid the crisp vellum sheet on a small writing table in the corner of the room and reached for the inkpot. ''Captain Hastings, if you will but sign first, then Mrs. Hastings. I am sure Martha will attest to the signatures, won't you, my dear? And Lord Audley also?''

Nodding, Adam took pen in hand to write in bold strokes, ''Adam Alexander Winfield Hastings,'' then passed the quill to her. She dipped it into the inkpot and signed ''Sarah Elizabeth Catherine Spender'' below. Devin Hastings followed with ''Devin, Viscount Audley,'' then stepped back to give Mrs. Wicklund room before he handed her the pen. She shot Sarah a look that plainly showed she thought the girl had wedded far above her station. Nonetheless, she wrote her name where her husband indicated, her small crabbed hand conveying much of herself.

That was it, then. Legally and for all time, Sarah was Sarah Spender Hastings, a wife now, a woman tied irrevocably to the man at her side. What God and a country vicar had joined together could now be sundered only by an act of Parliament or death. She took a deep breath and looked up at her handsome husband, who once again took her hand in his strong, warm fingers, pressing it.

''I suppose I should be relieved, Sarah,'' Mrs. Wicklund murmured as she placed the quill back in its stand. "I am certain that you and Roland would not have suited."

Ignoring the older woman, Adam turned to Sarah, smiling, his thoughts reflecting her own. "Well, for good or ill, you are this captain's bride, my dear—may I give you no cause to regret it."

"Do you stay to tea?" Wicklund asked politely as his wife snorted her disapproval. "I am sure that Martha has—"

"No," Adam answered quickly with a significant glance toward the door where Roland had exited. "I believe my mother has plans for Sarah."

"I am certain she does," Devin hastened to agree. Barely able to hide his own disappointment at Sarah's obvious happiness, he reached for his hat. "I shall see the both of you back at the Park. Until then . . . Adam, Sarah." Settling the ramillie over his black hair, he picked up his riding crop. "I wish you a good day," he told the Wicklunds.

"You should have ridden over with us, Dev," Adam said.

Devin's mouth twisted wryly. "Coming it too strong, and well you know it. I certainly should wish you at Jericho were it my wedding day."

"Such a charming gentleman." Mrs. Wicklund sighed as the front door closed after him. "Your father must be so very proud of him. Indeed, but 'tis rumored that Pitt shall direct the government if it comes to war, and everyone supposes that Lord Audley—"

"Aye." Adam cut her short, adding rather dryly, "We all take pride in my brother. Come, Sarah, we must not keep Mama and Mrs. Craven waiting." Then, with a smile calculated to add to Mrs. Wicklund's speculative gossip, he added, "And Papa also."

Once back inside the Westerfield carriage, Sarah leaned against the squabs and closed her eyes. Adam took the seat opposite, and for a time they were both silent. Finally he could stand it no longer. "My dear, you look as though you have regrets already," he chided softly.

"No." Her eyes opened and she managed a small

smile. "I am thinking that Roland will never forgive me, and I did not mean to hurt him."

"Of course you did not." He slid across the seat and took her hands in his. "Dev is right, you know—'tis but calf love and easily mended by year's end. He will fancy himself in love a dozen times and more ere he settles down."

Somehow the thought that Adam spoke from experience was lowering. "Did you?"

"Did I what?"

"Fancy yourself in love a dozen times and more?"

He appeared to consider the matter for a moment, and then his brilliant blue eyes took on a mischievous glint. "Are you asking if you have any reason to doubt my constancy, my dear—if there are any lights o' love I have failed to mention?"

"Well, I should suppose . . ." Her voice trailed off.

"Aye, you would be a strange female if you did not, wouldn't you?"

She nodded.

A slow smile spread across his face, warming it again. "None that ought to worry you." His strong fingers massaged hers, disconcerting her. "Oh, I won't pretend that I have been celibate, Sarah, for I haven't," he admitted honestly, "but I never found any I ever would wed."

"Oh." Her heart pounded from the awareness of him as she stared down at his hands. Even through her soft gloves, she could feel the vitality, and he suddenly seemed so much larger, so much more masculine than the boy she'd known.

He leaned closer until his face was but inches from hers, and his voice dropped softly. "I believe we will deal well together, Sarah, precisely because we *are* already friends." One of his hands left hers to lift her chin, forcing her to meet his eyes. "There is no need to discover the girl beneath the artifice, I think. I know more about you than if I'd stood up a hundred times to dance with you."

Although his expression was sober, something in those brilliant blue eyes drew her far more than any words. She could only stare into them, her heart wanting to believe he could somehow love her. Instead, he murmured gently, "I am the same Adam as you have always known, you know."

She knew it had been too much to ask for; he'd wedded her from friendship at best, pity at worst. She forced herself to smile at him, hoping he could not see how much more she wanted of him.

"That's better," he whispered. "For a moment I thought you meant to be blue-deviled on our wedding day."

Beneath his hand, her fingers pleated and unpleated the stiff taffeta, betraying her agitation, as her amber eyes searched his face. "But what if one day you should find a lady to love?" she asked finally.

"We can both hope that I already have." His breath, where it brushed her cheek, sent a thrill coursing through her, so much so that she had to close her eyes lest she reveal too much to him. But she could feel his hands slide up her arms, sending another shiver of anticipation down her spine. The taffeta rippled beneath his palms as he caught her shoulders, pulling her forward, and his lips touched hers lightly. Her eyes still closed, she pressed her mouth against his tentatively, hoping to rediscover what she'd felt in the stable. She felt his sharp intake of breath.

Time stood still, suspended in that moment; then the taffeta of her skirt rustled over her borrowed hoops as he moved closer, embracing her, folding her into his arms. And once again she was acutely conscious of his strength, of the hard-finished wool of his dress coat, of the gold buttons where they pressed through her gown, of the stiff lace that trimmed his collar and cuffs. But most of all she was intensely aware of him.

"Poor Sarah," he murmured tenderly as he nuzzled the crown of her hair, rubbing his cheek against its softness. "Can you not know that I have been as lonely as you?"

Tears welled, and an aching lump formed in her throat, making speech impossible. She tried to focus on one of the many gold buttons on his chest.

His free hand pushed his braid-trimmed tricornered hat

from his head, getting it out of the way, and then he leaned her back in his arms, cradling her as his head bent to hers. And this time, when his lips met hers, there was no light touching. It was as though an instant hunger had been kindled within him, for his arms closed about her almost convulsively and his mouth searched hers eagerly, eliciting an answering passion. She clung to him breathlessly, her hands moving to clasp his shoulders tightly, her fingers kneading the stiff wool over the muscles, aware only of a deep need to be loved by this man. She responded wholeheartedly, giving kiss for kiss, and wanting more.

He'd meant to go slowly, to woo her softly, gently, to court her like the virgin he knew her to be, but he found himself unprepared for the intensity of his own desire. He moved his hands over her back, stroking over the stiff fabric restlessly, feeling her slender body through the whalebone and taffeta. Her breath was rapid and uneven, and still he possessed her mouth, tasting, demanding more, urged on by her response to him, until his body ruled his mind.

His fingers skimmed her shoulder, then slid beneath the cloth to the warm skin beneath. And somewhere in the recesses of his mind he cursed the wire, whalebone, and hoops that kept a man from a woman. One hand moved to her waist, slipping between them to the laces that held her stomacher in place. Tugging at them, he felt the silk ribbons give way, loosening her stiff bodice. His mouth left hers to trail hot, urgent kisses along her jaw, the soft lobe of her ear, and then down to the hollow of her throat.

It was a heady thing to be held so close to a man, and headier still to be kissed like that. Caught up in the intensity of what he was doing to her, Sarah felt as though her whole body was tuned to his, that there was no other time, no other place than there and then. This, then, must surely be what she was made for. She felt giddy, more so than when she'd been given brandy to ease a sprain, and yet she felt a sense of power also. Heedless of the buttons that scraped her flesh, she gave herself over to his touch, arching her head for the hot kisses that traced fire over her throat, her neck, her shoulders.

Suddenly her stomacher gave way beneath his insistent hands, parting from her bodice as the laces loosened enough to slip it aside. As his mouth returned to hers, his palm rubbed over the cotton chemise underneath, pulling it taut over her breast. She wriggled as his fingers tugged at the soft gathers, then stiffened in shock when they found her nipple. Twisting her head, she tried to pull away.

"Adam!" she protested, clutching at his hand.

"Shhhhh." His hot breath rushed against her ear. "Just love me, Sarah," he groaned. "Love me now."

But she'd never been touched so intimately by anyone, and when his fingers played with her breast, she panicked. "Please, Adam, I . . ." She pushed at him frantically, trying to straighten up despite the disarray of her stomacher and her gown. "Adam, let me go!"

Between the small space and the hoops and petticoats, it was impossible anyway, and he knew it. And he was not, after all, an animal who slaked its lust at will. Reluctantly he released her, and tried to master his almost feverish desire. His blue eyes still dark, he exhaled slowly, whispering hoarsely, " 'Tis as it is supposed to be between us, Sarah."

She stared at him, seeing a stranger, then looked down at her loosened stomacher. Embarrassment, humiliation, and shame washed over her as she flushed to the roots of her hair.

Her eyes were enormous in her face, utterly devoid of passion now. He saw the parade of emotions pass over her, and the heat left him. This time, when his hands went to her waist, it was to tighten the laces there. He felt her sharp intake of breath and saw her stiffen. He'd botched the matter with his eagerness, and he knew it. Condemning himself for frightening her, he clumsily straightened the stiff stomacher, pulling it even with the bodice of her gown.

When her hands caught at his and her face flamed, he continued tautening the crisscrossed ribbons, moving from top to bottom, murmuring ruefully, "You find me

no hand at this, Sarah—I am far better at removing than
dressing, I fear.''

Words failed her. She'd let him touch her where she
scarce touched herself except in bathing. Her body as
rigid as the stomacher, she held her breath whilst he tied
the ribbon into a semblance of a bow, then sat back.
Unable to meet his eyes further, she turned to stare unseeing out the window.

She was mortified, and he knew it. ''I guess I rushed
my fences,'' he said quietly. ''I forgot what it must be
like for an innocent girl.''

''Innocent?'' she choked, swallowing hard. ''I was the
veriest wanton, and I know it.'' Her voice dropped to a
near-whisper. ''I liked it, until . . .''

''Until I touched your breasts,'' he finished for her.

''Yes.''

''Sarah . . .'' Not daring to take her into his arms
again, he reached his hand to her shoulder instead, touching her lightly. She shrank against the coach wall.
''Sarah, look at me.'' When she did not move, he slid
closer and tried to turn her head with a knuckle under
her chin. ''Silly goose,'' he murmured fondly. ''Don't
you know 'tis how it is supposed to be between us?''

She shook her head.

''Sarah, it pleases me that you are not overly missish—
truly it does. I don't want a cold female for wife.''
Silently cursing a society that mistook ignorance for innocence, he added gently, ''Poor Sarah—you've not had
a mother, have you? Would it help if I asked Mama to
speak to you?''

''I pray you will not.''

''You are not wanton, Sarah—you know not what wanton is. Come on, 'tis Adam,'' he coaxed, ''and I'd have
you look at me.'' With one arm slipping around her
shoulder and one hand under her chin, he slowly turned
her to face him. ''I'd teach you to love me, sweetheart.''

He made it sound so right. She dared to look up into
his face, seeing once again the warmth in those dazzling
blue eyes, feeling once again that shiver of excitement.

''Just let me hold you, Sarah.''

Before she could protest, he'd pulled her closer, wrapping his arms about her, easing her head against his shoulder. Leaning back, he smoothed loose strands of her hair with his palm. She turned her cheek into the scarlet wool of his coat, grateful that he could not see her face, for once again, reckless creature that she was, she wanted him to kiss her.

Instead, he told himself he was content to hold her, to smell the sweet, clean scent of the soap she'd used on her hair, knowing that he had the time to teach her to love him, secure now in the knowledge that she would prove an apt pupil. As the carriage turned into the Park's drive, he looked down on her auburn hair and felt a surge of protectiveness for her. If his father said one unkind word to her, he was going to take her back to his regiment with him, the gossips be damned.

10

Devin Hastings watched from the cross-paned window as his carriage rolled up the drive. Despite the fact that he'd witnessed his brother's marriage to Sarah Spender, he still felt something every time he looked at them—chagrin, regret, envy—he knew not quite what it was that he felt, but it was there. Oh, he was not foolish enough to believe he no longer wanted her, that somehow her marriage had ended her attraction for him, but he hoped it would not show. No, only time would overcome an infatuation as intense as any of his salad days. He'd just have to keep reminding himself that she was Adam's wife, he supposed, until such a day as it was over. Behind him, his father looked up irritably.

" 'Tis the same scene as has been there a hundred

years and more,'' he grumbled. ''I would that you would sit down and cease pacing ere you damage the carpet your foolish mother ordered from Brussels. Brussels!'' he snorted with remembered pique. ''Females! Never let one of 'em into your purse, you hear?''

''They are returned.''

''Who? Oh, I collect you mean the fool as wears his heart in his breeches, eh? Much good it did to offer to keep the gel, for all you'd have me do it. Well, I ain't pleased, I mean to tell you.''

''She is a Hastings now,'' Devin reminded him. ''For good or ill, she is one of us.''

''Humph! And I suppose he will think to drag her off to some godforsaken battlefield! Well, he'd best think again, for it ain't the sort of place to take a female!''

''I don't know.'' Devin shrugged as he dropped the window drapery.

The earl eyed his elder son suspiciously. ''And don't you be trying to tell me you are pleased with the match, else I'll know you for a liar, Dev.''

''No, of course I am not pleased. But 'tis done, right and tight, sir—I witnessed the marriage myself.''

''You, sirrah?'' For a moment the old man's color heightened dangerously, and it looked as though he were about to suffer a fit of apoplexy before he found his voice again. ''Nay, afore God, you did not!'' he roared. ''The devil you did! Of all of us, I thought you knew what was owed the Hastings name!''

''I did not wish to become estranged from him, Papa,'' Devin offered simply. ''I merely bowed to reality, after all. 'Twas plain as a pikestaff that he meant to have her.''

''Humph! As if she wouldn't have taken any as offered—and without the parson.''

''I would not say that to Adam, were I you,'' Devin warned him. ''And, no, she would not—I did ask her,'' he added dryly. ''York was preferable to me, you see.''

That gave his father a start. ''You? Nay, I'd not believe it! You ain't in the petticoat line!'' Then, realizing that his heir was serious, he sat back, stunned. ''Better Adam than you, I guess,'' he decided finally, ''for I'd not make the chit a countess.''

"There was never any question of that."

Devin heard the old butler and the housekeeper wishing Adam and Sarah well in the hallway. "No, Papa, we have to put the best face on the match. Whether either of us likes it or not, he's made her one of us."

"Damme, if you ain't a cold fish, Dev," the earl complained. "Your brother steals a march on you and plucks the plum himself—and all you've got to say is we got to stomach her?"

"Alas, aye. A man who fights a doomed battle is a fool, sir—and of all that can be said of us, we are not fools, I think." He walked to the cabinet and drew out a decanter of his father's best Madeira, then returned with it and two glasses. "He came home for her rather than us, you know." Setting down the glasses, he uncorked the bottle and poured the wine. "As much as I dislike the notion myself, I suggest you prepare to toast your new daughter, Papa."

"You want me to make the best of the baggage?"

The old man took the glass his son handed him, swirling the liquid before sipping it. His eyes met Devin's over the rim of the glass. "Think he'd stay home for her?" he asked hopefully. "I suppose if she was to keep him here, I'd not mind it so much."

"I think he ought to take her with him."

"And yesterday you thought as how I ought to keep her! Damme, Dev, if you ain't playin' Tom and Tilly with me!"

"Tom and Tilly?" Devin asked, lifting his brow.

"Aye now and nay then! And don't be trying to say you don't ken my cant, neither—mebbe you got Pitt's eye, but you are still a Hastings!"

"I know what I am," he replied shortly. "I just think he ought to take her with him, that's all. If he hadn't married her, I'd have had her stay, with an eye to separating them, but now . . ."

The old man turned around at the sound of laughter in the hallway and winced. "Listen to your mama—silly creature thinks they ought to be happy! Oh, what I could tell 'em—it don't last, you know."

A knock sounded on the door, and Adam called through, "Papa?"

For a long moment the earl did not answer, but Devin moved to open it, pausing as his hand touched the doorknob. "The decision is yours now, Papa—I made mine."

"Aye. Well, you might as well present yourselves!" he shouted back. "By the sound of it, the deed's done anyway!"

The door swung open slowly as Adam stepped inside, his hand still in Sarah's. " 'Tis too much to expect you to wish me happy, sir, but—"

"Happy?" the old man growled, interrupting him. His eyes raked over Sarah, who stepped forward, determined not to be cowed by him. "Well, well, Mistress Hastings now, is it? Come here, gel! Aye," he conceded grudgingly, "it ain't hard to see why, I suppose. You ain't in the common style, at least, I'll say that for you. Dev here thinks it ain't a complete *mésalliance*—or so he says." With an effort, he heaved himself up from the chair and hobbled closer. "You ever preside at table?"

"Papa never brought anyone home," she answered evenly, trying not to quail beneath his scrutiny.

"There are not many parties with an army, sir," Adam cut in stiffly.

"Parties is politics, boy!" his father snapped. "Aye, if you'd advance . . ."

"Charles, really," Lady Emma protested, "there is no sense frightening the child. I am sure that Sarah—"

"Be still, Em!" The old man's eyes never left Sarah. "She don't look cowed to me. You ain't frighted at all, are you?" he addressed her. "Dev, pour me another glass of the stuff, will you?"

"Charles, Mrs. Craven is come to measure her," his countess dared to tell him.

But he was not quite finished. Lifting the glass Devin gave him, he nodded to Sarah. "Well, 'tis done, in any event, ain't it? May you breed well, gel—I'd see more Hastingses ere I die."

"Charles!"

"Don't 'Charles' me, Emma! Gel's got a lifetime to squander his blunt without you helpin' her to do it! And

what the devil's wrong with plain speaking, I ask you?"
Waggling a finger at Sarah, he admonished her, "Don't
let her order up what you ain't needin', you hear? You
want to be a good wife, you don't waste a man's substance."

"I assure you that I do not need much, sir."

Adam, who'd expected a far more hostile welcome for
his bride, hastened to put his arm around her shoulder.
"I can afford anything she should fancy—and more."

"Adam, I am in mourning," Sarah reminded him.
"One black gown cannot be so very much unlike another, after all."

Her mother-in-law dismissed such heresy with a definite shake of her head. "Nonsense. One cannot live in
one dress, and you cannot wish to wear my old things.
Besides, you must have bride-clothes. Even Charles must
concede—"

"Charles don't concede nothing!" her husband retorted hotly. Turning once again to Sarah, he asked her
pointedly, "You don't want tricked out like a Lunnon
dove, do you?"

"I don't want but what my husband wishes to give
me," she answered simply.

It was the right answer to him. He eyed her critically,
taking in the plain black borrowed gown she wore. Despite the severity of it, she was a pretty girl in a whole-
some way—not a beauty, but decidedly pretty. She met
his gaze steadily, those strange eyes of hers neither brown
nor gold. Even the light sprinkling of freckles, which
should have been anathema, was not unpleasing. Aye, he
could see why Adam would want her. He turned back to
his wife.

"Well, ain't no harm in buyin' her one, I suppose. Tell
you what, Em—one muslin from us."

Sarah started to refuse him, then realized what it had
cost him to offer at all. "Thank you, sir," she told him
instead.

"Aye, and I ain't above buying a petticoat to put under
it, neither."

This unexpected turnabout stunned Adam, who'd been
prepared for battle. Not wanting to strain this fragile

thread of acceptance by testing it, he spoke to Sarah instead. "I am no hand at all in knowing what a female requires, Sarah—you'd be better advised by Dev or Mama—but I shall expect you to get whatever you like. Later, we'll go to London to visit the modistes there."

" 'Twill not be much," Sarah hastened to reassure him. "If we should be sent abroad, I cannot think I shall be expected to appear the fashion plate."

"Sarah, there is no need for economy."

"Here, now, that ain't the sort of thing t' tell a female, I'll be bound! Got to teach 'em to hang on to the blunt rather than spend it," his father protested.

"It is very much more to the point to see what Mrs. Craven can fashion, don't you think?" the countess cut in brightly. "But we tarry too long, my dear. I daresay she grows impatient waiting for us."

"Go on—go on with you gel! If they are ready to squander their blunt on you, I'll hold my tongue! But do not let Emma tell you you need ten pairs of shoes, you hear? And do not be listening if she wants to put you in ten petticoats either! A female don't need but one! It has got to where a man cannot get close enough to steal a kiss anymore, damme if it ain't!"

There was something daunting about spending Adam's money. Perhaps it was simply too new a notion. She looked at him and hesitated, her mouth forming an uncertain question. "Thirty pounds, do you think—for everything, I mean?"

"Thirty pounds!" Devin choked, and his mother looked at her as though she'd taken complete leave of her senses.

"You have my leave to spend a hundred, Sarah, but I'd not give it all to a village seamstress." Grinning, Adam squeezed her shoulder. "Go on—whilst you are fitted, I mean to get rid of this infernal wig. Unlike Dev, I do not keep a scratch hook about me."

As Sarah followed her new mother-in-law from the room, she could hear the earl telling Adam grudgingly, "Aye, she's passable—just wish you'd have found one with a little money, that's all."

11

It had been a long day, so much so that Lucie's filly seemed but a distant memory and her wedding but a dream. From time to time Sarah stole a sidewise look at her handsome bridegroom, thinking she must surely be living a dream from which she feared to waken. And despite the earl's grunts and Lady Emma's chattering during the meal, she found her thoughts wandering to the ride back to the Park, to Adam's ardent kisses—and more. Even now her blood rushed at the memory, and not all of it was from embarrassment. She had to avert her eyes lest any see her wanton, wicked thoughts.

His hand lay next to hers on the table, his strong fingers an odd contrast to the delicate Belgian lace at his wrists. A thin white scar ran across the back, something she'd not noted before, adding to the incongruity. And obviously, he was impatient of something, for from time to time his fingertips drummed the snowy tablecloth, betraying a nervousness not evident in his face.

She felt as taut as her laces, just looking at him, wondering what the rest of the night would bring. She'd liked being held close, and even now her body grew hot just remembering the feel of his mouth on hers. But there was more to it than that, else why would Miss Wallace have hinted so darkly at "a woman's distasteful duty"?

"Sarah," she heard her mother-in-law address her, "I vow you have not been attending me. Did you not think us fortunate to discover the *point-de-rose* lace? I mean, with this disagreeable thing with France, I daresay the lace trade will quite be cut off."

"Yes, madam—'tis quite fine."

"Humph! It ain't going to end, Emma," the earl declared flatly. "War or no, the Frenchies'll turn a profit, I tell you. Daresay we'll pay from the bottom of the purse for it, though—the demned smugglers expect recompense for their risk, they say." He leaned forward to look down the table at Sarah. "Pay her no heed, gel—she's had you buy the lot of it, no doubt, eh?"

"It was my extravagance," Sarah admitted. "I ordered just enough of it to trim out a petticoat."

"The one I bought you?" he wanted to know.

"No, my lord"—Sarah could not quite suppress an impish grin—"that one I commissioned plain."

"Saucy baggage, ain't ye?" But even as he said it, he sat back, pleased. "Damme if you ain't got more sense than Emma."

"We bought her a simple black silk with a stomacher of cream bow-knots," the countess murmured.

"Thought I told you muslin! Dash it, Emma, but—" He stopped mid-sentence, sighing. "Aye, but 'twas too much to expect of you, I daresay. And the gel don't get wedded but once—eh, mistress?"

"No, sir."

Thankfully, Devin changed the subject to politics finally, letting her go back to her own thoughts as he inquired of his father if he'd write to His Majesty urging a ministry for Pitt. And when the old man allowed as he wasn't asking the "demned German" for anything, the discussion between the two of them grew animated.

Adam's hand crept closer to Sarah's, then covered it, and once again she was surprised by the warmth of his skin. And even as he touched her, her whole body knew it. A shiver of excitement sliced through her. His fingers massaged hers against the smooth cloth.

"Cold?" he murmured.

"A little," she lied.

Disconcerted, she spooned the thick syllabub into her mouth, letting it melt slowly, trying not to betray what his very presence did to her.

He was watching her almost lazily, speculatively, as his fingers continued to stroke hers. Embarrassed, she drew her hand away, and hoped none of the others had seen. Adam looked faintly amused.

The candlelight reflected in his blue eyes and burnished his dark blond locks with gold, making him handsomer still. Let others think Lord Audley the comelier of the two—she knew better. Surely no Greek god of antiquity was better-favored than Adam Hastings.

"Tired, my dear?" he asked, leaning closer.

"I own I am, but I have had such a day."

"Perhaps you will wish to retire as soon as the covers are removed."

Sudden apprehension went through her as she realized he'd probably go up with her; then she reassured herself that he was her friend as well as her husband. And if what went after was anything like his kisses, she had nothing to fear.

"Yes."

Almost as though signaled, a liveried footman began clearing the plates. Lady Emma looked to Sarah and started to rise, but Adam shook his head. Lifting his glass to his bride, he smiled at her, offering a toast. "To Sarah—may I give her happiness."

"Humph!" Nonetheless, the earl lifted his glass, adding, "And may she give the world more Hastingses—more to the point, I should think." He drank deeply, draining the wine, then looked at Adam soberly. "Mayhap you will choose a better profession when you have dependents."

Devin, who'd scarce looked at Sarah through the entire supper, finally met her eyes. Holding up his own drink, he merely said, "To Sarah." He finished his drink in one gulp, then lurched to his feet. "If you will pardon me, sir, I mean to look to Lucie ere I join you for port. Your servant, Mama. Adam. Sarah."

His father turned then to his second son. "Adam? A little port tonight?"

Intensely aware of Sarah all evening, Adam considered even a few minutes in his father's company an unbearable delay, but he'd not forgotten how he'd rushed his fences earlier. No, he had to give her time. Reluctantly he nodded. "One glass, I suppose. I expect Sarah would prefer

Mary's help to mine," he said lightly, his eyes on his bride. "Besides, Mama—"

This time, the countess rose quickly and beckoned to Sarah. "Come, my dear—I know when we are being dismissed. Besides, Mary will have to find you one of my prettier nightrails."

"She don't need one! Dash it, Em, what can you be thinking of?" the old man snorted. "I mean, they are but wedded!"

"I am well aware of that, Charles, but I daresay she is not," Lady Emma retorted hastily. This time, she took her daughter-in-law firmly by the hand, hoping to escape before her husband said anything to embarrass the girl further. "You must not mind him," she murmured in a low undervoice. "Sometimes men are crude creatures, I fear."

"Crude, is it?" The old man's heavy brows lifted. "Time was, Em, when you did not think so, I'll be bound," he called after them.

As they trod the stairs, the countess fell silent, trying to decide how best to broach the matter Adam had charged her with. To Sarah, it was as though she pondered some great problem. Finally, at the top, the older woman turned to her, sighing, then plunged into her task as though she would execute it quickly. "I regret you have had no mama to speak to of this, child, and I cannot think that Wallace woman—no, of course she would not— she is an unmarried female, after all."

"Miss Wallace had a dislike of the male sex."

"More's the pity there. Well . . ." The countess sucked in her breath and let it out slowly, fixing her gaze on the wainscoting behind Sarah. "Well, what I am trying to say is, if you should have any questions about what to expect, or . . . That is, I should be happy to answer . . ."

For a moment Sarah could only stare while the older woman groped uncomfortably for words, and she was overwhelmed by her concern. "Dear ma'am, I assure you . . . That is, well, it cannot be so very bad, can it?" Then, realizing how stupid she must sound, she had to ask, "Is it?"

"No, of course 'tis not bad! Oh, dear, did I sound as if it were? 'Tis just a shock at first—or so it was for me. But actually 'tis not even unpleasant—quite the contrary, indeed." By now the countess's face was red, but she persevered gamely. "Though I cannot but think it *sounds* rather unpleasant—until one gets used to the idea." She glanced furtively about them, then blurted out, "Just remember you are not to appear disgusted, no matter where you are touched, Sarah, and think that you are pleasing him above all else. There—I have said more on that head than my mother said to me."

"But—"

The countess embraced her quickly, whispering, "At least you have Adam to instruct you, and I cannot think I have reared him to be anything but kind." With that, she released Sarah and fled.

Inside the chamber, a small fire had been laid to chase the night chill, but it had died down until it was little more than a bed of popping embers. The countess's own maid was waiting to undress her, something that no one had done for Sarah since she was a small child.

Self-conscious, she stood still while Mary unhooked the bodice of the black taffeta, separating it from the stiff flat panel underneath and pulling the outer gown over her head. The woman's hands worked deftly at the lacings, releasing the embroidered stomacher. Sarah gave a sigh of relief with the removal of the tight corset and breathed deeply. Stepping out of the borrowed panniers that had given the wide skirt its shape, she felt as though she'd been freed from a cage. But when the woman reached for the lawn chemise and underpetticoat, Sarah stopped her. "I can manage myself now, thank you."

"But, madam—"

"That will be all, I think. I'd very much rather do the rest. Besides, Lady Emma will expect your attendance on her."

The maid shrugged. "I have laid out your nightrail on the bed, madam."

Madam. Even the sound of it was rather daunting. Nonetheless, she was not about to let anyone know how taut her nerves were. It was, after all, ridiculous to fear anything Adam would do to her, particularly after what she'd experienced earlier. No, if she were truly afraid of anything, it would be that she would shame herself in his eyes.

Her hands shaking, she walked over to the bed to pick up the borrowed nightshift. It was of finest cotton lawn, quite a dear fabric these days, and it was lovely with its rows of exquisite lace and tucks at the neck, wrists, and hem. She ran her fingertips lightly over the soft, thin fabric, knowing she would feel nearly naked wearing it, wondering if Adam would think her pretty in it.

"Thank you," she repeated. "That will be all."

"Yes, madam."

The door closed behind the girl, leaving Sarah alone to wait. She slowly removed the underpetticoat and the chemise, then turned to see herself in the mirror, something she'd never really done before. Despite the fact that she was a slender girl, ridges could be seen where the lacings had cut into her chest. Above them, her breasts formed rose-tipped peaks. Her whole body flushed as she remembered how he'd touched her there. *'Tis as it is supposed to be between us, Sarah. You are not wanton, Sarah. Love me now.* Well, he had the right to do anything with her. How had the countess stated it? *Just remember you are not to appear disgusted, no matter where you are touched.* That gave her pause—just what would he expect to touch? Her breasts again?

Her thoughts flooded her with embarrassment, causing her to pull the thin cotton lawn nightrail over her head and tie the ribbon at the throat hurriedly. The awful thought that she'd seen her papa's hunting dogs mate once crossed her mind, but she discarded that quickly. It could not be the same—they had four legs, after all, and were but animals.

She was brought up short by the sound of footsteps coming down the hall. Without waiting to see if it were Adam, she dived into the bed and pulled the cool sheets up to her chin, clutching the hem with both hands, telling herself yet again that no matter what, she would not be disgusted.

He walked rapidly, loosening his neckcloth as he approached the chamber door. For hours he'd been able to think of little else but Sarah. All the time he'd endured his father's bawdy comments over his port, he'd remembered how she'd responded to him. Finally the old man had snapped, "Go on up and be done—I can see you are mad for the gel, and you are no company anyways."

But just outside the closed door, he stopped, wondering what she must be thinking. Had he given her such a fright earlier that she'd fear him? He'd need to go slowly, to make his mind rule his body, and that was not going to be an easy thing to do. Despite what he'd said about other women, it had been some months since he'd had one, and he was eager now, ready now, to give his body ease.

"Adam, is that you?" she called out uncertainly.

He knocked lightly, then opened the door. The room was softly lit by braces of candles flanking the fireplace and at either side of the bed. At first he'd thought to find her waiting up, but then he saw her.

His mouth twisted into a crooked smile as his gaze traveled eagerly over her. "I'd thought you might still be up." Even his voice did not sound like his own.

Nonplussed by what she saw in his eyes, she hugged the covers to her. "Well, as I have never been wedded before, I was not entirely certain just where I ought to be," she admitted, while her pulse sounded like a drumbeat in her ears.

He tried to still the surge of desire he felt at seeing her propped there among the pillows, her auburn hair streaming over her shoulders, spilling like dark red silk over her white rail. And her amber eyes seemed almost gold.

"Well, you are in the right place."

He closed the door and threw the latch. Then he slipped off his shoes and walked casually toward a chair, removing his coat all the while, telling himself to go slowly, to let her become accustomed to him. He draped it over the chair, then turned his attention to his vest, cursing the fact that it had some twenty buttons. His fingers felt clumsy as they struggled with the tight-fitting buttonholes. A mild oath of exasperation escaped him.

Realizing that he usually had a batman or a valet to

help, she asked almost shyly, "Would you have me aid you? That is, I should not mind it."

"Well, your hands are smaller than mine." He spied the brandy decanter on a cabinet near the bed. "Would you care for some brandy, my dear?" he asked conversationally. "Or have you had some already?"

"No."

"You don't want any, or you have already had some—which is it?"

"Adam," she murmured huskily, her eyes fixed on his face, "if whatever it is we are to do is so distasteful that I must needs be disguised first, then I don't want to do it." But even as she spoke, she smiled at him.

It was all the encouragement he needed. A slow grin spread over his face as he walked to the bed. "Did Mama say it was distasteful?"

She looked up at him, her heart pounding still. "Actually, she said I was not to appear disgusted, no matter where I am touched."

That brought him up short, reminding him that women viewed the physical side of marriage differently. The grin faded from his face. "I see," he muttered dryly, wishing he'd left well enough alone. "Leave it to Mama to botch the matter. 'Tis a wonder you are not under the bed rather than in it."

"Adam, I may be green, but I am not a coward."

"No—no, you are not, are you?" he said softly as he dropped to sit beside her. "You are this soldier's wife. Sarah . . ." He would have drawn her into his arms, but she reached to the buttons on his vest instead, making it difficult to hold her close. Her head bent almost to his chest, he felt rather than saw her hands as they moved downward.

It gave her a chance to avoid his gaze now, to hide the intensity of her reaction to him. While she was more than a little nervous, she was also more than a little eager for his embrace. He must not know that she was just as afraid of disgusting him.

Her fingers moved deftly, slipping button after button from the holes, feeling the solidity, the muscled tautness of his chest beneath. " 'Tis small wonder soldiers need batmen," she observed as the last gold disk came free. "There."

But he did not move back from her, nor did he take off his vest. Instead, his hands came up to clasp her head, tilting it for his kiss, and his fingers twined in her hair as his mouth eagerly sought hers. Her eyes widened, then closed as she felt the rush of his warm breath against her face.

"I'd love you, Sarah," he whispered against her lips.

This time, it was different, and she knew it. There would be no denial, no drawing back, no matter what he did to her. Her lips parted, giving him possession of her mouth, and he was tasting her, demanding and getting an answering passion. With a deep sob born of something exquisitely akin to pain, she threw her arms around his neck, returning his kiss wholeheartedly.

Neither her nightrail nor his shirt was a barrier to the heat of his body where it touched hers. His hands dropped to her shoulders, then to her back, molding her, pressing her against him, eliciting an eagerness to match his own. Heat flooded through her, leaving her hot and breathless, yet wanting more.

They clung to each other, savoring the building intensity of each kiss, until the blood pounded in her ears. She didn't even care when he tipped her back against the pillows, then followed her down, stretching the length of her. His mouth left her lips, moving to her ear, whispering hoarsely, "Let me love you."

There was no need to ask. Shivers raced through her body, raising gooseflesh on her arms, as she nodded, hoping that he would not think her wanton.

In the shadows of the candlelight, her closed eyes were shrouded beneath bluish lids, but the intensity of her expression betrayed her desire. Even as he stroked her arms and shoulders lightly, she moved beneath his touch, restless and wanting. His Sarah was as eager for union as he was.

His hands found the ties at her neck and impatiently tugged them loose as his head bent lower, first to press hot kisses the length of her neck and into the sensitive hollow of her throat. She moaned low as she felt the fabric of the rail give way, baring her breasts. This time, she did not stiffen, but gave herself up to the strange sensation of his palm brushing her nipples lightly. They hardened, intensifying the urgency she felt deep within. She tried to bring his head back to hers, but instead he bent lower, this time to tease her aroused nipples with his tongue. She gasped involuntarily, then clasped his head against her breast, her fingers caressing the thick waves of his hair restlessly.

His hands seemed to be everywhere, urging her on, sliding down her over her flat stomach, stroking along her hips and thighs, easing up her nightrail between them. And still his mouth and tongue moved over her breasts until she thought she could stand no more.

"Adam . . ." It was somewhere between a whisper and a moan.

"Shhhhhh."

He raised his head to possess her mouth again, and as he did so, his hand sought and found the wetness below. She stiffened in shock momentarily, then lay back as his fingers stroked. This time, it was a definite moan that escaped her as she began to move beneath his hand. He kissed her mouth, her neck, the hollow of her throat—all of them again—caressing her all the while, until she thought the center of her being must surely be there.

Everything else had been but as child's play to this. Her embarrassment fled in the ecstasy, the utter agony of what he was doing to her. Unbearably hot, she strained against his hand, thinking she surely must shatter into pieces ere he was done.

Suddenly he pulled back and began removing his clothes. She was afraid it was over, and yet her body cried for more. "Please," she whispered, turning her head so that he could not see how much she wanted him to come back to her, how shamelessly she'd enjoyed his touch.

Vest, shirt, knee breeches, and stockings landed softly on the floor beside the bed, and then he was back, covering her hungry body with his own. "Love me, Sarah," he urged her. "Love me now."

For answer, she twined her arms around his neck and

gave herself up to him. And as he took possession of her body, she gasped at the tear. He lay quietly for a moment, waiting for her, until her fingers tightened on his shoulders once again, and his body would obey his mind no longer. He began to move within her, slowly at first, drawing out the exquisite, excruciating pleasure as long as he could. He looked down, seeing her damp face as she clung to him, clutching and unclutching his shoulders, moaning and writhing beneath him, no longer aware of anything beyond her own need.

He'd meant to be gentle, but she demanded more of him. Her hands raked his shoulders and back, straining against him, mindlessly urging him on as her own desire consumed her. His hand grasped her hip, holding her as his body drove him home and he cried out, his own animal cries mingling with hers.

His whole body shuddered as she felt the warm flood; then he collapsed over her, resting his weight on his elbows. A sated, exhausted peace descended. Finally he rolled over, wrapping her in his arms and holding her close while they fought for breath. As she became once again aware of herself and him, of how their naked limbs twined together, she was afraid to look at him.

His passion spent, he felt an overwhelming tenderness. for her. She had given him more than most men got in a marriage, and he was glad he'd taken her rather than the icy heiresses that had been thrown his way. His own hair tangled over his shoulder, he eased himself up just enough to release it, then lay back down to brush the damp tendrils back from her temples.

"I am glad I did not disgust you," he told her, smiling.

Relief flooded over her. Stirring in his arms, she turned to see his face, and the warmth in his eyes was all she needed. "As if you could," she murmured happily.

Beneath her head, his chuckle rumbled, resonating deeply. "Is that an invitation to try again, madam wife?"

"Well, did you not expect to?" she countered hopefully.

"Saucy baggage," he murmured fondly, pulling her closer. "Aye—and often."

12

With rumors of imminent war abounding, Adam concluded it would be useless to find Sarah lodgings near his regiment, particularly when he expected the Thirty-Fifth Foot to be one of the first sent out of the country. And for the first time in his career as a soldier, he relied on his family's considerable influence to gain an extension of leave to spend with his wife. Not that he'd actually asked for either his father's or his brother's aid in the matter, for he was loath to do that, but he'd not been above having Dev frank the letter for him so that the envelope bore Audley's signature. The result was another fifteen days with Sarah, with the understanding that he would remain at the Park in case his commanding officer should need to recall him.

In the ordinary way of things, 'twas the last place on earth he would have chosen to be, but his deepening love for Sarah made it bearable. Even his father, beyond his customary grumbling, seemed reasonably pleased to have them there, once again urging that Adam sell out and stay home where he belonged before war broke out. And for a time, he'd considered doing it, but in the end, he knew he was above all a soldier. The military suited him, offered him the chance for advancement beyond what his name and his father's money could buy him, and gave him a very real sense of purpose. No, he would rather be an officer in His Majesty's forces than Westerfield's younger son, knowing that whatever status he achieved, it was a result of his own effort. If he did anything, he would purchase his promotion to major so that Sarah could have better accommodations with the army.

But even that was not certain. He'd always prided himself that he'd bought nothing beyond his first commission, that however far he'd risen, he'd done it on merit rather than money. And since he was no coward, he felt certain that he could distinguish himself enough to rise higher. The battlefield had made more than one career, after all, and hopefully it would make his. He supposed, if the truth could be admitted, that his desire to rise on his own came from a need to prove to his father that he could do it.

While he waited for Sarah to change into one of his mother's discarded riding habits, he sought out his brother. Devin was busily clearing papers from the desk in the bookroom when Adam knocked and entered. By the looks of it, whatever word the dispatch rider had brought was sobering. He had a hollow, sick feeling in the pit of his stomach even before he asked, " 'Tis ill news?''

Devin looked up, his expression graver than Adam had ever seen it. "Aye. I am called to London." He held out a sheet of paper, its lines heavily crossed with cramped writing. " 'Tis from Pitt—ere the week is out, he expects the king's ministers to meet over the articles of war."

As much as he'd known it was coming, Adam was nonetheless stunned. All he could think of was how little time he and Sarah had had in peace. "I'll have to return to my regiment," he decided finally.

"No. If Pitt can be believed—and I have no reason to doubt it—Lord Loudoun is to be appointed commander of the forces for America. And from all I have ever heard of him, his men call him Caution."

"Aye." Loudoun—John Campbell, Earl of Loudoun—as general for the American colonies? Aloud, Adam managed to ask, "What happened to Shirley?"

"Governor Shirley is being recalled, and General Abercrombie is in command until Loudoun reaches New York."

"But Loudoun's a damned hedonist! We shall be

marching with his hairdresser!'' Adam exploded. ''Who chooses him?''

''I don't know—Pitt, Newcastle, Cumberland perhaps. But I own you surprise me—I'd expected you to be pleased.''

''Pleased! How the devil should I be pleased? We shall dally and dilly whilst he dines and fornicates, and the French shall own America from Quebec to Boston!''

''Pitt thinks rather highly of him, you know. And I should expect he will travel in enough comfort that you can take Sarah.''

''And expose her to his ladybirds?''

Devin shrugged. ''Well, I do not know that he means to take even one.''

Adam forced himself to consider Lord Loudoun more dispassionately. He was being unjust and he knew it, for he was in truth unacquainted with his lordship by anything more than reputation. And despite his reported amours and his penchant for luxury, Loudoun was acknowledged to be more than just another fancy gentleman soldier. It was just that he did not quite fit Adam's notion of a general in wartime. Aye, by reputation, John Campbell could be expected to plot his campaign against the French as meticulously as he planned his wardrobe.

''I suppose we could do worse,'' he decided grudgingly. ''At least we shall know we are well-supplied.'' His eyes met Devin's. ''Is there any word on individual regiments?''

''Not yet, but I had it of the new paymaster that the Thirty-fifth will go to New York if war is actually declared. But you knew that, didn't you?''

''I'd heard.''

''You could sell out,'' Devin ventured casually. ''I mean, if 'tis war, there will be positions to fill in the government as the hotheads rush to buy themselves uniforms and commissions.''

''Thinking they shall look elegant in Vienna, no doubt,'' Adam retorted. ''No, for good or ill, my future is with the Thirty-fifth, Dev.''

''And what does Sarah say?''

''I have not spoken of this to her. She'd have me stay,

I expect, but I should be useless in a sinecure. I have not the temperament for dissembling, Dev,'' he admitted ruefully. "This way, I am confident of advancing by how I lead rather than on whom I have misled.''

Devin held a certain admiration for his younger brother, for Adam had always seen some sort of destiny beyond pleasing their father, gaining for himself a certain freedom that Devin himself lacked. But he did fear for him. To lighten the mood between them, he forced a smile.

"No doubt you expect to become a general, then.''

"If I leave a captain, I'll try to come home a colonel.''

"You are certain this is the course you wish? I mean, war is not without its casualties, you know.''

"I know. Dev . . .'' Adam hesitated to put thought into word, afraid to give voice to fear. "Dev, if anything should ever happen to me—that is, I'd not ask Papa, but if you could look to Sarah . . .''

For a long moment Devin was silent. Unbidden, her image came to mind. "You cannot have spoken of this to her,'' he decided finally.

Adam shook his head. "No, but I mean to.''

"She may prefer Papa's aid over mine.''

"No one could prefer to Papa to you.''

"I don't know. Sarah and I do not deal well together,'' Devin hedged. "She does not appear to care much for me, you know, and—''

" 'Tis that she knew you did not want me to wed her, but that is over and done. She is Sarah Hastings now, Dev—wife to me, sister to you. I'd ask you to accept her.''

"Do you not think I have?'' Devin demanded harshly. "I lost the fight, as you will recall—aye, and I have been all that is proper to your wife, but—''

"Then promise me you will take care of her if I fall.''

"She will not wish it! Dash it, but can you not see that she and Papa deal together better than she and I?''

"I'd not leave a dog in his care,'' Adam responded evenly. "I'd thought better of you—truly I had. 'Tis always the way it has been between us, isn't it? We quarrel, come to fisticuffs even, and then 'tis settled and forgotten. I'd expected this to be the same, but I guess it isn't.''

He moved closer, standing over his brother. "I'd see to your wife, Dev."

Devin looked up, seeing not the man Adam had become, but rather the boy who'd shared a childhood with him. How could he tell him that he had wanted—still wanted—Sarah for himself? For a long moment he considered it, but when he spoke, he merely muttered, "You won't fall—you are too stubborn to die."

"But if I should?" Adam persisted relentlessly.

There was no help for it then. He sighed and nodded. "Aye—she'll want for naught, I swear to you."

It as a great relief to Adam, and he relaxed visibly. "When all's said and done, you are the best of brothers, Dev."

"Lud, but what a foolish pair we are today, brother mine," Devin observed, glad enough to end the subject, "for not only will you not fall, you will return victorious to receive His Majesty's commendation and vast rewards." He returned to the papers on the desk, searching for his quill amongst the uncharacteristic disarray. "Let me write to Loudoun and secure a place for your wife in his train."

"No."

"Adam, I have never heard of his debauching his officers' wives."

"I should rather ask him myself."

They were interrupted by the sound of footsteps; then Sarah peered around the door. "I thought you wished to go riding, Adam. The day is far too pleasant to spend inside."

Both men spun around at the sound of her voice. She came into the room swinging her small whip, and once again Devin felt a pang of envy for the brother who had her. Her hair was pulled back from her face and held by a black ribbon at her nape, accentuating the fine bones of her face. It was a masculine style that only a pretty woman dared, but she did not seem to know it. Her borrowed habit was of a deep forest green, with a jacket, banded at collar and cuff in black grosgrain, that she carried over one arm easily. The white cambric of her shirt fit loosely, but not so much so that the curve of her breasts could not be seen. She moved closer to Adam.

"Would you tie my stock, if you please? Mary is with your mother, and I have made a sad muddle of it, I fear." She raised her chin much as a child about to be dressed.

He undid the lace-edged ties and looped them awkwardly over his fingers. " 'Twill be backwards, you know, for 'tis quite different to do it on someone else."

"Not to mention that you are more adept at taking them off than putting them on," Devin murmured, coming up behind him. "I say, but you are cow-handed at that."

"You do it, then."

As Adam moved back to give him room, Sarah opened her mouth to protest, but the words died on her lips. She could hear Devin Hastings' breath catch. It was as though the room had suddenly gone silent. And then he stepped forward, his face utterly devoid of expression.

He saw her recoil before he even reached out. With an effort, Devin forced himself to pick up both ends of the stock. Sarah stood like stone, silent and still, while he carefully tied the snowy cambric at her throat, adjusting the ends to cascade into a fall of Brussels lace above her breasts. He did not think she breathed until he stepped away.

"You should have been a valet, my lord," she murmured finally, and her meaning was not lost on him.

"Oh, he is much more adept with the ladies," Adam told her as he winked at his brother.

"I own I had not noted that."

Devin considered that he'd been set down, but he managed to flash her a smile that did not begin to warm his eyes. "Alas, Sarah, but you would wound me."

"But 'tis the way of things, is it not—that one seldom truly notes one's own relations?" she shot back, unrepentant.

"Are you quite ready, my dear?" Adam asked.

"Yes."

Devin waited until he heard the door to the front foyer close, then moved to the window to watch as they crossed the lawn to where ostlers held two horses. Adam boosted

Sarah into his mother's sidesaddle and helped her loop the wide, full overskirt over her hand. The sun caught in her hair, burnishing it, making it almost copper. He couldn't hear what his brother said to her, but he could hear her responding giggle. He turned away, certain that the sooner Adam took her off to New York with Loudoun, the better it would be for him.

"Adam, is something wrong?"

"Hmmmm?"

"We have ridden some distance since last you spoke," Sarah chided him.

"Well, mayhap I was thinking of you."

She reined in and cocked her head to study him. "Mayhap—but I do not think so."

As she watched him, her hazel eyes appeared amber and her auburn hair shone in the sunlight. And once again he was struck by just how very lovely she was. The same Almighty who had given him Charles, Earl of Westerfield, for a father had somehow allowed him to take Sarah for wife and therefore had blessed him, evening the scale. His mood lightened perceptibly as he looked at her, and an infectious smile warmed his face.

"Mayhap I was thinking of last night," he teased wickedly.

"Well, if you were, it made you rather sober, which ought to worry me, you know." She tried to sound cross, but she could not conceal the color that had risen in her cheeks.

For answer, he edged his horse closer, and leaning from his saddle, managed to brush a kiss across her lips. "I assure you that if I wasn't, I am now."

Despite the fact they'd been married for two weeks now, she felt an incredible thrill every time he touched her or even looked at her just so. It was beyond everything that he could actually be hers. For a moment she closed her eyes and held on to her sidesaddle to still the sudden desire that sent her pulses beating wildly throughout her body.

He felt it also, so much so that he considered turning back to the Park, but there was so little privacy in a house

full of family and servants. Instead, he straightened back
in his saddle and, keeping his voice as light as he could,
clicked his reins.

"Race you to Spender's Hill."

She had not been there since that day she'd left with
him in what seemed another age, and she hesitated, afraid
to go back. The place was empty and deserted now, a
shell of the home she'd loved. But Adam was already
ahead of her, his big bay horse stretching its legs. It didn't
make any difference—that part of her life was over anyway, she told herself. She flicked her riding whip and
shouted after him, " 'Tis not fair—you are astride!''

He reined in again at that and waited for her. "Tell
you what, then—I'll give you to the hill ere I come after
you!''

The wind had blown his dark blond hair, whipping
strands from the black ribbon that held it at his neck, and
the escaping tendrils lay across his cheek, softening the
planes of his handsome face. The eyes that watched her
were as brilliantly blue as that rare, clear sky above them.
She glanced down to where the full-sleeved French shirt
lay open at his neck, and another thrill of remembered
passion coursed through her. No, she didn't need Spender's Hill anymore—she didn't need anything except Adam
Hastings.

"Fair enough!''

He gave her farther than that, drawing back and waiting until she was out of sight. His sense of fairness demanded that, for she was right: a sidesaddle was a distinct
disadvantage. Why Anne of Bohemia had been able to
foist the contraption on her adopted nation those centu-
ries ago was beyond him. But that long-forgotten queen
had, and out of a need to prove to the earl and countess
that she was indeed a lady, Sarah had taken to using it.
He much preferred to see her as she was, capable of
riding astride with abandon, able to take hedgerows as
though she'd been born to the saddle.

When he judged she must be almost to the fork in the
road, he spurred after her. The thick mane of her hair,
having somehow lost its ribbon, tangled wildly in the
wind as she leaned forward, holding on tightly, all the

while urging his mother's mare to run. Aye, sidesaddle or no, she was a game one, his Sarah, and he'd misjudged just how hard she'd ride to win.

He did not catch her until they were halfway up the lane to Spender's Hill and the mare had begun to lose stamina. Sarah's hair blew into her eyes when she turned back to see how close he'd come. Not wanting to outdistance her by much, he held the big bay back.

She shook her head, reaching to pull her hair back. "No!" she shouted back at him. "I am not a child you must let win!"

He surged past her less than two hundred yards from the old house, leaning to catch her reins as he did, and they slowed to a walk just as they reached the abandoned stable. She clutched her precarious perch for a moment. He dismounted quickly and reached for her. She slid the length of his body as his arms closed around her. For a moment they stood together, breathless and exhilarated from the ride.

As she caught her breath, she became acutely aware of the strong masculine arms that held her. Through the unbuttoned jacket of her borrowed habit and the fine cambric of their shirts, she could feel his heart beating. The mood changed subtly between them. She started to step back, but he shook his head.

"There's none to see us now, love," he almost whispered as his head bent to hers.

Her eyes widened at the implication; then she lifted her face for his kiss. "No . . . no, there's not, is there?" she murmured softly.

"Nobody but us."

His hands came up to catch in her tangled hair. She sucked in her breath as his caressed her cheek. He nibbled gently, tenderly, first at the corners of her mouth and then at her lips. They parted, soft and yielding, to give him possession, and gentleness was forgotten in the blaze of desire kindled by his kiss. Bathed in the beauty of rare English sunlight, surrounded by naught but grass and air, they clung to each other shamelessly, partaking fully of that passion.

But it wasn't until his hand slid beneath her jacket to

work at the waistband buttons of her dust skirt that she realized he meant to take her there. Her eyes flew open to stare into his.

"No!" she gasped as his fingers loosened the full over-skirt and it fell at her ankles. "Not here . . . Adam—"

For answer, his mouth burned the hollow of her throat and his hands moved between them to the neck of her shirt. She caught at his strong fingers and shook her head.

"Don't make me wait until tonight, Sarah." His voice was hoarse, his eyes deep blue.

"Not here," she whispered. "Not where someone could ride up and see."

Nodding, he lifted her. The dust skirt rose as it caught at her ankles, then fell away, leaving his mother's deep green habit clinging to her legs as he carried her into the stable. The warm smell of dried hay wafted around her as he held her above the clean mound at the back of the place. Working almost feverishly, he pushed the skirt and underpetticoats down, fanning them out beneath her to cover the prickly hay, and then he laid her upon them. Her bared skin sank deeply into the cambric-covered mound. As she reached up to him, he pulled his shirt over his head and unbuttoned his breeches to free himself. Quickly he shed the rest of his clothes, flinging them into a corner beneath dusty tack.

The look in his eyes as he knelt beside her sent a shiver of exquisite anticipation to the very center of her being. She felt unbearably hot even before he touched her again. It was going to be good between them, and she knew it. He reached to the neck of her own shirt.

"I'd see all of you this time, Sarah. I'd have nothing between us."

She nodded, raising up slightly to remove the jacket and shirt of her habit, taking them off herself with an eagerness that matched his. She wanted to feel every inch of his body against hers. As the last of her clothes fell to the side of the hay, she lay back, waiting.

He lay over her, resting his weight on his elbows, holding his body just above hers, so close that she could feel the heat of it. She closed her eyes.

"Don't," he whispered. "I want to watch you. At night, I cannot see what you feel."

She thought she could not stand it. He'd not touched her yet, and already her body was wild with the wanting of him. She had to turn her head away to keep him from seeing how wanton she was. "Please . . ."

He shook his head. " 'Twill be too soon over. Just let me touch you first."

But she was having none of that. Not now—not this time. She reached her arms to clasp his neck and pull him down to her, demanding his kiss. Her hips settled in the hay beneath his as she brought her legs around his. He hesitated only until her mouth opened beneath his lips, and then he was lost. Some other time, he would love her as he ought, but now his intense need had the upper hand. She moved urgently beneath him, tilting her hips to receive him.

This time, she needed no gentle wooing—her body was on fire—hot and wet and clamoring for ease. Her eyes, when they met his, were like pools of dark amber, dusky with desire. His control deserted him as he plunged inside her, joining her in a mindless, ceaseless, rhythmic striving for the attainable ecstasy. She writhed and moaned, her hands raking his bared back, urging him onward until she cried out beneath him, a cry that descended into a whimper as he shuddered in release. It was over quickly, but neither seemed to mind.

They lay, legs and arms tangled, sunk deep within the hay, and neither wanted to be the first to pull away. As he came back to earth, Adam looked again into her eyes, seeing the contentment there. They were warm and smoky now, the coals left after the fire. The pulse in her neck beat steadily and the rise and fall of her chest beneath him gradually slowed. She caught her lower lip with her teeth, sobering as he watched her. Then she smiled—not the shy smile he was used to, but rather the smile of a woman loved. She moved her hand from his back to his temple, pushing the hair away from his face with her fingertips.

"Now you can touch me all you want," she murmured huskily. "And you can take all the time in the world."

He rolled away at that, turning on his side to face her. He stared in wonder, thinking himself the most fortunate fellow on earth. She met his gaze unblinking.

Slowly, deliberately, he brushed the palm of his hand over first one breast and then the other, watching as the nipples hardened. Easing his body down in the hay, he positioned his head between them, sampling both in turn. As he heard her involuntary gasp, he felt a resurgence of his own desire. Later, much later, he'd discover the means to tell her about the war. But for now, they'd take what time they had.

"I mean to. I don't think I could ever get enough of you, Sarah—not ever."

13

It was late afternoon when they rode in. Devin looked at the clock on the mantel and frowned before he moved to the window to watch them again. As ostlers took away the horses, Adam stopped to pick hay out of Sarah's thoroughly disordered hair. Giggling like a girl still in the schoolroom, she stood on tiptoe to do the same for him. It took little imagination to decide why they'd gone alone and where they'd been.

Just before they reached the house, she turned her face up to receive her husband's quick kiss. Devin let the drapery fall and stepped back. Resolutely he stifled the surge of jealousy he felt. It was a good thing that he would be leaving for London at first light, for he did not know how much longer he could stand to see her with his brother.

He heard them going upstairs together—no doubt to

make themselves presentable before they were seen. Briefly he wondered if Adam had told her about the ministers' meeting; then he doubted it. No, war was not the sort of thing to make anyone laugh. He himself approached the prospect of having Adam maimed or killed with a dread that sickened him deep inside. If anything happened to Adam . . . Well, he could not face losing his only brother—no more than he could face having a widowed Sarah in his house.

Unwilling to contemplate either eventuality, he turned resolutely back to the work on the desk. He'd struggled hours with the figures his secretary had sent him, so much so that they were but a blur, but he had to be prepared to present costs to the paymaster of the forces before Parliament met. And it did no good to remind anyone that the cost of good serge was rising. Well, when he reached London, he would have Mr. Clark research the matter further. In the meantime, he would prepare the rest of his recommendations.

By the time everyone came down to supper, Devin had finished his report and sent a copy of it to Pitt in the Foreign Affairs Office. Although his old mentor was no longer in charge of military expenditures, it never hurt anything to keep him apprised. If rumor ever became fact, Pitt could well form the next government—and when he did, Viscount Audley most certainly should be given a conspicuous position in it.

Over dinner, he attempted to prepare his father for the coming conflict, announcing almost casually, "I heard from Pitt today."

"Eh?" Turning to his younger son, the earl beamed proudly. "Told you he had Pitt's eye, didn't I? Well, well, out with it—what did he say?"

" 'Tis war, I am afraid."

"War? Oh no!" Sarah went pale.

"War?" the earl echoed. "Then 'tis settled—the boy sells out," he declared flatly.

"Papa, I am not a 'boy.' I am four-and-twenty and past my majority," Adam reminded him. "And I am a soldier."

The old man ignored the edge in his younger son's

voice as he leaned across the table toward him. "Aye, you are selling out—I mean to see you do. Why, sirrah, you should be a fool not to!"

"Sir—"

"Time you was advancing yourself, making a name for yourself, rather than captaining a company of foot! Aye, you'll get your head blowed off if you don't."

"Sir—" Adam warned again, casting a significant look to where Sarah sat.

"No, damme if I'll be silent in my own house—you ain't going, and that's that! If I have to write the war minister myself, I'll see you stay!"

"And do what, Papa?" Adam asked with deceptive calm. "Be naught but a wealthy wastrel—is that what you want?"

"Get Dev to find you a position," his father maintained stoutly.

"No."

"Perhaps the Home Guards . . ." the countess ventured rather timidly, sensing she was once again to be drawn into a conflict between her husband and her younger son. "I daresay 'twould not be—"

"No, Mama."

"No? *No?* Damme, boy, but I forbid going, I tell you! I did not rear a common soldier—I did not send you to Oxford for nothing!"

"There is nothing common about fighting for one's king," Adam retorted stiffly. "And my mind is set on the matter. Will someone pass the peas, if you please?"

"Foot soldiers is common, I tell you!" the old man all but shouted.

"I am thinking of asking Loudoun for a position on his staff."

"Loudoun?" the earl choked. "Never say they are giving an army over to John Campbell! The fellow's a demned hedonist! How's he to fight a war, I ask you—from the boudoir?"

" 'Tis not so, sir," Devin contradicted his father, rising to Adam's defense. "Regardless of his reputation for ease, he is a meticulous soldier—and more than qualified to take over from Shirley."

The earl turned to his elder son. "Never say you are against me in this, Dev? You hear that, Emma? Audley's defending Loudoun!"

"Charles, please, your digestion . . ." the countess tried feebly.

"You may save your choler, sir," Adam interrupted him. "I expect to be on the ship that carries Loudoun."

"Adam!" Sarah gasped. "You would not! Surely . . ."

The earl's eyes were intent again on Adam. "Aye, he would," he muttered, "if for naught else but to spite me. You see the gel, boy? She don't want you to go neither!"

Devin swallowed a mouthful of the peas and quickly washed it down with wine before facing his father. "Sir, perhaps we ought to discuss this after we have eaten."

"No, I ain't done! Look at the gel—she looks half-sick at the thought, don't she? Besides, the way things has been between them, what with all these calf looks . . . well, 'twouldn't surprise me if she ain't increasing already."

"No!" Sarah colored beneath the earl's sudden scrutiny. "That is, I shall go with my husband, of course— wherever he chooses to go."

"Now, I know he ain't got any sense, but I'd hopes of you Mistress Hastings!" He leaned across the table toward her and lowered his voice, coaxing, "You don't want him t' take a French ball, do you?"

"Of course I do not, but—"

He leaned back triumphantly. "See, the gel don't want you to go neither—too young to wear widow's weeds by half, anyways."

"Papa—"

"Stay home with her and give over this nonsense. Thing to do is to see there's more Hastingses—more to the point, I'd say."

"Please, Charles," the countess pleaded, " 'tis dinner, after all, and you know how quarreling over food makes you dyspeptic."

"Then you tell him he ain't going to fight in some godforsaken colony, Em!"

It was going to take some time to get the old man used to the idea, time that Adam did not have, and Devin knew it. It was better to let the idea lie for a few days now that it had been introduced. He reached for the bread basket, asking politely, "Does anyone care for some of this while 'tis still fresh and warm? And, Mama, you really must tell Cook she has outdone herself with the pasties."

"Thank you, Dev." Adam broke off a piece of the bread with the same determination. "I find myself quite famished."

"Aye, and if you'd a been here to nuncheon, I daresay you'd be in better case," his father grumbled. "Where you could find to ride the whole day away, I am sure I don't know."

"Charles, please," Lady Emma intervened again. "The child looks as though she has the headache. Perhaps I should call Mary—"

"Dash it, Em!" Her husband eyed her suspiciously. "Now, I ain't going to have you making an invalid out of the gel whilst she's in my house, you hear? 'Tis bad enough to have two ailing females much of the time, anyway! And I'll not have you addicting her to burnt feathers, I tell you! Stinks up the house and *gives* me the headache, if you must have the truth of it!" He looked down the table at Sarah. "You ain't increasing yet, are you?"

"Charles, really!" Lady Emma protested.

"Well, it ain't impossible, you know," her husband announced baldly. "And as randy as the boy acts around her, I'm surprised she can sit. 'Course, 'tis early days, I admit it, but naught's to say the crop ain't been sowed already."

Adam started from his chair, but Sarah laid a hand on his sleeve to stop him. Her face flaming with embarrassment, she faced her father-in-law. "You, sir, are as disgusting as German George," she managed between clenched teeth. "Were I not so hungry, I should leave, but I see no reason to punish myself for your want of manners."

At first the earl did not think he'd heard her aright. The room grew silent as family and servants alike stared. Adam, who'd been about to say much the same, felt intensely proud of her for not being cowed by the old man.

A faint smile played at the corner of Devin's mouth, while the countess appeared totally shocked. The earl's eyes narrowed and his scowl deepened, but Sarah met his gaze squarely. He looked for all the world as though he'd like to strike her, and then suddenly he threw back his head and laughed outright.

"Damme if I don't like you, gel—you ain't one of them simpering, quavering females, are you? Here"—he reached down the table to her—"hand me your plate. I won't let you starve in my house."

The tension dissipated, released by her outburst, and talk fell to safer subjects—the unseasonable warmth and sunshine, the health of Lucie's foal, Roland Wicklund's sudden departure from the neighborhood. The latter gave Sarah a pang of guilt, but there'd been no help for it. It was Adam she'd loved from the beginning, and now that she'd been loved by him, she could not imagine feeling that way about anyone else—not ever.

After dinner, the earl surprised them all by suggesting that instead of the usual port in the library, the women should join them for a hand or two of cards. And when Devin protested that there would be an odd one left over, his father allowed as how either Audley or his mother could watch. Later, after Sarah had won more than her share of hands, he growled at her, "Think you are a Captain Sharp, eh? Well, Mistress Hastings, let us see if you are willing to wager on it."

"I have no money, sir."

"I'll frank you, my dear," Devin offered behind her.

"No. I'd not play if I cannot pay, my lord."

"Play you for that comb in your hair, then—silver, ain't it?"

It was not worth above a few shillings, for the greater part of it was tortoise, but she shook her head. "It was my mother's."

He eyed her with disfavor for a moment, then sighed. "I would take your voucher, then."

"Alas, but I could not redeem it."

Adam, who had been sitting across from her, reached into his coat. Drawing out a thin leather folder, he retrieved a banknote from it. "Here—I'd see you play."

"But—"

"Go on," he urged her.

"The whole thing?" she asked doubtfully.

"Let me get the money box—I daresay I can break that down," Devin offered.

It was settled then. Seated behind a stack of small coins from the box, she watched the earl shuffle. When he pushed a piece into the center, she matched it. She lost the first game and he chortled. It was one of the few times he won.

"If you were a man, I'd think you cheated," he muttered as he pushed his remaining coins out.

"Well, as there was naught else to do at Spender's Hill, I played cards with the grooms, my lord, until Papa let them all go. Then I played myself—one hand against the other."

"And that woman allowed it?"

"Miss Wallace?" Sarah grinned impishly at the old man. "Oh, I can assure you she did not know of it."

"Sly baggage! Well, well, I suppose 'tis the last go-round, ain't it?"

To his chagrin, she won that also, taking the rest of his money. Scooping the pile into both her hands, she held it out to her husband. The countess, who'd nearly dozed for the last several rubbers, passed a tired hand over her eyes.

"Really, Charles, but you are keeping the child up too late."

"Dash it, Em—the gel's beat me! Tell you one thing, all of you: Mistress Hastings ain't a bad gamester—not by half, she ain't."

"Mayhap if all else fails Adam, she can set up a gaming establishment," Devin offered dryly.

"Now, it don't hurt to let her play at home a little. Er . . . don't suppose you'd try something a little deeper next time?" he asked Sarah.

"Alas, but whist's all I play."

"Heartless jade. How's a man to come about, I ask you, if he's only to play your game?" Turning to Adam, he added, "You'd best watch her, boy, else she'll have a settlement won of me yet."

"Maybe she'll make me rich on campaign by winning my fellow officers' pay."

"No." The old man's good humor faded abruptly. "I ain't going to let you go."

"Sir—"

"Charles, I think you ought to retire," Lady Emma spoke up hastily. "Your gout—"

"My gout pains me there as well as here, Em, and well you know it," he growled at her.

"I'll get the laudanum and help you to bed, sir," Devin responded promptly. "Then I am for my own. Unlike Sarah and Adam, I did not spend my day riding, but I find myself overtired." Sarah colored at the strange emphasis he put on the word "riding," but when she dared to look at him, his expression was bland. "Good night, my dear. Good night, Adam. Mama, if you will take Papa's other arm . . ."

Adam waited until they'd helped his father from the room. Then, turning to offer Sarah his arm, he leaned over and murmured for her ears alone, "Speaking of riding . . ."

She blushed to the roots of her hair, but she managed to nod. "If 'randy' means what I think it does, your papa knows you better than you think."

"If you are overtired—"

"Oh, no," she countered hastily. A saucy smile curved her mouth and warmed her amber eyes. "Captain Hastings, I have hopes of becoming a *bruising* rider."

14

His Majesty's ministers met and drew up the articles of war against France in mid-April, and Parliament agreed, making it official. And although Pitt was formally out of office, his influence was felt in that 'twas decided to make America and India the main thrust of British strategy, leaving much of the prosecution of the European war to England's allies. And, as expected, the Thirty-fifth Regiment of Foot, or the Royal Sussex, as it was commonly known, received orders to America with General Lord Loudoun.

Both Adam and Devin spent much of their time away from the Park, each deeply involved in the war effort. But as the June departure date set by Loudoun drew closer, Adam came home as often as possible. Sarah, who'd hoped to return to his regiment with her husband, had to be content to remain with his family, since the almost frenetic military preparations left Adam with no opportunity to find lodgings elsewhere for her.

For once, everyone had united against her in that small matter—a bachelor officer's quarters were deemed totally unsuited to a lady of quality. And so she'd been able to see her husband for only two or three days at a time, whenever he dared absent himself from his regiment, which was not nearly often enough to suit either of them. To both, it was as though they were given but brief stolen moments of passion before they would be thrust into the maelstrom of war. The separations were merely temporary, they told each other, since Adam had already made arrangements for Sarah to make the crossing to New York in the comfort of Loudoun's own ship.

But in late May, Sarah began to fear the plans she and Adam had made lying in the hay at Spender's Hill would come to naught. For a time, she determined to hold her tongue and keep her secret until she reached America. Then it would be too late to send her back alone.

Lord Audley also came home from London from time to time, escaping the intense political pressures of supplying an army embarking across the seas. Politicians became vendors, ready to profit on everything from cloth to muskets, and every one of them was only too eager to pressure Devin to influence the paymaster of the forces. There were fortunes in bribes to be made every day, but true to Pitt's confidence in him, he resisted the blandishments of merchant and peer alike. Despite his intention to stay away, he found himself drawn to the Park more often than was wise.

But to him, it seemed that his ancestral home afforded less respite than he would have hoped, for every time he saw Sarah, he was acutely aware that if he'd played his game differently, she would have been his rather than Adam's. He was torn between wanting to see her go and wanting to keep his brother safely in England. One moment, he would toy with the notion of asking high-placed allies in the War Office to reassign Adam to the Home Guards, and the next, he would hope that Adam would take Sarah as far away as was possible. The result was that he did nothing and assuaged his conscience by reasoning rightfully that Adam would resent his interference.

But Sarah still occupied his mind far too much for peace, and he was beginning to resent both her and Adam for their blatant happiness. A woman ought not to affect a man so, for was not one female much the same as another? he asked himself over and over. And each time he argued the matter in his mind, he convinced himself that she was no different from the rest of her sex.

On one particular Saturday, he rode out alone in the direction of Spender's Hill. The air lay heavy with unshed rain, prompting Devin to rein in and look upward at the cloudy sky. It seemed unseasonably hot, probably because of the moisture and the lack of wind. In another hour or so the darkening clouds were going to pour hard, pelting the earth with the sort of rain that ran off rather than soaked.

He removed his felt hat to wipe his brow with the back of his hand, thinking he ought to try for the Park before the storm hit. But he was almost to Spender's Hill, and he'd hoped to explore the place with an eye to building himself a fine home there. If the rains did in fact come, he supposed he could always take refuge with the pigeons in the abandoned house. Resetting his hat, he clicked the reins and nudged the horse down Spender's Lane.

It was not until he'd made the last turn that he saw the two horses—and then he saw Adam and Sarah. He halted and watched, reluctantly drawn by the scene before him. They were locked in an embrace, oblivious of his presence. As he stared silently, Sarah pulled away to remove her jacket and drop it into the grass. Then she unbuttoned the protective dust skirt from her habit, letting it fall to her ankles. As Adam reached out, untying her stock, opening her shirt almost to the waist, exposing the fine lawn chemise beneath, Devin's breath caught painfully. And when Adam's hands touched the lacings at her breasts, his mouth went dry. But she pulled away, laughing, and ran for the stable, stopping to lean seductively in the doorway. His eyes on her, Adam bent to pick up the discarded dust skirt, then carried it after her.

So that was where they disappeared every day Adam was home. For a moment Devin allowed himself to imagine what it must be like to possess her, and his pulse raced with desire. Then, his rational mind reasserting itself, he forced his thoughts from what must be happening inside, telling himself fiercely that it served no purpose now to think of her like that.

What he needed was a woman, an eager woman who knew how the game was played. Aye, what he needed was a new mistress to make him forget how badly he'd bungled the business with Sarah Spender. And London was full of exquisite creatures all too ready to share their

favors with a rising politician—beautiful, sophisticated
women far more accomplished than a green country girl.

He turned back toward the road, resolved to return to
London the next day. He'd been spending too much time
at the Park anyway, at a time when there was glory to be
gained in government. He belonged in London.

The earl was sitting on the wide porch when he rode
in, and the first thing he said was, "Postboy brought you
a letter from London."

"I am expecting to hear from Pitt."

"You ought to be there rather than here, you know. A
man can't advance himself by being least in sight," the
old man grumbled, echoing Devin's thoughts.

Audley dismounted, throwing the reins to a stableboy,
and mounted the steps to take the envelope. "You didn't
read it, did you?"

"Of course I did not! Not that I did not think to if you
had not come home." The old man's eyes narrowed for
a moment. "It ain't about Adam, is it? You think on what
I asked?"

"I have not read it yet," his son answered evasively,
ripping the seal. It was nothing, merely Pitt's recounting
of Whig positions on the prosecution of the war, and a
request for his support in a crucial vote before the Lords.
Beyond that, his mentor casually mentioned the American expedition, but contributed nothing that Devin did
not already know. Refolding it, he slipped it beneath his
coat.

"Well? Ain't you going to tell me what he says?"

"There is not much to tell—'tis policy mostly, and
word that Loudoun sails for New York next month."

"Campbell? Humph! That I should like to see!" the
earl snorted. "John Campbell is as like to command as
I am!"

"He will do better than Shirley now that war is declared," Devin maintained loyally. "Shirley was forever
being drawn into petty quarrels with the colonials, you
know, and we were always receiving two sets of reports—
one from him and one from his enemies."

"Well, Loudoun won't find colonial life much like what
he is used to, unless he's given to consorting with Indi-

ans. And by the looks of them as came over to pay hom-
age to Queen Anne, Indians is a bit ugly for his tastes.
Fellow's a demned hedonist—what's he to do in America,
I ask you?''

Devin smiled faintly. "Oh, I should expect him to remain one. But who's to say that there are not pretty
women in New York, after all? Besides, I would not be
surprised if he did not take one with him."

Abruptly the old man changed the subject. "Is that all
Pitt had to say—nothing about your brother?''

Devin drew in a deep breath and exhaled it slowly. "I
did not ask him, Papa. 'Tis already done and too late to
change it," he lied. "Adam sails with Loudoun."

"The devil he does! Nay, I'll not have it, and so I told
you both!"

"Papa, he is determined to go." Devin dropped into
a chair beside the old man. "He is a soldier by profession, whether we will it or not. Is not the fact that he
bought his own commission proof of that?''

"He did it to vex me," the old man admitted heavily.
"If I was to say he had to be one, he'd insist on something else."

"Try it—tell him that, then."

"On whose side are you?" The earl glared briefly, then
looked away. "What if he went anyway?''

"I am on Adam's."

"Aye, conspire against me, the both of you! I'd expected better of you at least."

"He asked Loudoun himself."

"And knew I'd not be pleased, I'll be bound."

"It would not surprise me if he came home a colonel,
sir, and if he distinguishes himself, 'twill reflect favor-
ably on the family. A military hero could advance my
career, you know."

The old man's bushy brows knit suspiciously; then he
shook his head. "Coming it too strong, Dev—if he ain't
in the thick of it, how the devil's he to advance? And as
it ain't you as is going, I fail to see how that aids you."

"Loudoun."

"Well, I don't like it, and so I am telling you right
now."

" 'Twould be better if you wished him well, sir.''

The earl fell silent, his thoughts still on his younger son. "No." He spoke slowly, almost absently. "I do not know where he gets it. There was a time I thought your mama had played me false with him—was sure of it, in fact, until I asked Wilmington why he did nothing for the boy. Said it wasn't any of his affair.''

"You should have asked Mama—she could have told you that years before.''

"Couldn't bring myself to do it." He looked up defensively, then lashed out, "Dash it, Dev! How the devil was I supposed to ask if he was mine? What if she'd lied to me? At that time, I thought she'd been with Wilmington—rumors was everywhere! And her own papa wrote for me to come after her!''

"Mama and Wilmington?" Devin choked. "Sir the man's a dashed bore—there is naught in Adam to remind you of him.''

"Well, he ain't like any of your mother's family, and—''

"Did you never consider that mayhap he is much like you, Papa? That he is as stubborn as you are?''

"I ain't a fool! Aye," he conceded, "I know he is my son now, but 'tis too late. Thing is, he didn't look like me—he ain't dark like me.''

"Neither am I.''

"You got the hair at least. But done's done, ain't it?''

"Not if you give him your blessing.''

"He ask you to speak to me?" the earl demanded suspiciously. "He ask you to gain my permission for this nonsense?''

"No.''

"I suppose not—he don't care what I think anyway," he grumbled. "But what's to do about the gel, I ask you? He's got a wife now—a penniless wife at that. No matter what I have said to him on that head, I cannot wish her any harm—like the gel, in fact—even own he could have done worse.''

"He'll take her with him.''

"And what am I supposed to do if he is killed? I've

only two sons—only two, mind you, and you ain't even got a wife!''

"Loudoun will keep him as safe as he can.''

"Humph! And what about the gel? What business has she following an army, I ask you?'' He paused as though struck by inspiration. "Aye, 'tis the answer, isn't it? If he don't stay, he'll come home to me if she is here.''

"He's made arrangements for her to sail on Loudoun's ship.''

His father looked away, knowing he was defeated. '' 'Tis all settled, isn't it? Aye, and I don't suppose she'd stay anyways. For nigh two months now, I've watched him ride posthaste home to see her, when time was that he'd not spare a thought for me or the Park at all. Aye, and I see 'em makin' sheep's eyes at each other, and it don't get any better, I can tell you. If she ain't increasing, she ought to be. No, he ain't going to leave her behind just because he's asked.''

"Wish him Godspeed, Papa.''

The earl sat very still, pondering the notion. "But I do not want him to go,'' he repeated, his voice dropping. '' 'Tis not what I want for him.'' Then, sighing heavily, he turned back to his favorite son. "Aye, you have the right of it, I suppose.''

It was as though the old man shrank measurably. Devin reached across to him, then dropped his hand. "You could be proud of what he does—'twould heal the breach between you.''

His father shook his head. "He hates me, Dev. But how was I to know he wasn't Wilmington's? An old man with a young wife has got a right to his suspicions, and Wilmington was particular in his attentions, you know. Then she came home to Milbrook Park to have the boy.''

"I think it was all a long time ago, Papa.''

"Aye.'' Acknowledging the truth of that, the earl returned to the matter at hand. "Still, he ain't like to forgive me the mistake, don't you know? Thing is, can't make it up to him anyways, and don't mean to try now. I'd feel like a fool explaining how it was.''

"He could scarce help knowing something was amiss.''

"Pitt ought to send you to argue with the Frenchies,

you know,'' his father grumbled. ''The War Office is the wrong place for you—'tis in State you belong. But 'tis too late for recompense, I tell you, and I mean to let it lie.''

The first large raindrops splattered against the stone steps, wetting them. The old man rose unsteadily and Devin caught him, holding him until he got his diseased knee into just the right position. Then, bearing much of his father's weight, he helped him inside.

''It ain't going to be easy letting him go, though—not now's I know—not now that she's brought him home to me,'' the earl muttered.

The rain hit just as Adam was boosting Sarah into her saddle. And the wind came up almost immediately, swirling the huge drops at first and then turning them into a sheet of water. Sarah slid down, and they ran hand in hand for shelter, reaching the house just as lightning cracked nearby. The horses shied and bolted for the open stable.

For the first time since Adam had taken her away from it, Sarah stood inside and realized just how badly the house had decayed in her absence. Either that, or she'd grown accustomed to the richness of Milbrook Park. She walked across the small open foyer, hearing her footsteps echo eerily throughout the house. It was as though she were in a strange place now. She walked into her father's study to look out into the garden beyond. Water seeped in through one of the cracked panes and trickled downward to form a small puddle on the faded floor. The outline of where the rug had once been remained, with the wood darker there.

Adam came up behind her and began picking bits of hay from her wet hair. But she was not attending him as she stared absently at the pelting rain, watching it shatter the petals of her mother's flowers, scattering them on the ground.

''Mama did so love her roses. I suppose when he has the house razed, he will plow them under. It seems a shame . . .'' Her voice caught as she turned away.

''I know.''

"I loved them also."

"Perhaps we could save them—replant them at the Park."

"No."

"Sarah, if I could, I'd restore your house—you do know that, do you not?" he offered helplessly.

"For Devin?" she asked bitterly. "Aye, 'tis he who will live here—not me."

"You dislike him, and I have never understood why."

She started to speak, then thought better of it. Finally, sensing that he had intended it as a question, she answered, "No. No, I do not dislike him, Adam."

"He's been all that is proper to you."

"Yes, I cannot complain of his behavior since I have been at the Park," she agreed carefully. "Indeed, he has been all that is kind."

His hands clasped her shoulders, then slid down her arms. "Good. It would pain me greatly if you could not be friends, Sarah. You and he are the ones I love best in this world." He fingered the wet material of her sleeve. "You and he make my life here bearable."

She pulled away and turned to face him. "But then it scarce seems fair that he has Spender's Hill, does it? Adam, he does not value it in the least."

"You wrong him, Sarah."

"Still, 'twas in my family for two hundred years. Could you not ask to buy it of your father? I mean . . ." Her eyes met his, then looked away quickly. "No, of course—and I should not ask it of you."

"I'd not beg Papa for anything. Sarah . . ." He reached out to her again, turning her back to face him. "If I thought he would do it, I would ask him for your sake—but he'd not sell it to me. Of if he would, he would bargain my independence from me."

"No, I suppose he would not," she admitted.

"If he gives it to Dev, I should ask my brother to sell to us. As you said, it cannot mean anything to Dev."

"Why does he dislike you so? Your father, I mean?" she asked suddenly, not wishing to consider Audley.

Adam turned from her to stare into the steady rain. "I'd not speak of it, Sarah. I'd take you and go to New

York—far away from here—where there's none to care if
I am a Hastings.''

"I'm sorry, Adam," she whispered softly, coming up
behind him, sliding her arms about his waist, and leaning
her head against his back. "You do not have to tell me
of it. I should not have asked."

He was silent for a moment and then turned back into
her embrace, closing his arms around her, holding her
close. " 'Tis the rain, Sarah, that blue-devils us. How
can I think of him when I have you?''

She leaned into his arms, savoring the warm closeness
of him, feeling the rush of gratitude for all he'd given
her. "I should rather have you than anyone, Adam—
Spender's Hill means little against what I feel for you.''

For a time, he stood there just holding her. "It will be
hard—following an army, I mean. Oh, New York will be
pleasant enough, but if we are sent inland . . ." His voice
trailed off. "Well, the French do not fight like gentlemen
in America, Sarah. I may have to leave you in New York
if that happens.''

"Adam, do you have to go to war?" she asked, suddenly afraid of losing him. "Could you not sell out?"

"No."

She sighed and turned her head into his shoulder. "No,
and I should not have asked that either.''

"What would I do—live in Papa's pocket, or become
a politician like Dev? I could not be an idle gentleman,
Sarah. I could not be content to wear satin breeches and
spend my time in witty conversation with other fribbles.
You behold a man more suited to battlefield than diplomacy. No, unlike Dev, I cannot dissemble before my
enemies." He smoothed her shining hair. "Besides, with
Loudoun's permission, I shall be able to take you with
me.''

She clung to him, loath to broach a matter that she
feared would change everything. But she could not hide
it forever. "Adam, will you sell out when we have children?" she asked carefully. Her heart seemed to stop
while she waited for his answer.

His hands, which had dropped down to rub along her
spine, stilled. Finally he answered, "No, then I should

try to advance up the ranks with distinction. I'd give my sons and daughters a pride in my accomplishments.''

"Oh.''

"Sarah, is something the matter?''

"No, of course not,'' she replied hastily. '' 'Twas curiosity merely. But we'd best get back, don't you think? By the looks of it, the rain has lessened, and I'd get out of my wet habit.''

15

Sarah lay silent, listening to the ticking of the ornate clock on the bedchamber mantel, unable to sleep. Beside her, Adam slumbered deeply, unaware of the turmoil in his wife's mind. He and Devin had spent the evening closeted together after dinner whilst she and the countess had entertained the earl with yet another night of whist. This time, her heart had not been in her game and the old man had actually won a few rubbers. But her supper had not set well, and when the countess had called for orgeat, she'd made herself sick trying to down the syrupy stuff, ending the evening.

But it was that sickness that bothered her. When first she'd experienced it, she'd thought it the heat. Then, on reflection, she was sure it was not, and she'd been glad, thinking it would somehow keep Adam from going to war. Now she knew it would not, and she could only hope to keep her secret long enough to go with him. But the thought of pitching to and fro on rough seas made her queasy all over again.

Finally she could stand the disjointed imaginings, the fears magnified by the stress of a wakeful night, no longer. She eased out of bed, taking care not to wake her sleeping husband, and stared morosely out into the star-studded sky. Life was not fair, not at all. The joy she'd known since her marriage was tempered now by the knowledge that unless she concealed the child from him, he'd have to leave her behind. The brief hope that he might somehow be persuaded to leave the army had been dashed. A child would not turn him from what he perceived to be his duty. And if she asked him outright to stay with her, she had no certainty that he would do it—or if he did, that he would not come to despise her for the asking.

Perhaps if she appealed to Devin . . . No, she could not, for despite the filly, despite the many courtesies he'd offered since, she could not quite forget what he'd thought her. And despite his pleasant demeanor now, she still felt wary in his presence.

What about the earl? A shiver coursed through her at the thought of asking him. The fact that the old man did not want Adam to go seemed to be part of her husband's determination to leave. Besides, she did not think he'd wish to aid her.

The night breeze blew her rail, billowing it around her. She hugged her arms to her chest. But if she hid the child she carried, what then? When he discovered it, would it change things between them? Would he resent the added burden? Did she have the right to expect him to fight a war and worry about her and a babe? She was being selfish, and she knew it, yet she did not think she could bear a separation from him.

There were no easy answers, or if there were, she was too agitated to discover them. It was too soon, early days even, for her to get used to the idea herself, and much too soon to test his love for her. She stepped back from the window and looked to the bed. Adam turned in his sleep, his form deep in shadows.

Sudden hunger gnawed at her insides, a reminder that she'd lost her supper with the orgeat. Perhaps that was it—her fevered imaginings were but the product of an empty stomach. A little milk or some cheese, something to ease her—aye, that was the answer for now.

She pulled on her wrapper and found her slippers in the dark, then padded noiselessly to the door. The hall was silent, illuminated by sconces whose candles flickered eerily as the wicks floated valiantly in a sea of wax. She slipped down the back stairs and made the turn for the kitchen.

"Who goes there?"

To her alarm, the door to the earl's study was open and a triangle of light spread across the hallway before her. At first, she considered flight back up the stairs, but then realized he'd probably already seen her. Instead, she edged gingerly toward the open door.

"Well, do not be skulking outside—come in, come in." He beckoned imperiously, forcing her to face him.

"You startled me," she admitted.

"Aye." His eyes raked over her, taking in the wrapper and the lace of the rail that peeked out the neck. "Cannot sleep either, eh?"

"I'd thought to get some milk."

"Milk curdles this time of night, gel." His eyes narrowed when they reached her face. "Still not feeling the thing, are you? Best take a little dry toast instead, though where you'll find it this time of night is beyond me." Abruptly his scowl softened. "Guess I could wake up Mrs. Cross."

"Oh, no, I shall merely get myself some bread."

"Sit down." He indicated a chair across from him. "I cannot sleep also, so we might as well be company for each other, don't you think? Gout pains me," he added for explanation. "And I don't want any of the demned laudanum—gives a man unnatural rest."

"I am sorry."

"For what? It ain't your fault m' leg's bad, is it? Go on, sit down. Here . . ." He leaned to reach the table next to him, removing the lid from a dish. "Got digestive biscuits, and I don't want any more of 'em." Before she could demur, he'd dropped two into a napkin and passed them to her. "The doctor Emma keeps rich with m' money says they are good for stomach complaints. They don't do much for gout, but I daresay they ain't going to hurt what ails you."

"Really, but I—"

"Got your own bread in the oven, ain't ye? Aye, I thought as much when you wasn't eatin' yesterday. Then tonight . . . well, I knew it then. It ain't like you to let an old man beat you."

"The heat—"

"Heat be damned! This is Westerfield, gel!" he roared at her. "Aye, I have seen Emma in just such case—five times—and each one as bad as the other. After the last two was stillborn, we just quit the business."

Sarah's heart sank. For a moment she considered denying it, but he stopped her before she could form the words.

"No, don't dissemble with me, gel—I won't have it, you hear? Thing is, we got to put our heads together, don't you know? You ain't wanting him to go, and I don't either."

"You won't tell him?"

"Of course I mean to tell him! Dash it, you're what's going to keep him here for me!"

"But you do not understand—you do not understand! This changes nothing!" she cried out in alarm. "He will only leave me!"

"Nonsense! Are you daft and blind also? The boy's mad for you, gel! Thing is, you've got to go about the matter right, that's all."

"How? He has already said that if I were to increase, he'd stay in the army. I fail to see . . ." Sudden tears welled, threatening her composure. "I pray you will not—I pray you will not say anything, sir."

"Dash it, you are a Hastings now, gel! Stifle those sniffles—don't go watering the plants around me! I'll not have you and Emma both acting like wetgooses. Here, now—eat the biscuits and let us think."

She bent her head and bit into one of the dry wafers. It tasted like flour in her mouth, but somehow she managed to swallow. He was right: she had to think.

"You could go to Dev," he ventured soberly. "I don't carry much weight with the boy, but he does. Two of 'em's been inseparable since they was in leading strings—until Adam got the maggot in his brain that he ought to be a soldier, anyway. Thing is, if anyone could make him stay besides you, it'd be Audley, don't you see?''

"Then why have you not asked him—Devin, I mean?''

"Because he won't do it for me! Oh, he's biddable enough except where Adam is concerned. Thinks it his duty to protect the boy—from me!''

"Then I fail to see what I—''

"Then's when you cry, gel! Appeal to his generosity—tell him about the babe—ask him to aid you! Dash it, for a pretty girl, you don't seem to know how to go on, do you? Tell him you'll be desolate without your husband—or some such fustian as that!''

For a moment Sarah's second bite tasted like ashes. She could not go to Devin—she could not. She closed her eyes to the wave of nausea that washed over her. "He would not listen to me,'' she managed as it passed.

"Females!'' He rapped the table in disgust, banging his cane against the wood. "He ain't proof to you, I tell you! He gave you his filly, didn't he?''

At first, Sarah was not sure she'd heard him right. "Sir, what you are suggesting is repugnant in the extreme!''

"Eh?'' It was his turn to stare. Then, as her meaning sank in, he threw back his head and laughed uproariously. "You and Devin? No, no—damme, gel, but he ain't lost to propriety! And you ain't neither, I should hope!''

"But if you could make your peace with Adam, if you could ask rather than order . . .'' she said desperately.

The laughter died abruptly, replaced by a look of intense pain. "Because it won't fadge,'' he muttered, turning his head away. "He and I don't deal together—never have, never will.''

"So he has said. But if you would but try—''

"You don't know anything about it! There's naught anybody can do about it now—too much ain't been done for me to ask him.''

"But why not attempt the matter? Can you not forget—can you not attempt a peace between you?''

"Nay. Suffice it to say I ain't been like a papa to him—he'd not understand now. 'Tis too late for it.'' He shifted in his chair, easing his swollen leg down from the footstool. "You'll have to speak to Audley, I'll be bound. If you don't, I mean to tell Adam about the babe."

"Then we shall both lose, my lord."

"It ain't going to be like that at all," he maintained stubbornly. "You are going to make things right—you and Devin, you hear?" He hobbled to his feet with an effort and reached again for his cane. Leaning heavily on it, he picked up the tray of digestive biscuits. "Here, might as well have the lot of 'em—I ain't going to eat 'em." Then he walked slowly toward the door, his shoulders stooped over the cane. Turning back briefly, he managed what passed as a smile for him, added gruffly, "And don't be thinking I ain't happy about the babe, 'cause I am. I mean to do better by the grandson, you know."

She sat for a long time, pondering what he'd said. He was right, of course: if she indeed wished to keep Adam in England, Devin Hastings was her best hope. Perhaps Adam would stay and not hate her for it if Devin asked him. And yet she was loath to approach Audley. What if he denied her? What if he humiliated her? And what if Adam would not listen to him? Finally she finished the dry biscuit and rose to go upstairs, resolving to try anything else first.

Adam shifted as she eased back into bed, then came half-awake. "Is aught amiss?" he asked sleepily as he reached to pull her close.

"No," she lied, snuggling close to the warmth of his body.

"Good. There is so little time to be happy," he murmured.

"Oh, Adam, I love you so much," she whispered into his shoulder. "I do not think I could stand being away from you—'tis miserable enough when you are at Tunbridge."

"Ummmmmm."

"Adam—?"

"Uhnnn?"

"Suppose we were to have a child—I mean, what if we were? I'd go with you anyway—I would."

He yawned above her head and wrapped his arms more

tightly around her. "Too hard for you," he mumbled drowsily. "Couldn't ask you to."

"Adam!"

"Huh?"

"Adam, what I am trying to tell you is that I am increasing."

He came awake with a start, struggling to sit up. She pulled away and stared miserably at the reflection of the moonlight off the clock. It was as though time paused. The knot in her stomach felt unbelievably heavy.

"What? The deuce you are! Sarah . . ." He groped in the semidarkness to turn her around, and the faint illumination from the window shadowed her face. "Oh, love . . ."

"Does this mean that I cannot go?" she asked miserably. "For if I cannot, I know not how I shall go on without you."

"I don't know. I'd have to think . . ." One of his hands crept to comb through his hair as though he could somehow clear his head.

She looked down at the tangled covers and tried to put into words what she felt for him. Her hands pleated the wrinkled cloth nervously. "Adam, all my life has been as naught until you brought me love. You are the first person ever to love me—except Mama, of course, and that was so long ago that I can scarce remember it."

"Sarah . . . Sarah . . ." He pulled her onto his lap and cradled her as though she were a child herself. "Do you think you are not everything to me also? Until you, I never had anyone but Dev."

"I shall become big and ungainly, I know, but . . ."

He grinned foolishly and brushed her tangled hair back from her face. "And I will still love you."

"But—"

"Sarah, I love everything about you—your eyes, your hair, the way the sun freckles your nose, the noises you make when we love each other, the—"

"Stop it! Adam, I am asking you to take me anyway. If you cannot stay, I mean to go."

"I don't know . . . 'tis too sudden . . ." His voice trailed off as he considered the difficulty of what she asked. "An army sometimes moves fast, over rough terrain, forced marches . . . I don't know, Sarah. I'd not risk you or the child, and . . . and the surgeons who travel with us are little more than butchers. You'd have to stay in New York," he decided. "We'd have to engage a companion and take lodgings for you."

"Then you are saying I must stay," she answered for him. "You are saying this changes everything."

"It would be hard for you. We'd have to discover a midwife—and what if something goes wrong? Not that I should expect such a thing," he added quickly. "At least you'd have Mama here."

"Then stay with me! Stay in England, Adam, and do not leave me!" she cried.

"I cannot. Sarah—"

"You could if you wished it! You could if you loved me!" She felt him stiffen, and her voice dropped in pleading. "Please, Adam—please."

"Sarah, my orders are already given and Loudoun has chosen me above a dozen others. I cannot just say I have changed my mind."

"But . . ." It was a useless quarrel, and she knew it. He'd been a soldier when he offered for her—and he'd never pretended otherwise. No, it was she who owed him everything, she reminded herself. Without him, she'd be teaching sums to unruly schoolboys in York. And it was wrong to make him choose. He would go and she would stay.

"Sarah, I am sorry. Perhaps we should have waited to wed—perhaps 'twould have been kinder to you—but I wanted to marry you, love. Perhaps it was selfish of me, but I wanted you to love me."

"No." Somehow she managed to smile in the darkness. "If we'd waited, you would have left me without the memories I have to sustain me whilst you are gone. I shall be in no worse case than other wives, I must suppose," she managed, hoping she sounded braver than she felt.

"Sarah . . ."

"And when you are come home, there will be a small Hastings to greet you." She slid her arms around him to clasp him tightly. "Oh Adam, I shall miss you so!"

He lay back, pulling her down with him. "Just let me hold you, love. You should be asleep."

"No." She pulled away and turned on her side. Reaching to trace his profile with a finger, she shook her head. "No, Adam, I'd rather you loved me," she whispered huskily.

For answer, he cradled her head with his hands as he bent to kiss her. Her lips parted beneath his, drawing an answering desire from him. When at last he left her mouth to trace a burning trail from her ear to the hollow of her throat, she moved against him, molding her body to his.

But I wish you were not going, she cried silently as his hand slid to the hem of her nightrail.

16

Once they accepted the inevitability of separation, they were determined to live their remaining time together to the fullest. Adam took Sarah to London to stay at Westerfield House the last week before he left. Devin greeted their arrival pleasantly enough, but managed to absent himself frequently, apologizing that he had a rather full calendar of engagements. It was just as well, as it gave Adam the opportunity to show Sarah the sights of the city.

She gazed in wonder at the beauty of Westminster, admired the work of Wren at St. Paul's, viewed the menagerie at the Tower, and quite generally enjoyed herself. And as his young wife gaped at the wonders around her, Adam reveled in her pleasure, wishing he'd thought to bring her to town earlier. As special treats, he took her to Drury Lane to see David Garrick in *Macbeth,* and to Ranelagh Pleasure Gardens, where they supped and watched spectacular fireworks after a concert by an Italian tenor.

And everywhere they went, there was evidence of war fervor. In preparation for His Majesty's review of troops, flags were patriotically placed atop every lamppost from Westminster to Hyde Park, and hung from houses and hovels everywhere between fashionable Pall Mall and Gin Lane. Adam, in his scarlet dress uniform, found himself hailed and applauded on the street by strangers, many of whom urged him to "bag a Frog" for them. Their joviality, Sarah complained privately, made one think she was sending her husband off to a hunt rather than to a war.

On the last day before he left with his regiment to sail from Southampton, Adam persuaded his brother to secure Sarah a grandstand position for the parade and troop review, and she found herself watching the display of military pageantry with an august company of Whigs, including Mr. Pitt and his wife, Hester, the Duke of Newcastle, the Earl of Chesterfield, and Sir George Grenville, from a seat not fifteen feet from where His Majesty King George sat beside the Prince of Wales.

She could not help staring at the king, recalling the gossip of Mrs. Lynch, who claimed he'd taken a succession of ugly women simply because he thought that princes ought to have mistresses. More to the point, Sarah wondered how he persuaded the females, for he did not look courtly in the least. But then, she supposed the chosen ones were more flattered by his royalty than by the man himself.

It was an odd group, with Newcastle and the king determined to keep Mr. Pitt from the center of power, when all the world knew that before long German George would have to ask him to form the government. Mr. Pitt, it seemed, was most vocal in his approval of the war and in his criticism of how it was to be prosecuted, and the tide of public opinion was with him. But this day, no one would guess that there was any animosity between any of them. Mr. Pitt, in keeping with the festive air, was jovial, but then, why wouldn't he be? It was obvious, to King George's and Newcastle's probable chagrin, that Pitt was extremely popular with the masses. Mr. Pitt, it was said, was perhaps the only man ever to have held the powerful position of paymaster to the forces who did not use the office to enrich himself. And for his honesty, he'd been shunted out of that office into a less visible place in the War Office, where his stinging criticism of his own party was becoming more and more embarrassing. The king, when he'd arrived, had merely nodded frostily as he passed Devin and the Pitts. His warmth was reserved for Newcastle.

It was a lengthy parade, beginning with the blue-coated Royal Horse Guards, followed by the green-coated Sixth Regiment of Horse, then the Dragoon regiments, the Mounted Grenadier Guards, the Light Infantry, the Musketeers, the Royal Artillery, the Royal Scots Fusiliers, and finally the infantry, each regiment with its own drummer to beat out the march, with the exception of the Highlanders, who were accompanied by the eerie sound of their bagpipers. The colorful display, with its precise formations, was awe-inspiring. Sarah craned her neck, trying to catch sight of her husband as the foot regiments came into view. Finally she glimpsed the red and blue of the Thirty-fifth, and in her excitement she clutched Audley's sleeve.

"There he is! The mounted officer on the left!"

Devin, who'd been merely polite rather than attentive, followed her gaze briefly and caught sight of his brother. Adam sat tall and straight in his saddle, resplendent in the blue-faced scarlet coat, the gold of his gorget, braid, and buttons shining in the sun. And beneath the braid-trimmed black ramillie, his perfectly powdered peruke displayed the requisite two curls over either ear and the neat pigtail in the back. Lud, how Adam hated that wig. It would be a surprise if he ever wore it once he reached New York.

He looked down at Sarah, her hand still clutching his coat sleeve, her face flushed with the eagerness of the moment. Her auburn hair was pulled back and piled atop her head in fashionable curls now, but there was still something unfashionably appealing in her enthusiasm. There'd be none to dub her the Ice Mistress, he was certain. No, she was lovely in a totally unsophisticated, un-jaded way, and she was completely unaware of the effect she had on him. With an effort, he reached to remove her hand from his arm, but as his fingers closed over her black lace gloves, he found himself merely covering hers, holding them there.

The gesture brought her back to the present, and for a moment she was unsure if she ought to pull away. She'd no wish to make a scene before these powerful men, and in the end, she merely looked down at his hand. Abruptly he removed it and turned his attention studiously toward the parade.

"'Tis quite grand, is it not?" she murmured rather lamely.

"Aye."

"He looked particularly splendid, did you not think?"

"Splendid," was the all-too-terse reply.

She fell silent then, until Mrs. Pitt leaned across her husband to address her. "Was that Captain Hastings? The tall one with the bay horse?"

"Yes."

"How fortunate you are, my dear—and how terribly proud you must be of him. Mr. Pitt says General Loudoun values him quite highly already."

Sarah wanted to cry out that she did not consider herself fortunate that her husband was going off to a wilderness to fight a war against savages. She did not count herself fortunate that he was leaving her. But instead, she forced a smile and nodded. "Yes—of course, I *am* quite proud of him."

"Yes, well . . . 'tis a signal honor for one so young to be chosen to the general's staff."

Sarah wondered how Mrs. Pitt would have felt if Loudoun had chosen Mr. Pitt, but again she held her tongue. "So I have been apprised, ma'am. My husband seems quite pleased by the appointment."

Just then, the caissons rolled to a halt before the reviewing stand and the king stood to receive the customary salute of guns. Everyone in the grandstand rose to cheers from the common crowd; then a hushed stillness of anticipation fell over them. With great ceremony, the royal gunners rammed false charges and wadding into the barrels and set the fire to the cannon. It was a marvel to watch—the drumrolls and flourishes, then the simultaneous firing of the big guns. The burst was nearly deafening, accompanied by clouds of acrid blue-black smoke that wafted toward the stand and seemed to hang in the air.

A wave of nausea from the smell washed over Sarah, making her suddenly weak and clammy. She sank back into her chair and tried hard not to be sick. A second volley followed immediately, and the ground seemed to sway beneath her. Closing her eyes against the rising gorge in her throat, she wondered if she were going to disgrace herself and Lord Audley in front of everyone.

Devin looked down when she sat, and one glance at her closed eyes and white face told him that she was quite suddenly and very thoroughly ill. Silently cursing, he leaned toward Mrs. Pitt to inquire if that lady would lend him her fan. And the very circumstance that Sarah feared the most occurred: she was instantly surrounded by a sea of faces that swam before her as everyone crowded around solicitously. Devin took the exquisite lace-edged fan and began waving it before her, whilst Mrs. Pitt searched for her vinaigrette. Producing the small gold case, she lifted off the top and held it beneath Sarah's nose.

The combination of smells was devastating. Sarah barely had time to lean forward and cover her mouth before she gagged. Devin alertly whisked off his hat and held it beneath her, all the while trying to support her with his other arm. Wave after wave of nausea assaulted her, bringing up the remnants of a hearty breakfast. She knew she was humiliating him, but she was too ill to care.

As soon as she finished retching, he thrust the ruined ramillie beneath his seat and helped her to stand. "Can you walk, do you think? I've got to get you out of here."

"I don't know . . . Yes."

He slid an arm around her shoulders and walked her toward the end of the stand, and all the while the guns continued to fire their salute to King George. When Mrs. Pitt would have followed them, Devin shook his head.

"She is merely increasing—'twill pass. I shall send a servant to dispose of the hat."

Somehow he got her off the platform and they stood for a moment behind it. She leaned her head against the wooden supports, hoping she was not going to be sick again. When at last the terrible nausea passed, she mumbled miserably, "I am so sorry, my lord."

" 'Twas the smoke. I ought not to have let Adam talk me into bringing you. Here . . ." He drew out his handkerchief and wiped her damp face impatiently, but then she appeared so miserable that he relented. "And you are not the first female to become ill from it, I should expect." Discarding the dirty linen, he again slid his arm beneath hers. "Got to get you to the carriage before the crowd disperses and we are caught amongst the mob."

They passed behind the unwashed spectators, whose bodies added to the stench of the smoke; and Sarah began to gag again. Devin muttered a curse under his breath as he held her over a straw-filled ditch, and when she was done, he picked her up and carried her past the curious. She was too sick to care. Oblivious of the cheers and howls, she turned her head into his shoulder and held on.

The crush of carriages was such that it was amazing he was able to find his own. His driver, who'd been dozing, came awake at the sight of his master carrying the young mistress, and nudged the coachie off the box. The boy sprang to open the carriage door.

Devin thrust her inside, waited for her to crawl across the seat, then climbed in after her. She turned to lean her head against the coolness of the door pane on the opposite side, swallowing visibly. Out of breath from the effort of carrying her all the way from the grandstand to the parked coach, he leaned back against the squabs to rest.

"Well, you are not so slight as I had once thought," he observed dryly. "Nor as healthy."

Her eyes opened, betraying her utter embarrassment. "I'm sorry, my lord—I guess I disgraced us both, didn't I?" Her voice dropped to a mortified whisper. "But I did so wish to see Adam, you know."

She was so pale that her eyes seemed darker, and she

looked so forlorn that Devin, who'd been thinking much the same thing, shook his head. "Do not refine on it—I doubt the others will, after all. You are not the first female to increase," he added shortly.

She fell silent, and he was not inclined to speak either. Instead, he let her stare out the window, watching her as the carriage weaved between other equally magnificent equipages, hoping fervently she did not shoot the cat again. But somehow she didn't, and by the time they were on the street, her ashen color had receded and she looked as though the sickness had passed. When she finally turned back to him, she managed a small rueful smile.

"Do not think I am ungrateful, my lord. Had you not been so prompt, I daresay 'twould have been much worse." When he did not say anything, she sighed. " 'Tis not easy to apologize to you for anything."

"No, I suppose not," he acknowledged, leaning forward.

"I own your kindness surprised me."

That elicited a faint smile in return. "If you mean to be civil to me, Sarah, I shall not know how to go on. Suffice it to say that I could scarce abandon Adam's wife."

"I guess 'tis time to cry peace with you, isn't it?"

"I thought I'd done that with Lucie's filly," he reminded her, "but, aye, 'tis overtime, I'd say."

His smile did not reach his eyes, but that didn't matter. In her way of reconciling balances, they were almost even now, and for Adam's sake, she hoped 'twould stay that way. She nodded.

But even as he looked across at her, he knew that he dared not attempt friendship with her, for deep within, his foolish passion still lingered. And until it was conquered, there could not be enough distance between him and his brother's wife.

17

It had been a long, grueling day, and yet Adam was loath to see it end, for on the morrow he'd be leaving Sarah. There'd been a time when he'd have welcomed the adventure, the chance for advancement, but now he was torn between what he perceived to be his duty and his wish to remain with his wife. And it was taking all his resolve to go.

Despite the fact that his bones ached from hours of sitting ramrod straight in his saddle, and his head pounded from the discomfort of a wig worn beneath the summer sun, he tried to appear cheerful as he trod the stairs to his bedchamber. It was, he reminded himself, his last night with Sarah, and she was obviously as downcast as he was.

During supper, she'd been unusually quiet, so much so that Devin had suggested she retire. To his surprise, she'd gone, and then Dev had told Adam how ill she'd been at the review. Now Adam felt the veriest brute for wanting her so, for thinking of little else this last day. He'd wanted to lie in her arms and forget that it would be months, mayhap years even, ere he saw her again. If ever.

He tried not to think of that possibility, for it served nothing now to dwell on it. He'd done what he could, entrusting his will to Dev, consoling himself that if he perished, he would at least know that she'd never want for anything money could buy her again. He reached the hallway before their door and stopped. It was tenderness, not lust, that she needed of him now. To stall until he was master of himself, he loosened the cravat that had suddenly become far too tight.

Sarah heard him pause in the hall, much as he'd done that first night, and she had to close her eyes for a moment to hide the intense wave of desire that flooded through her. Her brush, held by now nerveless fingers, stopped, its bristles still caught in her hair. She sat quite still as she heard him open the door.

The room was filled with long shadows cast by the brace of candles beside her dressing table. She was still up then, still preparing herself for bed. Her back was to him, her auburn hair rippling down over the white Egyptian cotton of her nightrail. She'd been brushing it, burnishing it, until it seemed to have captured the flickering candlelight, holding it in a warm halo. She was so very lovely.

He stared at her, taking in every detail, engraving it into his memory, storing it for those long months away from her. And the familiar desire returned, washing over him, coursing through him, setting his pulses racing. His body felt unbearably hot, his mouth too dry for speech. And for an intense moment his body warred with his mind.

She knew he stood there, but she was strangely loath to face him just yet, not when she knew he'd be far too tired to want her. She'd not have him think he had to love her. But even as she reasoned with herself, her body rebelled, telling her differently. Just one last time—she'd have him love her this last time.

With an effort, she dragged the bristles the rest of the way through a snarl. The room was utterly still except for the faint crackle of her hair when it followed the brush. Why did he not come closer? She felt as though she were so tense, so taut that she could shatter into pieces, and he merely stood there watching her. Did he not know how badly she needed to be held, to be loved by him—that she needed one more memory to sustain her when he was gone?

He felt it also, and when he could bear it no longer, he spoke, his voice as strained as his body. "I thought you'd be abed."

"My hair was tangled from the pins." Then, admitting the real reason, she added, "And I wanted to wait for you."

He closed the door behind him and crossed the thick carpet, stopping safely a few feet from her. "Dev told me you were sick from the heat today."

She grimaced, remembering again how she'd disgraced herself in front of King George and his ministers. "I very much wish he'd not spoken of that. I shall never, ever face any of them again."

"Nonsense." He moved closer, daring to lay a comforting hand on her shoulder. " 'Twill be soon forgotten."

"Forgotten? *Forgotten!*" She twisted beneath his hand and leaned forward. "*I* shall never forget it, I assure you. Adam, had it not been for Audley, I should have ruined the day for everyone! As 'tis, we had to leave under what can only be described as the most mortifying circumstances, and he missed a great deal, I fear."

"I don't think I had quite the whole story—he merely said you were ill and he brought you home."

"It does not bear repeating."

She closed her eyes again, that he would not see what even his merest touch did to her. Despite the fabric of her nightgown between them, her skin was afire beneath his fingers. She raised the brush again.

"You are tired—I'll do it for you." Before she could demur, he'd taken the silver-backed brush from her and begun long, deliberate strokes through her hair, lifting it and letting it fall like strands of silk against her back. "I don't find any tangles." But he did not stop the rhythmic brushing. "You have such lovely hair, Sarah—I'd remember it like this, you know."

"Thank you."

"Sarah—"

"Please . . . I'd not speak of your leaving," she choked out. "Not tonight. And I'd not have you work my hair either. I . . . I shall have months to do that when you are gone from me."

He laid aside the brush and bent to nuzzle the shining crown of her head. "Come to bed and let me hold you until you sleep,'' he murmured softly. "You are fagged beyond bearing, aren't you?"

"No," she answered baldly. Ducking away from him, she twisted to look up at him. "I want more than that."

Her voice had turned seductively husky, and her amber eyes reflected the flames. The desire he'd thought to conquer flared anew, flooding his body with renewed heat. As he watched hungrily, she rose to face him, moving closer, until they almost touched. And the answering passion in her eyes sent his senses reeling.

"Please, Adam—give me this night to remember forever."

His arms closed convulsively around her, crushing her against him. "I'll try, Sarah—believe me, I'll try."

She twined her arms around his neck, pulling his head down to hers, and her lips parted eagerly beneath his. All thoughts of tenderness were consumed in the urgency of mutual desire. Words were superfluous—touch was everything. She pressed and twisted against him, molding her body to his, heedless of the buttons and stiff gold lace that cut into her flesh through the thin cotton nightrail. Her hands moved incessantly over his dress coat, clutching and stroking his shoulders and back through the scarlet cloth.

He slid his hands over her hips to cup her against him, rubbing her body with his. She moaned low and leaned her head back in his arms, giving him access to the sensitive hollows of her throat and neck. But when he began easing the rail up between them, she pulled away, leaving him thoroughly aroused and panting. Her eyes were dark, her voice almost hoarse with passion.

"No—I'd see you first this time."

Nodding, he removed his coat, dropping it to the floor beside him, and reached to his vest. But as he struggled with the long row of buttons, his hands made clumsy by eagerness, she reached out to help, her fingers working feverishly to free him. The vest joined the coat in a tangle of scarlet, blue, tan, and gold at their feet. Leaning her head against his shoulder, she turned her attention lower, fumbling for the buttons at his waist. His flat abdomen quivered, then tautened beneath her touch, and his breath caught and held.

"The boots," he gasped, groaning as her fingertips moved lightly over his body. He felt brittle, ready to break. Every fiber of his being was tensely alive to her—agonizingly taut and yet wanting to prolong the exquisite torture as long as possible. His breeches slid down to hang over the tops of his boots.

Her mouth found his again for a deep, breathless kiss, and this time when he lifted her nightrail over her hips, she made no protest. Her skin was as hot as his, feverishly dry except where his fingers probed, and there she was enticingly wet and ready.

"Love me now, Adam—love me now," she urged huskily. Her voice trailed off into a guttural moan as he stroked between her legs.

His mouth trailed hot, wet kisses over her throat, her neck, and her ears, and his breath rushed like a torrent of wind against her ear, sending shivers through her as she clung to him, aware only of what he was doing to her.

She twisted and writhed against his hand, moving incessantly, her eyes closed, her face damp and intense until he brought her the pleasure she sought. Then her head went back, and her quick, breathless moans turned into that primordial cry of release. She shuddered against him, and then she was quiet. He held her close for a moment, trying to control his own body. She buried her head in his shoulder, not daring now to meet his eyes.

"Adam . . ." she said finally, her voice muffled in his shirt, " 'tis not to be like that, is it? I mean . . ."

"Aye."

"But you—"

"Oh, I quite intend to, love." He set her back enough to look at her, and his blue eyes still burned with his own desire. "But first there is the matter of my boots. I'd have you finish what you have begun, Sarah."

She stepped back, embarrassed now by her former boldness, and watched him sink into the nearest chair, where he stretched out his legs. His masculinity still stood at attention above his bared thighs, and as she stared, she felt the renewal of passion and wondered how, sated as she was, she could want more. Hastily she dropped to her knees to pull at his boots, removing them with effort, then discarding them. He rose, towering above her, and pulled off his shirt, dropping it. Her eyes traveled the length of him, and her heart pounded so hard she felt she could not breathe. As though she were in a trance, she slowly unbuttoned her nightrail and took it off.

Wordlessly he bent to lift her, cradling her in his arms, and carried her to the canopied bed, where he followed her down. Together they sank within the feather mattress. His mouth lingered but briefly on her lips, then moved to her breasts, tasting first one, then the other, before drawing deeply of her nipple. And she felt the familiar ache deep inside. Her fingers caressed his thick hair as she arched her back for more. This time, when his hand slid lower to touch the wetness, she rolled against him, whispering, ''There is no need. I'd have you now.''

He kissed her deeply, exploring her mouth hotly with his tongue, and pulled her over him, entering her body as she straddled him. She gasped in surprise, then began to move, tentatively at first, controlling her own pleasure, looking down at his face, seeing what he saw every time he loved her. His hands stroked her back, pulling her down to give him access to her breasts. And as his tongue teased and sucked, she rocked and slid against him, harder and faster, as he rocked and moved beneath her. It was good, better than anything that had gone before, and she didn't want it to end, not yet.

Her brow furrowed with the intensity of her effort, and her face was contorted as though she were somewhere between agony and ecstasy. She was panting hard, and still she moved, urging both their bodies toward that final, complete release. Perspiration dampened her forehead above her closed eyes. He watched her, his own enjoyment enhanced by hers, until he could wait no longer and he was plunged into the mindless maelstrom, bucking wildly beneath her. He exploded in wave after wave of his own ecstasy, scarcely aware that she cried out over and over again above him. And then it was as though the seas calmed, leaving an indescribable serenity after the storm.

When he came back to the world of mortals, she was lying quietly over him, her head resting on his shoulder. His arm held her close, and his hand still stroked her back, this time with a gentleness far different from what they'd just experienced.

"I love you, Sarah," he said simply.

"I know." She raised up slightly and smiled down at him. " 'Tis quite a memory you have given me."

" 'Tis mine also." His fingers combed lightly through her hair, discovering the snarls. "I think you brushed for naught, love."

"I don't care. I just want to lie here with you whilst I can."

They were both silent at that, neither wishing to speak of the long separation they faced. So, legs and arms entwined, they merely savored the warmth and closeness of each other. Outside, the watchman called out the hour of midnight, prompting Adam to finally ease away.

"You'd best brush and braid your hair, else you'll never get it untangled in the morning. Besides, you need your sleep."

Reluctantly she rose to clean herself, then sat once again before the dressing table to struggle with the thick mass of hair. The candles were gutted now, the room dark save for the moonlight from the window. And as the clock ticked, Sarah felt the precious time slipping away. She hurriedly made a loose single plait down the back of her hair, and returned to bed. She didn't want to sleep—she could do that when he was gone—but he had a long journey ahead of him, and she had not the right to keep him awake also. She eased closer, snuggling against his back.

He turned over, pulling her into the crook of his arm and pillowing her head with his shoulder. His other hand stroked lightly over her nightrail, touching her breasts, her ribs, and tracing along her still-flat abdomen.

"What are we going to name her?" he asked suddenly.

"Her? I have hopes 'tis a son."

"Well, I should be pleased with either, you know, but I rather fancy the notion of a daughter much like you."

"I suppose we ought to have one of each—names, I mean," she decided. "What did you think—Adam if 'tis a son and perhaps Mary if 'tis a girl?"

"Mary?"

" 'Twas my mother's name," she reminded him.

"Well, neither is my favorite," he admitted slowly, "and I'd certainly not wish for another Adam, but if your heart is set on Mary, then Mary 'tis."

"Oh, no! That is, I'd wish for something pleasing to you also. But if 'tis not to be Adam, what do you want?"

"I rather favor Devin."

Devin. She might have known that, she supposed. Well, there was no saying that one Devin must be much like another, was there? She sighed, unwilling to defy him in so small a matter. "Then of course he shall be Devin." A new thought struck her, making her add, "Devin what? I refuse to add John for my father, you know—do you perhaps think Devin Charles?"

"No!" he answered with unwarranted harshness. "Choose any other name you would wish—Spender even—but I'd not call a son of mine for my father."

Devin Spender Hastings. "Anything else you'd add to it—beyond Devin Spender, I mean?"

"Winfield and Alexander are from my mother's family, if you care for either of those."

Devin Alexander Spender Hastings. Devin Winfield Spender Hastings. Devin Spender Winfield Hastings. She tried all of them in her mind, then aloud, deciding, "I rather prefer Devin Alexander Spender Hastings, I think."

"And poor Mary—do you give her anything else?"

"Mary Emma . . . or Emma Mary . . . or perhaps Mary Margaret—I don't know."

"Mary Margaret sounds like a nun, my love," he chided.

"Well, I daresay I have enough time to think of something else. I shall write to you ere I choose, anyway."

"There'd not be the time, Sarah. 'Tis a month over

and a month back in good weather—she'd have teeth ere she was christened. No, 'twill be your choice, my dear.''

A month over and a month back in good weather. It was another reminder of how far away he'd be from her. She felt like crying, but there was no sense in ruining the hours that remained. Instead, she changed the subject abruptly, asking that ancient question between lovers.

''Adam . . .''

''What?''

''I know you wedded me out of pity, but when did you come to love me?''

''I never wedded you out of pity, Sarah.''

''Friendship, then.''

''I don't know—mayhap I've always loved you—'tis difficult to say. I only know that when Roland wrote to me that you'd been left without a farthing, I came home. And when you said you were going to York, I couldn't let you do it.''

It had been but two months and a fortnight since then, but it seemed such an age ago—almost as though it had been in another lifetime. And she could not remember when she did not love him. She turned slightly in his arms and looked up at him.

''I have always loved you, Adam.''

He stroked her arm lightly. ''You knew nothing else. You had not the chance to discover anyone else, you know. Now, if you'd been to London and met all the beaux there, you'd have discovered what an ordinary fellow I am, Mrs. Hastings—and once they'd seen you, I'd have been Jack Fortune to have ever gotten close enough to speak with you.''

''Spanish words, sir—but I like them excessively anyway,'' she admitted.

'' 'Tis the truth,'' he protested.

On the street below, the watch bellowed out one o'clock, and Sarah forced herself to ease away from him. ''You must sleep, Adam, else you'll be weary long ere you reach your ship.''

''No.'' He rolled over to prop himself up on an elbow and look down at her. ''I cannot sleep, love—no more than you can.'' The faint moonlight from the window reflected in his eyes as he smiled crookedly. "Unless you choose to object, I would very much rather make memories."

18

Devin Hastings shifted his tired body against the velvet squabs of his traveling carriage and picked up his newspaper once gain. The misting rain outside gave a grayness that made for difficult reading, but there was naught else to do, after all. Across from him, Sarah sat silently staring out the window, her spirits as dismal as the day. And so it had been much of the journey.

Not that his mood was much better, he reflected soberly, for he'd seen his only brother off to a distant war but yesterday. And despite an unwillingness to speak of it, he too could not help thinking it might have been the last time he'd ever see the boy who'd followed him so fondly for nearly as long as he could remember. Aye, Adam would have his twenty-fifth birthday somewhere at sea, far away from them, and Devin devoutly hoped it would not be his last. But Fate was such a fickle creature, picking and choosing who should live and who should perish, without apparent reason.

Resolutely he opened the paper, but full half the news was of the war, turning his thoughts yet again where they were loath to go. What if Adam did not return? What happened then? As executor of his estate, Devin would be the same as guardian to Sarah. He looked at her again, seeing her stony profile, her amber eyes fixed on some distant thing, her auburn hair almost hidden beneath the feather-trimmed black hat. She looked so very different now from the girl he'd admired at Spender's Hill, for gone were the faded gown and the wildly tangling hair. His eyes strayed lower taking in the new fullness of her breasts, so demurely covered by her pleated stomacher. If anything, she was even lovelier now than then.

Momentary jealousy washed over him as he remembered how Adam had stolen her from beneath his nose, offering her what he himself had not been prepared to give. 'Pon reflection, he ought to have done it differently, and would have if he could relive that awful day. He'd misjudged her—he admitted it—with the result that she was his brother's wife instead of his.

But how could he have known that she would have shown to such advantage? Aye, even Pitt had complimented Adam's taste, saying that she would be an asset to her husband's career. And before she'd heard of Sarah's condition, Mrs. Pitt had wondered aloud if he meant to make his sister-in-law his hostess whilst Adam was gone. Well, he did not—he was not made of such stern stuff that he could sit back and watch her daily and not want her. 'Twould be the path to his destruction, and he knew it.

And that was all there was to the matter, he reminded himself dryly. A man did not dream of what he could not have with any good result. And even if she came into his power—if, God forbid, that Adam should die—his foolish infatuation was and would remain impossible. It was still against the law to wed one's brother's wife. That he thought of it at all ought to damn him.

"Do you think they will set sail in this?"

Her voice, low that it was, gave him a guilty start. Recovering, he nodded. " 'Tis scarce a storm at all."

"He says 'twill take a month to cross it."

He straightened in his seat, not daring to look at her lest she read his thoughts. "The sea? 'Twill depend on the wind and weather. I have heard of it being done in as little as three and as many as seven weeks."

"And if anything should happen to him, we should not know of it for a full month and more." She sighed unhappily and looked again to the window. "Aye, there's the horror of this, you know—he could die, and we'd not know it.''

"Sarah, such thoughts are bad for the child,'' he chided. "You must not dwell on such things.''

"And how am I supposed to avoid my fears?'' she cried, lashing out with sudden fury. "I shall be immured in the Park with naught else to do but think!''

"Sarah—''

"No! For his sake, I did not tear at him, but I cannot help worrying, my lord!'' She reached across to snatch his paper from his hands, waving it in front of him. "Every day there are accounts of French or Indian atrocities—read them—no doubt there is yet another tale of the fall of Oswego in this! Or some tale of farmers axed in their beds!'' She let the paper fall and covered her face with her hands. "I know not how I shall bear it—I know not how,'' she finished helplessly.

It was as though all the fears she'd kept from Adam burst out. Her shoulders shook as she turned her head into the squabs. For a time, he said nothing, letting her cry. There was so little to say anyway—she'd but given voice to his own fears. He stretched his hand out, thinking to comfort her, then dropped it lamely, knowing he dared not touch her.

"Sarah, you must not—''

"I cannot help it! Ever since he left London, I am haunted! I . . . I cannot think I shall ever see him again!''

"He is a soldier.''

"But he does not have to be!''

"Sarah, tears serve nothing now—I cannot bring him back to your side, you know. You must think he is safe enough with Loudoun.''

She sniffed and nodded at that, straightening up shakily. And despite her watery eyes, she managed a twisted smile. "Aye, 'tis foolish of me, isn't it? I mean, if the general can take his linen tablecloths and his mistress, he must not expect to be fighting Indians.''

"I shouldn't think so.''

"They have colonials for that sort of thing, don't they?''

"Aye. Every colony sends troops against the French,

and now there are the rangers. Ten to one, Adam will but guard New York.''

Chastened, she turned her attention to the countryside, watching as they turned onto a familiar road. In a matter of a few minutes they'd be at Milbrook Park, and there she'd stay to await the birth of Adam's child soon after Christmas. She sighed heavily, then told herself that Audley was right, of course: she had to consider her babe and devote her love and attention to it. She could not spend all of Adam's absence feeling sorry for herself.

When she looked up again, Devin was watching her over his paper, an enigmatic expression on his face. As he met her eyes, he smiled wryly and shook his head. ''I was wondering, you know, what I must do to persuade you to call me Audley. I have quite despaired of hearing 'Devin' cross your lips, Sarah.''

''Well, I expect you shall hear it often once the babe arrives,'' she answered. ''Adam is determined that his son shall be another Devin.''

''And you?''

''I'll not gainsay him.''

''I am honored.''

For a moment she wondered if he mocked her, then chose to accept what he said. ''But he refuses 'Charles.' ''

'' 'Tis a pity—'twould help heal the breach between them.''

Privately she thought it was up to the earl to reach out to his son, but she held her tongue. As she was now alone amongst her husband's family, she had no wish to roil the waters. ''That,'' she said simply, ''I leave to Adam.''

''You could be the bridge between them, if you wished.'' Then, looking out, he noted, ''But 'tis your affair, after all, and by the looks of it, we are arrived at home.''

The great country house loomed ahead, huge and gray in the mists. Home? Never. Her home was with Adam.

Sarah's second welcome at the Park was far different from the first. Adam's father hobbled out into the hall to greet them, rounding on Devin that he ought to have taken the journey in easier stages for Sarah. She was a trifle peaked, he said, and had lost weight in less than a fortnight. Devin cut him short, reminding him that she was more than a little blue-deviled.

As for the countess, she embraced Sarah warmly, kissing her on the cheek. Charles had missed her, becoming even more testy than usual for want of a card partner, she murmured. And now that Meg was not to be home before fall, she herself was delighted to have at least one daughter beneath her roof.

"Meg remains in Bath?" Audley asked, betraying his surprise. "I'd thought she was to be back this week."

"M' sister Trowbridge does the impossible," the earl admitted almost gleefully. "Got Chatwick's boy a-dangling after her!"

"Harry? Sir, he's a Tory!"

"Don't care if he's an atheist!" the old man retorted, eyeing his heir unfavorably. "Dash it—his fortune's respectable enough, ain't it? Besides, it don't harm anything to have both sides covered, as I see the matter. And don't you go postin' off there, thinkin' to put a spoke in the wheel, you hear?"

"Of course not."

"Good. Liza says she ain't tongue-tied round him, though what they got to say, I am sure I don't know. Damme if I ain't going to behave handsomely to the gel, after all. Chatwick! Ain't an earl's son, of course, but that don't signify—at least she ain't going to lead apes in hell." Then, realizing that Sarah knew nothing of the young man, he leaned across his cane to confide, "Heir to Viscount Chatwick—Devonshire title, but I ain't a-holding it against him"

"You must be very pleased."

"Of course I am pleased! Gel's nigh a spinster! And he ain't a half-pay officer like I'd expected, after all."

"Charles, Sarah should be resting rather than standing in the hall," Lady Emma reminded him.

"Eh? Aye, 'tis the right of that, I'll be bound. Well, well, don't be standing when you should be sitting, gel! Stubbs! Fetch Mrs. Cross t' take the young mistress up! Aye, and tell the demned cook to send her a tray—you hear?'' To Sarah he admonished, ''Rest yourself—ain't no need to come down to dinner if you don't feel quite the thing. And if Cook ain't got what you was to fancy, we'll send for it.''

''Really, I—''

''Poor Sarah,'' Devin murmured sympathetically. ''Papa means to cosset you—if he has to bullock you to do it.''

''Aye, but I have not the least intention of lying abed to suit anyone's notion of how I ought to feel. I shall, of course, be down to dine.'' Then, realizing how ungracious she must sound, she added to the earl, ''And you, sir, have you no wish for a rubber or two of whist after supper?''

His bushy brows drew together; then he threw back his head and roared. ''Damme if Adam ain't got himself an Amazon, Dev! First female I ever heard of what don't want to be an invalid! Here, now—anytime as you are feeling Dame Fortune smiling, gel, you come play the pasteboards with me.''

''You will make her wish herself back in London,'' Lady Emma warned. ''Indeed, but if the Park becomes tiresome, I daresay we may travel there to shop, anyway. I am sure Devin will not mind it.''

''Dash it, Em! The gel's increasing! Got no business traveling!''

Stung, his countess argued, ''But we are scarce sufficient to entertain a young girl, Charles. And there is nothing to say that she could not be amused with small private dinners at Hastings House, after all.''

''Emma—''

''Well, six months is quite a long time to be cooped up in the country with naught but a gossip and a grumbler for company,'' Emma persisted. ''Besides, the gossip's thin these days.''

''Humph! And I s'pose I am the grumbler? I ain't having it, Em! I told the boy me and Dev'd see to her, and I ain't going to London! You want gossip—pay morning calls in the neighborhood, you hear! Aye, take yourself over to the parson's and get an earful of prattle, if you've the stomach for that.'' He raised his cane to poke at his wife. "Do not be thinking I ain't knowing your game, Em, 'cause I do. It ain't her as wants to go—damme if she didn't just get back, anyways—'tis you!"

Devin, who'd witnessed far too many such scenes before, cast a significant look at the housekeeper. Mrs. Cross responded with alacrity, turning to Sarah. "Daresay you are overtired from the trip, Mistress Hastings. "If you will not consider a nap, perhaps a warm bath, followed by some tea and cakes—'tis the very thing to revive you."

She was tired—Sarah admitted it. The night before Adam had left, she'd not slept at all, and last night she'd tossed and turned alone. She followed the housekeeper up the stairs, thinking that perhaps a bath and a nap would be welcome, after all.

But even after a soothing soak, sleep did not come easily. Lying between the cool sheets, she still struggled to accept the separation. It was not fair, she cried bitterly into her pillow. Why was it the female who was always left behind? Why had she conceived so soon? Another month or so and she'd have gone with him, instead of being left to rot at Milbrook Park. But finally reason reasserted itself. Devin was right: Adam had had to go. He'd not wanted to leave her, and she knew it. And she *was* in no worse case than thousands of other wives, who sent their men off to war as reluctantly as she did. And she was not entirely alone—she did have his babe growing within her. After Christmas, it would be born, flesh and blood for her to love.

Resolutely she turned her mind to better things than self-pity, remembering anew how Adam had come to Spender's Hill, how he'd asked her to wed with him, and how it had been to be his wife. She had so many memories to cherish. She lay there letting her body grow hot as she recalled that last night spent with him. Aye, she had the memories. And, God willing, she'd have her husband back when this accursed war ended. With that comforting thought, she finally slept.

When she awoke, it was almost dusk outside, and the smells of supper wafted upward from the kitchen at the back of the house. Her stomach growling, she hastily rose and dressed without calling for a maid. Dragging a comb through her hair, she twisted it and pinned the thick curls to the top of her head.

They all seemed surprised to see her when she presented herself at the table. But the earl merely inquired if she felt more the thing, adding she did not look half so hagged as when she'd arrived. A footman promptly produced another place beside Lord Audley for her.

There was no mention of Adam, Devin having warned them that she was quite cast down. Indeed, all of them were subdued through most of the meal. Finally the earl gestured in her direction with his fork.

"Emma would have it that you'd like some new dresses, gel. If 'tis so, I ain't against payin' to have the Craven woman measure you for one or two—nothing extravagant, you understand, but a little finery might be just the thing for a female's spirit."

"I have all I need, sir, and nowhere to wear what I have. But I thank you for the kindness," Sarah added politely.

"Ain't goin' to stay thin, you know—got to think of the babe," he reminded her. "Aye, don't be one of them females as corsets herself until she cannot breathe, you hear? Ain't nobody but me and Em here much of the time, and I don't care if you swell up like a toad."

"Really, Charles, but—"

"Time enough to trick yourself out in a cage afterward, I say," he continued, ignoring his wife. "Make yourself comfortable—get that as feels good—and I'll sport the blunt for it. Always thought Em lost the last two 'cause they was crushed and couldn't grow."

"Charles!"

"Well, you would not listen to me," he retorted. "You was always a-pullin' the strings tight so's you was swoonin'—and don't be thinking I don't remember it. Dash it, Em, a female's got to fatten, and it don't matter if she does. A man don't think an increasing female's ugly."

"Some things, Charles, are not suited to discussion over dinner," his affronted countess declared.

"Ain't nobody but family here." He speared a piece

of roasted mutton and carried it to his mouth. As he chewed, he turned back to Sarah. "Don't mean to offend your sensibilities, you know."

"I assure you you have not. And I shall not wear my stays when they are uncomfortable, sir."

"Good gel. Got the babe to think of, you know. Time'll be over afore we know it. Best find out what Adam wants to name him, though—'Charles' would not be amiss, I'd think."

"Really, Charles, but 'tis their affair, don't you think?" Lady Emma protested.

"Why? First Hastings in a long time, ain't it? What's wrong with 'Charles'?"

"Actually, we'd thought to name him Devin," Sarah admitted. "And besides, he could well be *she,* you know."

"Well, you must not think to call her Emma," the countess cut in quickly. "I never liked the name, and I cannot think she would either."

"I suppose 'Dev' ain't half-bad—thought of it myself when Audley was named." Unable to completely hide his disappointment, he considered the possibility of a girl. "And what about that—you got a name for a female?"

"Mary."

"Mary! 'Tis a Popish name!" he roared.

"It was my mother's."

"Let us hope 'tis a boy," the old man muttered. "We are God-fearing Church of England in this house."

"As was my mother."

"Yes, yes, well, dash it, there ain't no Marys in the family!" Just as he was about to say more on that head, he caught the mulish set of her chin. "Daresay there could always be a first one, though," he conceded, unwilling to overset her. "If she has your spirit, a gel ain't unwelcome."

"Thank you, sir."

His faded blue eyes brightened briefly. "Yes, well, if you ain't feeling sickly, I don't suppose as you'd humor an old man with a rubber of whist, would you?"

"Charles, she is but returned from London. 'Tis early days yet, and she needs her rest."

"Aye, I suppose. But, dash it, Em, the gel's got a tongue—if she don't want to play, she can say so."

Devin, who'd been strangely aloof throughout the meal, spoke up finally. "If she is half so tired as I am, I doubt she wishes to play. Indeed, but as soon as dessert is done, I mean to seek my bed."

"Aye. Don't know why you are going back on the morrow, anyways. War or no war, seems as though you could be spared just now."

"Pitt has asked me to speak in Lords on behalf of his bill, and I am unprepared."

"Eh? Damme if I don't wish I was there to hear you." Then, recalling the matter of whist, the earl reluctantly conceded that Sarah needed her rest. Sighing, he looked to his wife. "What say you, Em?"

"Me?"

"The devil, Emma! Do not be coming the coquette with me! Of course I meant you—said so! You ain't Sarah, but you are a fair gamester yourself—what say you to a rubber or two? Play you for that new gown you was wanting, if 'twill get you to agree."

Lady Emma looked at him as though he'd taken leave of his senses. "I was thinking of going up with Sarah, but . . ." She hesitated uncertainly.

"She ain't an invalid. And she can find her way up, you know. It ain't like she was a guest, is it? Gel's at home!"

"But 'tis late, and your gout—"

"Gout be damned! 'Tis company I am wanting! Besides, daresay gambling's as addictive as the opium, Em, and I'd as soon lose my blunt to you as to anyone. And, " he added with an uncharacteristic twinkle to his blue eyes, "who's to say I'll have to pay? You ain't a Captain Sharp like she is, you know."

"Do not listen to him, ma'am," Sarah encouraged her. "If you will but realize that the more he scowls, the better his hand, you will win."

"If that don't beat everything! You hear that, Dev? The gel wants to help my wife fleece me!"

Later, while the earl and the countess repaired to the front saloon for cards, Sarah found herself walking up the steps with her brother-in-law. They were both silent until she reached her door; then he stopped also.

"I shall not be coming home nearly so often now," he said finally. "I expect my duties to detain me in London more."

"You are an important man, so I daresay your father will understand."

"And you?"

It was an odd question. "Well, I shall wish you Godspeed," she answered. "Really, I shall be as content here as anywhere."

"Aye."

He walked the rest of the way down the hall to his chamber, leaving her standing there. As she went into her room, she could hear his door slam hard behind him and wondered briefly what ailed him.

19

It rained nearly every day for three weeks after Sarah returned to the Park, but for the most part she managed to maintain a pleasant mien. Despite the fact that she still tossed and turned at night, wishing desperately for Adam's love and comfort, she told herself that she could not let herself succumb completely to the blue devils. As the earl kept reminding her, it was not good for her babe.

Being summer, the days were long as well as gray, and with the weather enforcing a captivity of sorts, Sarah spent much of her time with Adam's parents. The countess, attempting to take her mind off his absence, had her stitching and embroidering small baby gowns, something for which she lacked much in the way of skill. Miss Wallace, never having had a home or husband to call her own, had been more inclined to Latin verbs and mathematics than sewing. And, as often as Sarah had to pull out her mistakes, she was heartily glad she hadn't learned the skill. Plying a needle was an abominable bore.

And the countess's habit of lying down for hours at a time made Sarah restive. At first she'd tried sitting with her, reading from books purloined from the earl's library, but she soon discovered that her mother-in-law's taste in literature ran to heavy-handed moralism. She started reading aloud from Richardson's *Clarissa Harlowe*, but quickly abandoned it when Lady Emma, who'd proclaimed her great affection for the seven-volume tome, began to snore. For Sarah, the struggles of a female to withstand an unprincipled male's blandishments were almost as boring as needlework. No, give her the adventure of the Greek classics or of Shakespeare's dramas any day.

And so it was that she began to turn to the earl for respite. With him she whiled away hours each day at whist or reading things that suited her. He never raised a disapproving eyebrow to discover her poring over anything, whether it be Ovid's poetry or Caesar's commentary. She discovered that if she made a few allowances for his temper, she could almost like him. And he in turn relished her company, speaking quite improperly to her of anything that crossed his mind. If Charles Hastings held an opinion, and he did on nearly everything, he was not the least bit reticent to share it. But she didn't care—she much preferred his temper to Lady Emma's invalidism.

Not that she herself felt all that well, but she simply would not give herself over to the malaise that went with her pregnancy. If she lost her breakfast, which she did quite often, she waited a few minutes, then ate another, something that Lady Emma could not understand. But she was not unwell, she told herself fiercely—she was merely increasing.

But on this particular day, she was having greater difficulty convincing herself. She'd awakened with a gnawing ache in her back that would not go away, and nothing seemed to ease it. Had it been pleasant outside, she would have attempted to walk it off, telling herself that it was merely a cramp from sleeping wrong. For the first time since she'd come back to the Park, she actually considered going back to bed.

"Play you for some of that lace Emma's a-wantin'," the old man offered just as she was about to go upstairs.

This time, she was more vexed than happy to see him. Could he not know that 'twas only the countess who wished for more finery than she could wear? she asked herself, turning back to him. But there he was, leaning heavily on that cane of his, waiting expectantly. She was about to snap peevishly that she was heartily sick of cards, but something in his face stopped her.

"Oh, I know it ain't going to chase the dismals, but then perchance it might make 'em a bit easier, do you think?" He limped awkwardly to the door of the front saloon, telling her, "I ain't met a gel yet as didn't feel better for something pretty."

She hesitated, knowing that whatever ailed her was not likely to be improved by bed. Sighing, she came back down. "I should rather play for points, sir. There's none to see me, and one black silk is very much like another, regardless of how 'tis trimmed."

"Points, is it?" He shook his head. " 'Tis too tame by half, gel. Tell you what—you best me and the money goes to the babe. We'll begin with ten pounds for Devin Charles—or whatever 'tis you mean to name him."

So that was the lay of it—he meant to bribe her to name the child after him. "You, sir, are of a devious mind," she accused him, but his effort nonetheless brought a grudging smile. "You know very well that Adam—"

"No, no. Call him what you want—and if it ain't 'Charles,' I'll come about. Just cannot give the money to Adam for him, don't you see? For one thing, he'd not take it from me." His breath short, he managed to get into his chair, where he leaned back to rest. "Ain't right for God to keep a mind going when the legs is gone," he gasped. "Got to have the demned laudanum."

She looked down to his cross-bandaged knees, and

even with the wrapping, she could tell they were swollen,
one horribly so. The buttons at the bottom of his knee
breeches were undone above his silk stockings. Briefly
she considered trying hot towels to ease his legs, but
knew he'd not stand for it. Yet she could not in conscience dose him with much more of the opium.

"How much have you had?"

"Too much, but it ain't helped."

"Willie!" she called out to one of the lower footmen.

"Dash it! I don't want him—and I ain't going t' bed!"

"Of course you are not." She moved the footstool over
and lifted his leg to rest his foot on it. Kneeling, she
began unwrapping the bandage on his worse knee.

"Here, now—it ain't seemly," he protested.

"And when have you ever cared about that?" she
countered. When Willie appeared in the doorway, she looked
up. "If Cook has the bake oven going, tell her I'd have
some hot towels."

Cold sweat appeared on the earl's forehead, and his
hands were clammy where they gripped the arms of his
chair. "No—'tis not a pretty sight," he told her through
clenched teeth.

He was right. In addition to the swelling, there were
suppurating ulcers where the leg had either been bound
too tightly or been burned by liniment. She almost
gagged.

"Don't—"

"You are fortunate you have not lost it," she muttered,
trying hard not to retch. "Has the physician seen this?"

"What's he to do? He'll want to cut it, and I ain't going
t' let him."

As soon as Willie returned with the hot towels, she
sent him off again for a basin of water and some talc.
"At least we can clean it, my lord, and mayhap ease
you."

"The laudanum—dash it, got to have it."

"All right."

It was not difficult to find a bottle of the opium, for
there was one in almost every room. She poured a small
amount in a wineglass and added a little of the wine. He
gulped it, grimaced, then leaned back.

Willie held the basin while she washed the sores and sprinkled talc over them. Discarding the bandages, she shook her head. "Our old groom was always used to say he'd not bind the horses after he fomented them—that the Almighty heals best with nothing. But I think that perhaps the warmth will ease your knee just now. Later, we can leave it uncovered."

Twice she sent Willie for more hot towels, and together they wrapped the worse knee. The old man laid his head back and closed his eyes until the last of the towels cooled. Then he looked up at her.

"You owe me a game for this."

"I think you ought to send for the physician."

"So he can cut off m' leg? Nay—play or pay, I say."

A sharp pain shot through her back, then spread across her abdomen. With an effort, she straightened up and took the chair across from him.

The laudanum was taking effect, mellowing him. "Feels better, anyways." He picked up the pasteboards and began to shuffle them. "My son's going to come back to me—got to—stands to reason he'll come back for you. And don't think I ain't grateful for that."

The pain subsided into the nagging ache that had plagued her all morning. She played poorly, losing the rubber, wishing she'd taken the laudanum herself.

"Dash it, but how's a man to provide for his grandson if you are to lose? Put your mind to the game, gel!"

"Your pardon, sir."

He eyed her knowingly. "Heart's not in it, eh? Aye, I remember how 'twas after Dev was born . . ." His voice trailed off for a moment; then he shook his head. "Aye, 'tis hard when you are left—no matter what the reason." When she didn't say anything, he went on, "You got to tell yourself he's coming back—be home before you think. At least you got yourself a vigorous husband. Em—" His mouth snapped shut abruptly, cutting off the thought. "Well, it don't signify now, I guess."

"She is content enough, I think," she said quietly.

"No, she ain't. If she was, she'd not be dosing herself half the time, running from one demned doctor to another, wantin' one of 'em to discover something fatal, don't you know?'' He leaned forward, putting his elbows on the table between them. ''You want to hear what an old man thinks? You listen to me, gel, and I can tell you a thing or another.'' He waggled a crooked finger at her. ''When he does come home, don't you be a-takin' yourself off to your chamber alone. Even when you are angered, you make him go with you—you hear? And don't be a-burnin' feathers and hiding from him neither.''

Something had set him off, the laudanum perhaps, and she thought he was rambling from the effects of it. But his blue eyes were almost bright as they stared at her. ''If things is not as they ought to be, and you want to know how to hold him, you come to me—I'll tell you the truth of it. Don't go lettin' Emma fill your head about making him pity you. Pity,'' he pronounced heavily, ''is a poor substitute for affection.''

''Sir—''

''Nay, you hear me, Sarah. There ain't nothing as drives a man away like thinkin' his wife don't want him in her bed.''

The pain crossed her back again. She tried to fight it by holding her breath, but he did not seem to note anything was amiss. And then it subsided.

''You think I am crossing the bounds of decency, don't you? But you ain't got anyone as'll tell you the right of things, gel. I'll tell you one thing every female ought to know, and I doubt a one of 'em does—there ain't a man born as wants to be made to feel like a beast for his appetites.'' His piece said, he sat back and eyed her. ''But I suppose I don't need to tell you—I mean, Adam don't seem to disgust you.''

''No.''

''Good. Should have known that, I guess. Well, stands to reason, the way the bread got into the oven right quick.'' He watched her flush uncomfortably. ''Guess I ought not be so coarse about it, eh? But damme if I got any patience with pretty manners that keep a man from saying what he means.''

''No one shall ever accuse Westerfield of that, sir.''

''The monarch sets the tone, mistress,'' he retorted, ''and don't you be forgettin' that. If German George can talk like a lout and rut like a blind boar, then manners is a waste.''

"Audley seems to think the Prince of Wales a paragon, sir,'' she reminded him.

"But he ain't king yet. Daresay I'll have to learn to mend my tongue when he is crowned.''

This time, the pain that hit her took her breath away. She clutched at the table, exhaling sharply, but it did not ease. "I . . . I think you'd best send for the physician, sir.''

"Ain't—'' It was then that he saw the color had drained from her face. "Sarah—''

"I am going to be ill.'' Unable to stand the searing pain that tore across her abdomen, she tried to rise, then sat back. "Get Willie—please.''

"Loosen your stays! Willie! Willie!'' he bawled. "Damme, where is everybody? Send for the demned doctor! Aye, and fetch her ladyship!'' Somehow he managed to get his foot down and stand up. One of his hands clasped her shoulder and the other the back of her chair. "You are all right, gel—Emma will see you are out of those stays and into bed. Just cannot breathe, that's all.'' But even as he said it, he knew it was not so.

And she knew it too. Tears collected in her eyes, spilling over. She reached up to hold his hand as yet another pain convulsed her. "After he looks to me, my lord, I pray you will show him your leg,'' she whispered.

Two footmen ran in, one still with the plate-polishing cloth in his hand, and stopped to stare at the young mistress and the old man. Lady Emma, *en déshabillé* in her wrapper, pushed past them.

"Sarah . . . whatever . . . ?''

"Dash it, Em, what does it look like?'' her husband snapped. "Get the demned doctor! Aye, and send for Audley!''

Feeling an utter failure, Sarah shook her head. "No . . . 'twill pass.'' This time, when she rose, she thought she was better for a moment. "I should like to lie down, I think.''

The countess looked to her husband. "Charles, do you truly . . . ?''

Sarah had taken but two or three steps when she doubled over. The two footmen hastened to catch her, and Willie supported her, helping her from the room.

"I think, Em," the earl muttered dryly, "that the gel's either poisoned or lost the babe. Go on up with her. I'll write to Dev—'tis all I am good for."

He walked, each step agonizingly painful, to his bookroom desk and dropped heavily into his chair. For a time he could only stare blindly. He knew what was happening—he'd seen it too many times with his own young wife years ago. It wasn't the sort of thing one forgot, after all. Finally he reached for a sharpened quill and dipped it into his inkstand. He'd so wanted this babe, more than any of them suspected. Aye, he'd hoped to atone for his own terrible mistake through Adam's child.

The pen scratched across the sheet of paper before him. "Dear Audley," he began, "I'd have you come home posthaste. In the absence of your brother, you are needed to tend to his wife. 'Tis not confirmed, but I am expecting the babe to be lost. I pray you will make all haste, for 'tis a sadness to all, and I doubt your mother's or my ability to console her." It was, he reflected as he sealed it, the first letter he had ever written to either of his sons. He sent it to London by a rider.

Sometime later, an hour perhaps, the countess's physician arrived to confirm their fears. It was too late to stem the bloody flow, and naught could be done about the child. About all he could offer was laudanum to ease the mother's mind and body, and let it happen, he said. Twelve drops in water, repeated as often as she roused, should make her sleep. Aye, it ought to, the earl told Emma, for it had taken him two years of use to accommodate such a dose. And the countess, feeling her husband's pain, turned a tear-streaked face into his shoulder. He stood for a time, patting her awkwardly, then dropped his hands.

"Got to sit, Em—can't stand m'leg anymore."

20

Devin Hastings hovered, ignoring the protests of the servants who tended her, watching Sarah lie still in the postered bed. Her auburn hair spilled like tangled skeins of silk across the snowy pillowcase, seeming dark where it touched her pale face. Her eyelashes were smudges over the bluish hollows beneath her closed eyes. She looked smaller, thinner, more vulnerable in sleep.

The maids had difficulty getting the laudanum down her, spilling it when she choked. He lifted her, bracing her back with his shoulder, and held the cup to her lips, urging her to drink. Her nightrail fell open at the neck, slipping off one white shoulder, giving him a glimpse of creamy breast. His hands eased her down, sliding over her arms, and then he released her beneath the housekeeper's frown.

He was torn—he'd not wanted to come, but his promise to Adam overruled his resolve to avoid her. And now that he'd seen her, lying there so white and silent, her plight touched his heart more than he cared to admit. It did no harm to help her, he told himself, for once she revived, he meant to leave. But for now she needed someone, and neither his mother nor his father was able to deal with the loss of Adam's child. Already one of them had taken to her bed with camphor and burnt feathers, and the other sat below in a stupor from either opium or brandy or both. It was his duty, he rationalized, to stay with her.

His hand crept to her hair, ostensibly to get it out of her face, but as his fingers stroked lightly along her temple, she moved slightly, turning her head until he could feel her breath on his palm. And for a moment he allowed himself to imagine what it must be like to wake up beside her, to see the warmth in those amber eyes. Then reason reasserted itself, and he drew back, shamed by his thoughts. She was his sister, his brother's wife, and nothing more to him. He would not touch her and want again.

Sarah's memory was hazy, clouded by the opiate. She knew not how long she slept, only that whenever she roused, someone was there to give her the foul-tasting drink. More than once she'd tried to protest, to no avail. At first the pains were merely eased, but later they ceased entirely. She'd been in a world where mind and body seemed to separate, floating dreamily apart, and part of her wanted to stay there. Murmured words of comfort penetrated from time to time, then faded as she slipped in and out of the blissful oblivion.

"No more," she finally heard a masculine voice say as she struggled to come awake. "Would you have her addle-brained?"

"But I was told to give twelve drops whenever she stirred," a woman protested.

"No. She does not appear to suffer now."

Sarah's eyes and limbs were heavy, unresponsive to will, too much so, and the effort too great to make anything move. She slept fitfully now, and with each passing bit of consciousness she became more and more aware of where she was. She tried to touch her head, and someone, thinking it must pain her, placed a cool compress on her brow.

"Can you hear me, Sarah?"

"Aye," she croaked. "Adam?"

" 'Tis Dev."

For a moment she could not comprehend. "But Adam . . ."

"Is with Loudoun. They should be in New York next week."

"Oh."

Finally she managed to force her eyes open. The room had gone dark again save for a brace of candles drawn close by the bed. Audley sat back, his face lined with fatigue, and passed a weary hand over the stubble of his dark beard. It was odd, but there was a trace of powder still in the hair that fell forward over his forehead.

" 'Tis night?"

"Aye. Poor Sarah," he murmured softly, "you are not feeling at all the thing, are you?"

"No."

Her hand crept to her abdomen. It did not seem so very different, and for a moment she dared to hope. It had been but an awful dream—she'd eaten something that had made her sick, that was all.

The gesture was not lost on him. "Do you remember anything, Sarah?"

She closed her eyes and swallowed hard. "I was ill."

"Papa sent for me."

The words, quietly spoken as they were, hung in the air, confirming her worst fear. There was no need to say more; she understood that his father would not have bothered him for anything less than a disaster. And yet she could not quite believe it.

"But I am all right. I mean . . . ?"

"You are all right, Sarah," he answered.

"And the babe?"

There was a sharp, audible intake of his breath, and then he shook his head. "No." He leaned over to clasp her hand between his. "I am sorry."

"I see."

He'd not meant to touch her again, had promised himself that he wouldn't, once she waked. He released her hand self-consciously and sought words of comfort. "You are young, Sarah—there will be others."

It was the wrong thing to say to her. She turned away, drew her knees up against her chest, and pressed her knuckles against her teeth. If Adam did not come back, she'd not even have his child. Tears rolled down her cheeks, spilling onto her pillow, spotting it. He sat there helpless, yet wanting to aid her somehow.

"Would you have a bit of laudanum?" he asked finally.

"No."

"Would you have me get Mama?"

"No."

"Do you want me to write to Adam?"

"No."

"It would reach New York within the month."

"No."

"Sarah—"

"I shall write to him—later," she whispered so low he almost could not hear her. "Not now."

He, who moved in the highest circles of His Majesty's government, who participated in decisions that determined England's course, was helpless in the face of her grief. Finally, unable to think of anything else to say, he laid a tentative hand on her shoulder. And it was as though a dam broke beneath his touch, for she gave vent to her anguish, sobbing almost uncontrollably. He began stroking her, rubbing along the bones between her shoulder and spine.

"There will be others—you'll have others, my dear. You and Adam . . ."

She shuddered and choked. "N-not if he d-does n-not come b-back!"

"Sarah . . . Sarah . . . Sarah . . ." He eased himself onto the bed, leaning over her back, whispering, " 'Twas not your fault, Sarah—none will fault you for this."

She hiccuped back a sob as yet another tremor passed through her. "You . . . you d-do n-not un-understand. What if . . . if he does n-not come back? What if he dies? Then I sh-shall have nothing!"

She was shivering uncontrollably now, so much so that the bed shook. Without thinking, he lifted her, drawing her onto his lap as though she were a child. She turned her head into his shoulder and held on, clinging to him as though she were drowning. The crying subsided, but the shaking did not.

"My lord . . ."

He looked up, feeling suddenly guilty, to meet the stern disapproval in Mrs. Cross's eyes. His arms still around Sarah, he murmured rather apologetically, "I have told her, you see."

The woman's expression softened. "Aye, 'tis hard to understand. Do you think she'd mind his lordship's coming? He was wantin' t' speak with her." Then, her gaze turning to the girl in his lap, she added pointedly, "I told him she was awake."

"Aye. Sarah . . ."

Unable to meet anyone's eyes, Sarah stared into the soft cambric of her brother-in-law's shirt, wanting very much to stay there rather than face the old man. He'd fault her for the loss of the child, she was sure of that, and she did not think she could bear his censure just now. And Devin's arms were reassuring, reminding her of Adam's.

"Tell him she . . ." He groped for words to placate his father. "Tell him she is still unwell."

But the earl had managed to come up, when walking was such an effort for him, and despite her reluctance to face him, her conscience pricked her. She sat up and wiped the back of her hand against her wet cheek. She still shivered as though it were cold in July.

"No." Her voice husky, hoarse almost from crying, she spoke low. "I'd not send him away."

"Aye." Mrs. Cross looked to where Sarah's nightrail slipped on her shoulder. "If your lordship will pardon us, me and Annie'll have her clean and fresh in a trice."

His gaze followed hers; then he resolutely looked away. "Of course," he murmured, releasing his brother's wife. "I am in need of a bath and shave myself." To Sarah he added, "I'll speak with Papa first."

Gratitude washed over her as she looked up at him. "Once again I find myself in your debt, my lord." Something, disappointment perhaps, clouded his handsome face, and she nodded. "Devin."

The housekeeper waited impatiently, leaving him nothing to do but rise. "You'll come about, Sarah—and we'll both pray for Adam's return," he promised. "Until then, you must look to yourself."

He started to leave, crossing the room slowly as almost unbearable weariness settled over him. Behind him, he heard her say, "You are more like him than I once thought, you know."

"Thank you," he answered bleakly.

* * *

Under Mrs. Cross's direction, Annie had changed the sheets again and bathed Sarah with scented water from the washbowl. And the countess's dresser came in to brush out her hair. Sarah lay back amongst a bank of plumped pillows, her clean nightrail demurely tied at her neck, and waited for the earl.

She was tired—the laudanum had robbed her of her strength—and she did not want to see him at all. But there was nothing he could say that she did not think of herself. If she'd but stayed abed, if she'd rested more, perhaps it would not have happened. They'd all warned her, hadn't they? Neither his father nor his mother had thought she ought to travel to London before Adam left, and even Devin had appeared to be against the trip. And then, when she'd returned, everyone had treated her as though she were an invalid—everyone but the old man, that was.

The door creaked openly slowly, and the earl limped in, stopping to shake off Willie, who held one arm. "Be gone with you—ain't no need, I tell you! Got to walk whilst I can."

He seemed old, more so than she'd noticed before, and his cane wobbled from his weight. His wig sat slightly askew, betraying dark hair heavily streaked with gray. He looked to be in sadder case than she. She held her breath nervously as he made his way across the room to take the seat Devin had pulled close to her bed. Would he be the first to tell her the fault was hers?

Unwilling to wait for him to task her, and unable to stand it if he did, she spoke first. "Did you let the doctor look at your leg, sir?"

The question took him aback and touched him deeply. That she could put her own misery aside to ask of his was almost more than he could bear. He dropped his bulk into the chair and caught his breath. For a moment he had to close his eyes against the hot pain that shot through his legs as they bent.

"Aye," he said finally. Mopping his brow with his kerchief, he leaned closer. "Surprises you, don't it? But I ain't here to speak of that, mind you—'tis of you I'd hear."

"I am all right, sir."

"Of course you are!" he uttered bracingly. "And so I told Em, but she wouldn't listen t' me. Damme, I says to her, but the gel's got strength! Aye, I know 'tis a disappointment to you, but it ain't like 'twill be your last babe, Sarah." He hesitated as though he'd like to say more, but then fell silent. His faded eyes were strangely bright and rimmed with red.

She'd been prepared for his censure, but not his sympathy, and the lump in her throat tightened. Swallowing hard, she bit her lip and shook her head. "Not if he doesn't come back," she whispered finally. "But—"

"Here, now, we ain't thinkin' like that, you hear? He's got to come back—stands to reason he will. Loudoun ain't going to risk my son's neck, don't you know? Aye, I'll have Dev write to him today—tell him Westerfield wants his boy home." He tried to smile, but it looked more like a frown. "Boy won't like it, of course, but what's that to anything? When he sees what case you are in—"

"No." With an effort, she shook her head. "He'd never forgive either of us, my lord, and 'twould be said he hid behind your coat."

"Aye, so I suppose. But I'd do it for you, don't you know? He'd blame me rather than you."

"No."

"You are a strange gel, Sarah, damme if you ain't. Well, I blame meself for what happened, I suppose. I could see you wasn't wantin' to play—guess you wasn't feeling quite the thing then."

"Did the doctor tell you that?" she asked incredulously. " 'Tis beyond the bounds if he did."

"The old quacksalver? Nay—said 'twas certain to happen if it happened—as if that's an explanation for a body!" he snorted derisively. "Says them as tries but don't get lost comes into the world with club feet—or some such idiocy!" Then, fearful of oversetting her with the notion that her babe wouldn't have been quite right, he hastily changed the subject. "Aye, but I did ask him about m'leg—showed it to 'im even. Told him I wasn't to be bled, also."

"Surely he did not wish to cup you for that."

He nodded. "Aye. Was goin' to put the leeches below to pull the blood down into the leg. But I allowed as how as big as the thing is, there's enough in it now. Then he wanted to cut on it—to send me to London to see the surgeon. That's when I sent the fool packing."

"But if it were drained, perhaps . . ."

"He was going to leave me a stump. Now, what's an old man who can't get about with two legs t' do when there's only one, I ask you?"

"Does he think 'tis gangrenous?"

"Nay."

"Then why on earth—?"

"Because he's a quack! They are always a-wantin' to cut off what they cannot cure! Don't know where Em finds 'em, and so I told her, damme if I didn't." He sat back, adding defensively, "Besides, 'tis better. Been having Willie keep hot towels for me, and it seems to ease it. Aye, and the sores are a-drying out."

"Since yesterday?"

"Yesterday?" Then realizing she did not know how long she'd been abed, he shook his head. "Been nigh to three days, gel. Audley's been here two. Twenty-second of July today—twenty-third come morn."

"You should not have troubled Lord Audley, my lord."

"Got to. It ain't like I was wantin' to, mind you, but I promised Adam me'n Dev'd see to you—and I know 'twas Dev he wanted for the task. Eased his mind o'er leaving, thinking Audley'd take care of you, since he didn't trust me as is his papa t' do it."

"No."

"Gave me a fright, I can tell you, gel. I thought as if anything was t' happen to you, he'd not forgive."

The door opened again and Lady Emma stepped in, followed by Annie bearing a tray. "Devin says she is awake," the countess said to her husband. Then, seeing Sarah sitting up amid the pillows, she burst into tears. "Oh, my dear child! I am so sorry! What Adam is to think—"

"Dash it, Em! I ain't standin' for this! If you can do naught but water the plants, you can go back to bed yourself! The gel's already cried o'er the business enough, you hear?''

The countess sniffed. "What an unfeeling thing to say, Charles. What Sarah must think—''

"She don't think she must weep to mourn! Gel's tired, Em! Go on—and don't be coming back until you got the water stopped! Give her peace, if you can.'' He saw the tray Annie set beside him. "Aye, and let her eat—make her feel more the thing than hearing you blubber o'er her.''

Moving around him, the maid lifted the cover off a bowl of gruel. "Something to sustain ye, mistress.''

"Eh? What the devil is that?''

"Doctor ordered it, my lord.''

He looked into the bowl and shuddered. "You hungry, gel?''

"A little," Sarah admitted, eyeing the gruel with misgiving.

"Take the pap back to the kitchen and bring her some of the mutton we had at supper—aye, and a bit of the calf's-foot jelly and cream also.''

"Charles!''

"Go back to bed, Emma.''

Adam's parents stared each other down for a moment; then the countess seemed to shrink. "The consequences, I am sure, will be laid at your doorstep, Charles," she said finally.

"I got a wide door." He sighed, relenting slightly. "But if you was to have a more cheerful look to you, I'd say stay.''

"If Sarah does not mind it, I think I should rather see her in the morning," his wife answered, still miffed.

After she left, he appeared preoccupied for a time. "She ain't always been a fool," he observed finally. "Time was when she was a taking thing—pretty as you are.''

"And you were much like Audley, I suppose," Sarah responded.

"Eh? Nay, I was the fool then. Audley ain't a fool for any petticoat—he knows what is owed his family.'' Then, realizing what he'd said, he quickly added, "But I ain't blaming you or Adam, and you must not think it. I've come round a bit now that I know you, gel. Adam did all right for himself in that quarter.''

''Thank you.'' Could he not see that she had no wish to discuss Adam's family just now—that she'd be left alone in her grief? She wanted to cry out, to ask him to leave her alone, but she could not.

''But Dev'll be Westerfield, don't you know?'' he went on. ''And he's got to have a wife as advances him before the world.'' Out of the corner of his eye he saw Annie returning with a full tray. '' But enough of an old man's prattle—'tis food and rest that'll mend you. Emma's going to be up here come morning, and if she vexes you, send word you want to see me or Dev, you hear?'' He struggled to his feet and held on to the bedside for a moment before reaching for his cane. ''If m'sister Trowbridge wasn't there, we'd go to Bath to take the waters, Sarah. I could sit in 'em, and you could drink 'em, and mayhap we'd both be the better for it. But I ain't visiting the Old Tartar—don't like her above half—never did, in fact.''

She watched him go with relief, then turned her attention to the contents of the tray. She did not in truth want to eat, but she knew she should. For a moment she considered asking Annie to take it back, then considered that they'd all be at her. Resolutely she cut into the meat. She knew that the mutton was good, but it seemed tasteless in her mouth, and the calf's-foot jelly not cold enough to suit her. She managed to eat a little before pushing the tray aside. Clucking over the waste, Annie carried it out, pausing only long enough to douse the candles as she went.

Alone in the darkness, Sarah lay listening to the steady ticking of the clock, feeling an intense, aching sadness. There were no tears to be shed, just that empty feeling when she considered this last blow. Life didn't seem to have been fair with her at all. She'd lost her mother, her home, and her child, and she'd endured enough loneliness in her nineteen years to fill a lifetime. There was no end to it—if she'd been superstitious, she'd have considered herself cursed.

No, that was not entirely true, she had to admit. She'd been given Adam, and that was recompense for all else. What happiness he'd brought her in those brief months. As long as he came back to her, she could survive anything. As long as she had him to love.

And with memories of him to comfort her, her grief was nearly bearable. No, she must concentrate now on her husband. Adam must not come back to a dreary, self-absorbed wife. Now that she had not the child to think on, she would have to consider how best to further her husband's desires. She would have to use his absence to increase her usefulness to him.

It was a long time before sleep came again. She lay there, not making plans for the babe as she had so often done, but rather examining how she might become a political wife capable of advancing her husband. Finally, her mind exhausted, she cradled her head in her arm and drifted off.

21

Albany, New York: August 1756

The colonial city, if it could be called that, was almost unbearable in the summer, or so Adam had been told often enough. And as he stared into the hot, humid darkness, he felt as though he'd come to hell. And it was a hell as much of spirit as of body, for he yearned for Sarah as he'd never wished for anything before. The isolation he'd felt as a boy at the Park was but child's play to what he felt now.

Closing his eyes did little good, for his body burned at the thought of her. With a groan he rolled out of bed and groped for his flint. Sparking it against the cottony nub of a candle wick, he worked until there was a soft glow. Blowing softly while cupping it with his hand, he managed to get the wick to catch. The small flame bulged, first a small drop of blue-violet, and then it grew until it licked, a flickering red-orange light that teased the night with its daring.

Carrying it to the small table he used for nearly everything, he found his journal and tore a blank page from it. He would write to Sarah, pouring out his love for her, putting the words of his loneliness to paper. She would understand, he hoped, and perhaps the constancy of his letters would somehow make up to her for all the things he'd not said when he left. And she could draw comfort from him whilst she waited for the babe.

He was in the process of mixing the ink when one of Loudoun's other aides, Captain Wilcox, tapped on the door and identified himself. Without looking up, Adam called out, "Come in."

"I thought you had retired, but then I saw your light."

"I had, but 'twas too hot to sleep."

James Wilcox eased himself into the room, looking around. "I wasn't certain I'd find you alone."

Adam's eyebrows rose. "And whom did you expect to find?"

"Well, as the general sets the tone, I'd not have been surprised to discover a ladybird."

"No." Adam forced himself to smile. "You behold a married man, Jamie."

"With a wife left in England." Wilcox sighed, nodding. "Aye, but I know how it is—'tis the fifth time I have had to leave Elizabeth behind. And with four daughters now, I cannot afford to bring her."

The smile twisted, turning one corner of his mouth down. "But you did not come to see if I had a soiled dove here, I think. You are as alone as I am, aren't you?"

"Aye. Actually, I have been thinking."

Not wishing to seem inhospitable, Adam rose and lit a large lantern across the room. An eerie red-yellow glow bathed the small room, casting long shadows against whitewashed walls. "And I am to guess your thoughts?" he asked, turning back to Wilcox. "My dear Jamie, you find me too wearied by my own. You'd best just open your budget.''

"Do I look like a ranger to you?" the older man wanted to know.

"Not at all. For one thing, you are neither drunk nor unprincipled, and for another, you are obviously a soldier. You look like an officer and a gentleman," Adam answered sincerely.

"I hate it here."

"You are not alone in that. If I never see another supply list, 'twill be too soon, Jamie. We are sent to fight a war, but he prepares and prepares—supply is everything to an army, he says.''

"And it is. The forts will fall if they cannot be supplied.''

"Forts fall when they are not reinforced with troops, also," Adam retorted. " 'Tis time to move men."

"Well, 'tis none of our affair—those decisions come from above," Wilcox decided. "Though how we are to oust the French ere they have the whole must be decided soon.''

"We outsupply them," Adam answered dryly. "Ask Loudoun if he does not mean to do that."

Wilcox shrugged. "Aye, I chafe under his eternal planning also, my friend—and I mean to do something about it. There is money to be made in this war, Adam."

"Aye, and soldiers become rich," was the sarcastic response to that. "If you bought your commission for gain, you'd have been better served to have invested your money in the funds.''

"What do you know of Robert Rogers?"

Adam was impatient with the way Wilcox meant to lead him. "Cut line, Jamie—I am in no mood to play at this tonight.''

"But you have heard of him?" Wilcox persisted.

"Of course I have heard of him!" Adam exploded. "Who over here has not? Rogers' Rangers, is it not? Sixty ruffians who spy and scout and scalp under the guise of fighting a war—aye, I have heard of Rogers"

"Abercromby is authorizing the formation of five more

ranger companies." Wilcox let this sink in before adding pointedly, "Do you know what they are paying them?"

"No."

"The enlisted men will make twice what the regulars do, and 'tis to be supposed that the officers will fare well also."

" 'Tis a waste—the wrong people are rewarded," Adam muttered.

"Aye, but they serve a purpose unlike any other," his friend argued. "And these are to be employed in the Champlain Valley—they will attempt to separate the French from their Indian allies. Wreak disorder on them, you know."

"Somehow, Jamie, I cannot quite see you taking a scalp."

"I cannot see myself sitting here, my musket rusting, whilst the French take everything all the way to Albany. 'Tis easier to keep what you have than to fight to get it back, you know. Besides, I think I could spy rather well."

For a moment Adam thought he jested; then, perceiving he did not, he was incredulous. "You cannot wish to join a pack of knaves, Jamie—think! You are trained to lead men into battle."

Wilcox shrugged. "Why is it more civilized to line up in formation, our scarlet coats marking us for targets, and be killed rather than to meet the enemy with its own tactics?"

"Because 'tis uncivilized!"

"Be that as it may, Lieutenant Colonel Gage is to form a company—as are others. And Abercromby is looking for officers from the regular army to train and fight with them—at higher pay." Wilcox walked to where Adam stood. "I do not know about you, of course, but my girls could use more money, my friend."

"What do you know about fighting Indians?" Adam demanded; answering himself: "Nothing—and neither do I, if that is what you are suggesting."

"For the money, I mean to learn. Just thought I'd share what I mean to do, that's all." The older man shrugged expressively. "Beyond that, 'tis your affair." Then he added slyly, "But I do not mean to sit here planning every minute detail of every troop movement as though it were a chess game between masters. That I shall leave to the other poor fellows unlucky enough to be honored by Loudoun.''

"You will not find the rangers to your liking, Jamie. You like to be clean,'' Adam reminded him.

"I'll manage. I can tell you one thing: I do not mean to stand up and fight Indians who skulk behind trees. Have you read the field reports of this last year? As much as I hate to give them credit, the French know what they are doing here. We outnumber them twenty to one and yet they have won again and again.''

"I think you are mad.''

"Mayhap, but I shall be sending more money home to my wife in the bargain.''

"Indians are but savages—think on that while you are about it. Aye, and whilst you are reading the field reports, note the atrocities. You look better with hair and skin, Jamie.''

"And I am just as dead whether from French musket or Abnaki hatchet,'' Wilcox countered. "Besides, Abercromby says he means to make the new companies as independent as Rogers'—without giving up English discipline.''

"I should like to see that.''

After Wilcox left, Adam sat for a time, trying to compose the letter to Sarah. But words beyond ''My dearest wife'' would not come. There was so little to tell that did not sound maudlin or had not been said before. His pen scratched across the page, writing, ''My heart is torn by this separation between us.'' Aye, but she knew that— he'd said so even before he left her. ''I long . . .'' There were no words capable of conveying the longing he felt, the ache that nearly consumed his soul when he thought of her. ''. . . for the day when I shall see you and the child,'' he finished lamely.

Frowning, he considered reminding her of those days spent in the stable at Spender's Hill, or of that last night in London, but then thought better of it. For one thing, such memories set his body on fire with wanting, and for another, he was certain his mother would wish to share Sarah's letters.

He dipped the quill in the ink and continued on safer ground, telling her of Loudoun and the crossing, of the French and the Indians, and of the rangers.

They are an undisciplined lot, dearest Sarah, ruffians from every gutter in Europe and unschooled farm boys eager to take scalps in revenge for the horrible atrocities the Indians have committed. They come in all manner of clothes, most of them unwashed, and yet the hopes of the colonials are with them. The argument is that they fight as the French do—without regard for decency—which goes against all I have been taught.

But I sympathize with their desire to punish, for the French, particularly the priests and the *coureurs de bois,* incite their Indian allies to unspeakable savagery. It has reached such a pass that we now offer bounties for some of the more notorious. Indeed, but I have heard that the governor of Pennsylvania promises money for the scalp or person of one Etienne Reynaud. Would you think it possible for one presumably civilized man to buy the scalp of another?

He stopped to read what he had written and shook his head. It would be difficult for those back in England to understand the bitterness that existed against the French missionaries. And it would be equally difficult to explain the savagery of the Indians against those they captured. He dipped his pen yet again, writing of mundane things such as the fact that whilst Loudoun was a stickler for paperwork and discipline, there were other areas in which he was lax. Adam had to wear the hated wig only at muster in the mornings—the rest of the time, he kept it in a box. That was the one thing he envied the rangers: none of them seemed to possess one. And he wrote of one junior officer who'd had his dressed quite neatly with tallow and powdered it with flour, only to be embarrassed by the swarm of flies that followed him everywhere. That ought to remind her of Roland and his honey.

He had to stop to blot where the ink would run, then

plunged ahead, adding, ''But wherever I am and wherever I shall go, I take you with me in my thoughts. I
thank you for the wonderful memories that do and will
sustain me. Keep me with you in spirit as I shall you,
and know that I pray for you and our child. May God
grant you are both well.''

He signed himself ''Your loving husband, Adam,'' and
waited for the pages to dry. In the course of writing, he'd
hoped to ease his loneliness, but it had only made the
longing more painful. The relative idleness gave him far
too much time to think, and the days crawled when he
was away from her.

He folded the letter finally, sealing it with wax from
the candle. This time, when he returned to his bed, he
stripped the nightshirt off and lay down on top of his
sheets. The hot, moist air was like a heavy blanket over
him.

For a time he tossed and turned on his narrow cot,
trying not to think of her just yet. His mind tumbled with
impatience, and still he put it off, forcing his thoughts to
the present, to his dislike of Loudoun, to Jamie Wilcox's
strange decision to join the rangers.

But finally he drifted into that confused netherworld,
that last semiconscious bastion of thought, and there
Sarah came to him, loving him, her rich auburn hair
spilling over him like silk, cool against his hot skin. His
arm went around his pillow, pulling it closer, holding it
until at last he slept.

Far too soon, he was awakened by the sound of insistent pounding on his door, followed by Lieutenant Carswell's shouts of, ''Captain! Captain Hastings! General
Loudoun's orders, sir!''

Adam came awake with a groan, realizing that the sun
was rising. ''I thought hedonists stayed abed at least until
six,'' he muttered. Aloud he called out, ''Tell the general
I shall be there as quickly as I can make myself presentable!''

''Aye, sir.'' There was a slight hesitation; then Carswell added, '' 'Tis over rangers, sir, and I'd . . .'' Again
he stopped, as though he feared to put it to the touch.

Finally he blurted out, "I'd have your recommendation, Captain Hastings."

The devil you would, Adam thought to himself as he forced his feet to the floor. Groaning, he reached for his breeches and stockings.

"Sir?"

"Aye?"

"My wife's increasing, and I could use the money, sir," Carswell persisted. "Captain Wilcox will vouch for me also, I think."

"Will he, now?" Adam eased his body into his breeches, standing to pull them up and button them. "Fools seek company, then." He smoothed his stockings and pulled the buff-colored fabric down over them.

There was a pause on the other side of the door; then the boy said, "Beg your pardon, sir?"

"Nothing." Adam sat to draw on his freshly blacked boots, feeling a sense of ill-usage. The open-necked shirt caught as he yanked it over his head, and his fingers hastily tied the stock without regard to order.

"Colonel Sir William Johnson is come also," the lieutenant added conversationally as he waited outside. "Aye, and the French have moved down into Pennsylvania, sir— 'tis rumored amongst those who have come in that Fort Granville has fallen."

An oath escaped as Adam grabbed his coat and wig, jamming the latter onto his head without so much as a glance into his mirror. If western Pennsylvania was defenseless, mayhap Loudoun would move now.

He emerged from his quarters still pulling on his coat, and walked quickly beside Carswell, his mind racing. Ever since he'd arrived in New York, there'd been speculation that the French might launch a new offensive ere autumn, but so far scouting reports had proved unreliable. But if Johnson had come, perhaps his Mohawks had told him something worth noting.

Loudoun looked up irritably as Adam entered the general's meeting room. "It took you long enough," he observed sourly, wincing as his eyes traveled over Adam's wig and stock.

"Your pardon, sir."

"Aye." John Campbell turned back to the man who lounged against the wall. "You think Montcalm means to attack Oswego, then?"

"Momentarily," was the answer.

Adam stared at the stranger, observing his strange dress. Almost as an afterthought, Loudoun gestured toward him and Carswell. "Gentlemen, I make known to you Captain Hastings. You have, I believe, met the lieutenant. Captain Hastings, Colonel Johnson brings us most disturbing news, I fear," he murmured, not bothering to speak to Adam's face.

This, then, was William Johnson, self-styled baronet of the Mohawks. Adam eyed him curiously, wondering if half the tales he'd heard of him were true. 'Twas said that when he was amongst his Indian allies, he became more Indian than they were, sharing their rituals and their women.

Johnson cleared his throat, and the men gathered in the room fell silent. "Gentlemen, as you know, Chief Red Head of the Mohawks is dead, leaving a more agreeable leadership. I am just returned from the mourning ceremonies, where I have heard that not only have the French and their Menominee allies moved into Pennsylvania, but that they are at this moment traveling down the Champlain Valley, presumably to lay siege to Fort Oswego and Fort George." He half-turned to address Colonel Bradstreet. "Did you not encounter them?"

"Aye."

Bradstreet rose to describe the attack he'd suffered on his way to Albany, answering terse questions as Loudoun interrupted him from time to time. The French thrust would surely be the valley, but he did not think they would attempt Saratoga, Fort Edward, or Fort William Henry, for between them, these camps boasted some ten thousand soldiers, well over twice as many as the French had at Fort Carillon.

Then it was another's turn. A man Adam could only describe as little better than a savage himself took the floor. He was unkempt and unshaven and looked as though he'd not slept in days.

"Beggin' the general's pardon, sir, but Carillon's not

completed yet. I was there but three days past, and the defenses are not closed. A body of troop could—''

''Captain Rogers''—Loudoun's expression was pained as he cut the fellow short—''there is naught to be served by precipitate action.''

Both Rogers and Johnson gave a start, and even Bradstreet appeared uneasy. ''If you do not reinforce Oswego, my lord, 'twill fall,'' Johnson predicted glumly. ''And if Oswego goes, much of New York is vulnerable, ready to be caught between there and Carillon, I am afraid.''

The meeting was strained as John Campbell stared down his nose at the baronet, but Johnson did not waver. ''You, my lord, are but lately arrived from England, and cannot know how the French military is deployed here. The French we deal with are not gentlemen, I am afraid. And if we do not protect our outposts, Englishmen will lose their lives and their hair.''

Both Bradstreet and Rogers voiced agreement, and even Captain Wilcox of the general's own staff nodded. It was obvious that Loudoun wished to take the matter under advisement, but in doing so, he risked alienating the very men who'd helped bring his predecessor down. Grudgingly he ordered Colonel Webb to move the Fortyfourth Regiment out to reinforce Fort Oswego. Muttering something about a barbarous land, John Campbell adjourned the early meeting and withdrew once again to his quarters.

As the meeting broke up, Johnson moved to greet Adam. ''Audley's brother, I collect? You must tell him that his efforts on our behalf are not unnoted here. Aye, and if Pitt were but to take the ministry, I have not a doubt as to the successful prosecution of the war.''

''I try not to involve myself in policy,'' Adam answered.

It was Robert Rogers who spoke up at that. ''Over here, errors of policy are costly, sir. If you would know how badly the French want to rule, you have but to travel amongst the savages and see the harm they do there. They are little better than the Indians, Captain.''

Johnson rubbed his chin thoughtfully. ''Not a bad notion, when one thinks on it—Hastings' brother has some influence with Pitt, or so I am told. If he were to know how things really stand with us, I daresay Parliament would back us with more than promises."

"Gentlemen—"

"Got nothing to lose beyond your hair," Rogers offered, snorting.

James Wilcox, who'd been listening quietly, shook his head. "He's Westerfield's son—there'd be hell to pay if anything happened to him."

Johnson appeared to digest that before he spoke again. "Aye, I had not considered Westerfield in this. He'll want his son safe."

They drifted off, leaving Adam with Wilcox. "Jamie," Adam muttered tersely, "I don't thank you for the service."

Wilcox shrugged. " 'Tis true enough, isn't it? With your brother in the paymaster's office and your father Westerfield, I doubt Loudoun would wish to be charged with losing you."

"Neither my father nor my brother has the ordering of my life," Adam retorted, walking away.

A slow smile played at James Wilcox's lips. "Does this mean you are going?"

Adam stopped, but did not turn back. "It means that I do not dance to Papa's tune—nor yours, Jamie," he answered evenly.

"You'll tire of Loudoun's paperwork soon enough," the other man predicted.

And the trouble of it was that he was right. But Adam was not going to be goaded into anything—not yet.

22

Adam surveyed his new company of men and wondered if the quarrel with Loudoun had been worth it. Aside from Lieutenant Colonel Gage's still-forming Eightieth Regiment, there were several other new ranger companies still needing the discipline of regular officers. Adam had asked for assignment to Gage's, but instead had been given command of his own, if command it could be called.

His men were for the most part no more than a motley assortment of adventurers who'd signed on to fight "Injuns and Frenchies" on the northern frontiers. And Adam was dismayed to discover among them a number of Irishmen, Spaniards, and seamen as well as trappers and farmers looking for a place to spend a hard winter. Between the lot of them, there was not so much as the semblance of a uniform, nor was there an issued weapon. His men carried knives, hatchets, much-repaired muskets, and in the case of one farmer come up from the south, a Pennsylvania rifle that was the envy of his fellows. They wore ragged breeches ranging from wool to buckskin, coats of all descriptions, some long-tailed, some short, and everything from buckled shoes to knee boots. And there was not a one of them that did not view him with equal skepticism as they faced each other.

"Sergeant," he addressed Edward Byrd, the young man he'd brought with him from Loudoun's staff, "read the roll."

"Aye, sir." He cleared his throat and began. "Sean O'Donnell." When there was no answer, he looked up, directing, "When you hear your name, you will be pleased to respond, 'Aye.' Now, is Mr. O'Donnell here?"

"Aye."

"Rafael Estevez?"

"Aye."

"Benjamin Dixon?"

"Aye."

"Thomas Kirk?"

"Aye."

"John Peters?"

"Aye."

"Francis Burton?"

There was no answer. Byrd looked around him, then repeated, "Francis Burton?"

"He's here!" someone shouted.

"Mr. Burton must answer for himself."

A big burly fellow with limp brown hair sauntered forward. "Allowing as you was to ask for Frank Burton, I might be here," he told Byrd, spitting at his feet.

Adam groaned inwardly. He was going to earn every penny he got for his service. He stared coldly at Frank Burton. "You will be pleased to address Sergeant Byrd as 'sir.' "

Burton looked him up and down contemptuously, taking in the scarlet coat and polished brass buttons, before spitting again. Then he looked at Byrd. "Sir." He sneered, sauntering back to lounge against a wall.

"Sergeant Byrd, you will order that man's pay forfeit." An ugly murmur spread through the sixty men before him, but Adam was too angry to note it. "Any man who has no wish to show the proper respect to a superior should withdraw now. Otherwise, those who choose to remain will face disciplinary action—is that clear to all?"

A freckle-faced sandy-haired boy spoke up from the group. "Beggin' yer honor's honor, but d' ye mean to wear that ter fight Injuns?" he called out to Adam. " 'Cause if yer do, I ain't goin'—I ain't follerin' no redcoat into no trees." The crowd tittered. "I came here to

fight for Rogers, and yer ain't 'im, mister!'' The laughter
grew louder.

Adam's jaw tensed visibly. Briefly he considered having the boy flogged, but letting someone else discipline
him would have no effect on the rest of them. It would
appear as though he hid behind the whip. The laughter
faded to silence as everyone waited for him to respond
to the boy's insolence. And he knew instinctively that to
these ruffians his manhood was in question. He was
naught but a rich man's boy come to play soldier with
them.

"No, I am not," he admitted tersely. "Sergeant Byrd,
your musket, please. O'Donnell, you will step forward."

For a moment the Irish boy's eyes widened, and then
with the bravado of youth, he swaggered forward, grinning. "Yer can't shoot the lot of us, can yer, now?"

Instead of answering, Adam reached for the paper cartridge in his belt. Holding it, he took the musket from
Byrd, half-cocked it, and opened the pan deftly. He bent
his head to bite off the end of the paper, poured part of
the powder into the priming pan, closed the cover, and
tapped the gun butt on the ground. The rest of the powder
he poured down the muzzle, inserted the bullet and paper, ramrodding it down. In an easy motion, he shouldered the gun and pointed it toward where O'Donnell
stood. The boy went white behind his freckles.

"The horse ring," he answered as he fired.

O'Donnell dived to the ground and rolled, certain he'd
be hit, and then he scrambled toward Adam while he
reloaded. But he'd lost the crowd. To a man, they'd turned
in awe toward the horse rail. Frank Burton ran rather than
walked to examine it, then motioned the others over.

"Damme, but he hit it!" He turned back to Adam,
open admiration on his face. " 'Tis nigh fifty yards, sir.''

"Stand back," Adam ordered him curtly. Having reloaded, he raised the musket again, took aim, and fired.
The sound of the ball hitting the ring seemed to rever-
berate through the drill yard.

"Gor!" Sean O'Donnell breathed, standing shakily.
"I ain't never seen the like of that."

"Twice he did it," someone reminded him. "Aye, and fired fast."

Adam handed Ned Byrd back his musket, observing quietly, "Your flint's worn—you'd best replace it. And you may proceed with the roll."

Later, when all sixty men had been counted off, Adam addressed them, telling them that he had no use for those unwilling to submit to discipline. They'd fight like rangers, but they'd behave like soldiers, or else they could seek another company. They'd drill until they were sick of it, and then they would drill some more, not because they would stand and fight in formation, but because it would teach them to fight together. And he expected to learn as much from them as they learned from him. The objective was to defeat the French and not each other. Their assignments would be irregular, requiring not only a great deal of self-reliance but also an absolute trust in their fellows.

His piece said, he dismissed them and turned to leave. As he started across the parade ground, Sean O'Donnell caught up to him. "Beggin' yer honor's pardon, but I ain't never seen shootin' like that—sir," he added quickly as Adam's eyebrows lifted. "I thought the regulars just pointed the barrel and fired."

"We do. There is no need for a full formation to aim," Adam admitted. "The thinking is that if everyone fires in the same direction, something will be hit."

"But—"

"My expertise comes from hunting."

"Still . . ." The boy hesitated. "Beggin' yer honor's . . . sir . . . but could yer show me?"

"I expect to show everyone. You shall practice until you can hit a moving target at thirty yards and a fixed one at fifty." When the boy looked skeptical, he added, "The Indians, I am told, do not stand still and wait to be shot."

"How fast can you load—sir?"

"About five times per minute."

"Gor!" He fell in beside Adam, heedless of the difference between officer and recruit. "I'd thought yer meant ter shoot me."

"No. I considered flogging, but I am opposed to it. However, if I'd missed, I was prepared to thrash you in front of the lot of them." Adam's blue eyes betrayed a hint of amusement now. "I hope you will remember that, in case you are inclined to disrespect again. I can give you more than a stone in weight, you know."

The young Irishman watched him disappear into the long, low building reserved for officers, and not once did he think that Captain Hastings could not have done it.

That night, Adam wrote to Sarah again:

My command is as crude a bunch of fellows as I have ever seen, dearest wife, but I have hopes of them. They are, after all, more to the purpose than a drawing-room dandy in this sort of war. My greatest worry is that they shall think me but a fashionable fribble. A clean uniform around here is suspect, so much so that I shall have to acquire the requisite buckskins favored by the fur trappers, I think.

We have much to do, my men and I, in the way of accommodating each other. There is not a one of them that I should speak to on the streets of London were we to meet there. But now my life is dependent on their goodwill and theirs on mine.

Do you recall my writing of Jamie Wilcox? I should not expect you to meet her, but if you do, I pray you will tell his wife he is well. The wretch got me into this business, you know, and has been given command of a company under Abercromby himself, whilst I am of the more irregular sort. My company, as I understand it, will not fight pitched battles anywhere, but rather will be used for spying and pacifying the Indians. I expect my first assignment within the week, and 'tis rumored that we shall divide into parties for the purpose of observing French activity in the area of Lake George. Others will move into Pennsylvania under the pretense of being French trappers.

As for Indians, I met my first true savage yesterday. Colonel Johnson introduced me to his brother-in-law, who is full-blooded Mohawk and a fierce-looking fellow. And Johnson himself dresses like him, wearing leather shirts and leggings even into our councils.

I must close for now and get to bed, darling Sarah, and I cannot tell you what a lonely place that is for me. I console myself with the thought that you are well and that the babe will soon be company for you. In the meantime, I hope that if you have need of anything, you will apply to Devin.

Forever yours,
Adam

He finished writing and sanded the pages, drying them, before he readied them for the post packet. He'd forgotten to tell her he was no longer at Albany, but he supposed that her letters would be forwarded by Loudoun's staff. There were a lot of things he'd not told her—of how he'd been goaded into quarreling with the general, of how he'd not wanted to hear how he owed his position to his family's influence, and of how Loudoun's overattention to detail had finally pushed him to volunteer for the new companies.

One blessing that came from his new assignment was that he had not the time to dwell on his loneliness so much. Now it overwhelmed him only at night, and that was something. He rose, flexing tired muscles. He had to sleep. There was so much to do before the harsh winter set in. Already the September nights were cold and there was a chill dampness that gnawed at one's bones. But the colonials insisted that nature would give forth one last warm, pleasant week or so before winter's storms rolled over New York's mountains. Indian summer, they called it.

Blowing out the last candle, he rolled into his cot, pulling his blanket around his shoulders, and thought of Sarah the way he liked to think of her. And he could almost smell the hay and see the sun from the open hayloft brightening her red-brown hair as it streamed over her bare breasts. Her amber eyes welcomed his touch, betraying a passion that matched his. The memory of her body was an exquisite torture for him. But she would not look like that now—not now that the babe grew within her. He tried to imagine her with rounded belly and full breasts.

And he tried to imagine the child. Would it be fair with amber eyes or would it have the blue eyes of the Hastingses? Would its hair be blond like his or warmed with red like hers? Whatever it looked like, he was certain he would love it. No child of his would ever be denied as he himself had been.

But when he slipped closer to sleep, the face that floated before him was not Sarah's—it belonged to Sean O'Donnell. He'd been lucky enough to have impressed his ragtag group with his marksmanship this day, but could he in truth make them follow him? Or would he have to prove himself to lads like O'Donnell every day?

The answer was no clearer in the morning. Ned Byrd awakened him with the news that some of his men had wandered off in the night, whilst others had gotten drunk and taken either one or two Mohawk girls to bed with them. Colonel Johnson was not amused, Byrd said, and awaited him.

It was not an auspicious beginning for a day. William Johnson, whether one liked him or not, was a power to be reckoned with in New York. A member of the Governor's Council for many years, he was also a colonel in the colonial militia and held a royal commission as superintendent of all the northern Indians in British America.

"Does he accuse any of them of rapine?" Adam wanted to know as he exchanged his nightshirt for his clothing. "Does he know who is responsible?"

"Aye."

"Well?"

"Francis Burton was seen with one."

Adam had a problem not easily faced at any time, but in this case he had to deal with men who distrusted his ability to lead at all. And on the one hand, stories filtered in almost daily of settlers' wives carried off by Indians somewhere, while on the other, Johnson expected everyone to treat his Mohawks like white people. Adam hadn't heard the whole story, but already he knew it was a devil of a coil.

He washed and shaved quickly, emerging into the pale pink light of a morning not yet fully arrived. The air was chilly, yet heavy with the smell of smoke from dozens of fireplaces. He found Johnson pacing in the deserted parade yard, and he was flanked by two Mohawks of obvious standing, for they wore scarlet tunics rather than traditional buckskin, and beads and copper hung over their breasts.

"Colonel Johnson."

"Captain."

"I collect there has been a disturbance involving rangers assigned to me? Indian girls, I believe."

"Aye. There is the matter of a girl taken against her will by a man she knows as Frank."

"Burton."

Johnson spoke to the two Indians, who answered in a few guttural syllables and left. As Johnson turned back to Adam, he half-apologized. "I know you cannot very well hang him, but neither can you fail to punish him for it."

"No. But you are certain 'twas but one female?"

"And it will not set well with the locals, but if we fail to address the complaint, we lose credibility with the Indians. Aside from the Six Nations, Britain has no allies among them. And I am told there was but one girl," he answered finally.

"But she was unwilling?"

"Her father says so."

"Very well—they shall have their justice. Sergeant Byrd!" he called across the quadrangle. "Assemble the men!"

They came, some stumbling from the aftereffects of too much government-issued rum. Almost none made any attempt to stand at attention before him. He walked in front of them, stopping before Francis Burton. "Burton!"

"Huh?"

"Sir. The response is always 'sir'!" Adam snapped. To Byrd he ordered, "Arrest this man."

"Sir," Burton added contemptuously.

"Colonel Johnson lodges grievous charges against

you—the taking of a female without her consent or that of her tribal elders."

For a moment the soldier blinked as though he could not believe it. "Naw."

"For a two pence, soldier, I'd give you to the Mohawks. As it is, you are remanded to the stockade until such time as a case can be brought against you."

There was a disgruntled murmur amongst his men. "But he was drunk!" O'Donnell burst out.

Adam's jaw worked as he sought to control his temper with them. "And, Sergeant Byrd, you will see to the disposal of all the rum. You can pour it into the creek."

"I say, but—"

"No buts!"

Someone in the back muttered, "It ain't like it was a white woman."

"Speak up! Louder!" Adam ordered, his eyes on the man.

"Huh?"

"Sir! Do not address me without that, you hear? Now, out with it, soldier—what did you say?"

"It ain't right—it was an Indian . . . sir!"

Adam turned back to Burton. "Do you deny it?"

"I was drunk . . . sir!"

"But do you deny it?"

"She was an Indian, sir!"

"We was just havin' fun, sir, and she was drinkin' the rum," O'Donnell protested. "If you was to lock up Frank, you'd have to lock up more'n him, sir."

"How many of you had her, soldier?" Adam demanded.

"Now, wait. She drank my rum. It ain't—"

Emboldened by the support of the others, Burton grinned. "Well now, Captain, you goin' to lock all of us up—sir?" The hesitation gave a derisive inflection to the word "sir."

It was not a situation easily won, and Adam knew it. There would be little support for courts-martial against those who had merely forced a female with little legal standing, particularly when the Indians themselves had a reputation for promiscuity, and yet he could not let them go unpunished and maintain any order at all. It went against his very nature to do it, but he'd have to mete out some punishment or other. Even a whore ought to choose her custom, he supposed. He exhaled slowly, then looked to Johnson.

"Bring the girl, that she may identify them, and invite her family to watch." Walking to face Francis Burton, he let his eyes travel the length of the man, his contempt evident. "And we will see if your back is half as strong as your mouth. Aye, 'tis twenty-five lashes to every man she picks—and fifteen more for Mr. Burton's insolence. And, Sergeant Byrd, you are to punish any man who fails to meet a roll call with the loss of one month's pay."

"But—" Francis Burton seemed to shrink before his eyes. "Nay, but—"

"Would you rather that I gave you over to her family? Do you think you would fare as well with them?" He watched the man turn apprehensive eyes at Johnson's Mohawks, who stood scowling at him. "Just so," Adam murmured.

He turned on his heel and walked past the now utterly silent company of men. It had been a mistake to think he could lead rangers, he told himself bitterly. Those he'd been given were little better than the animals who inhabited the menagerie at the Tower of London. He was not an officer—he was a keeper holding his men at bay with a whip.

Johnson caught up with him. "Do you report on this, or would you rather I did it? 'Twill not be popular, you know, and I am already known for my stance on the Mohawks."

It was a generous offer, but Adam shook his head. "If I would lead, my actions must stand before my men and my superiors—though I find myself loath to call the knaves I am given men."

The tall buckskin-clad colonel turned for a moment and looked back toward Adam's company. "A rough lot," he agreed, "but I have seen worse. Rogers once told me that it takes a mean and violent man to fight a mean and violent war with Indians. The Abnaki and their allies observe none of our civilized rules, I am afraid."

"Rogers' men take scalps," Adam retorted.

Johnson shrugged at that. "It is something that the Abnaki—or even the Six Nations—understand far better than civilized warfare. Taking a warrior's scalp lessens his chances of eternal reward, you know."

Adam watched him rejoin the two Mohawks, speaking the grunting, guttural language of the people he'd adopted. And as they left the grounds together, he could not help but wonder at the man. It was as though Johnson condoned the savagery and accepted the need for England to counter with the same.

"Captain Hastings?"

He swung around, ready to confront yet another disaster, but the boy who hailed him was obviously only a messenger. He nodded.

"There is a packet of letters for you in the colonel's office, sir. They have been forwarded from Albany." Then, as an afterthought the boy added, "When I was looking for you, I found the letters you had prepared for dispatch, sir, so I have already sent them back to the general. Briggs says he will include them with Loudoun's reports that they may get back to London within the month."

"Thank you."

Adam walked quickly, so quickly that the boy could not match his long strides. After nearly four months of waiting, he'd received his first word from home. His anger with his men forgotten, he felt a surge of almost boyish eagerness to hear of Sarah.

The colonel's aide looked up and grinned, pointing to the canvas-wrapped package. " 'Twould seem all England misses you, Captain—Johnson does not receive so much even when the government is vexed with him."

But Adam wasn't attending. Instead, he tore at the protective canvas, opening it clumsily. There were letters, all right—letters from Sarah, Devin, his mother, his sister, and from his Aunt Trowbridge. There was even a short message from Roland Wicklund.

Sarah's letters he put back, wanting to savor them in the privacy of his crude room. Instead, he broke the seal on Devin's first and read quickly, his eagerness fading as his eyes traveled down the page.

"Bad news, sir?" the boy who'd come for him asked.

He had to read it twice to believe it. Sarah had lost the child, and was naturally despondent, but would surely mend in time. He looked at the date—5 July, 1756—a scant three weeks after he'd left her. He tore into his brother's second letter, this one dated 20 July. Devin had had to return to London, but he thought Sarah was better. "I know you would not credit it, but Papa and she deal well together, consoling each other, she him over his poor legs, he her over her loss. Indeed, but she has lightened his black moods considerably." Then, almost as an afterthought, Devin had added, "You cannot know what hopes Papa had for the child—it has been a bitter blow for the both of them."

"Are you quite all right, sir?"

"Hmmmm? No, not really," Adam answered absently. "No, not at all."

He needed to be alone to read the rest of them. Poor Sarah. How abandoned she must feel to have been left behind because of the child, only to have lost even that. He picked up his packet and walked slowly back to his quarters.

His writing supplies were still on the table where he'd left them, reminding him that he'd written to her just last night. And that letter had already gone, another one that spoke of the babe that no longer existed. A sense of guilt washed over him. If only he'd known . . . if only . . . What? Aye, as Shakespeare had said, there was the rub, for what could he have done about it? He was thousands of miles from home. An ocean separated him from her.

He sank into the crude chair and reached to open her letters. And as he read them one by one, he thought he could not bear it. At first, there was pain in every word, then acceptance, and finally a wistful regret as she spoke of the child that would not be.

Without waiting to read the rest of the packet, he reached for the inkstand and quill. And taking paper, he began to write to his wife.

My dearest Sarah, wife of my heart as much as of my body,

Mere words cannot express the sorrow I feel upon learning of your suffering. You must not grieve for the babe we cannot have, but rather comfort yourself with the thought that we shall have another.

I am decided that when this accursed war is ended, I shall return to you a gentleman farmer, and neither of us shall ever again have to suffer this hell others call a separation. If you like, I shall attempt the purchase of Spender's Hill from Papa or Dev, and you may tend your mama's roses there once again.

In the meantime, I ask that you keep yourself as well as may be for my sake. You are never out of my thoughts and prayers.

As he reread it, his words seemed woefully inadequate to express the grief he shared with her, a grief compounded by the knowledge that he'd been thinking of the child long after it had ceased to be. But he could not write to her of that—not when she'd already had the time to adjust somewhat to the loss.

A knock sounded on his door; then Ned Byrd called in, "The girl has chosen five, sir—do you mean to witness the floggings?"

He knew he had to, that his presence was the best reminder of whence the punishment had come. With an effort, he heaved himself up, leaving his unfinished letter on the table. Unpleasantness had to be dealt with first.

They were assembled at attention when he walked into the open yard. Burton and the others had been stripped bare to the waist, and Burton's hands were tied to an overhead branch. The muscles in his broad back were white in the autumn sun.

Adam took a deep breath, then nodded. Sergeant Byrd read the charge and judgment against the man, and stepped back. The drummer beat the roll as everyone seemed to stop breathing; then the man who'd drawn the short straw lifted the whip. With a quick look to Adam, he struck the first blow. Burton flinched as the lash cut across his back, but Adam forced himself to stare impas-

sively while Byrd counted out the rhythmic beating. By
the end, Burton's back was laced with welts and the blood
oozed, shining a fresh bright red in the sun. He sagged
when his wrists were freed, then was helped to the side,
where the boy O'Donnell stood ready to rub salt into the
stripes.

Mercifully, it did not take long to finish the floggings,
and when it was over, the men were dismissed, parting
silently as Adam passed. Leading these men, Adam reflected grimly, was going to be the challenge of his life.

23

Although the time dragged, Sarah managed to keep
reasonably busy between entertaining the earl and
reading everything she could find on the war, the colonies, and the political situation. If she did naught else in
her husband's absence, she meant to learn enough to become useful to his career. Had not Devin once told her
there was as much politics in His Majesty's army as in
Parliament?

Adam's first two letters arrived in September, and she
could tell by the forced cheerfulness in them that he was
as lonely as she. He wrote of Loudoun's meticulous planning, saying that if naught else was certain, the general
could not be accused of Shirley's faults—whereas that
unfortunate commander had kept few records before his
recall, Loudoun meant to leave volumes. And so Adam
chafed beneath a mound of paperwork, saying he felt
little more than a secretary. Even as she read it, she could
sense his frustration with the lack of any real activity.

Then, in his second letter he mentioned the rangers,

describing them almost contemptuously, yet envying them their freedom in the matter of dress. She had to smile at the way Adam still hated the requisite wig. Some things never changed.

Both times, he commended himself to her, saying that his thoughts were never far from her and their child. He'd not gotten her letter yet, then. As much as she'd been able to put it from her mind, a stab of pain cut through her as she read. By rights, she ought to be fat now, heavy with his babe. But that was over, done, and beyond remedy.

She'd written often, so much so that the earl had chided her for it, saying she'd make the pouch heavy, but he nonetheless franked them for her. Surely one of her letters would reach Adam soon—or perhaps it already had. Her spirits lowered again at the thought of the distance that separated them. He was in another world, one far from her experience, and already she wondered if he would come home a stranger. She had to remind herself that there had been years in the past that she had not seen him at all, but that was before they'd married, before he'd meant quite so much to her. The love she'd had for him then was but a poor weak thing compared to what she felt now.

As she finally laid his letters aside, she became aware of a commotion in the hallway below. Annie tapped on her door, then stepped inside, saying, "Mary says I am to tell you Lady Margaret is come home, mistress."

She was early. They'd not expected her before the morrow. Sarah rose quickly and with some trepidation, for she had never been well-acquainted with Adam's sister. And from what she could remember, she and Margaret Hastings were not at all alike. She wondered briefly if the other girl would consider her an interloper.

She pinched her cheeks and smoothed errant strands of hair back from her face, then adjusted her skirts over her full petticoats before she went down. Black, she decided for at least the hundredth time as she passed her mirror, did not particularly become her. She paused at the top of the steps before going down.

Willie and two others struggled with trunks as Lady

Emma and the earl came out to greet their only daughter. The girl stood back almost shyly, whilst the young man with her bowed over her mother's hand. She'd brought Henry Chatwick to the Park.

He was the first to look up, and a warm smile lit his face. He was not handsome—his wig overshadowed a thin face, giving him the appearance of having recovered from an illness. But his clothes were of the first style, bespeaking wealth. He moved to the bottom of the stairs.

"Venus descending," he murmured, sweeping off his exaggerated ramillie in a grand gesture.

It was not the sort of thing to endear her to her only sister-in-law. Margaret's face froze into the coldest smile Sarah had ever seen.

" 'Tis Adam's wife," she told him shortly. "There was nowhere else for her to go."

"Come on, gel! You will recall Meg, no doubt—aye, and 'tis young Chatwick also." The old man beckoned her down, turning back to Margaret's fiancé. "Gel's been with us since m' son left, and very good thing she is—keeps an old man tolerably occupied at whist."

Henry Chatwick bowed over her hand, kissing her fingers. "Mrs. Hastings."

"Sir."

"Come, Meg, give the gel a kiss," the earl urged his daughter. " 'Tis the only sister you are like to have—unless Chatwick's got some."

"Aye, there are two, but neither can compare to this lady."

"You are too kind," Sarah murmured, removing her hand.

"La, but how you have surprised us, dearest Meg—I vow Sarah and I had planned a better welcome." The countess's brow furrowed. "Did I mistake dear Liza's letter? 'Twas tomorrow you were expected."

"The roads were better than usual, ma'am, and I saw no need to spend another night on the road," Chatwick answered. "Besides, Margaret's abigail does not travel well—poor thing suffered so much that I decided to get it over with."

"Well, you are always welcome, of course." She eyed

the trunks that had accumulated in the hall. "Never say that Liza has ordered your trousseau," she said with dismay. "Oh, but, dearest, I'd hoped to take you to London for that."

"Emma . . ." the earl said warningly.

"Really, Charles, but she cannot be married with nothing, and—"

"Nothing!" he exploded. "What the devil do you call this?" Then, recalling the presence of Chatwick, he spoke more calmly. "Dash it, Em, but don't be a-spendin' the blunt until you know what she will require."

The girl's face fell; then she turned to her mother, choosing to appeal to her instead. "Really, Mama, but you cannot know what is needed to be fashionable until you have been away from here. Aunt Liza said I was the veriest dowd ere she took me in tow. You behold but what a Bath miss must have, and that does not take into account what—"

"Nay! Nigh to a thousand pounds I spent on your come-out, missy! If you was a dowd, 'twas not the clothes! You had the finest as them London modistes could provide, and don't you forget it! Aye, and a hundred pounds on flowers alone! I paid for gewgaws as I never saw! Aye, fifty pounds for jeweled shoes you did not wear—you recall that, missy?"

The girl's face reddened in embarrassment. "Papa, please—Chatwick is not used—"

"Nay, I'll not be silenced in m' own house! Look to Sarah here—she ain't a-wastin' a man's money on what she don't need."

It was the coffin nail in any friendship that might have grown between them. Lady Margaret's chin quivered dangerously, and rather than defy her father openly, she chose to attack Sarah.

"But then, she had naught when she came here, did she? Aye, she was but an impecunious baron's daughter, after all, and no doubt counts herself fortunate to have discovered my brother."

"Yes, I do," Sarah responded quickly. "And as I am in mourning for my father still, my needs are few." She turned to the earl, telling him fairly, "Had I had a proper wedding, sir, no doubt I should have required more."

He stared, then relented slightly. "Well, I should expect to do the proper, of course, but I ain't paying for what she don't plan to wear. You hear that, Em? You watch what you are a-spending! Now, Chatwick, d' you join me for a brandy whilst they sort this out?" He leaned toward the young man. "There is a small matter concerning the settlements. My solicitor sent 'em to me, but I ain't decided on a point or two."

"You have not kissed Sarah yet," Lady Emma reminded her daughter after they left. "Come, she has been eager for your company."

"I cannot think why," the girl muttered, dutifully bussing Sarah's cheek with the enthusiasm she'd reserve for a stick. "She seems to have Papa's, after all."

In the weeks that followed, Sarah's attempts to befriend Adam's sister were rebuffed more often than not. Once Chatwick left, the girl retreated into a meekness before her parents that changed to sullenness when she and Sarah were alone. And when Sarah politely inquired of Margaret's fiancé once, she was roundly accused of wishing to steal him, "for you have quite taken over Mama and Papa from me—is that not enough?" After that, Sarah left her alone, choosing to retreat into the earl's bookroom whilst Lady Emma planned her daughter's extravagant wedding. And there she either read or kept the old man company.

"Been thinkin'," the earl announced over the card table one afternoon. "Em is wishful of taking Meg to town—says the gel's got to have a London modiste make her wedding dress—Craven ain't good enough."

"I am certain she wishes to appear proper before Mr. Chatwick's family, sir," Sarah murmured noncommittally.

"Aye. And I'd not have 'em thinking I am clutch-fisted neither, but I ain't paying for that as she don't need, don't you see? Em gets there, and she don't *think!* She'll discover something one place and order up a dozen of 'em, then two days later like something better elsewhere, and

the devil of it is that she ain't above getting more! Put
my foot down the last time—told her she wasn't going to
town again." He sighed and shook his head, muttering,
"So now I get the demned bills from the tradesmen
here."

"Perhaps Lord Audley—"

"Audley ain't got the time! He ain't' even got the time
to come home—we've not seen him since you was sick!
And since it looks like Newcastle's stumbling, I don't
fault him for it. Pitt is where the future is—and he's dan-
gling attendance on him much of the time, or so he writes
t' me—don't know what he says t' you."

Not very much, she thought to herself. It was odd how
Devin had come home when she'd lost the babe, then all
but disappeared. His letters were cordial enough, and he
was conscientious in his duty as he saw it. Adam had
asked him to see to her, so he wrote each fortnight, inquiring as to whether she was in need of anything. And
occasionally he passed on some news of the war or a
particular debate in Parliament. Sometimes when she answered, she'd request a book, but nothing more. He'd
always responded promptly, sending anything she asked,
and once he'd even included an exquisite ivory-handled
India fan.

"He does not say much to me," she admitted, "but
then, he has little reason to bother with me, after all."

"Aye." His fingers tapped the table for a moment, as
though he were reluctant to broach something to her.
Then he met her eyes defensively. "Guess I got to let
'em go, what with the wedding coming, but they ain't a-
going alone."

"Well, there is Mr. Chatwick."

"Damme if you ain't foolish sometimes, Sarah! Nay,
but I ain't sending him with them—'twould be like setting
the cat in a barn full of mice. You ain't seen what he got
of me in the way of settlements—fellow'd not cavil at
spending my blunt, I can tell you. 'Tis you as has to go."

"Me?" Even as she said it, she shook her head. "I
have never visited a modiste in my life, sir, and I should
not know how to go on. I'd not know whether the cost
was cheap or dear at London prices."

"Damme, but you are a female, ain't you? And you can ask Dev—daresay he's bought a gown or two. Stands to reason he has—the high flyers expect it, don't you know?" Then, realizing what he'd said, he coughed apologetically. "Guess I ought to wrap it up cleaner than that, but you ain't a total innocent, after all."

"No."

"That's what I like about you, gel—you don't dissemble! Oh, I daresay we've argued a bit now and again, but a man can speak his mind to you. Adam wasn't the slow-top I thought him when he brought you here."

A smile quivered at the corners of her mouth. "Spanish gold, sir—you think to turn me up sweet enough to go with kind words."

"Nay—mean everything I say. Don't think I ain't watched you, neither. Ain't empty-headed like my Meg—I'd like to see her pore over the paper like you." His voice lowered, coaxing her. "I cannot make the trip, Sarah—and if I could, they'd be impatient waitin' for me t' take the steps. Besides, I don't know what the gels is wearing these days."

"I do not believe that Lady Margaret would welcome my interference, sir," she admitted honestly.

"Gel's jealous—envies you your looks. Don't think I ain't seen it, 'cause I have. Aye, the first time Chatwick took his hat off to you, it was done betwixt you."

"No, my lord—I think she envies me your company."

"Eh? The devil she does! Me and her don't deal any more'n me and Adam. Gel's got no tongue—and no brains neither. 'Tis a pity she did not get Emma's face at least, but she didn't."

"Perhaps if you did not bullock her so—"

"Bullock you, and it don't make you dumb," he countered. "Just hope my fortune keeps Chatwick blind until the deed is done." He threw down his unplayed hand and leaned back to watch her. "But you ain't answering me—do you go or not?"

"I'd rather not, sir."

"Damn!" His face reddened and his temper rose. "Don't ask you for much, do I?" Then, perceiving that 'twas the wrong tack to take with her, he tried appealing to her boredom. "Great deal to do there—get Dev to take you about, don't you know?"

"I am still in mourning, my lord."

"Buy yourself some gowns, then. Damme if I won't pay for 'em."

"I thought you wished me to save your money rather than spend it," she reminded him.

"Buy you two or three—keep Em from beggarin' me with two dozen! Besides, I'd take it as a favor done to me if you was to go. It ain't no life for a young woman sitting here with me. Get Dev to show you Lunnon, discover the bookstores, meet them as can help your husband."

She truly did not want to go, but she was not entirely sure why. That Lady Margaret did not like her was something she accepted. And certainly she was as eager for new gowns as most females. But the last time she'd been to London, she'd gone with Adam.

"A comely female as has brains can advance a man's career, Sarah. When Adam comes home, you could know them as has the appointments. Let Dev guide you—be happy to do it. Young female still in mourning for her papa, husband's gone to fight in the war—bound to make Pitt sympathetic to you."

This time the smile broadened into a grin. "Just which is it that I am to do, sir—restrain your wife or flirt with Mr. Pitt?"

"Well, if you was to do one, you'd be useful to me, and if you could manage the other, you'd be a gem in your husband's crown."

"I think I have been bamboozled, sir."

"But you'll go—don't have to stay long, you know. When Em and Meg comes home, you come also."

"All right."

"Give you a hundred pounds for the service."

"No. Lord Audley banks my allowance from Adam. I shall merely apply to use some of it."

"You ain't spent it?"

"Why should I? As I have said before, one black gown, my lord, is very much like another." Her eyes warmed mischievously. "Besides, I am saving it for *my* visit to

the modiste come March, you know. I have hopes that
my husband, when he sees me, will be utterly smitten all
over again.''

"Fool if he wasn't,'' he murmured. "But you ain't got
to worry on that head.'' He half-turned, twisting toward
his desk. "Get me m' box, will you? If you are going to
Lunnon, I'd have you get Emma something from me for
Christmas. There ain't nothing around here as I'd give
her, you know—if there was, she'd already have it. Besides, do you good to make the rounds of the shops—it
ain't right for me to keep a young female dancing attendance on an old man.'' He picked up the scattered cards,
stacking them, then cut them for another shuffle. " 'Tis
settled, then. You set Mary and Annie to packing for you
so's you can leave afore the end of the week. I don't like
for females to be on the road when the weather gets
bad, you know.''

"And what will you do until we return?'' she asked,
reaching for the cards he dealt her.

"Wait for you to come back. 'Tis the lot of the old,
my dear: we wait for everything—e'en death.''

But even as she examined the pasteboards, she felt a
sense of unease. As much as she'd hated coming there,
she discovered now that she didn't want to leave the Park
until Adam returned for her.

24

It was late when Lord Audley returned to his house,
terribly tired and slightly foxed. For well over a week
he'd been embroiled in negotiations with his fellow
Whigs, and the process had been trying. Newcastle was

shaky—his margin of support was eroding almost daily—and yet King George's obstinate dislike of William Pitt stood in the way of a new government.

Well, like him or not, the old man would have to bow to public opinion sooner or later and ask Pitt to form the government, or so Devin thought. The strategy that had emerged after much argument was to launch a barrage of attacks on the war effort, charging that it was too little too late. And as undersecretary to the paymaster of the forces, Devin was to speak out in Lords. Aye, Newcastle would have to bend or break. But it was a chancy maneuver, for what if the king looked to the opposition instead?

The house appeared dark and still as the watchman called out the hour behind him. "One of the clock and all's well." Only one? The way his body felt, he was surprised.

Letting himself in, he stood for a time staring up the tall staircase at the dimly lit hall above. No doubt his mother and Meg and Sarah had long been abed, exhausted from yet another round of frenetic shopping. Already the lower footmen had been complaining of the pile of boxes that overflowed the storage closet. The surprising thing to him was that so few of them belonged to Sarah.

Loosening his cravat and shrugging out of his coat, he wondered how long they meant to stay. Not much longer, he hoped, for Sarah continued to cut up his peace. He'd left the Park to avoid her, after all, only to have his mother bring her to town, tempting him again with what he could not have. And he resented her presence in London, for in his efforts to avoid her, he'd become nearly an exile from his own house. Over breakfast, if he could discover her alone, he meant to ask his mother quite pointedly how long they meant to stay.

He had one foot on the steps when he noted the slim slice of light beneath his library door. A servant had failed to douse the lamp, he supposed wearily, turning back. If he'd not feared burning up in his bed, he'd have gone on up, but poor Addington had perished in just such a way the year before. Mentally vowing to punish the miscreant, he threw his coat over his shoulder and groped his way back down the shadowed hall.

He'd scarce opened the door when he saw Sarah, her head bent so low over his desk that her rich auburn hair touched the polished mahogany, one deep, dark red against another. Apparently she'd once been to bed, for she was in a green silk wrapper, the white cotton of her nightrail peeping out at neck and sleeve, and her long hair was brushed out until it rippled over her shoulders and back, reflecting the light from the candelabrum on the desk. He stood transfixed, watching her as she wrote, thinking that he ought not to disturb her, that he ought to go on up. Her pen scratched over the vellum, pausing from time to time whilst she thought. And then she would dip it again and continue on.

Reason told him to leave, but this time the draw was too great. Perhaps 'twas the excess of brandy he'd consumed, but some small part of his mind insisted that he stay. Thus, he waited for her to finish her task before he spoke, watching her, thinking that she seemed particularly lovely this night.

The candlelight left much of the room in near-darkness, illuminating only the girl and the paper on which she wrote, haloing her face and hair. The stillness was broken only by his own pulse in his ears and the sound of the quill crossing the page. His mouth was suddenly far too dry. To break the spell, he forced himself to move forward.

She felt rather than heard his presence, and turned around to see him in the door. A rueful smile turned one corner of her mouth down.

"Alas, but I am caught, my lord."

"You might as well finish the task." Discovered, he left the door ajar and crossed the room, his coat still over his shoulder. "But you ought to be abed, you know. You'll scarce be fit company for Mama and Meg when they set out to cheer the linen drapers."

"I know, but I could not sleep." She sighed heavily and turned back to the paper on the desk, blotting it carefully to dry the ink before she inserted it into the envelope. "It seems so long since I have heard from Adam that I cannot help worrying, you know. I write and write to him, hoping that he will find the time to answer, and yet there have been so few letters in return. It has been nigh two months and no word . . .'' Her voice trailed off; then she caught herself. ''Well, I daresay he has things of greater import than me on his mind, don't you think?''

''I think the mail pouches are filled with military dispatches these days, so perhaps with all the bad news, there has not been room for anything else.''

That ought to have comforted her, but it did not. She pushed away from the desk impatiently, rising to pace before the embers of a dying fire. ''And perhaps he is unwell—or hurt somewhere. 'Tis the lack of knowing that tears at me, Devin.''

''Aye. You do not fear alone, Sarah, but there's naught to do except put it from our minds.'' Again reason told him to say something polite and withdraw, but he could not. Instead, he walked to face her. ''You must not dwell on the uncertainty.''

''I cannot help it!'' she cried out desperately. ''Sometimes I think my letters to him and his to me must wash overboard at sea.'' She looked up at him, her amber eyes deeply troubled. ''You have not heard from him either, have you?''

''Once.''

''But not since he must have heard about the babe.''

''Nay.''

''My lord, it has been nigh five months since he left. Surely in that time—''

'' 'Tis a war, Sarah,'' he reminded her gently. ''And Loudoun has moved to winter quarters in Halifax, so letters may have gone astray.''

''He isn't with Loudoun! Do you not understand? He is not with Loudoun! And we cannot know if he is dead— or worse! You told me he wasn't with the general!'' She spun around to stare into the coals that glowed and faded in the dim light. ''I would he had not done it, my lord.''

''Do you think you are alone in your fears, Sarah?'' he asked her gently. ''You are not, you know.''

''Sometimes I think I must be the only one to miss

him, that your mother and Meg are too busy choosing whether 'tis the rose or the lavender gown that they spare not a thought for him.''

"Poor Sarah—they try you, do they not?'' he murmured sympathetically.

"They do not seem to care that he is gone, my lord.''

Clearly she was overset, and whatever she'd been writing had only made it worse. Not knowing what else to say, he threw his coat into a chair and moved to the brandy decanter, reaching for two glasses. "Well, Meg is caught up in her own happiness, you know, and Mama has always denied as much unpleasantness as she can. For her, Meg's betrothal is a blessing in more ways than one. And you cannot wholly fault Meg, for she and everyone else expected her to fail. 'Tis her one success, my dear.''

Not wanting him to see her opinion of his sister, she picked up the poker and jabbed savagely at the charred logs, stirring them until the coals beneath them brightened and a small valiant flame once again licked between them. She sensed that he'd come up behind her, but she did not turn around.

"I wish that I were a man—I'd have gone also, then.''

" 'Twould be a pity if you were, Sarah.'' He stepped in front of her and held out a glass. "Have a drop of brandy, my dear—'twill help you sleep, I promise you. And on the morrow, matters may seem better.'' When she did not take it, he coaxed, "Come—'twill ease your mind for a time at least.''

She hesitated, wary now of his presence. "I am not at all certain 'tis proper, and—''

"Who's to know but you and me?'' he said softly, handing her a glass.

"If Meg knew, she'd surely write to your father that I had been disporting myself in my wrapper, drinking with abandon in the bookroom,'' she reminded him.

"And do you think he'd believe her?''

"No, but—''

"But she dislikes you,'' he finished for her.

She nodded. "Your pardon, my lord, but I should not have said that.''

"Do you not know there is no need to dissemble with me, Sarah?"

She did not answer, choosing instead to take a small sip of the brandy, holding it in her mouth before slowly swallowing it. This time, she knew better than to gulp. And even at that, it was hot all the way down to her stomach.

"You must remember that Meg has spent her life in terror of Papa," he mused aloud, "and I think it chagrins her to see that you do not fear him in the least."

"I do not know what it is, and I do not dwell on her dislike of me, my lord." Her eyes met his over the rim of her glass as she took another sip. "I am very much more concerned about my husband's safety than whether or not she discovers a dress to match her eyes."

"She envies you, you know," he murmured, drinking deeply. "She thinks herself plain."

She sat at that. "Well, she need not envy me—Chatwick is here and Adam is God knows where," Sarah retorted. "Besides, I have not the least claim to beauty or fashion."

Cocking his head sideways, he appeared to consider her, then shook his head as he dropped into the chair opposite. "You really do not think so?"

"No."

"Well, your mirror ought to tell you a different tale, Sarah."

She made a face at him. "My mirror tells me, sir, that my hair is neither red nor brown, my nose is far too long and covered with freckles, and my chin too sharp for beauty. And there you have it, I fear," she added, as though she dared him to dispute her observations. "Furthermore, I am not blond, which puts me sadly out of fashion."

"Beauty, thou are blind to thyself."

"No." A slow smile curved her lips and warmed those lovely eyes of hers. " 'Tis Adam who is blind, my lord, for he loves me as I am." Then, recalling her letter, she lifted her drink in the direction of the desk. "I'd meant to be done earlier, that it could have been posted, but we were late getting home from the milliner's."

"Give it over to me, and I'll frank it for you—or leave it there and I'll have Mr. Stone send it out over my name tomorrow."

"Thank you." She finished her brandy and set the glass on the polished mahogany side table. "I suppose I must go up, for your mama has a list of linen drapers, mantua makers, and glovers to be visited today. The shoemakers," she added tiredly, "are for the day after. And I know not why your papa sent me, as I have not persuaded anyone to economy yet." She rose, facing him. "Good night, my lord."

"Don't go—I'm not quite done with mine." Even as he said it, he leaned over to reach for her empty glass. "Share another with me, Sarah—I find myself too tired to sleep."

She shook her head, then relented as she read the appeal in his eyes. It was difficult to refuse him, particularly since it seemed to her that he was the only other person in London to share her concern. And he appeared so terribly, terribly fatigued that she could not help feeling sorry for him. It seemed he'd changed so much in the months past, revealing himself to be far more than the shallow lecher she'd refused. Perhaps the war had sobered him as much as it had her.

"All right, but not too much," she decided finally, sinking back down into her chair. "You work far too hard, I think. 'Tis you who should be abed."

"If I were, my mind should be full of what I mean to say in Lords tomorrow. I am chosen to speak where Pitt cannot, and I mean to fire a volley that will arm the opposition against us as well as embarrass the duke."

"Newcastle?"

"Aye—his prosecution of the war is a timid one, and whilst he half-arms, half-supplies, and half-delays, the French take more and more everywhere."

" 'Tis a risk, isn't it—such a speech, I mean?"

He looked up, surprised that she would realize that. "Aye, for if I say too much and Newcastle does not survive the next vote, the king may well ask a Tory rather than Pitt."

"But the Tories are even less likely to bring the weight of England against the French!"

"Precisely."

"And King George cannot be brought to see that? I mean, with the Germans against the French, one would think that he would wish us to act as decisively as they. Indeed, but I read the article by Mr. Robinson before he was given his position, and if he can be believed, the king's paramount consideration would seem to be how policy affects Germany rather than England!"

He stared in fascination for a moment, then nodded. "And if a green girl from the country can see the matter so plainly, one has to wonder what the devil is the matter with the government."

"Has no one made the point with the king?"

"Believe me, but there are many as have tried, my dear," he answered dryly. "The fact remains that he does not like Pitt and will not see that the prosecution of the war lies elsewhere rather than on the Continent."

"America and India." She sipped more brandy, warming to the subject. "If we could best them where they are not so entrenched, they would either have to divide their resources or choose to lose all but their continental possessions."

"And you agree with Pitt, then?"

"Of course I do! For one thing, it disturbs me to read that we are manufacturing Pennsylvania rifles for use on the Continent, whilst our troops in America are given the weapons that we ourselves consider less satisfactory. We ought to be providing the best where 'twill do the most good."

"Where heard you this?"

"I read it."

" 'Twould seem you have read a great deal about the war."

"Well, I am decided that if my husband truly wishes to be a soldier for his life, then I ought to be conversant enough to help him, don't you think? After all, 'twas you who said that there was as much politics in the army as in the government."

"Did I say that? Well, 'tis true, of course, but I cannot recall when you would have heard it."

"You told your father when he objected to Adam's being attached to Loudoun. You said 'twas a very good thing, for the general was in a political position to help him." She drew her knees up beneath her wrapper and partook of more of her brandy. "And there is naught else for me to do, is there? One cannot be forever spending money on clothes and gewgaws that one cannot wear, after all."

"I would that Robinson and Newcastle could hear you, my dear, for they are not as proof to a pretty face as Pitt."

"Alas, but I doubt they should listen to me," she reminded him, smiling. "You forget His Majesty's review of his troops. To them, I should but be a silly peagoose who knew not enough to stay home when she was ill." She drained her glass and put it down again.

"Still . . ." He stretched toward his desk to take one of the unused quills from the stand. Poking it into his powdered wig, he scratched his head. "Wigs are a nuisance," he muttered. "Now . . . where was I?"

"If you were Adam, you'd already have that off."

One of his black eyebrows lifted. "A gentleman, my dear, endures much in the name of fashion. I should be thought a veritable hayseed without it."

"Ah, but you are at home now, sir. At home, I should think a man ought to be forgiven his comfort." The reflected firelight danced mischievously in her amber eyes. "I know that if I were a man, I should not choose to wear one here."

"Afore God, but I think you are right." He reached up to lift the peruke from his head, exposing his own dark hair, which was sadly plastered from the weight of it. "There. Now that I look a horrid fright, you have my leave to laugh. Damned thing itches like the devil, you know."

Under ordinary circumstances she would never have thought to touch him at all, but perhaps it was the effect of the brandy on a near-empty stomach. She rose and moved behind him. "Adam said it was an invention of the devil—he was certain of it. Indeed, but he was forever having me do this." To demonstrate, she reached her hands into his thick dark hair, rubbing through it, combing the flecks of powder from it. Her fingertips massaged his itching scalp, easing it, then moved to his temples. Applying gentle pressure, she worked toward the back of his head. He closed his eyes, feeling first the relief, then the easing of tension from his tired body. "Lean forward," she ordered as her fingers moved toward his neck. "You work far too hard, my lord," she murmured, working at the tight muscles in his neck.

It felt good, so good, that for a moment he dared to forget about Pitt and Newcastle and the king—so good that he dared to forget she was Adam's wife. The brandy, the popping embers, the soft candlelight, the silence—all seemed to suspend the moment in his mind as he savored her touch on the bare skin of his neck. And as the fatigue receded, it was replaced by an acute awareness of the woman behind him.

His hair was thick where it fell over her hands, but unlike Adam's, it appeared almost black in the dim light. His skin, like Adam's, was warm and alive to the touch. Ever so briefly, she dropped her hands lower to move over his cambric-covered shoulders, and closed her eyes, dreaming that somehow she touched her husband once again, and a yearning born of the long separation washed over her.

"Sarah . . . Sarah . . ." he murmured ever so softly, "where have you been all of my life?"

It was enough to break the spell. Exhaling sharply, she drew back as though she'd been burned, and her face flamed from her thoughts. She moved away quickly, speaking a trifle tartly to hide her embarrassment.

" 'Twas Spender's Hill, my lord."

Disappointed, he felt the awkwardness that had sprung between them, knowing that the intimacy had passed. He straightened his shoulders and managed a rueful smile.

" 'Tis a wonder that Adam could have left."

"He never led me to believe that he was anything but a soldier, you know," she answered slowly. "And I have tried very hard to understand his duty, believe me. But," she added, recovering her composure, "I am in no worse case than other soldiers' wives, or so I must tell myself."

"No." Impulsively he refilled her empty glass, knowing that he ought not to, and held it out to her. "If you would aid the war effort, you ought to get to know Pitt, my dear. He'd find you quite useful, I think."

"Me? Coming it too strong, my lord—I am but a green country girl, after all." Nonetheless, she took the glass.

"Sit down, my dear, and let me welcome you to the world of policy and politics. Between us, we just might be able to do something about this war."

"I fail to see . . ." She sank into the chair and sipped deeply of the brandy, savoring the warm, secure feeling it gave her.

"I need a hostess, Sarah—someone who can appear guileless and yet plant useful ideas in the minds of my fellows, someone with an understanding of what must be done." When she said nothing, but merely stared at him over the rim of her glass, he plunged ahead. "Sarah, if you've a mind to do it, you can make a difference for Pitt."

It was a heady thought—and one which she dismissed quickly. "As I am in mourning until March, Devin, I fail to see how I could do very much."

"Oh, there could be no routs or balls or overt social engagements, of course, but that's not to say that you cannot preside over my table." Even as he watched her, he warmed to the task of convincing her. "You are a pretty woman, Sarah—no, do not deny it. I merely intend to invite my fellow Whigs, particularly those whose support wavers, to dine with us. You will ply them with food and plant ideas, my dear."

"My ideas or yours?" she asked suspiciously.

"Ours. I'd not ask you to say anything you do not believe."

"I . . ."

He leaned closer, his eyes meeting hers steadily, his voice earnest. "Think, Sarah. Would you have the money and supplies go to North America, where Adam fights— or would you have it diverted to the Continent? Would you bring this accursed war to a quick end?"

"You know the answers."

"Then join me in the effort, Sarah."

"Your mother . . . Meg . . ."

"Do you truly wish to return to the Park—to watch my sister and my mother plot and plan a wedding?"

"No, but your papa—"

"Leave Papa to me, Sarah. He understands politics far better than you might suppose."

"Politics," she murmured, slurring the word slightly. "But I am too foxed to decide just now, I think. I shall consider it in the morning." Yawning widely, she pushed her heavy hair back from her face. "Indeed, but I ought to retire whilst I can still take the stairs."

"Nonsense. A few brandies are scarce the end of an evening, Sarah."

"Then I plead fatigue. Perhaps 'tis the combination of the two that makes me dizzy, sir."

"I'd still have your company, my dear."

"You must surely be the only one. Even my husband cannot be brought to write to me, can he? Four months and two letters," she murmured, returning to the beginning of their conversation. "Tell me . . ." She leaned forward, resting her chin on her hand. ". . . do you think a man can forget a woman in five months?"

"You *are* dizzy, Sarah, if you think a man could forget you," he answered quietly. "No doubt his letters are lost amongst the dispatches."

"Tell me, my lord"—her amber eyes were fixed on his face now—"if you were wed, would you not write your wife?"

"If you were my wife, Sarah, I should write every day."

"No, you would not, but 'tis what you think I would hear." She yawned sleepily again, then forced herself to rise unsteadily. "Unless you are wishful of throwing a shawl over me, I'd best seek my bed. I suspect I shall have a devil of a head as it is, for I do not think I was meant to drink spirits at all."

He watched her weave unsteadily from the room, thinking he ought to help her up, but then he did not want to risk waking his mother or Meg. Besides, he didn't wish to retire—not yet. He poured himself yet another brandy and stared into the glowing coals.

He was a fool and he knew it. He'd set himself on a course for hell. He closed his eyes and remembered the feel of her hands in his hair, of her fingers as they moved along the tense muscles in his neck. And he could smell again the clean, fresh scent of lavender water. For a moment he'd thought she was as aware of him as he had been of her, but then it had passed.

But she was his brother's wife. And yet it was as though he'd been led to lie down beside the water and bidden not to drink. And what if Adam did not come home— what then? He still could not have her—'twas forbidden to take one's brother's wife.

He lurched to his feet, suddenly angry at Adam. Damn him! He had had no right to wed her and leave her! He had had no right to expect Devin to look and not want! His eyes caught sight of the letter she'd written to his brother, and he groped his way to his desk. For a time he sat there staring at her letter, seeing her again as she wrote it, her hair brushing low over the mahogany wood. Then his fingers tore open the envelope. He read it, turning the page toward the gutting candles, seeing her love and anguish bared there, words reduced to mere ink on paper, and yet still unbearably poignant.

He couldn't stand it. He stood unsteadily to fling the envelope into the hot coals, where it slowly curled into ashes. Then he refolded her letter and slipped it beneath the false bottom of the top drawer.

And once again he stumbled to his feet, feeling an impotent fury with the both of them. Damn Adam! Damn her! They had not the right to cut up his peace so! If he were any kind of a man at all, he'd send her packing back to the Park, and be done with her. And yet as surely as he breathed, he knew he was too much the fool to do it.

25

It was so cold that Adam thought they'd surely freeze, and yet they dared not make fires, lest they alert any lingering enemies. It was expected that Montcalm would retire to quarters in Canada, and the rangers were engaged in reconnaissance, particularly in the woods around Fort Edward and up toward Fort Carillon, which the English still called by its Indian name, Ticonderoga. When Montcalm moved, it was hoped that they could harass him all the way to New France.

And after the disastrous year just past, Loudoun considered it imperative that they attempt to learn of Montcalm's plans for the following spring. That meant that small groups of rangers were constantly in the field with orders to send back any prisoners for interrogation.

Adam's command of the French language, gained from an emigrant tutor, had brought him notice from William Johnson and Robert Rogers, both of whom insisted that since he spoke it fluently, he was an invaluable intelligence asset. And so it was that General Abercromby, Loudoun's second in command, had ordered him to take five of his men from Fort Edward up Lake George to Carillon to observe French troop movement. It was presumed that since the weather had turned cold and unpredictable, the Indian allies of the French would soon withdraw to their longhouses, making spying an easier task.

Easier for whom? Adam wondered irritably. Certainly not for those who trudged through the light early snow, carrying canoes on their backs. At least temperatures had not dropped long enough to freeze the lake, rendering the canoes useless. That would come later, and others would be making the trip on snowshoes with poles to test for drifts as Rogers said he'd done the year before.

His breath clouded and clung to the wool scarf he wore pulled over his face. Beside him, the boy O'Donnell complained, "Beggin' yer honor's pardon, but if the Injuns is gone, it don't make no sense that we can't have a fire."

"And if they ain't, your hair'll hang on a scalp pole," Frank Burton retorted.

"I ain't seen an Injun yet."

That was not entirely true, but Adam refrained from reminding them of the village they'd skirted the day before. It had been a close thing, but with the characteristic relief born of survival, they chose to forget that.

They were still a relatively green lot, all of them, himself included. Only Burton had had any experience fighting the Indians at all, and his came from surviving a raiding party in western Pennsylvania, a circumstance that left him with an abiding hatred for the race. Jeremy Cook, on assignment from Lieutenant Colonel Gage, did not care much for Indians either, and took it upon himself to regale the others with recounted atrocities whenever the occasion arose. O'Donnell, on the other hand, tended to view his assignment to the rangers much as a jolly good adventure and nothing more. Ben Dixon, who'd been born of an Iroquois woman and an English trader and educated at Albany, said little to either Burton or Cook, but Adam suspected he resented having all Indians painted with the same ugly brush.

And then there was Thomas Kirk, a quiet Scotsman who had come down from Nova Scotia for the express purpose of earning enough money to purchase a woman's indentures from his uncle. They'd all teased him for his thrift, only to discover that every penny not needed to sustain life was sent home to buy his wife. Beneath that solemn, unsmiling exterior, there existed a man smitten.

"How far to the lake, Captain?" O'Donnell asked suddenly.

Adam squinted up into the glaring sky, figuring the

time, then guessed, "Not more than another two or three miles."

The boy groaned. "And we ain't making above seven or eight of 'em a day."

But Ben Dixon had stopped and raised his hand in warning. As he did so, his canoe slid silently to the snow. His face intent, he inhaled deeply, letting the air out slowly, as though he searched for something. Cook shook his head in disgust, but Adam waited, his own breath drawn in.

"Smoke," Dixon grunted finally.

"Jesus," Burton muttered. "Where?"

It was a credit to Burton that he recognized the half-breed's ability, something that Cook was not inclined to do. The others stood stock-still, waiting as Dixon sniffed the air again, turning slowly as though he could follow a smell so faint none of them could detect it.

"By the water."

"Which side?" Cook asked sarcastically. "And how many do you see camped there? Really, Captain, but—"

"The fire is small. Like us, they fear detection."

"Aw, Captain, 'tis but his breath coming back to him," Cook jeered. "He ain't got no powers, and—"

But Adam's mind was racing ahead. If they'd encountered a *coureur de bois,* or perhaps a couple of them, the information might prove more than useful. But if it were Indians, he wanted to give them a wide berth.

Ben turned to him. "Do you want me to see, sir?"

"Aye."

Despite Cook's grumbling, they made a small camp in the shelter of a wooded hill. Piling the canoes together and heaping them with dead leaves for cover, they scooped out a circle on the ground away from the wind. While they waited, Adam opened his sack and took out his food. It was the same as he'd had the day before and the day before that, but it was beginning to taste better. If anyone had ever told him that he'd be sitting on cold, wet dirt, eating dried venison and berries, clad in oily, smoky buckskin and fur, with at least a week's growth of beard, he'd have disputed it. But he was. Following his lead, the others ate silently.

"What if he don't come back?" O'Donnell asked finally.

"Then we cut back and come up the other side of the lake."

That brought forth a collective moan, for it meant another day, perhaps two, of carrying the deadweight of the canoes.

"And we don't move until nightfall," Adam added.

It seemed like hours before Dixon returned, and when he did, he was breathless from running in the cold and snow. Dropping to the ground amongst them, he tried to collect himself, but by his manner, Adam could see he was excited.

"*Coureurs*—four of 'em," he gasped. " 'Tis Reynaud."

"Reynaud? Naw, he ain't—"

"Are you certain?" Adam cut in, interrupting Cook impatiently.

Ben Dixon nodded, still trying to gain his breath. "Aye, I saw him when he came to my mother's village to speak against the British."

There was no need to ask which Reynaud. Reynaud was Reynaud—called the Fox by allies and enemies alike. Etienne Reynaud, to be precise, and his name struck terror among settlers throughout the Champlain Valley. It was said he had a scalp belt to rival that of an Abnaki chieftain, and when the Iroquois spoke of him in council, it was with the awe reserved for a dreaded adversary. He was a white man whose savagery rivaled that of the Indians he led.

"Gor!" O'Donnell breathed.

"Any Indians with him?" Adam demanded abruptly.

"No, but by the looks of it, Captain, they mean to rendezvous."

"Captain, he cannot know that—'tis but speculation!" Cook protested. "Even if 'tis Reynaud, which I'd be doubtin'."

"Why do you think 'tis a rendezvous, Ben?"

Dixon swallowed, still trying to catch his breath. "He's chosen good portage, sir—bateaux can put in there."

"That don't mean nothing!"

"But you saw no others—other than the four of them?"

"No, sir, but they was looking like they meant to stay awhile." Dixon gulped again. "Got a fence, sir."

A low whistle of appreciation escaped Adam. Abercromby wanted French prisoners, did he? Well, he wondered what the general would think of Reynaud. "We take them, then," he murmured aloud.

They recoiled as though he'd suggested they grasp live snakes bare-handed. Even Ben Dixon stared. But it was his antagonist that put it into words. "Beggin' the captain's pardon, sir, but there ain't but six of us!"

"And four of them!" Adam snapped back.

"But 'tis Reynaud! Even if we was to take him, we'd not get him back, sir," Burton reasoned. "I mean, the longhouses'd empty and the woods'd be thick with savages if we was to try it, don't you know?"

"Pennsylvania's got a scalp bounty on 'im—and they're offerin' a hundred pounds sterling for the bloody bastard," Cook remembered. "Got to be a reason why nobody's collected the money."

"Aye, and there's been none to think of getting any of it," observed Burton dryly.

"Gentlemen, I mean to truss Monsieur Reynaud up like a bird and carry him back to Fort Edward."

"But—"

Only Thomas Kirk seemed inclined to think it could be done, but Adam was adamant. Finally, amid much grumbling, they listened to him outline his plan. And then, with the bright sun reflecting off the snow, they rolled up into their blankets behind the wall of canoes and tried to sleep until night fell.

The moon was but a sliver against the starlit sky, and the air was cold and still as Adam put his lone canoe into the icy water of Lake George. Beneath his blanket lay his musket, fully primed and ready to fire, hopefully not before it was needed. And in his belt, he wore a wicked dagger, while a smaller dirk rested reassuringly against his leg.

The oar cut the cold water like a knife, smoothly, barely rippling, as the canoe glided as quietly as possible up the lake. In the distance, he could see the small glow of a campfire, and he headed straight for it, taking care to remain as long as possible in the open water to avoid the thin sheet of ice that bobbed like broken eggshells along the shore. Then, when he was nearly even with the light, he stared beyond it, hoping that his men were close. A piece of ice shattered like twigs crackling against his canoe.

"Qui êtes-vous?" someone called out.

"C'est Bourget!" he shouted back, pushing at ice that eddied around him. The canoe slid aground, nearly turning over, then righted itself. He stepped ashore to face a French musket. Despite the pounding of his heart, he grinned at the man holding it. *"C'est comme ça que vous saluez un ami, monsieur?"*

In the chill darkness, his eyes traveled over the four men, noting the slight, almost imperceptible inclination of the tallest one's head, a gesture that indicated he was the leader. This then must be Reynaud. Adam brushed the musket barrel aside, murmuring, *"Je ne croyais pas ça de vous, Etienne."*

There was a pregnant silence; then one of the others picked up a burning stick from the fire and carried it forward for light. The tall man took it, staring at Adam with narrowed eyes that glittered eerily with the reflected fire. And for a moment Adam knew a fear as intense as any he'd ever experienced. The hairs at the nape of his neck pricked uncomfortably. Though the man's eyes were as blue as Adam's and his hair a wild blond mane, his face was painted grotesquely, obscuring his natural features. Even his dress betrayed nothing of the civilization from whence he had come, for he wore a heavily ornamented deerskin shirt, leggings and breechclout, and winter moccasins. But it was those cold, merciless eyes that made a man want to cower.

A stocky Frenchman, his face greasy and soot-stained from the small campfire, drew an ugly knife of the sort that William Johnson's Indians carried, the sort that ripped a man's skull bare. Rather than show fear, Adam said nothing.

It was Reynaud who broke the silence. "You are mistaken, Monsieur Bourget," he said shortly.

Thinking it was like the game where one's entire fortune lay on the table, Adam shook his head. *"Mais non, monsieur,* but I would recognize you anywhere." His mind raced for a plausible explanation. "I was with Montcalm."

The tall one's eyebrow lifted. "In Montreal?"

Fearing a trap, Adam guessed differently. *"Non*—at Carillon."

"A member of La Marine perhaps?"

"Non. I carried a message to the general from Governor Vaudreuil."

"Vaudreuil—bah!" Reynaud fairly spat the word as though it were bad food.

Adam shrugged expressively and smiled again. "I was but traveling that way, *monsieur.* You behold one but lately come from France."

The tall one's gaze was contemptuous. "Another bastard come to make your way with furs? Did you believe Vaudreuil's lies also—that you will be rich beyond your dreams, Bourget? If so, you'd best go back to France and leave New France to those of us who were born here. You even speak as a foreigner."

"My birth is of no concern," Adam responded stiffly.

"Non? Every fool here seems to think being a lord's bastard ought to make him somebody." He leaned closer until Adam could see the flash of white teeth. "I know, Bourget—I *know,* for I am one also, the difference being that my noble father abandoned me here." Then, turning his head sharply, he demanded, "You are alone?"

"I lost my companion to the Onandagas."

"Where?"

"In the valley. Warraghiyagey incites them." He used William Johnson's Indian name in hopes it would sound as though he knew what he was saying.

"The Onandagas are women!" Reynaud snorted. "And Warraghiyagey is the greatest squaw of all! He thinks the Six Nations will stand between us, but they will not—they fight no battles they cannot win."

"Tell him either to put away his scalp knife or use it, *monsieur.*"

"Eh?" Turning to his companions, the tall one nodded. "Armand."

The blade flashed, then disappeared into a sheath that hung from Armand's belt, and Adam dared to relax. Reynaud started back to the fire, still carrying the makeshift torch. "I thought perhaps you were English, Bourget," he flung over his shoulder, "but you do not cower sufficiently." Dropping the burning wood back into the small firepit, he muttered, "Warm yourself, then, but do not expect Reynaud to be your nurse. If you had sense, you'd go back to France."

"I thought perhaps if you proved to be French, I'd go with you, *monsieur.*"

That brought another sharp look from Reynaud and then a shake of his head. "Jesù! Another fool, Armand. *Mais non*—discover for yourself another fiefdom, Bourget, for tonight you stand on mine—do you hear? Mine!"

The thought crossed Adam's mind that he was mad. In the distance, a shrill bird call broke through the night. The Frenchmen all listened intently as it was repeated, then Reynaud cupped his hands over his mouth and emitted a high-pitched screech that dwindled to a warble. And once again Adam's skin crawled.

Reynaud sat back on his haunches, apparently satisfied. "Abnaki," he announced tersely. "They leave their longhouses for one last sortie ere the lake freezes." Then, turning pale eyes on Adam, he asked softly, "Would you have sport with the poor devils who dare to settle in my valley?"

Adam shook his head. "I abandoned my furs to the Onandagas. I'd replace them ere I return to Montreal."

The Frenchman looked him up and down again, shaking his head. "Fool!" he spat at him. "You'll be forced into La Marine come spring, for Montcalm means to come again, and this time he will not leave until we have Albany itself. Warraghiyagey's scalp," he boasted, "will grace my belt—as will Wascaugh's. The Six Nations will cower before my Abnaki and their allies." He indicated the glistening lake with a wave of his hand. "Far better

to fight like men than to strain like animals in the bateaux, Bourget.''

"Vaudreuil supplies another invasion?"

"Bah—Vaudreuil! He robs us! But Montcalm will prevail. Come spring, the English forts will fall, and we will
occupy Albany.''

The eerie, piercing sound of another call, closer still,
cut through the night, echoing off the nearly leafless trees.
Reynaud stopped to listen, then answered in kind, as
Adam's blood went cold. When the Fox turned back to
him, his eyes glittered and his voice gloated.

"Until then, we bring an army of Indians, Bourget—
my Abnaki are joined by hundreds come from New
France: Hurons, Ottawas, Chippewa, and Menominees.
By the morrow we shall be four hundred strong! While
Montcalm withdraws safely, we soak this ground with
English blood.''

"And Montcalm knows this?" Adam asked with a lift
to one eyebrow.

Reynaud shrugged. "War is war, Bourget—Montcalm
will ask no questions, I think. So, would you count a
different pelt, do you think?" He lifted his hand toward
a long pole that had been set like a standard, its grisly
collection bearing mute testimony to the suffering he'd
wrought. In the firelight, the waves of what must have
been a woman's glory shimmered.

Unwilling to acknowledge the revulsion he felt, Adam
merely questioned, "You raid south, then?"

"All the way to Pennsylvania," was the grim reply.

"Then I am for Carillon." He eyed the scalp pole
again, forcing himself to grin. "I'd not see French hair
there by mistake.''

"For a moment I thought you were a man." Reynaud
sneered, turning to his companions. "He runs to New
France with Montcalm.''

Adam knew he had to escape, to get away before Burton and the others attempted to take Reynaud. And he
had to get back to Albany to warn William Johnson.
Hopefully, the baronet could get his Mohawks to stand
between their age-old enemies and the settlers.

He stretched his hands toward the fire, warming himself. "We also serve who merely trade. You will remove the English and I will profit." Looking back to where his canoe rested in the mud, he sighed regretfully. "In the meantime, I must eat, and therefore I am for Carillon tonight."

Reynaud's expression never changed. He lifted his shoulders slightly, settling them, then nodded. "So be it, Bourget. You will, of course, give my regards to the general?"

"Would you have me tell him anything?"

"*Non.* The less he knows, the less he will interfere, I think. Armand, give Monsieur Bourget some food for his journey. Carillon lies many leagues over water, and he will have need of it. You'd best keep to the east side, Bourget, else you will encounter my Abnaki," he advised softly. And as he said it, his white teeth flashed eerily in the darkness.

"*Merci.*"

While the Frenchmen watched, Adam eased his canoe back into the cold waters and began paddling northward, praying that somehow he would encounter his men before Reynaud or the Indians discovered them. Once again, the shrill bird cries cut through the night, shattering the stillness, and yet he dared not appear to be trying to escape.

When he was about thirty feet from shore, a musket shot rang out, and he felt the searing pain as it tore into his left shoulder. As he slumped over, he could hear one of the men ask Reynaud, "Would you have me bring him in?"

"*Non.* He will not survive. It is enough that he carries no tales to Montcalm."

"Still the coup—?"

"His scalp? *Mais non,* Armand—I would not separate a Frenchman from his soul."

The canoe drifted shoreward with the lapping waves, oblivious of the crackling ice, until it hit a partially submerged log and capsized, dumping Adam. With the sudden shock of impact as his head went under, he revived somewhat, only to realize that he could not live more than a few minutes in the cold water. His body went numb, and the last thought in his mind was that he would never see Sarah again.

26

He came awake slowly, aware only of the intense cold in his bones and the jarring motion of his body. And then there was the pain that pounded his shoulder almost rhythmically. His other senses returned warily. He smelled the oil and the sweat, and despite the nausea and the pain, he opened an eye. His head was lower than his body and his left arm hung uselessly toward the ground, a numb deadweight.

"Praise the Almighty," he heard Cook say, and the movement stopped abruptly. "I think he's coming round."

It was then that he became aware that he was being carried. Thomas Kirk leaned down until he was almost at eye level with him, and told him, " 'Tis a rare fright ye've given us, Captain Hastings—aye, but O'Donnell'd have it you were dead."

"Well, I didn't think he was breathin' when Burton pulled 'im out," the boy retorted. "Know he wasn't."

"We was comin' in to get you, sir, but Ben said he heard a raidin' party," Burton added apologetically "Had to come back south to avoid 'em—the woods is full of Injuns, Captain, and there's boats of 'em coming down."

"Aye." It was little more than a croak.

Burton unshouldered him, sliding him to the ground, and stood over him, flexing the muscles in his big back. "Didn't have time to rig a carryin' pole, sir. Kirk, get the captain a spot o' rum—aye, and I'd have a bit my-self.''

''Got to get him warm.''

''Aye.''

It was still dark, so much so that it was easier to see a man's breath than the man. Ben Dixon knelt beside Adam and began a careful rubbing of his limbs. ''We couldn't wait for the clothes to dry, sir—wasn't any time, so Burton and Kirk put you into what we had to spare between us.''

''I guess you must've swooned from the water being so cold,'' O'Donnell told him.

'' 'Twas the ball,'' Burton cut in shortly.

''Reynaud must've found you wasn't French,'' Cook muttered. ''The bloody bastard shot you.''

''Nay.'' Adam's hand crept to his throbbing shoulder, discovering a wad of cloth there. ''He didn't care—didn't want me to report to Montcalm.'' He turned his head toward Ben Dixon and groaned as the half-breed finished working along his legs. ''Got to get word to Johnson—cannot wait until spring—they mean to lay waste to the settlements.''

''Now, sir? 'Tis too cold.''

Adam nodded weakly.

Burton gave a low whistle. ''Then it ain't Montcalm as we've got to worry over.'' He lifted Adam by the other shoulder, bracing him, and held the flask to his mouth. ''If this don't warm, a man don't care anyways.''

Adam choked and tried to wipe his mouth. ''How far have we come?'' he asked.

''From Reynaud? 'Bout three miles or so, I'd think.'' The big man laid him back and shook his head. ''Wound's not too bad—didn't hurt anything but flesh, Captain—and the cold water kept the blood slow.''

''Got to keep moving,'' Adam insisted, trying to rise.

''Nay. Ain't nobody comin' after us,'' Cook insisted. ''Heard 'em myself—think you are done.''

Despite the change of clothing, Adam was still cold, and it didn't seem like the rum would warm him. Shaking, he tried to pull the blanket Kirk threw over him closer. Burton gave him another sip. His eyes met the big man's.

"My thanks, Frank—I owe you for this."

"Naw, I'd not let a dog perish like that, Captain," Burton mumbled, ignoring the fact that he'd just carried him on his back for miles. "Besides, I used a limb to hook you, so's it ain't like I risked anything, now, was it?"

"How's the color in his feet?" O'Donnell asked of Ben Dixon. "He ain't going to lose 'em, do you think?"

"Nay."

"We've got to get out of here, got to warn—"

"Ain't going nowhere till we get a litter made—Frank cannot carry you all the way to Albany," Cook pointed out reasonably.

"Reynaud numbers his Indians in the hundreds—not twenty or thirty to a party—says they are come from Canada and the West. Ottawas—"

"Ottawas? Old Pontiac? Reynaud was bamming you!" Cook scoffed. "They ain't—"

"They come," Adam murmured tiredly. "He had no reason to lie to me. Aye, and the Hurons." His face clouded as he tried to think. "Menominees and Chippewa."

"By all the saints!" O'Donnell breathed.

"Save your heathen popism for the frogs!" Kirk snapped. " 'Tis God's grace we are in need of."

"You've got to flee for Fort Johnson—the colonel's got to rally the Mohawks." Adam twisted his head to look down at Ben Dixon, who'd finished rewrapping his feet. "Ben—"

The young man's black hair gleamed in the faint sliver of moonlight. "Aye, sir?"

"Can you make it to Fort Johnson?"

"Fort Edward," Burton protested. "For Johnson's too far. I say we alert the troops there first—Campbell's got an army there."

"Aye, but Johnson needs to rally the Mohawks also. Ben?"

"Aye, sir."

"Kirk—"

"Captain?"

"I'd have you and Cook set out for William Henry whilst 'tis still dark—tell them Reynaud raids. And, O'Donnell, you and Burton are to seek out Rogers—his men are coming upriver. I'd warn them."

They looked at one another as his meaning sank in; then O'Donnell blurted out, "Beggin' your honor's honor, sir, but we ain't leaving you."

"Burton—"

"Nay." The big man flashed a grin. "The next bastard might order a hundred lashes—sir. Me'n you and the Irishman'll float down together—sir. Me, I want to see Rogers' face when you tell 'im you met with Reynaud and lived t' tell the tale." Burton looked the others over. "Well, what the devil keeps you? Go on, you shiftless Iroquois—'tis for Fort Johnson you are bound! Aye, and tell Sir William if he don't move, his fancy house'll be ashes, you hear? And don't give him any peace until 'tis done."

"Warraghiyagey will know."

A high-pitched screech rose in terror, then was cut short, leaving a painful stillness in its wake. O'Donnell crossed himself furtively, then turned away. "Poor devil," Cook muttered under his breath. Ben Dixon drew his knife and crouched, listening. Apparently satisfied, he turned back, intoning words in his mother's tongue; then he shouldered his canoe and bedroll and moved noiselessly toward the river below the lake.

"The savage cursed ye or blessed ye, I'd say," Kirk decided.

"Else 'tis some sort of charm," Burton countered. "But I ain't disputing it—not when I'd keep my hair." He looked down at Adam. "We got to go, Captain—sir."

"Aye."

The next several days were a blur in Adam's memory. All he knew was that the big man carried him, keeping to the river's edge until it was judged they were far enough south not to meet any stragglers come to join Reynaud's savage army. At some point, Kirk and Cook left them to go on ahead, but from time to time O'Donnell's voice penetrated his consciousness. And then they were on the water, he recalled, for the pounding stopped, replaced by a rocking. He heard shouts and knew that someone loaded and primed a musket, but he was too hot to care.

When he awakened the last time, it was in another world. His first sense of it was the thick bearskin that covered him; his second was the smell. Forcing his eyes open, he stared up into the immense bared pendulous breasts of an old woman who sat cross-legged and silent over him. Her stomach hung over a calico breechclout that lay between two hamlike thighs. Seeing he roused, she leaned closer, her straight gray-streaked hair brushing across his face. Her breath smelled of rotten teeth, her body of the bear grease that mingled with her sweat. A callused hand felt his brow, then moved to his shoulder. She half-turned to grunt something to someone he could not see.

A younger woman, her body covered incongruously in a frilled calico shirt that came not quite to her knees, moved closer and knelt at his other side. All of Cook's stories of what squaws did to captives crowded his mind at once, but he knew enough not to betray fear. The girl pulled the bearskin away, baring his naked body, then reached for a pot that appeared to contain cooked weeds. Murmuring something unintelligible, she dipped her hands into the mess and smeared it across his shoulder. The old woman nodded her approval.

The unbearable heat and the nightmares were gone, leaving him weak but clearheaded enough to wonder where he was. He was afraid to speak, not knowing whether he should use French or English, and yet he had to discover what had happened to Burton and O'Donnell. The girl solved part of the problem for him. Sitting back on her heels, she placed her hand over her breast, saying, "Jo-anh-ha." When he did not respond, she repeated, "Jo-anh-ha."

Jo-anh-ha. Joanna. He stared blankly, wondering if he had understood her.

She searched his face solemnly, then tried again, this time with, "Bar-clay." When he still said nothing, she appeared at a loss for a moment. "Je-sus man."

Barclay. The Jesus man. It dawned on him that she

must have been one of the children Reverend Barclay had
tried to teach, for he'd rechristened all of them with English names. And yet the girl was scarcely conversant in
English.

He moved his good arm to his chest. "Adam."

"Ad-dam."

It did not exactly roll off her tongue, but he didn't
care. At least he knew now that he was among English
allies. She had to belong to one of the tribes of the Six
Nations. He struggled to sit, but she pushed him back,
shaking her head and speaking once again in the chanty
cadence of another language.

"Sean . . . O'Donnell," he tried.

"Sha-won?"

He nodded. "Aye, and Frank . . . Frank Burton."

"Burr-ton?"

He nodded again.

She turned to speak to the other one, and the huge
mass of flesh lumbered to her feet. Moving ponderously
to the door of the longhouse, she called out loudly. Within
minutes they were joined by others, who ringed around
him, staring at his nakedness. The girl addressed a young
buck, whose decorated deerskin leggings appeared rather
strange with his British officer's frock coat. His black hair
was long and straight in contrast to the usual Indian fashion of cropping it into the center mane of the Iroquois
nations.

He dropped to sit cross-legged where the old woman
had been. A broad smile split his face. Pointing to himself, he said proudly, "Kan-en-dey-ah." He spoke
slowly, letting Adam digest each syllable.

"Kan-en-dey-ah."

The black head bobbed appreciatively and the smile
seemed to widen even further. "Barclay taught me." He
touched his breast again, this time saying, "An-drew."
His eyes traveled to the girl, who still hovered over Adam.
"Her name is Jo-anh-ha." He said it with the precision
of one who had been drilled to say it.

"You speak English?" Adam asked hopefully.

"Aye. 'In the beginning was the Word, and the Word
was God.' "

Leave it to missionaries to teach Indians something useful, Adam thought. "You attended Barclay's school?"

"Aye." He pointed at the old woman. "She is Tak-ey-don-wah-ti, but we call her . . ." He groped for a word and found it. "She is Ancient One in your tongue. Her chosen name was Girl Who Sees Much, but she is no longer a girl." The white teeth shone against his dark skin. "Jo-anh-ha would be as Degonwadonti and choose a great warrior." When Adam's brow furrowed, he explained, "The English and Warraghiyagey call Degonwadonti Molly Brant." He appeared to consider the girl, then shook his head. "Woman Who Watches the Water has been to Fort Johnson," he added, as though that ought to enlighten Adam.

But Adam had other things on his mind besides a girl who apparently wished for Molly Brant's position as concubine to William Johnson. He had to know if any of his men were safe.

"Sean O'Donnell . . . Frank Burton . . . ?"

The young buck snorted derisively and waved his hand impatiently. "The big one would not stay amongst us for fear we meant to take his scalp while he slept, I think. They would not have left you, but the fever had taken your"—again he appeared to search for a word before continuing—"your thoughts."

"They had to reach Rogers near Fort Edward."

The girl Joanna, called Woman Who Watches the Water in her own tongue, moved between them, carrying a decorated gourd. Kanendeyah edged out of her way but did not leave.

"She wishes you to drink, Ad-dam."

He was thirsty, probably from the fever. Propping himself up on an elbow, he took a swallow and almost had to spit it out. All of them broke into laughter except the girl, who pushed the gourd to his mouth again.

"Boiled bark water," Kanendeyah announced. "It cools the skin."

The Ancient One, seeing him drink, bestirred herself to poke at a pot on the fire. Spearing chunks of meat with a knife, she dumped them into a trader's bowl and carried them back to the girl. Her blue-black hair brushing over her shoulders, Joanna cut the chunks into smaller pieces, then held out one to him, indicating he was to eat.

Recalling that Johnson had said Indians were very conscious of their hospitality, Adam let her feed him. The first bite was greasy and chewy, but the flavor was no worse than the dried venison he'd eaten before. He swallowed it, knowing better than to ask what it was.

"Warraghiyagey comes," Kanandeyah offered conversationally as Adam ate. "He would have us wear English war belts."

"You are Wolf People, then," Adam murmured between bites, thinking they were Mohawks.

The buck shook his head. "Onondaga."

It didn't matter. Mohawk, Onondaga, Cayuga, Seneca, Oneida, or Tuscarora—they were all Iroquois when it came to taking or refusing the war belt. Adam finished eating and fell back exhausted.

"The big one lies, I think," Kanendeyah said finally.

He must have still been speaking of Frank Burton. Adam closed his eyes. "How?"

"He said you fought Reynaud and lived."

Damn Frank. He must have been striving to give him status with the Onondagas, but Adam had no wish to live a lie. And yet he ought not to lose all face.

"No. I spied on him, and we both lived."

"It is the same thing," Kanendeyah said simply. Rising, he addressed the others in the rhythmic, run-on cadence of his own language. There was a murmur of curious approval. When Adam opened his eyes briefly, they were filing past respectfully. "Mend well, Ad-dam Tecawrongati."

"Wait—how long have I been here?" Adam asked suddenly.

The buck spread out his hand, folding down his thumb. "This many days."

And then they were all gone except Woman Who Watches the Water. She settled once again, sitting crosslegged, her back against the rough-hewn wall of the longhouse. She'd been wrongly named, Adam thought as he drowsed once again; she ought to have been called Woman Who Watches Man.

With sleep came dreams, pleasant ones, for the first time since he'd taken the ball in the shoulder. Gone were the tortured nightmares, gone was the fire that had rivaled hell, and in their place there was Sarah. Sometime in the night, she came to him. Her rich auburn hair spread over his chest like soft silk, and her amber eyes looked into his, sending the familiar, oft-remembered thrill through him. He was home in England, home in her arms. This, then, was reality. Loudoun and Reynaud and Indians were but bad dreams.

Her bare flesh was pressed against his so closely that he could scarce move. He turned to ease his shoulder and woke with a start. The silken hair was thick and straight and smoky from the fire, and the naked body next to his was strong and supple. She stirred as he moved, then followed him, snuggling closer.

"Ad-dam's wo-man," she said, lifting his hand to her breast.

"No." Rolling away, he wrenched his shoulder, pulling at the healing tissue. With an effort, he sat up.

Bewildered, she sat up behind him. "Ad-dam's woman," she insisted, as though he'd not understood. Then, grasping for the few words she'd learned at Barclay's school before she'd sickened and returned to her people, she tried, "Wife."

He didn't want to offend her, but neither did he wish to mislead her. From snatches of information gleaned from Johnson and Burton and others, he knew the Indians did not view sexual liaisons in quite the same light as Europeans. Johnson had boasted once that before he'd discovered his Molly, he'd been with dozens of others. Indian women, he'd asserted, were not nearly so reticent about such matters as their English sisters, and they knew how to give a man pleasure. And amongst the Iroquois nations, they had enough status to choose their men.

"I have a wife," he said finally. "Her name is Sarah."

Perplexed, the girl rose, oblivious of her naked body, and poked at the embers of the fire. Heaping handfuls of twigs onto them, she managed to rekindle the blaze and add a log. She padded back to the bearskin pallet proudly, stopping in front of him to display herself. She was slender but full-breasted, and her oiled skin gleamed like polished bronze in the firelight. Even by European standards, she would be attractive.

His hand went to his shoulder. "Sick. Ill. Hurt."

He was relieved when she turned away to search for the pot. But she came back with more of the boiled weeds and dropped on her haunches to rub some of them over his wound. Her hands smoothed the mess over his chest, plastering the hairs against his skin.

Thinking he'd convinced her, he lay back down and eased the fur over his shoulder. She wiped her hands and returned to the pallet. Easing herself down behind him, she was still for a moment, and then he felt her hand creep over his hip and slide between his thighs.

"No." He caught at her hand and drew it away, holding it stiffly at his side. "I have a wife, Joanna," he tried again. "I have a wife in England."

She moved against his back, her bare flesh warming him. "England far away."

"I am sick—I'd not have you touch me." It was hopeless and he knew it. Nothing he'd said made sense to her. Still holding her hand, he told her, "I would rather sleep."

It seemed like an eternity that they lay like that, but finally, when he thought she slept, he released her hand. This time, she merely rested it on his shoulder, but the last thing she said was, "Ad-dam's wo-man."

He wasn't a monk, but he'd never so much as thought of another woman after he'd wedded Sarah. He stared into the darkness, trying to recall every detail of her face, hoping it would blot out the heat of Woman Who Watches the Water's body. And he prayed that William Johnson would come soon.

27

Devin watched Sarah across the crowded room, his pride in her evident. The entire Whig leadership, with the possible exception of Newcastle, thought her a credit to him, and it was easy to see why. Gone was the country hoyden, replaced by a lovely woman. Even in her black mourning gowns she turned heads, and when she exhibited a superior grasp of politics also, men listened. And once she came out of mourning and he could gown her exquisitely, she'd be the political hostess of the *ton.*

Indeed, there'd been those who'd already noted her influence. Devin leaned smugly against the wall of his drawing room, observing the way some of the younger Whigs crowded around her. He felt a nudge at his elbow and turned round.

"Hallo, Wilmington."

"Audley." The baronet studied Sarah much as Devin had been doing. "Fine-looking female, ain't she?"

"Aye."

"Got a good head too."

"For a country-bred girl," Devin admitted. "She has proved an apt pupil."

"Didn't know a Whig from a Tory ere she came to town, did she?"

"Spender was a Whig."

Wilmington looked again at Sarah and sighed. "Aye—more's the pity she's in mourning for Spender. Daresay the old buffer didn't spare a thought to the gel ere he cocked up his toes." He flicked open his exquisitely enameled snuffbox, offering Devin some of his sort. "And even more's the pity she ain't yours. Devil of it is, your brother's going to come home and spirit her off to the country somewheres, and where's that leavin' us, I ask you?" When Devin declined the snuff, he snapped the box shut. "Ain't another Whig wife I'd put up against Mrs. Hastings—look at 'em over there, hanging on every word she says. You think Pitt's wife'll fill the void—or Newcastle's?"

"No," Devin answered shortly.

Unaware of the speculation, Sarah smiled at Lords Revenham and Rothwell. "But you will agree, gentlemen, that to send our poorest weapons to the American front is folly, is it not? How is it that the French, who are said to use their worst, seem to be winning at every turn? We should not," she emphasized clearly, "knowingly send anyone to fight with less than our best. To do less is to sacrifice lives on the altar of economy."

" 'To sacrifice lives on the altar of economy,' " Rothwell repeated after her. "A ringing condemnation of policy, would you not say, George? Madam, I should like to use those very words in my next address in Lords should you not mind it. 'Tis time we spoke out on the ridiculous waste. Cheap goods, particularly in arms, save us nothing."

Sarah smiled. "Exactly so. And of course you have my leave to say anything that you feel will aid the cause."

Revenham nodded agreement, beaming at Devin. "Brilliant stroke to keep Mrs. H. in town, old fellow— says what ought to be said. Rest of us are hampered by the dead crow at the top, waiting for him to fall off the branch. Any news of the king yet? If he don't move, we're going to topple ourselves. The Tories is already sniffing victory in Commons, don't you know? 'Tis a damned crisis!"

"The king has met with Pitt—more than that I cannot say," Devin admitted.

He didn't have to explain himself. It was as though an instant ray of hope had struck them. "But will Robinson step aside without a fight?" Rothwell wondered aloud. "If so, Newcastle could name—"

"Just so, gentlemen," Devin answered smugly. "Who else is there? Fox cannot get along with Newcastle, and Pitt cannot get along with the king, but who else is there?" he asked again rhetorically. "The antipathy between Newcastle and Fox is an old one, and yet the Whigs still hold sway in Parliament. The paramount importance then is to give the portfolio to someone in Commons who can keep the two houses in harmony. The king's wishes cannot alter that."

"Will Newcastle swallow Pitt?"

"Rather than Fox."

"And the king?"

"We are losing the war, gentlemen. The government is in crisis."

It was a credit to Sarah's growing influence that Revenham turned to her. "And what do you think, Mrs. Hastings?"

"I think the king cannot continue to lose. Public opinion dictates that a government cannot be formed without Mr. Pitt."

"What about Devonshire? Surely a compromise—"

"Well, I am but a female, sirs—however, I fail to see how someone who does not control the votes in Parliament can expect to govern. There is the matter of a mandate, after all." She looked to Devin for confirmation and read the approval in his eyes. "If Devonshire is chosen, we merely postpone the inevitable."

"Dear lady, may I use that also?" Rothwell asked.

"Of course."

She was so tired. She sat in her room, reliving the dinner party as the maid Devin had engaged for her unpinned her hair. If anyone had told her even a month before that she would be supervising at least one large dinner per week for a group of Whig politicians, she'd have thought him insane. But politics seemed to be the lifeblood of her existence now, occupying her thoughts, keeping her from despair.

She still had not heard from Adam. All the news she gleaned of the war came from the papers and from Devin, and none of it was good. Oswego had fallen, as had

a number of the outlying forts, and there seemed to be
nothing except the winter to stop New France from encroaching on New England.

And there was so little that she could do. She and other
wives of MP's had participated in collecting warm coats
and blankets for the harsh American winter. The government, she reflected bitterly, did so little—each man had
but two changes of clothing and one blanket, the costs of
which were deducted from what could only be described
as meager pay. So by day she joined those who attempted
in some small way to see to the distant troops, and by
night she attempted to persuade dandies, fops, and bored
peers to push for a more active prosecution of the war.

And all the while, she wondered where Adam was—if
he were safe, if he were alive even. Sometimes she could
only hold her arms tight against her breast until the terrible urge to cry passed. And sometimes she lost the battle and sobbed helplessly anyway. It was so difficult not
knowing.

Devin had said that Adam's name had come up in the
paymaster's office among the rangers, and that was most
likely the reason she'd not heard from him. But instead
of consoling her, it made her feel even more isolated,
knowing that he was in constant danger from the heathen
Indians. From what had been said of them in England,
they could have captured and killed him, leaving his
maimed body to rot where there was none to find it.
What if he did not come back? What if they never knew
what happened to him? Already it was as though he'd
disappeared from the earth.

Unable to bear such thoughts further, she pulled away
from the brush the girl stroked through her hair. She
could not sit and think alone—she could not. And she
could not simply go to bed and hope yet again that her
fatigue would somehow drive her nightmares away. It
never worked that way—quite the opposite, in fact.

And the warmed milk Devin's housekeeper provided
didn't work either. Nights of tossing alone in the great
postered bed were an agony to be postponed as long as
possible. For there, in that netherworld between the conscious and the unconscious, memories of Adam left her

hot and wanting, and once she slipped past time, sleep brought dreams of a very different sort. Then every atrocity she'd ever read of or heard came to life in vivid color until she awakened too panicked to breathe, her body covered in sweat. Sometimes she found herself thinking longingly of the opium they'd given her when she'd lost the babe, but Devin did not seem to have any in the house.

Perhaps the brandy. Not much—just enough to soothe the senses, to dull the knife that cut at her peace. She rose from before her mirror, murmuring, "That will be all for tonight, Bess."

"But, mum—"

"I can turn down my own covers, and you've waited up far too long. Seek your own bed."

The maid withdrew, and Sarah stood before the mirror staring at the stranger she had become. She felt older, far older, than the girl who'd stopped on the way to the Park to shed her petticoats. And so terribly lonely. It had been cruel of him to love her, then leave her behind in a place where she could only long for the comfort of his touch, for the ecstasy of his embrace. She closed her eyes briefly and the terrible hunger washed over her.

Then she mastered herself and moved to the small writing table Devin had bought for her. Opening the drawer, she drew out the few precious letters, all of them months and months old, reading them once again, drawing from them what strength she could.

My dearest Sarah, wife of my heart as much as my body . . . I shall return to you a gentleman farmer . . . You are never out of my thoughts and prayers . . .

That was then. What about now? Did he ever think of her anymore? Did he burn as she burned, longing for her as she longed for him? Or was he dead? That thought sent a shudder through her.

She had to escape the confines of the room. She had to have a glass of Devin's brandy—aye, that was it—she needed to soothe an overactive mind, to depress her foolish imagination.

Pulling on her wrapper over her embroidered lawn nightrail, she flung herself from her bedchamber. Her bare feet trod noiselessly down the carpet runner on the stairs to the hall below.

Devin was still up—the door to his bookroom was open and the light illuminated a wedge of the hall. For a moment she considered going back, but she knew she could not. Perhaps he'd join her in a brandy, giving her the excuse.

"This time 'tis you who should be abed, my lord," she said softly from the doorway.

He looked up, startled, then hastily shoved something into his desk drawer. Smiling ruefully, he rose.

"I am caught working at an ungodly hour."

" 'Tis better than fighting nightmares."

"But what are you doing down? I'd thought you in bed long ago, my dear."

"Actually, I am come back to purloin a spot of your brandy," she admitted baldly. "I cannot sleep."

"You look fagged."

"Fatigue does not bring rest, I fear."

"Then we can be souls together, I suppose," he offered, grinning.

When the light struck him just like that, haloing him from behind, he looked much like Adam. His hair, tousled from where he'd removed his wig, was darker, but it lay almost the same. And his eyes seemed to bear his thoughts like Adam's. Her eyes strayed lower, to where his stock had been untied and his snowy shirt lay open at the throat, revealing dark curling hair. No, he was not Adam.

Turning to look for the decanter, he said, "You might as well come the rest of the way in, my dear. By now you surely must know I'd not devour you."

"No, you are very different from what I once thought."

He poured two glasses and held one out to her. "As I have a recollection of that opinion, I shall not be cast into transports by the compliment, Sarah. But you must admit that we deal well together, do we not?"

"Yes." She looked down into her glass, seeing he'd filled it almost to the brim. "Is this what you call a spot, my lord? I shall be quite disguised."

"Nonsense. Sit down, and I'll put another log or two on the fire."

Dropping wearily into one of the chairs he kept close to the fireplace, she sipped the fiery liquid, letting it warm her. "Do you really think Pitt will make all that much difference?" she asked to his back.

"Aye."

"I sometimes wonder if any of it matters."

"Why would you say that?" His task completed, he stood and brushed his hands against his thighs. "Sarah, are you blue-deviled again?"

"Very."

"Why?"

"Why not?" she lashed out. "Why would I not be? Dev, I have not heard of my husband in months! I know not if he is safe, if he is sick—I know not if he thinks of me even!"

In an instant he was behind her, laying his hand on her shoulder for comfort. "Sarah, he thinks of you—why would you say such a thing?"

"Because I am a weak, foolish creature! Because I don't *know*—because sometimes I miss him so much I cannot think!"

"Sarah . . . Sarah . . . you are merely overtired. You must not overset yourself so," he murmured soothingly.

"By day I tell myself he is all right, but at night I lie abed and think, and I . . . I cannot bear it, Dev." Her voice dropped to a low whisper. "I cannot bear it."

Both her hands clasped the bowl of her glass tightly and her shoulder was rigid beneath his hand. "Lean forward—I can do no less for you than you did for me. Here . . ." His fingers separated her thick hair, discovering her neck, then began rubbing, starting behind her ears, as his thumbs worked down from the base of her skull. "Breathe deeply and let it out slowly, my dear. How does this feel?"

"It feels quite good, my lord."

Gradually he massaged the muscles, moving lower, from her neck to her shoulders, slipping under the soft woolen wrapper. "Would you like me to engage a physician to see if he can perhaps prescribe a sleeping potion?''

"No. I'd thought of laudanum, but I cannot be asleep forever, can I? Besides, what if I should come to like it too much?" She closed her eyes, savoring the soothing motion of his hands over her tired shoulders. And for a moment she dared to pretend it was Adam whose warm hands touched her. He wasn't dead—he was alive and with her. His fingers loosened the wrapper, easing it off her shoulder, as they kneaded the bony ridge and slid over the top.

She was so very, very close—he was actually touching her smooth flesh, looking down on her soft, pale skin—and yet she was so very far away. How could she sit there, so warm, so alive, and not know how much he wanted her? How could she look at him a dozen times a day and not feel it? His whole body was aware of the heat of hers, so much so that it ached.

He forced himself to break away, to step back. "Better?" he asked in little more than a croak. With shaking hands he reached for his own brandy and took a drink.

She was disappointed, for he'd brought her back to reality. She colored in embarrassment at the way he'd made her feel again. "Much, thank you."

He sprawled into the chair opposite and sat drinking deeply from his glass. The clock on the mantel ticked, suddenly seeming quite loud, as though it would have them note each creeping second.

She was the first to speak. "Do you truly think he is all right?"

In that moment he almost hated his brother. Could she, after all these months, think of naught else? He did not want to think of him at all. Why did she have to force him to do it? But aloud he answered, "Of course I do."

She finished her brandy and rose to pace, stopping to stare into the licking flames of the fire. "I would that I knew," she whispered. "I would that I knew."

"Sarah—"

"If you have heard anything, I beg that you would tell me—even if 'tis bad news, Dev."

He'd intended to put his hands on her shoulders, but

she spun around just as he reached her. "I need your help, Dev, else I cannot survive."

His arms closed around her, holding her. "Would it help if you wept, Sarah?" he asked softly. "I've no objection to tears."

She turned into his shoulder and held on, shaking her head. "If I cried, I'd never stop."

He held her, acutely aware of her body where it touched his. Had she been any other female he'd wanted, he'd have already taken her to bed, but for him this time was different. He wanted more than a casual liaison—he wanted her to love him.

It felt so good to be held by a man again, to know the warmth and the security of a man's arms. Sarah leaned into him, closing her eyes, remembering Adam. His arms tightened around her, molding her against him so closely that she could hear his heart beat through the snowy cambric of his shirt, and once again she dared to dream of another time, another place, another man. She slid her arms around his waist, returning his embrace.

He rubbed his cheek against her hair, smoothing it, smelling the lavender she wore, and he closed his eyes momentarily also, pretending they were as any man and woman. It was not enough for him, and he knew it. Touching her only made his rebel body demand more. His hands came up to twine in her hair and cradle her head as he lowered his mouth to hers.

Whether the brandy made her foolish or it was merely the intensity of the moment, she let him kiss her. It had been so long she'd almost forgotten the headiness of a man's passion, the flood of heat as her body answered it. She let his hands move over her back, smoothing her wrapper and gown over her hips. Through her shift she felt his body rise against hers, and realized what was happening between them.

She broke away, breathless and panting, staring at him, too shocked for speech. Slowly she touched her mouth, unable to believe what she'd done. Her eyes wide, she backed away.

"Sarah—"

"No!"

"Sarah, I'm sorry." He stepped toward her, his hand outstretched. "I did not mean . . ." But she shook her head, retreating further. He dropped his hand helplessly.

Afraid that he meant to touch her again, afraid of her shocking response to him, she all but ran for the safety of the door. It was not until she had had her hand on the knob that she dared to turn back.

"The fault was mine, Sarah," he said finally.

"No, it was mine also, my lord. I wanted you to be Adam."

"Sarah—"

"No, I pray you will not think you are to blame."

With that, she fled to the safety of her room, where she lay upon her bed staring into the darkness, wondering what was wrong with her. She'd very nearly played the wanton with her husband's brother.

After she left, he picked up the two brandy glasses and savagely tossed them into the fire. The few drops left in one ignited as the glass shattered, and then the room was again still—except for the infernal, eternal ticking of the clock. His body was still taut with wanting, ready to shatter like the glass in the fireplace. He was driving himself to madness keeping her there, and he knew it, but the very thought that she might leave sent a chill to the core of his being. And if she ever discovered what he'd done to her, she'd despise him, he was sure.

He stood staring long into the flames, seeing not the red and yellow and orange and blue glow, but rather hell itself licking at his soul. But he'd felt her response to him, he'd known ever so briefly the heat of an answering passion, and his body demanded ease from the torment of his mind.

What if he went after her? What if he took her to bed, slaking her need and his? What then? He'd damn the both of them.

He walked to his desk and pulled out the drawer, lifting out the false bottom to stare at the disordered pages of Adam's letters beneath. He was torn between consigning them to the fire and giving them to her. But if he did that, how could he ever explain their existence? How could he tell her that he'd not meant to keep them from her—not at first, anyway—that it had just happened. First, it had been just the one, and he'd thought to hold it back but a day or so—just until a favorable vote. But then in her isolation, she'd turned to him, and he dared to think the impossible, he dared to think she could be his. After that, the deceit came more easily. Now she'd hate him if she even suspected what he'd done to her, what he'd done to Adam.

The clock struck the hour of three, jarring him. In the end, he closed the drawer and left it. Nay, 'twas done. He'd gone too far to turn back entirely. He merely had to learn to wait.

What he needed was someone who did not complicate his life, who did not force him to make such awful choices. What he needed was a woman to hold him whilst he plunged deep inside her again and again until his body wanted no more. Aye, he'd ease his body, if naught else.

He tied his stock quickly, his fingers working almost clumsily, then searched for his discarded coat. He knew a woman or two who would ask no questions if he showed up on the doorstep. And for a price, they'd do anything he asked.

28

Sarah had considered the possibility of returning to the Park, but then she would have had to explain her sudden arrival there. Moreover, she would once again be caught up in Meg's wedding plans and forced to deal with the girl's dislike of her. The only other alternative was to remain in Audley's house and hope to achieve a pleasant discourse with him, one utterly devoid of any physical contact.

It was the brandy, she'd concluded the next morning, and hopefully his memory was more befuddled than hers. She was spared discovering that, however, when he did not come down to breakfast. Neither was he there for dinner. In fact, she didn't see him for almost a week—not until they were expecting to entertain again.

This time, it was to be a small, intimate dinner with two gentlemen she did not know beyond the fact that they were not supporters of Mr. Pitt. Since she was not notified otherwise, she went on with plans, ordering geese and a joint of mutton from the butcher, peas from the greengrocer, and tarts from the baker. The rest would have to come from Audley's well-stocked pantry.

He came home midafternoon, retreating to his own chamber almost immediately, sending his valet to inform her that he'd be down about a quarter past seven to review with her cogent information about their guests. That was it—no explanation of where he'd been or why he'd been gone. But then, she was not, after all, his keeper, she told herself somewhat resentfully.

The space of a week had not lessened her mortification. It was with some trepidation that she dressed for dinner, donning her best black silk gown, the one with the cream-colored brocade stomacher laced in black satin ribbon across the front. She'd never gotten over the way silk swished over her petticoats, giving her a sense of elegance she'd not had in all those years of faded calico dresses.

As Bess put the last pin in the curls on top of her head, Sarah surveyed her image with some satisfaction, wondering what Adam would say if he could see her just now. Would he think her prettier? she wondered. Surely he would—if he ever saw her again.

"Oh, mum, 'tis lovely ye are!" Bess assured her, stepping back. "Lord Audley cannot be but pleased."

"Lord Audley is scarce at home."

"He's a busy man, mum." Bess glanced down at the street below, seeing the lamplighters struggling with the oil lamps. "Look, 'tis beginning to snow. 'Tis swirlin' about the lamps like yellow bugs."

Curious, Sarah rose to see. The street was still clogged with carriages and pedestrians, but Bess was right—it was indeed snowing lightly. "Maybe they won't come," she murmured.

"Oh, they'll come, all right—'tis Lord Audley who asks 'em, ain't it? James says his lordship's going to be the paymaster himself when Pitt goes in."

Even the servants were not above gossiping over the crisis in government, it seemed. Sarah sighed and turned away from the window.

"I might as well go down, I suppose—there's naught else to do, after all."

The girl watched her, shaking her head. The other young mistresses she'd served were glad enough to sit and preen themselves, but not Mrs. Hastings. She was as restless as a cat on hot coals, and the winter wasn't but begun. 'Course, it wasn't the weather that ailed her, Bess allowed—it was the absence of her husband. Of course, ladies didn't own up to the passions of the poor, but Bess'd wager her fifteen pounds per annum that Mrs. Hastings, for all her fine clothes and manners, just needed a man.

Sarah could hear Devin cursing as she passed his door, and by the sound of it, he was more than vexed by the set of his wig. Words like "lying bastard" and "Judas" punctuated the air. Forgetting her earlier chagrin, she tapped on his door.

"Audley . . . Dev, is everything quite all right?"

There was a soft scuffling of shoeless feet on the carpet; then Devin himself opened up. "No, nothing's right!" he almost shouted at her. "The war . . . Pitt . . . Adam . . . you—nothing's right, I tell you!"

She went white. "Adam?"

He groaned and ran his fingers through his disordered hair as though he could clear his head. He'd not meant to tell her like that. His temper faded at her stricken appearance. He held the door wide.

"Come in."

"Here?"

"Bates is here, and I will leave the door open if you like."

Peering around him, she could indeed see his valet holding up two waistcoats to the candelabrum as though he were checking for spots. Recalling their last encounter, she suddenly felt rather foolish. Nonetheless, she stepped inside the door.

He nodded toward an assortment of papers scattered on his bed. "I was just going through the dispatches before Pitt's messenger came."

"The dispatches?" She glanced eagerly at the disorder. "Was there mail in them?"

"No."

"Oh."

"Which disaster would you have of me first, Sarah?"

"Adam—"

"Reports are vague as yet, my dear, but 'twould appear he has not returned from spying in the Champlain Valley."

The room spun around her. She had to close her eyes and swallow to fight the awful fear that sliced through her. "He . . . he's *missing?*"

"Unaccounted-for."

She groped her way to his bed and sat down, heedless of the papers that slid to the floor. " 'Tis the same thing, isn't it?"

"Reports from his men indicate that he is not a prisoner."

She had to cover her face with her hands. In an instant he was beside her. "Sarah, 'tis not as you think! Apparently the mission was a success—Loudoun recommends a royal commendation for it."

She dropped her hands and looked at him. "Where is my husband?" she asked evenly. "I care not about commendations or anything else, my lord. I only want to know what happened to him."

"Loudoun sent a party of rangers, but Johnson insisted he was safe enough—that the ranger who made it to Fort Johnson said he believed they were taken by friendly Indians."

"Is there such a thing, Dev? Or is one savage very like another?"

"Apparently there *is* such a thing. William Johnson seems to think his Mohawks are more civilized than we are."

"I want to go there."

"Sarah . . . Sarah . . . these dispatches are a month old."

"And he could have been dead a month!"

"And he could be safely in Albany now. By now Johnson will have filed his report on the matter, and we shall hear soon. What if he is being sent back here? Would you pass him on the way?"

He spoke softly, yet matter-of-factly, and she had to own he made sense. She sighed heavily. "And there was nothing else?"

"No." He moved back, putting a great deal of space between them. "Sarah—"

" 'Tis all of a piece, anyway, isn't it?" she asked bitterly. "I've not known where he was or how he fared since shortly after he arrived there. I suppose another month of knowing nothing is but more of the same."

"Exactly. I wasn't going to tell you until I heard—I shouldn't have, in fact."

"I am not a dieaway miss, Dev. At least now I shall have a notion as to why he does not write. Before, I thought he had ceased to care." She drew in a deep breath and let it out slowly before meeting his eyes again. "And the other disasters, my lord?"

"Pitt has been asked to take a ministry."

"And you count that a misfortune?" she asked incredulously. "Have you taken leave of your senses, Dev? 'Tis what we have been striving for!"

"Aye, but not quite in this way. The cost has been too high. The first portfolio goes to Devonshire."

"Devonshire? But *why?*"

"I wish to God I knew." He combed his hair again with his fingers. "Probably because the German bastard had his way—and because Henry Fox quarreled yet again with both Newcastle and Pitt. This infernal squabbling amongst ourselves lets the king divide us."

She forbore reminding him that some of the squabbling had been brought about by Pitt's attacks on his own party's government. "I see," she said finally. "And the lying bastard?"

"George II had allowed us to think he would give Pitt free rein in the war."

"And the Judas?"

He smiled ruefully, and his expression was much like Adam's. "You heard that also?"

"I am scarce deaf, Dev."

"As you know, Newcastle resigned under pressure from the war hawks such as myself, but he still holds the majority in Commons."

"That was over a month ago, but the king did not replace him."

"Aye."

"And he still holds the majority in Commons, doesn't he?"

"But he will not use his power to Pitt's advantage!"

Privately, since Pitt's friends had been thorns under his saddle for months, she could understand that, but Devin's loyalty to the man made him blind. "So he is Judas?"

"Aye."

"But Pitt is not done yet, I think. If he has a portfolio, he can push the war."

" 'Tis the wrong portfolio! They give him secretary of state rather than premier! That lackey Devonshire is premier, Sarah!"

"Oh."

"But he has no support. 'Tis the king's doing, not the Commons' nor the Lords'."

"Well, if our criticism brought Newcastle down enough to consider Mr. Pitt, then we shall simply have to press the king to do otherwise," she decided practically. "Attack Devonshire."

"They've tied Pitt's hands behind his back, Sarah."

"But they have not tied ours."

He stared, ready to give her a set-down, then stopped as the idea took hold. "Sarah Hastings, you ought to have been a man. Ladies are not supposed to be schemers."

"Pooh. Females are born schemers, my lord." She

favored him with a twisted smile. "So what should I know about the gentlemen you have brought to dine? Must I appear to champion Mr. Pitt or not? Or should I sit meekly and hold my tongue?"

"Sarah, you could not hold your tongue with both hands."

"How very uncivil of you to say so, my lord."

"What a baggage you are." He slid off the bed and stood over her. "You have the instincts of a politician, you know," he added.

"Yes, well . . ." She stood to face him, smoothing her wide skirts over her voluminous petticoats. "My interest, my lord, is quite selfish. I will do anything to see this war concluded." Looking away, she sighed. "I only want my husband home. And I pray he comes back to me whole."

"He will." He moved to a table and lifted a gilt-covered box. "I'd meant to give this to you earlier, Sarah . . . er, before our . . . quarrel of last week. Go on—take it."

"Whatever . . . ?" She opened the box to peer inside. " 'Pon my word . . ."

"And do not be saying you cannot keep it—'tis small payment for all the politicians you have listened to. Besides, it behooves me to see you in your best looks, you know, for how else am I to keep young bucks like Rothwell swooning at your feet long enough to vote my way?"

She stared down at the long strand of perfectly matched pearls. Their soft sheen caught the light from the candelabrum, reflecting it warmly. "My lord, I cannot—"

"Sarah, a man gives his mistress diamonds and other precious gems," he explained patiently. "Pearls are the sort of thing one gives one's daughter or mother. They definitely are not meant to compromise your character."

"But I am not your mother or your daughter, Dev."

As much as it galled him to say it, he managed to smile. "No, you are my brother's wife."

To her it was a reaffirmation that everything was all right between them. She closed the box in her hand and nodded. "Thank you, Dev. I shall wear them tonight."

After she'd gone, he remembered he'd meant to put

them on her himself. He'd wanted to see how they looked
nestled in the hollow of her throat. But it was just as well
he hadn't. He couldn't touch her again—not for a long
time, if ever.

While Bates matched the waistcoat to dark knee
breeches, Devin stared out into the swirling snow. It
wasn't going to stick, it'd be just enough to snarl traffic,
he observed dispassionately. But as always, his thoughts
turned again to Sarah. She ought to have been a politician's wife. She ought to have been his.

29

"Sarah is . . ." He groped for words to tell her of
his wife. "She is more than merely pretty, I think.
Her hair shines red in the sun, and her eyes are like polished amber, more gold than brown, but it is more than
that. She's not missish—not overgiven to the false niceties that are so common to her sex."

He looked up to see Woman Who Watches the Water
sitting quietly watching him, and he wished he could
make her understand. But she merely sat there, her dark
eyes wide. She had a great deal of patience—he had to
admit that—for she had not given up on the notion that
she'd chosen him. So much so that she guarded him jeal-
ously from the curious stares of other Indian girls.

The nights had been the worst, for she lay naked
against him, waiting. And as his body had healed, it
warred with his heart and mind over her. She was his for
the taking—there was nothing to stop him from availing
himself of her favors, and if he did, he'd be no worse
than a hundred other soldiers and trappers. But he'd

pledged his heart and body to Sarah, and neither distance
nor time could alter that. And so he passed his waking
hours speaking of her, trying to bring her to mind, telling
a silent, watchful Indian girl about her, repeating the
same descriptions, remembering the same incidents over
and over again. His memories were his shield against the
temptation to take Woman Who Watches the Water.

Kanendeyah had come to him, speaking on her behalf,
asking him to wed her. Joanna wanted to go with him,
to live in his longhouse, to have status above her sisters
as Molly Brant had done. Practically speaking, Kanendeyah had argued, it would be a good thing for him. She
would cook, keep his house in order, and warm his bones
at night. But he had a wife, he protested. The Indian had
simply looked at him and shaken his head. But she was
not here, he said, and she could not want him to suffer
alone. And the way he'd said it almost made sense—until
Adam thought of Sarah.

"I remember the first time I noted her," he continued,
trying to ignore the girl's stare. "She was but six and
wearing a torn, dirty gown—it was pink, I think—but she
didn't seem to realize that she looked like a beggar child.
She was running barefoot across the small parkland at
Spender's Hill, squealing and trying to retrieve one of
her slippers from her father's hunting dog. I thought she
belonged to one of the tenants at the time."

"Ad-dam!" Kanendeyah stuck his head through the
narrow doorway, and for once betrayed excitement.
"Warraghiyagey is come, and Araghi sends for you." He
twisted his head to say something to Joanna, and her
dismay was immediately evident. She beat her breasts
and cried out, then wailed pitifully. Kanendeyah spoke
sharply, and once again she was silent. "Jo-anh-ha wants
to go with you," he explained.

"Tell her I have a wife."

"I have." Nonetheless, he addressed the girl, this time
more kindly. Two tears rolled down her dark cheeks as
she answered him. "She is saddened, but she would still
go," the young man repeated for Adam. The girl said
something else, and Kanendeyah shook his head. "If you
cannot take her for wife, she will be your sister."

"Tell her I would be honored to be her brother."

As his words were translated, she eyed him reproach-fully, then spoke haltingly to the other Indian. "She says as your sister she will take care of you in your house."

"Tell her I am honored, but I have no house."

They exchanged words back and forth until Kanen-deyah finally threw up his hands. "She still wishes to go with Tecawrongati."

Tecawrongati. The best translation he'd gotten of that was Man Who Dares or Man Who Defies. With the age-old defense of a man faced with the uncomfortable, he sighed. "Tell her I will think on the matter."

Still weak from the effects of fever and his wound, he stood unsteadily. He was unshaven and dirty, clad in grease-stiffened leggings covered with a ragged calico breechclout that came from God only knew where, bare-chested, and stained with Ancient One's medicine. But he was alive, and for that he was grateful.

Joanna brought him a woolen blanket of the sort that traders gave the Indians, draping it over one shoulder, lifting his arm to indicate how it ought to be worn. It was ludicrous—she fussed over him like a woman readying a child for church.

He stepped from the warm, smoky confines of her fam-ily's longhouse into the cold. "Araghi calls council in honor of Warraghiyagey," Kanendeyah murmured as he slowed enough for Adam to keep pace. "It is expected that he brings us English war belts."

Adam was unprepared for the awesome sight of Wil-liam Johnson in full regalia as Warraghiyagey. The En-glishman was transformed almost beyond recognition. As Adam was led into the council house, assembled dele-gates of the Six Nations sat cross-legged in a half-circle, at the center of which were obviously important chief-tains: one he recognized as Araghi, who'd paid him a visit at the longhouse; two others wore their scalp locks differently, decorating them with feathers and beads; and seated between them was an unbelievable sight. He was tall and big-boned, paler than the others, and his hazel eyes were circled with black and red paint, his cheek-bones striped with green. His black hair was not shaved on either side, but rather was braided in a single plait that started in the middle of the front and ended in a string of beads at the back. His broad chest was bare and painted, with stripes and zigzags of red, black, white, and green seeming to radiate from his nipples. A shiver went down Adam's spine as he recognized the strange design for the ceremonial war paint Cook had described. In front of the man lay six highly decorated belts, the leather thongs at the end of which were knotted with beads. In the center of each belt was painted a replica of the British flag.

There were perhaps twenty Indians in the council, and none of them spoke to Adam. Neither did Johnson. Instead, a clay pipe was produced with great ceremony and shared first by Johnson and the two chieftains Adam did not know. Then it was presented to Araghi. Kanendeyah leaned closer to Adam and whispered, "Warraghiyagey brings pipe to Rozinoghyata, high chief of the Onandagas. On the other side is Nichus, chief of the Mohawks, father to Degonwadonti."

This, then, was William Johnson's father-in-law, called Nicholas Brant by the English. Adam eyed him curiously. The old man sat very straight, his mien giving new meaning to the word "solemn."

"They sit on the sacred skin," Kanendeyah explained.

As the pipe traveled around amongst the assemblage, gifts were exchanged between what appeared to be the principal chiefs—six in all—and William Johnson. As the pipe moved from man to man, Kanendeyah identified each one.

The high chief of the Onandagas stood to speak, and once again Adam wished he knew the language, for the Indian's voice was rich as he waved his hands expansively and launched into what must have been a sermon to rival Cotton Mather. By his tone, he exhorted them, his voice rising and falling dramatically. There was utter silence as every man there hung on every word. Then Nichus rose and talked in much the same manner, followed by the other four high chiefs of the Six Nations.

There was a murmur as the last one sat down, and the floor was given to William Johnson. Adam listened spellbound, not understanding a word, as Johnson pleaded eloquently, stopping to lift the belts one by one, holding each high in the air, addressing a different chief with each belt. He spoke the Iroquois language so fluently that he did not even have to search for words.

In the end, he sat down, taking the pipe once again from Nichus. And, one by one, the other chiefs rose, each to take one belt.

A tall scalp pole was brought and paraded around the fire. One chief would call out something, and the pole would be raised almost in salute, its grisly mane of human hair waving above the smoke.

"We take Warraghiyagey's enemies for our own," Kanendeyah whispered. "We fight for your King George."

It was not until the meeting ended that Johnson spoke to Adam. "You are quite the hero of the dispatches, Captain Hastings," he murmured, walking across the room to greet him. "No—do not rise, sir—'tis not I who am wounded." Heedless of his breechclout or warpaint, he dropped to the hard-packed earth in front of Adam. "Aye—had you not sent warning, the whole valley would have been burned clean. As it was, the loss of life was terrible, but not so bad as it might have been. Albany and Schenectady overflow with terrified farmers, I fear."

"How many came—Indians, I mean?"

"Depending on whom is asked . . ." Johnson shrugged, then grinned. "To hear it from the settlers, 'tis thousands, but Rogers puts the number at less than five hundred."

"Reynaud said four hundred."

Johnson's eyebrow lifted. "Then it *was* true—you saw the French Fox, did you?"

"I blundered into his camp, thinking I could take him," Adam muttered, embarrassed at how wrong he'd been.

"You are fortunate to be whole, Captain. Usually we discover those who have encountered him in pieces."

"He thought I was a countryman." Adam touched his shoulder and shook his head ruefully. "Not that he's much kinder to his own—the bloody bastard shot me.

Odd thing was, he didn't come after me—said something about my soul," he recalled.

Johnson nodded. "Indians believe taking a man's scalp denies him eternity. It is the ultimate power over an enemy, you see." He looked to where Nichus displayed his war belt. "You did us a great service, whether you will admit it or not. Of the Six Nations, only the Mohawks would have fought until word came that the Ottawas are leagued against us. Pontiac's fame is great enough to make the Iroquois fear being called women if they do not stand before him." Abruptly Johnson rose. "Can you travel yet, do you think? Or would you have a travois made? I'd return to Albany as soon as may be, lest fools there make mischief in my absence. Loudoun is not one to move."

"No, he is not," Adam agreed dryly.

They walked out together. "Loudoun would have it there was the devil to pay when word came you'd been shot. Your brother's influence is felt over here, I fear. Oh—one of Loudoun's aides forwards your mail," Johnson remembered suddenly. He shouted at a boy, who disappeared for a few minutes, then returned carrying a bag.

Forgetting the baronet, forgetting the cold, forgetting his wound and all else, Adam delved into the bag, drawing out the fistful of letters. He recognized his mother's scrawl and his brother's neat, precise hand on several—there was even one from Meg. He sifted through them again, then examined the bag. "Was there nothing else?"

"Nay—I had them of Loudoun's man myself."

It was as though he'd been soaked with cold water. "I see." He had to get back to the longhouse, he had to be alone to read, to discover why there was nothing from Sarah. Perhaps she was ill. Aye—that had to be the explanation.

"Can you be ready to leave within the hour, Captain?"

"All I have is what you witness on me, sir."

"Not quite." Johnson gave him a sly wink and grinned. "Araghi tells me you have taken yourself a wife."

"I have a wife," Adam retorted stiffly.

"Indians do not expect monogamy, Captain Hastings.

Enjoy yourself, and when 'tis done, you can send her back to her people with presents. Man was not meant to burn, sir.''

"Is that what you have done?" Adam asked coldly.

Johnson shrugged. "From time to time."

"Even Degonwadonti?"

For a moment the baronet of the Mohawks was quite still, his expression arrested. "Nay. Molly is my heart, Captain."

"Sarah Spender is mine."

But back in the longhouse he'd shared with Joanna and her family, Adam sat on the bearskins and opened his mail, starting with his mother's, scanning each page quickly, looking for something about Sarah. But Emma Hastings' letters were as flighty and disjointed as she was, so he had to endure endless accounts of Meg's unexpected success. The girl had gotten herself a husband, after all, or so it seemed. It was not until he reached the one about London that he paid much notice. Then he read page after page of shopping expeditions, listing everything she and Meg and Sarah had bought, but he could not quite discern who'd acquired what—only the wanton extravagance of it all. By the sound of it, his wife was enjoying her endless round of shopping. There was not a word about her being ill.

Disheartened somewhat by his mother's gossipy, disoriented descriptions of what now seemed almost another world, he picked up Meg's, saving Devin's letters for last. Tearing it open, he began to read her self-centered recitation of her success in Bath. Well, he could not fault her for that—after all, her life at the Park had been next to miserable. But her rhapsodic recitation of Chatwick's perfection wore thin. When he reached the part that interested him, he was shocked to discover his sister's intense dislike of his wife.

"Sarah, my dear brother," she wrote spitefully, "seems quite content in your absence. Indeed, but she has both Papa and Devin thinking she can do no wrong. Your paragon rules the roost both here and in London." And it did not end there, as she continued:

Despite the fact that she is supposed to be in mourning, our dear brother has seen fit to establish her at Westerfield House, saying he has need of her there. And he is so lost to propriety in the matter that he quite forgets Baron Spender, for under the guise of his politics, he has her presiding at all manner of social events. I should not be surprised in the least to discover he has expended more money on her clothing than Papa has allowed for my whole trousseau.

Of course, the men all admire her greatly, even dear Chatwick, although he takes great pains to assure me that she is quite beneath him. I cannot entirely fault him, however, as Sarah does little to depress a man's pretensions. While you and Audley admire her artlessness, I cannot but think she would have been better served by a little discipline.

It was not difficult to fathom why she'd written of Sarah in such terms: Adam wagered Chatwick's attention was the root of the problem there. Poor colorless Meg could not expect to show to advantage in the same room with the vivid, vital Sarah. She ought to be glad enough that Devin had relieved her of his wife's company.

But he still had no word from Sarah herself, and that disquieted him. Dispensing with everything else, he picked up the envelopes from Devin. How like his brother to write in the same neat, precise manner in which he thought. Adam chose the one that had been franked first, noting the date of 15 October.

Like the others, he wrote of Mama and Meg and Sarah coming to London, complaining that it was a devil of a time to do it. He was so embroiled in the fratricide the Whigs were determined to commit amongst themselves that he scarce had time to spare for the women of his family. In fact, he wrote he would be heartily glad to see them return to the country "ere they spend you and Papa into the poorhouse."

That was odd—he'd never known Sarah to care about such things. But then, she'd never had much either, Adam reminded himself. Perhaps the opportunity had proved too much for her. Well, it did not matter; he could afford it, and if it consoled her after the loss of the child, it was money well spent. Certainly there was nothing in Devin's tone to indicate anything like Meg had implied. If anything, Dev seemed to regard Sarah as a burden.

And on 20 October Devin had written again, this time to tell that Sarah would be remaining in London. It was a terse note explaining that Pitt had thought that because of her concern for her husband's safety, she might prove useful in convincing doubting Whigs to increase the war effort. That was it—nothing particularly personal or enlightening as to why she had not written herself.

Then there was nothing until 5 November, and most of Devin's news had been political—all Newcastle and Robinson and Pitt and Devonshire and the king. The plot seemed complicated, with each politician doing his damnedest to stab the others in the back. Adam would not have given a farthing for the lot of them—with the exception of Pitt. At least he gave the appearance of being an honest fellow, having been paymaster of the forces without visibly enriching himself. Ominously, there was no word at all of Sarah.

Adam sat there on the pile of bearskins, at a loss as to what was happening. Had she not written at all? Was she so caught up in London life that she'd all but forgotten him? Had the loss of her babe been so devastating that she had put him and it from her mind? Had she found someone to console her in his absence? Meg's words, "The men all admire her greatly," rang in his ears. Had she in her naiveté, her inexperience, fallen prey to someone? He didn't know.

Just then, London and Sarah seemed so very far away, in another lifetime almost. Ever since he'd become a ranger, memories of Sarah seemed to be his greatest link with the past, and now they were growing fainter, unnourished by any word from her. He looked up, aware once again that Woman Who Watches the Water watched him.

"Ready?" William Johnson called through the door.

"Aye."

Adam scooped up his letters, dumping them into the dispatch bag, and stood up. As he did so, the Indian girl rose also, shouldering a pack that appeared to be blankets and clothing. It was then that he knew she meant to go with him, that nothing he'd said to her had made any difference. She'd chosen him.

"Look, I cannot take you. I have a wife, Joanna, and in my country we are allowed but one."

She searched his face solemnly, then nodded. Relieved, he started past her, only to discover she followed him. He sighed and turned back.

"Nay."

She touched her calico shirt over her breasts and smiled. "Jo-anh-ha. Sis-ter."

He knew he ought to be firm and just walk away from her, but the fact that she'd probably saved his life stopped him. Had not Kanendeyah said that when his fever was the worst, when his wound had putrified, she had sucked the poison from his body? Surely he must owe her something for that. And it was obvious that she wanted to return to the white man's world she'd glimpsed once in the past. But he didn't want to take her with him, and he didn't know what the hell to do with her if he did. He dug into the pouch Burton had left him, feeling the cold shillings there as Woman Who Watches the Water watched him hopefully, thinking to buy her off. But something in those dark eyes stopped him from insulting her.

He exhaled slowly and nodded. "All right. But when we get to Fort Edward, you will have to sleep in your own bed. Brothers and sisters do not share the sheets."

Johnson's face broke into a broad grin as the girl followed Adam out, but before he could say anything, Adam snapped, "One word, Warraghiyagey, and I'll send her to your Molly, and you can explain it."

"What are you going to do with her?"

"I don't know—send her to Barclay's school . . . let her do my laundry . . . hell, I don't know!" he exploded finally. "I can't even tell her to go away!"

"Everything but the obvious," the baronet murmured, shaking his head as though Adam were a fool.

They'd brought him a horse, a rarity in the woods, and as Adam swung his body into the saddle, he wondered how he could ever explain Joanna to Sarah. Well, he

would not be the only one needing to give explanations,
he supposed. He'd give a year's pay to know why Sarah
had stopped writing to him.

30

___

The winter was a harsh one in more ways than one.
The Indians raided unexpectedly even after the lakes
and rivers froze, and Adam and his men had to recon-
noiter on ice skates and snowshoes. He'd lost a couple of
men to bones broken while attempting to master the hated
skates. But it was a land that did not give itself to riding
horses, and even if it had, the snow would have been too
deep and the ice too slick to make the animals useful.

Still, despite the extremes of weather, despite the hardships of life beyond Albany, he'd grown to love this land.
It had a beauty, a rugged, pristine beauty so unlike the
neat, defined farms and estates in England. America was
a place where a man would be limited only by the scope
of his thoughts and his dreams. One only had to look at
William Johnson to see that. But even when Adam wrote
to Dev, he found himself unable to describe the affinity
he'd discovered for New York. Here there were no
younger sons, no limits of birth. The silliness, the inanity
of a useless aristocracy was borne in on him when he
lived daily by his own wits.

After the initial guffaws and laughter when Adam had
returned to Fort Edward with Woman Who Watches the
Water, his men gradually accepted her, calling her by
the name Barclay had used at her baptism, Joanna. And
she proved her worth nearly every day, cooking for him
and his men, mending their clothing, and teaching all of

them the basic Iroquois dialect common to the Six Nations. Every evening they were in camp on the rangers' forty-acre island outside Fort Edward, she would sit in their midst and pronounce the names of things. It worked two ways—she would also point to objects and expect to have them named in English. In two months' time, she could speak enough for them to understand basic things when communicating with each other.

When he and his men left the relative safety and comfort of Fort Edward, she accompanied them, proving an invaluable guide over the ice and snow. If Adam's relationship with her was cause for speculation, nobody was foolish enough to remark on it. He did not sleep with her even when the temperatures plunged and everyone rolled up into thick bearskins. In the wilderness she positioned her bedroll at his feet. At Fort Edward she slept on a cot against the opposite wall.

To ensure that nobody mistook her for one of the Indian females who'd discovered the ancient profession, Adam saw to it that she was properly dressed whenever they were at the fort. It had been a struggle at first to get her to cover her breasts in front of his men, but he'd literally put her into a corset and gown himself, lacing her up like a basted bird while she screeched and berated him with what must have been Iroquois expletives. When they were moving stealthily up and down the Champlain Valley, she wore what she pleased, the only requirement being that she keep her body covered.

There was no question that he'd given her status amongst her people. Whenever any of the Onandagas traveled far enough southward, she greeted them in her full-skirted muslin gown, curtsying as though she were a lady. The effect was not long-lived, however, for Adam often caught her displaying her corsets to her relatives, male and female alike, who inspected them curiously, poking about her body to discover how the whalebone worked to give her an artificial shape.

When one of the officers' wives from the fort had met her, Woman Who Watches the Water had pointed to Adam, then to herself, insisting, "Sister." And the affronted woman had looked her up and down haughtily, clearly disbelieving the relationship. But Adam didn't care; the only person he hoped would understand was in England. And he still did not hear from her.

Woman Who Watches the Water gave Adam status also—he was the only ranger who had his own thoroughly reliable Indian guide. And once he got used to having her around, it seemed perfectly natural that she should be there.

In February the snow was deep and smoke curled into the crystalline sky from the longhouses of every Indian village between Pennsylvania and Quebec. Rumor had filtered down through the Mohawks' relatives, the Caughnawagas, who were not part of the Six Nations, that Reynaud ranged far and wide, gathering tribal allies to the banner of France for a major assault in the spring.

Robert Rogers had just returned from a mission between Fort William Henry and Carillon, traveling some twelve miles of the trip by ice skates on the frozen surface of Lake George and the rest of the way on snowshoes. As luck would have it, they surprised a group of French coming to reinforce Carillon. Seven prisoners and three sleds were captured, yielding the alarming information that two hundred Canadians and nearly one hundred Indians were expected to join the six hundred regular troops there.

On the way back, Rogers' group was pursued and ambushed, with the result that a number of the rangers were killed and Rogers himself was wounded in the head. Out of the hundred men he'd taken into the wilderness with him, only forty-eight healthy and six wounded made it back to Fort William Henry, reporting that they'd been attacked by two hundred and fifty French and Indians.

Abercromby, acting as Loudoun's second, wanted to know the extent of activity in the valley and ordered numerous small parties to fan out, observe, and report. They were not to engage the enemy.

Adam, who'd been offered a promotion to major by Loudoun for the earlier encounter with Reynaud, had turned it down, saying it was undeserved since he'd not captured the Fox. Now he begged to go out again. The wound in Adam's shoulder, he argued with the ailing Rogers, ought to be avenged.

"You are still green!" Rogers snapped.

Adam looked down at the dirty buckskins and the fur-lined moccasins he wore, and shook his head. "Begging your pardon, sir, but I don't think so."

"Humph! Every fool as gets himself a concubine amongst them thinks he knows the Indians!"

In the end, perhaps because of Rogers' worsening wound, Adam got his way. He chose to take the same route Rogers had completed weeks before, hoping to discover the intent of the French movement the ranger leader had encountered. He chose the same five he'd taken before—and Joanna.

The night before he left, he wrote again to Sarah. With Joanna sitting on the floor before the fire, mending the fur that lined O'Donnell's cloak, he sat at the crude wooden desk and tried to compose his thoughts. Through the weeks and months he'd waited in vain for word from Sarah, he'd suffered depression and despair. His worry had slowly changed to bewilderment and, finally, anger.

Could she not know what she did to him? Could she not know how alone he felt at night? How terrible it was to be alone? When they'd wedded, she'd said she wanted someone to love her, and he had. Had she, as his sister implied, found another in his absence? Was she so inconstant she could not wait even a year? It was painful to ask himself such questions, to consider them even, but he'd reached the point where he had to admit something was very wrong.

Perhaps they'd wedded with too much haste, and perhaps they'd mistaken mutual lust for love. And they'd had so little time together before he'd left—just enough to make him hurt with wanting her every time he let himself think of her. Was he a fool to have thought her that different from her *ton*-ish sisters? Had she, like so many of them, taken a lover in his absence?

He had no answers and no means to discover them. If he wrote to Meg, she'd probably vent more of her spleen on Sarah, and he did not think he could bear that. And his mother would not know how to answer him. As for his father, how he would gloat to discover he'd been right about Sarah. No, that was not quite true, and Adam knew it—the earl had come to like her. He'd feel as betrayed as Adam if Sarah had a lover.

The most disturbing thing was the way that Dev had ceased to mention her at all. Did he know something he was not telling? Since he'd returned to Fort Edward, Adam had received two more letters from his brother, both ominously silent where Sarah was concerned.

He closed his eyes, shutting out the pain; then, squaring his shoulders, he looked again at the blank page and began to write. "Dear Sarah"—not "Dearest" anymore—he'd passed that a month and more ago.

Dear Sarah,

On the morrow I leave for Carillon, not knowing if I shall ever come this way again. The last party was ambushed, and full half of them perished, so I shall write to you in case it be the last time.

Meg writes that you are quite the social success despite your mourning. I should think that when you can wear the colors you favor, full half of London will be at your feet.

It has been months now since last I heard from you, so I can but imagine how things are with you. You are well, I think, else Dev should have written to me. More than that I do not know.

As much as it pains me, Sarah, I must ask how it is that those memories we shared have faded for you. Were they not enough to sustain? Did we perhaps wed in haste and repent too late? Or do you think you have discovered in another a more constant lover?

If that be the case, if the wait be too long, I pray you will tell me. I am a man grown, Sarah, and I can take much in the way of disappointment. The hell of not knowing is far worse than any blow you could give me.

He read what he'd written and felt sick. He sounded much as a green boy calf-sick with his first love. And the last thing on earth he wanted was her pity. Disgusted, he threw it on the floor and began another.

Sarah,
　　On the morrow I leave for Carillon on a mission of some risk. Should I perish, you will receive the customary one-third of what I have. Devin is my executor and will see that your needs are met until such time as my estate is settled.
　　It is with some sadness that I note a dearth of letters on your part, but I understand that in the fashionable world to which you have belatedly become accustomed, there is not that depth of attachment to which I had aspired. Meg assures me that you are having a jolly time of it in London and that the gentlemen are all clamoring at your feet.

He paused, pen poised above the inkpot, to read what he'd written. It sounded cold and by no means conveyed the awful pain and loneliness he felt. Instead, it accused her, but there seemed little else to do at this point. As he dipped the quill, he felt a surge of impotent anger. Forcing himself to go on, he wrote:

　　My life here has been a lonely hell, but I manage to fill my days with adventure. My nights I endure.
　　It is a wild, untamed place, America, but not without beauty. Here a man is known by what he can do rather than by who signs his baptismal register.

That was not precisely what he'd intended to say either, but perhaps it showed how much he had changed also, and it came to him that he was not the same man to whom Sarah had clung so tearfully. But that seemed to have been so long ago. He sighed heavily, reluctant to go on, yet feeling he must. Slowly his pen stroked over the page, forming the awful thought, giving voice to that which he'd been loath to face:

　　Should I return safely from Carillon, I shall write once again, asking if perhaps you are wishful of a legal separation. If you have discovered another, and he will not cavil at the scandal, I am not averse to allowing a divorce. I realize that long separations sometimes create a fondness for another, closer lover.

I shall direct Dev to tend to the matter, as I do not expect to return to England should that be your wish.

While the first letter had sounded unduly maudlin, this one was much colder than he felt. But how else did one discuss having one's happiness cut up? He felt as though he'd gone through hell, and if he could have gotten his hands on her, he'd have shaken her for what she'd done to him.

Joanna looked up. "Sa-rah?" she asked quietly.

"Aye."

Disgusted with himself for letting anyone cause him such pain, he swept everything from his desk angrily, sending papers, inkpot, and quills flying; then he lurched to his feet, oblivious of the spreading stain on the floor. Joanna blinked.

"Where you go?"

"Out."

She laid aside O'Donnell's cloak and rose gracefully to come up behind him, touching his shoulder.

"Ad-dam?"

He was in no mood to try to explain to her—the effort would be too great. He shook her off and started to leave, but she was quick. She stood between him and the door. Her dark eyes were troubled as she looked up at him.

"You no need sister, Ad-dam—you need wife." And as she said it, her fingers indicated the laces of her stomacher where they crossed her breast.

He stared at her a long silent moment, tempted—tempted to lie once again in warm arms, to feel the heat of bodies joined in passion. The muscles in his neck and jaw tensed and he clenched his fists at his side.

"Nay. I need no one," he told her harshly.

Joanna dropped her eyes and stepped aside to let him pass. A blast of cold wind and snow blew through the small room; then the door banged shut after him. She fell to her knees and gathered the strewn papers and quills, making order out of them. She could read none of what he'd written, but she'd seen the way he'd looked while his pen had scratched across the pages. Very carefully she collected and folded them, forcing them into the envelope Adam had addressed to his wife, much as she'd seen him do so many times before. The woman Sarah must know what she did to him.

Hours later, Sean O'Donnell came for his cloak, paying her three pence for her labor. And as he was about to go, she handed him the envelope.

"Adam wishes this sent?"

"Post."

He nodded. "I'll give it to Captain Wilcox tonight." He lingered, trying to think of something else to say to her. "Joanna, I . . ." But there was no encouragement in her eyes. His face inexplicably red, he gulped and clasped the envelope. "Good night, Joanna."

The candle in the dish was nearly gutted, now but a sputtering valiant flame in a sea of wax, and still she sat waiting for him. His packs were readied, his doeskin shirt oiled, brushed, and mended, and the stock of his new musket polished until it shone like a mirror.

The flame flickered, flared, then went out, leaving naught but coals in the fireplace. Finally, in despair, she unlaced her stomacher and pulled the stiff, white man's torture away, then drew off her full-skirted muslin dress. Stepping out of the many petticoats that were her pride, she padded naked to her cot.

The room was dark and silent when he stumbled in. She came awake as he lurched to stand over her, his eyes glittering. She shrank against the mattress, watching mutely whilst he shed his clothes, seeing his shadow loom hugely on the wall. His eyes less used to the darkness than hers, he groped for the cot and tripped over her discarded petticoats, falling. His body covered hers, crushing her with his weight. One hand, clumsy from too much rum, caught in her hair.

"You wanna be my wife, Joanna?" he murmured thickly against her ear. "You wanna love me?"

She lay stiff and unmoving beneath him.

"Whatsa matter? 'Tish what you want, ishn't it?"

She swallowed hard—he could feel it—but still she said nothing. And as drunk as he was, he knew something was very wrong. He rolled off her and staggered from her bed. Fumbling in the darkness, he found his flint and tried to spark the candle, cursing when the wick glowed and died amid the congealed wax. She rose silently and took a candle from the rough-hewn mantel. Bending over, she lit it from the dying embers of the fire. And as she held it up, he could see her cheeks were wet.

"Dammit, what *do* you want?" he shouted at her. "For months you led me to think . . . and then . . . What the devil is the matter with you?"

She dropped to sit cross-legged on the floor before the fireplace, staring at him. Then she spoke haltingly, stringing the long multisyllabic words together, but he had not the patience to try to understand a language he scarce spoke beyond merest commonplace.

"Speak English!"

Her chin came up. "Jo-anh-ha not Sar-ah, Tecawron-gati."

The heat faded from his body, leaving him ashamed and almost sober. "No. No, you are not," he said finally. "I'm sorry, Joanna."

Setting the candle aside that he might not see her face, she shook her head miserably. "Jo-anh-ha named wrong. Jo-anh-ha Woman Who Weeps."

He walked to take a blanket from his bed and, gently laying it over her shoulders, he tried to make amends. "Come, you ought to be abed—and I also."

Nodding, she wiped her face with the back of her hand. Looking up at him, she managed a small smile. "Ad-dam fall on arse with skate."

"Probably." Shaking his head at the way she'd said it, he asked, "Who the devil told you you could say 'arse'?"

"Sha-won O-Don-nell."

"Well, don't use that word."

Later, when Adam thought she slept, she spoke across the room, rousing him from his troubled thoughts.

"What call arse then?"

"Nothing."

"Arse called something," she persisted.

"Buttocks, but ladies don't say that either."

"But-tocks? Like 'arse' better," she decided definitely.

Despite everything, he had to smile. He turned over, cradling his head in his arms, and promised himself he'd speak to Sean O'Donnell.

31

With spring came decidedly mixed blessings. March marked both the end of Sarah's mourning and Adam's sister's wedding. And as much as she hated seeing Meg gloat over her "dear Chatwick," Sarah accompanied Devin to the Park. Thankfully, she had not been made part of the wedding party itself, for while she bore no real malice toward the girl, she did not think she could bear participating without Adam.

She'd taken great pains with both her wardrobe and her looks for this, her return to the Park, and the results had been gratifying. Her traveling gown of deep green lustring and her feather-trimmed hat of the same hue, both chosen with Devin's guidance, had turned heads wherever they had stopped along the road, and they did not fail to do so upon arrival.

"My, but don't you look fine as fivepence, mistress?" the earl had greeted her. "Em, you see what town bronze does for the gel? If it was to become you half so well, I'd let you go more often."

Meg gave her a dutiful buss, all the while assessing the worth of her toilette down to the last farthing. Sarah merely smiled and told Adam's sister she was looking well. It would never do to let the jealous girl know how much she hurt inside.

There was no question that Adam's father was glad to see her, and the countess allowed as how "Charles has been suffering from pique since you left, dear Sarah, for he counts poor Meg and me as quite inadequate substitutes at cards."

"Don't suppose as you'd want to try a rubber or two ere we sup?" he asked her hopefully.

"Charles! The child has but arrived!" Lady Emma protested.

"I know that! Been waitin' for her, in fact! But, dash it, Em, the gel's been sitting all day, ain't she?"

And so Sarah had drawn off her hat and traveling gloves to follow him into his bookroom, where the table was already laid with the deck of cards. A bottle and two glasses sat on his side.

"Best Madeira I could procure," he murmured, pouring a little into each crystal goblet. "And before you say you ain't wantin' any, you let an old man celebrate your homecoming, you hear?" He drank deeply of his, then smacked his lips with satisfaction. "Good stuff, eh? Go on—didn't buy it so's I'd drink alone."

"Are you hoping I will not be able to see the spots on the pasteboards?" she asked, smiling.

"Got to get an advantage somewheres, ain't I? I ain't forgot as you are a Mistress Sharp, you know."

"I have not played in months, sir."

"Daresay Dev ain't much of a hand at it—never was, anyways." He dealt deftly, then picked up his cards. "Got his mind on politics. Guess his hopes was all cut up when the German picked Devonshire."

"Yes."

"Well, it ain't going t' last, and so you can tell him—no, damme, I'll tell him meself."

She arranged her hand to suit her, murmuring, "The rumors are thicker than the fog, my lord, and I for one think Mr. Pitt's time has finally come. I mean, who else is there? With Fox piqued, Robinson ineffectual, and Newcastle leaning toward Pitt himself, what can the king do? If he persists in looking for yet another minister, he'll be booed in the streets. Pitt, sir, is the popular choice. I predict he will be given the prosecution of the war within the month.''

He closed his hand and stared. ''You do, eh? And you think he will make a difference?''

''Undoubtedly. I have heard him say the effort must be America, sir—if we cannot beat the French there, where they have the disadvantages of weather, corruption, and worse equipment than ours, we might as well run down the flag and surrender.''

''Fine words, mistress! They all say what we want to hear—always have, always will.''

''But Pitt understands the importance of America and India. Both are vast and rich, one in gold and gems, the other in land. What good does it do to soak Europe yet again with English blood, when in the end 'twill belong to the Prussians and their allies?''

''You have been listening to Audley.''

''I have been listening to everyone—Mr. Pitt, Mr. Robinson, Newcastle, and the others—and I happen to agree with Mr. Pitt.''

''And I suppose you ain't above letting a few Whigs know your mind, eh?''

''I've not been above putting fleas in a few ears,'' she admitted openly.

''So Audley wrote to me—said you had 'em all dancing to your pipe.''

''Well, I should not say that, I think. I should rather say I merely prodded a few consciences.''

''Sly puss!'' He played a card and sighed. ''If Adam had gone into government, you'd a been a gem for him. The way Dev tells it, you got the restless ones a-singing Pitt's song now.''

''I hope so.''

It was not until several rubbers later that he brought Adam up again. ''I don't hear nothing from the boy, you know—oh, not that I was expecting to, you understand. Just wish I knew he was all right.''

She sat very still, wondering whether he knew that Adam did not write to her either.

''Can't get nothing out of Audley—writes of demned

near everything else,'' he muttered. His faded eyes met hers. "The boy's well, ain't he?''

She considered lying to him, but could not. "I wish I knew also,'' she answered finally.

His eyes narrowed sharply. "What's this, mistress? You ain't heard neither? Now, I know that for a hum! Come on, out with it—'tis to Charles Hastings you speak! If he ain't all right, me as is his papa ought to know of it.''

"No.'' It was little more than a whisper, for her throat had tightened, and the hollow ache in her chest was almost more than she could bear. She swallowed hard, shaking her head. "What I know, Dev has had from dispatches,'' she managed, her voice low. "He . . . he is well, so far as I have been told.'' Then, unable to face his incredulous stare, she burst out, "Sir, you behold the most miserable of females!''

"Eh? Here, now, Sarah, didn't mean to put you into a taking—just wanted to know, that's all.'' He leaned forward until his face was but inches from hers, and his expression was unusually kind. "But if you are saying he ain't wrote to you neither, something havey-cavey's afoot, my dear. It ain't Adam as would neglect you.''

"Ask Dev—he can tell you how it has been.'' She dug deeply into the slits of her skirt and found the cambric pockets tied beneath. Pulling out a dainty lawn handkerchief, she blotted her eyes almost angrily. "Your pardon, my lord, but I should not trouble you with my concerns.''

"He didn't come to me from a fairy's basket, Sarah—I got a right to know what goes.'' But as he said it, his veined hand covered hers. "He's blood of my blood and bone of my bone, you know.''

"But I . . . I don't know why he forgets me!'' she cried.

"He ain't forgot you! Dash it, but he wrote after the babe was lost, didn't he?''

"But I've had no word since September, and then 'twas a month ere I got it!'' She stopped and blew her nose. "I know not what to think.''

"Letters got mixed up in the dispatches—aye, I warrant 'tis what—''

"No. I asked Dev, and he put forth an inquiry for

me." She looked at him through tear-wet lashes. "It is as though he joined the rangers and forgot me."

"Mayhap the frogs has got him—it ain't impossible, and—"

"No. So we thought also, but he has received a commendation from the War Office—Audley brought me the notice. And there was word he refused a promotion. More than that I have not heard."

The thought crossed his mind that if it had been Audley who was gone, he'd possibly discovered a ladybird, but it was Adam. Apparently his expression was transparent, for she asked him, "Do you think perhaps he has found someone else?"

"Adam?" The way he said it clearly indicated he did not. "The boy was head over heels for you!"

"Then."

He digested that and shook his head. "He ain't a here-and-therian, Sarah," he reminded her gently. "I'd wager the Park that ain't what ails him." His cards forgotten, he absently poured himself a glass of Madeira and pondered the matter. "Nay, it ain't that at all. You ain't given him no cause to doubt you, d' ye think? No—no, of course you ain't," he answered himself. Then finally he sighed. "I talked him into leaving you, ye know—he was wavering even with the babe and all, but I said you'd be safer here and I'd like to have you stay."

In the face of her silence, he explained, "I thought if you was here, he'd come back to me, don't you see? Was sure of it, in fact. Dev thought as how you ought to go, but 'twas me and Em as said New York was no fit place for an increasing female with no family. Dash it, 'twas not to be much over a year, anyways."

"And he proves he is so inconstant that he cannot remember me longer than three months," she decided bitterly.

"He remembers you! Damme, I know he does!"

"I have not your conviction anymore, sir."

"Nay. The mistake was mine, I guess—I ought to have considered as a wife belongs with her husband. Seems I didn't learn my own lesson," he admitted heavily. "Forgive an old man his foolishness, my dear."

His logic was confusing, to say the least. "Forgive you, my lord? 'Tis not your fault he does not write."

"Ought to have insisted you go. But don't you see? Before he brought you home to the Park, the boy hadn't been home above a week in three years. We don't deal together, he and I, and I thought with the babe and all . . . well, I'd hoped to make amends. But I guess he don't forgive me yet." His eyes were red and watery, and his old voice quavered slightly. "But how was I to know he didn't come to me by the side door? Emma'd left me, you know." Then, realizing what he'd said, he looked away. " 'Course he didn't—know that now, and many's the time as I tried to tell him, but 'twas too late. My foolish pride's lost m' son to me, Sarah."

"No."

His hand closed over hers again, squeezing it. "Don't let pride and ignorance lose him to you also, gel. Forget he ain't written—bound to be a reason for it, anyways. There's favorable winds now, don't you know? You book yourself passage over there and demand an explanation of him. Aye, and if you've spent your allowance, I'll sport the blunt meself." He released her hand and sat back. "All I'd ask is for you to tell him it ain't just you and Dev and Em as has a care for him."

Swallowing hard, she shook her head. "I could not bear discovering he does not want me anymore. Like you, sir, I have my pride."

"Then the two biggest fools in this house are in this room right now."

Meg's wedding was far different from Sarah's. As the only daughter of the Earl and Countess of Westerfield, she had in attendance full half the county as well as a number of lords and ladies of the *ton,* many of whom had traveled the length or breadth of the country. The church in the village overflowed with well-wishers come to witness her vows.

And Meg was radiant for a change. As she looked up at Chatwick, her happiness was so obvious that Sarah felt a pang of envy. Meg was living every female's dream.

As Sarah sat beside Devin, she could not help contrasting the pomp and ceremony with her own hasty wedding a little over a year before. But the words, after all, were still the same. She closed her eyes as Chatwick spoke the age-old vows, promising to love, to honor, and to cherish Margaret Emma Hastings so long as they both should live. And she could not help wondering if Chatwick would be more constant in his devotion than Adam had been.

When she looked up again, it was Meg's turn, and the girl pledged herself, her voice as strong as Sarah's had been in what seemed now to have been an age ago. Would Meg be more fortunate in keeping her husband's love than Sarah? As much as the girl obviously disliked her, Sarah could not bring herself to wish Meg anything but continued happiness. No female on earth deserved the misery she herself had suffered.

She became aware of Devin's eyes on hers, and once again she was struck by how much they reminded her of Adam's. His hand crept to where hers lay folded in her lap, and he held her fingers in his. How like him to attempt to comfort her. A sense of gratitude overwhelmed her as she realized he understood better than any how Adam's neglect had wounded not only her pride but also her heart.

She stole a sidewise glance at him, seeing his strong, handsome profile, thinking how very different he'd proved to be from what she'd thought him. And her mind again harked back to that fateful day when he'd visited her. How very different her life would be if he'd offered marriage then.

She'd have had to take him—she'd had nowhere to go, she recalled. But would they have discovered the intense passion she'd shared with Adam? Was it possible to feel as much for more than one man in one's lifetime?

As if he knew her thoughts, he leaned closer to whisper, ''I was a great fool last year, to my eternal regret.''

''No.''

His breath, warm and light where it touched her ear, sent a rush of remembered desire through her. For a moment she closed her eyes, telling herself she was wanton, that it was but her traitorous body's longing for a man's embrace. She sucked in her breath, letting it out slowly, then studiously watched as Reverend Wicklund pronounced the benediction over Meg's and Chatwick's heads.

Such thoughts could lead nowhere but to her shame, and she knew it. What she felt for Devin Hastings was but a friendship born of common interest, nothing more. Her hunger was loneliness—it had to be. And yet she sometimes wondered if she could not learn to love him. He'd taught her so much of the world these months past, sharing with her his hopes and ambitions.

Under his tutelage, she'd become far different from the green country girl Adam had wedded. Her hair, her clothing, even her carriage bespoke an elegance that turned heads, and she knew it. And the gentlemen Devin brought to dine came to look and stayed to listen. Her views were discussed and quoted in Parliament by Whigs and Tories alike, though with quite different interpretation, of course.

She and Devin worked well together, furthering Pitt's cause at every turn. And there was scarce a day to pass when he did not praise her efforts. Was this perhaps of greater importance than the intense passion she'd shared with Adam?

But he *was* Adam's brother. And that fact alone ought to make both of them draw back from the casual discourse that had sprung up between them. The reality of the matter was that even if Adam did not want her anymore, if Adam did not come back, there was nothing beyond the present for her and Devin. To take one's brother's wife was forbidden under law. And to engage in any sort of liaison would end Lord Audley's promising career.

Abruptly his hand withdrew from hers, and she realized the wedding was over. Music reverberated through the small, ancient church as Chatwick led Margaret out. The eight bridesmaids and eight groomsmen followed; then Devin slipped his hand beneath Sarah's elbow, guiding her from the family pew.

Outside, Mrs. Wicklund greeted her with more enthusiasm than she'd ever afforded Sarah before, murmuring,

"How very lovely you look, my dear Mrs. Hastings. 'Twould seem London life becomes you.''

"Thank you. And Roland is well?''

The smile faded from the woman's face. "Roland is in New York with his regiment.''

"Then I shall pray for his safety.''

"We take great pride in Captain Hastings' accomplishments,'' Mr. Wicklund said. "Village gossip has it he is quite the hero, and all of us read the article of General Abercromby's commendation with interest.''

"Well, I for one am thankful Roland has not been sent amongst the savages,'' his wife sniffed. "Why, I have heard that they—''

"We have heard the tales also,'' Devin cut in quickly. "Sarah, I believe 'tis Mrs. Lynch who tries to gain your attention. Aye, and there is Lord Rothwell also.''

"Rothwell here?'' Mrs. Wicklund was instantly diverted. " 'Pon my word! Is Mr. Pitt come also?''

"Alas, no. But I believe Devonshire is here.''

"You do not say!''

And while the lady cast about curiously, Devin propelled Sarah toward Squire Lynch and his wife. "Audley!'' that gentleman hailed him; then, "Egad—it cannot be! Never say 'tis Spender's chit! Mrs. Lynch, you ever see the like? 'Tis Sarah Spender!''

"Sarah Hastings,'' Devin corrected him.

"Eh? Oh, aye. Mrs. Hastings.''

Somehow Sarah managed to get through the social discourse with her former neighbors, enduring their curiosity as pleasantly as possible. Without exception, they'd all thought she'd wed above her, and she knew it.

"Buck up,'' Devin murmured, drawing her arm through his. "Soon 'twill all be over, and we'll be on our way back to London. I have told Papa that Newcastle will not survive Tuesday's vote in Commons, and I must be back to confer with our allies there.''

"I was thinking of staying, Dev.''

He stood stock-still, then shook his head. "Sarah, we are not done yet. We have come too far and striven too hard for you to draw back now. We are poised for victory this time, and I'd have you there to share in it.''

"As if it can make any difference to me now."

"It makes a difference to me. Sarah, do not let these country cows overset you with their questions of Adam. Just say he is well and leave it." ·

"I have, but—"

"Sarah, I still need your aid. What if Rothwell should waver? Or Revenham? Sarah, I rely on you to persuade them. They admire you greatly, you know, and have the highest regard for your opinion."

She couldn't tell him that she didn't want to go back, that she feared the growing attraction between them, that in far too many of her dreams Adam became him. He was watching her intently, his blue eyes entreating.

"All right," she said finally. "But once Mr. Pitt is named, I shall come back. Your father, I think, would like the company."

"Sarah, I like the company. Without you, London is dull and insipid." Then, despite the crush of people around them, he declared flatly, "I need your company— I need it, Sarah."

"But I am afraid of yours, Dev," she murmured, turning away. "And if you will excuse me, I see Miss Wallace."

He let her go, staring after her. The spring sun shone on the rich, deep green of her gown and brightened her auburn hair. *But I am afraid of yours, Dev.* Then she felt it also. A sense of exhilaration flooded over him. And in that moment, he didn't give a damn about Pitt—or Adam; he didn't give a damn about anything except her.

32

Devin's hands slid around her neck, fastening the clasp of his mother's borrowed emeralds, and lingered lightly, stroking the fine hairs at her nape. "You ought to have your own set," he murmured softly. "Emeralds become you."

She ducked away, trying to hide what his touch did to her. "It would not be seemly for you to buy them," she told him quietly.

"I tire of the seemly, Sarah. I tire of being the paragon brother." He turned and walked to face the fireplace, where a small fire warded off the chill of a spring evening. "You must know I love you," he said finally. His heart seemed to stop, waiting for her response, yet he dared not look at her.

"Yes," she said simply.

"At first, it was but lust—I saw and I wanted—but 'tis far more than that now."

What could she say? The truth would lead to disgrace and dishonor, and she knew it. Closing her eyes, she leaned forward to rest her head on her elbows, wishing very much that she'd not come back with him.

"Sarah, I cannot bear this! I tire of watching you from afar—I tire of seeing you suffer also!"

She swallowed hard, feeling as though she must surely break into pieces from the tension she felt. "I'll go away, Dev."

"No!" He crossed back to stand over her. "Can you not see that would be the greater hell? Sarah, I love you!

There—twice I have said it! Can you not find it in your heart to care for me?''

She dropped her head lower and stared miserably at the patterned carpet on the floor beneath her dressing table. "Sometimes I think I love you also, but—''

"There can be no 'buts' between us, Sarah. I'd give all I have for you to love me. I am a wealthy man, far wealthier than you might imagine. I can give you anything you want: diamonds, gowns, estates—''

Surely Satan never tempted anyone more. He offered an end to the terrible loneliness, to the aching emptiness she felt. He would hold her in his arms and love her as Adam once had done.

"Sarah, look at me,'' he pleaded.

"No!'' She pressed her palms against her temples as though she could shut out the temptation. "I cannot think! I would that you did not stand over me! Please, Dev—I would you would not.''

Reluctantly he backed away. She stood, turning almost desperately, seeking respite from what she felt. Her wide, hooped skirt brushed against him as she moved to the window and stared unseeing at the garden below. He ought to go slowly, to let her accustom herself to what he'd said, but he could not bring himself to do it. Instead, he came up behind her and laid his hands on her shoulders.

"Sarah, I see it in your eyes also. Do not deny either of us this happiness, I beg of you.''

"Happiness?'' She whirled to face him. *"Happiness?* How can there be any happiness in dishonor, Dev? 'Tis what you ask of both of us—to shame your family, to fly in the face of society—'tis a high price you would have us pay, my lord.''

"I'd wed you.''

"How? Have you forgotten Adam? Do you forget your own brother? And what of your parents? How do you think your papa will feel?'' she demanded almost hysterically. "You cannot wed me—I am your brother's wife!''

"Adam will give you a divorce, Sarah.''

"For what—adultery?'' Tears welled in her eyes but

did not spill. Her voice, which had risen, dropped low. "Even if I admit to loving you, I cannot."

"I'd not meant to tell you, Sarah—I'd wanted to spare you, but I'll not let you throw this chance away. Sarah, Adam is not alone in New York—he has taken an Indian concubine."

"I don't believe you."

"I have set inquiries afoot there, and 'tis true, I am afraid. It seems she nursed him back to health."

She stared at him, not wanting to believe, but those blue eyes so like Adam's were sober. He nodded. "Well," she said slowly, " 'twould explain much, I suppose."

"Sarah—"

"How long have you known? You had not the right not to tell me of this—I am not a child to be spared, my lord,"

"He brought her out of the wilderness with him some months ago."

It was as though he'd cut the last thread of the hope she'd clung to for so long. "I see."

"Sarah, I will introduce the bill myself, with his blessing. There'll be a devil of a scandal, but we can go away—I'll take you to Italy or Spain."

She shook her head. " 'Twould break your papa's heart."

"Not when he knows why."

"Your career would be over, and you'd come to hate me for that."

He reached out to brush an errant curl away from her face. It was a gesture that reminded her once again of Adam. A dull ache possessed her chest.

"I would do anything to have you, Sarah—anything."

"You cannot wed your brother's wife."

"I cannot wed my brother's widow, 'tis true, but 'tis debatable if you were divorced. If you like, I am willing to approach him about an annulment, since there is no issue."

Every fiber of her being cried out in denial. An annulment would say there had been no marriage, that they'd never loved so intensely that the memories burned her still.

" 'Twould be a lie!'' she cried.

"Merely an expedient. Then, regardless of the gossip, there could be none to say you were not my viscountess." He drew her resisting body into his arms, holding her as close as her billowing skirts would allow. A shiver went through her; then she leaned into him, taking comfort from his strength. "Sarah, I'd take care of you," he whispered into her shining hair.

"He loved me once—I know he did," she choked out miserably. "I hate this accursed war—I hate it!''

"Shhhhh."

"And what if you tired of me also?"

"I do not mean to ever leave you, love." He lifted her chin with his knuckle and searched her face. "Say you will wed me when you are free, Sarah." When she did not answer, he bent his head to hers.

His kiss was tender at first, so unlike that earlier time; then, as her arms slid around his neck, it deepened hungrily. She gave herself up to the moment, closing her eyes and savoring the strength of the man who held her. And when at last he left her mouth, he whispered softly against her ear, "I'd love you, Sarah—let me love you, Sarah."

It was what Adam had said. She stiffened and pushed him away. As the blood rushed to her face, she could not face him.

"You want me also—I can feel it every time I touch you. Do not deny us what we both desire," he said softly, reaching out to her again.

The appeal in his eyes tore at her soul. "Give me time," she pleaded. " 'Tis time I need, Dev. 'Tis too soon—I cannot even think.''

A soft knock sounded on her door. "Madam, there is Lord Revenham below. He offers his apologies that he is early."

Devin cursed under his breath as he dropped his hand. A great sigh of relief escaped Sarah. The interruption had granted her a reprieve from making the unthinkable choice. Her hands shaking, she moved to the mirror to pat her auburn curls in place.

"Sarah . . ."

She spun around. "A week—I ask a week, my lord, nothing more." Her amber eyes were grave, devoid of all passion now. "I wedded in haste once, with this unhappy result. I pray you will not allow me to make the same mistake twice over."

It was not what he'd wanted to hear. For two full days—ever since he'd received Adam's last letter—he'd wanted to approach her. Ever since Adam had offered to divorce her, he'd dared to think she'd come to him. Swallowing his disappointment, he nodded.

"All right. 'Tis fair enough, I suppose. After all, I am accounted a patient man." His smile twisted as she turned again to her mirror. "There is no need to look again, my dear—you are quite beautiful enough for any man."

Somehow, she'd managed to get through dinner, smiling and responding to the endless compliments of Devin's guests, listening to chatter that now seemed meaningless. Adam did not love her anymore. 'Twas why he had not written. He'd found another. And the pain that she thought had passed stabbed at her anew.

She excused herself as soon as she could, hearing Devin explain she was not feeling quite the thing as she slowly climbed the stairs to her bedchamber. There'd been a murmur of sympathy, followed by more of the eternal speculation on whether Devonshire would survive past the morrow.

She lay fully clothed upon her bed, staring into the darkness, heedless of the fact she crushed her hoops. Adam did not love her. Devin did. There would be those to think her the most fortunate of women, those to envy her Viscount Audley. And she could not deny a very real attraction to him. But when she closed her eyes, it was a young officer in a red coat that she saw.

How could he have forgotten her so quickly? The Adam Hastings she'd known and loved all her life had been a more constant fellow. A kind, generous man. Had his wound affected his reason? Had this distant Indian girl used some pagan art to enslave him?

As painful as it was, she relived her memories of him—of how he'd come to Spender's Hill and offered for her, of how he'd defied his family to wed her, and of the wonderful, tender, ecstatic moments they'd shared in their brief marriage. Even in the dark, her face flamed as she remembered those passionate days spent in the stable at Spender's Hill. And her body ached with wanting him still.

Was that what it was—had she turned to Dev to succor those memories of Adam? Sometimes she really believed she loved Devin Hastings also, but could a woman love two men? She knew Devin loved her—she had seen his regard deepen with the passing months—and yet she'd done nothing to avert it. Had she merely allowed herself to substitute him for Adam?

She had no answers. It was too soon yet for her to think clearly. If she had any moral fiber at all, she ought to do her thinking at the Park. But she could not bear the old man's disappointment any more than she could bear her own.

She still, despite everything, wanted to believe that Adam was a decent, honorable man. Perhaps he'd merely succumbed to loneliness as she had almost done. Perhaps he did not love this Indian girl.

She ought to take Devin. Reason told her he was right. And if Adam had found someone else to love, then she could also. If only he'd written to her of it—she'd have found the means to bear it—but then at least she would have heard it from him.

As humiliating, as painful as it would be, she decided she had to write to him one last time. Then if he truly wished to be free of her, she'd decide what she ought to do. It would be difficult to make Devin understand, but surely he would. And if he loved her—and if she loved him—time would make them sure.

She rose, pushing her hoops and petticoats out of the way, and searched for the candle dish. Groping along the mantel until she discovered the flint, she picked it up. Her fingers closed over the candle. Striking the flint, she set the spark to the wick, and after several tries, she was rewarded with a tiny glow. Cupping her hands around it, she sheltered it and watched it grow.

The one small flame was insufficient to her purposes, so she carried it to the Scottish cruzie, which was still filled with oil. She lit one wick from the other, then turned her attention to the brace of candles on her writing desk.

It was not so good as if she'd had a fire, but she had not the patience to light that, nor the wish to call anyone to do it for her. Instead, she pulled a fringed shawl about her shoulders and sat down to write.

The quill was dull, so much so that it spattered ink on the first page, and she could not find her small ivory-handled knife. In disgust, she threw it down.

The men were still in the front saloon—she could hear their voices rising in convivial disputation when she came down the servants' stairs. Ah, well, let them argue without her. She slipped inside Devin's bookroom and quietly closed the door. The coals were still alive in the fireplace, making the room warmer than hers. She picked up a piece of wood from the kindling box and threw it over them, hoping it would catch.

She noted with satisfaction that Devin's desk was unlocked, and seating herself there, she rummaged for paper and quills. Then she opened his inkwell, dipped his pen, and started to write.

"My dear husband." No, that was scarce the thing to begin with, not when he'd not bothered to write for seven months. She crumpled the sheet and threw it into the fireplace. Beginning again, she wrote, "Dear Adam." It seemed so impersonal, considering what they'd once meant to each other, but she had to start with something. She bit the feather tip absently, trying to compose her thoughts.

Bitter recrimination came to mind, but that time was past. "I trust you are well." She changed the period to a comma and went on, "for I have not had word of you since September last.

I know not how it has been for you, but my life has gone from heaven with you to purgatory and then hell in your absence. I know you are busy, that your duties take you into dangerous and wild places where there is no post, and I have tried to understand. But I have reached that place where your first two letters no longer sustain me. I would know from your own hand how you fare.

Devin has been most kind and considerate to me.

She stopped, wondering how to go on. She could not very well say his brother had fallen in love with her, that she was drawn to Devin also. Her pen moved slowly, deliberately over the page. "Indeed, I know not what I should have done without him, for there have been times I thought I could not go on, times when I despaired of ever seeing or hearing from you again."

The point broke, flattening against the page, leaving a blob of ink there. She reached into the drawer for another and found it jammed. Sliding her hand inside, she pressed down to release whatever held it. And as she drew the drawer out, she discovered the half-closed false bottom. It was, she supposed, where Devin kept documents of some importance to his office. But, looking down, she went cold to the marrow.

Page after page, each covered in Adam's bold, distinctive hand, lay flatly pressed in the shallow space. So Adam had written to Devin, after all. Then her heart nearly stopped beating as she saw: "Sarah, On the morrow I shall embark on a mission of some risk. Should I perish, you will receive the customary one-third . . ." Her eyes traveled quickly down the paper, resting on the words "It is with some sadness that I note a dearth of letters on your part . . ."

How could that be? Until the past few months she'd written often, and even after that, at least once per week, hoping that somehow he'd answer. But he hadn't. His last words on the page struck her as though he'd used a knife: "I am not averse to allowing a divorce. I realize that long separations sometimes create a fondness for another, closer lover."

How dared he? How dared he accuse her when he'd taken his Indian girl? With shaking hands she lifted the page, discovering another one, also addressed to her. She read it in disbelief, seeing, "Meg writes that you are quite the social success despite your mourning," and "I must ask how it is that those memories we shared have faded for you."

She fairly tore out the stack, reading through it, discovering well over a dozen, all addressed to her. And as she relived his growing doubt of her, her heart sank. He'd gone from consoling her about the babe, from sharing his dreams with her, to a stiffness that betrayed his growing bitterness also.

And in the back of the drawer were her letters, carefully kept in order. The envelopes were gone. And with the discovery came the sickening realization of what had happened. She took them out, fitting them in order with Adam's, seeing the parallel between their growing disaffection. She did not even hear Devin's guests leaving.

The door opened behind her. "Sarah, you are still up? You ought to be abed, you know, as it grows late," he chided.

"I have been reading, my lord." She turned around in his chair and held out the sheaf of papers. "These."

The color drained from his face. He stared helplessly, saying nothing.

"How could you do this to me, Dev? How could you be so false to your own brother?" she asked coldly. "Did you think we should never know?" She rose and advanced on him, the letters clenched in her hands. "Were you going to see to it that we never met again?"

"Aye." It was more of a croak than a word.

"I almost loved you, my lord."

"Sarah—"

"I shall require the carriage in the morning. If you refuse to lend it, then I shall simply book the stage."

She brushed past him, leaving him just inside the doorway. "Sarah! You cannot! He has another!"

"Does he? Well, if 'tis so, then I suppose I shall try to forgive him. After all, 'tis no worse than I was tempted to do more than once these months past."

"He will give you a divorce."

She stopped, but did not turn back. "If I discover it to

be too late to effect a reconciliation with my husband, I shall never forgive you, Devin.''

The gulf between them was unbreachable and he knew it. Her coldness was more defeating than if she'd screamed and railed at him. "While you were upstairs, a messenger came from the king. Pitt shall direct the war,'' he said finally.

"I suppose I ought to be glad for that at least, but I find myself strangely unable to feel anything. Good night, my lord.''

33

Albany, New York: May 5, 1757

Relieved to finally be there, Sarah stepped from the boat to survey the town curiously. The riverfront was filled with the bustling wharves and warehouses of Dutch merchants. And alongside the large barges were bark canoes piled with great stacks of furs.

It had been a long and arduous journey undertaken alone, but she'd come to face her husband, and she'd not wanted any other to witness her probable rejection. For five weeks she'd dreaded this final meeting and yet she'd come, armed with nothing more than her pride and two stacks of letters.

In New York she'd been told that all ranger companies had been ordered into Albany but two weeks earlier by General Abercromby on Lord Loudoun's orders. Rumor had it that Captain Rogers, Lieutenant Gage, and the other ranger leaders would meet with the general staff and representatives of the colonial governors to assess and interpret intelligence gathered over the winter. Most of the rangers were to be housed privately in the town, much to the dismay of the inhabitants.

Well, she'd come this far, and now was not time for faint heart. Leaving all but one small bag in the care of the boat's captain, she started down the crowded colonial street. All manner of people—prosperous merchants, German farmers, plainly dressed women, soldiers, an occasional Indian, and rugged, unwashed trappers in dirty buckskins—stopped to stare as she passed them.

A tall, strapping blond man, his face leathery from the sun, accosted her, smiling. "Vot iss viss? Fräulein iss lost?"

By his accent and appearance, he must have been German, probably a settler, she supposed. "Ah . . . yes. I should like General Abercromby's or General Loudoun's direction, if you please."

He appraised her boldly, taking in her expensive bronze silk gown and her cocked hat with its curved ostrich plumes dyed to match her dress. Clearly she was a vision beyond his experience. She met his gaze and smiled.

"I am Mrs. Hastings—Captain Hastings' wife, sir. I should like directions to General Abercromby's quarters, if you please."

His own smile faded to regret. "Iss over there." He pointed to a long, low building, its planked facade whitewashed. Spring flowers bloomed in boxes set beneath it.

Her heart pounded as she crossed the street. Would they know Adam? And would they laugh at her for journeying so far to see him and his Indian concubine? She entered the open meeting room, discovering several officers there. They rose respectfully at the sight of her.

"My husband is a ranger, and I have come to meet him," she blurted out quickly, before she could lose her courage. "I am Sarah Hastings."

"Mrs. Hastings." A gentleman well into middle age moved forward to greet her. "I am Robert Abercromby. May I make known to you my second, Lord Howe? And Colonel Sir William Johnson?"

This tall man then was William Johnson. He appeared neither as savage as his reputation nor as imposing as she'd supposed. His eyes raked over her appreciatively as he acknowledged the introduction.

Abercromby cleared his throat and called to a soldier who still labored over papers in a corner of the room, "Perkins, send word to Captain Hastings that his wife is here, will you?"

"I should rather go there, I think," she announced with a calmness she did not feel.

The uncomfortable look Johnson and Abercromby exchanged was not lost on her. It was William Johnson who spoke. "Dear lady, I should be honored to escort you there myself."

"But of course you will wish to refresh yourself with a cup of"—the general hesitated, then settled on—"tea."

"No," she answered baldly. "I should like to see my husband first."

Abercromby cleared his throat again, looking to Johnson. "Sir, I should take her by way of Mrs. Apsley, don't you think? The other is probably not so safe."

Nodding, the colonel took her bag, then held the door for her. "Dear lady," he protested when she began to walk vigorously, "there is no need to rush. I am not at all certain you will find him there at this hour anyway."

"Yes, but I'd not have him apprised of my coming—'tis somewhat of a surprise, you see," she answered sweetly, increasing her step. "And I suspect a messenger goes the shorter way, does he not?"

"No matter how wonderful the surprise, there are times a man ought to be warned," he answered dryly, keeping pace with her.

Adam, it seemed, was well enough known that he'd been given quarters in the home of a Hendrik Von Risling, an absent but wealthy Dutch trader. They arrived as the soldier she'd seen in Abercromby's office was leaving. He shrugged expressively, then turned the other way.

"Thank you, Colonel," she said definitely, extending her gloved hand.

"I think perhaps I ought to go with you, madam—in case you should decide not to stay," he added significantly. "Mrs. Hastings—"

"If you think I have not heard of her, you are mistaken, sir."

"Nonetheless—"

But she was already several steps ahead of him. Sighing, he followed her anyway, and waited with her as she rapped loudly.

As the door opened, Sarah held her breath, praying that Johnson was wrong, that Adam was there. But no matter how many times she'd considered the possibility, she was unprepared for the Indian girl who answered.

They stared at each other in mutual comprehension. The girl was not what she'd expected, not at all. Instead of a half-wild savage, Sarah faced a slender woman with straight black hair and intelligent eyes. Moreover, she was wearing a neat muslin gown with a stomacher laced tightly at her narrow waist. And everything about her was clean.

"I am come to see Captain Hastings," Sarah announced crisply.

"Ad-dam not here." The girl pointed to her breast. "Jo-anh-ha. Ad-dam sister."

"Mrs. Hastings—"

"I am well aware of the relationship, Colonel," Sarah cut in coldly. "There is no need to dissemble for my sake."

"Sa-rah."

It was a statement rather than a question. Sarah nodded. "Yes."

Johnson spoke rapidly to the Indian girl in her own language and was answered in kind. Whatever he'd said, she'd protested. Finally she opened the door wider.

"Sa-rah wait. Ad-dam come back."

"Mrs. Hastings, if you have need of assistance, you have but to ask," Johnson murmured as he handed her her bag. "I am sure General Abercromby can find you quarters should these prove unsatisfactory."

"Thank you, sir."

After he left, Sarah stepped inside and drew off her soft kid gloves. Looking around her, she was surprised at the simplicity of the place. It seemed to consist of but two large rooms, both whitewashed and heated by huge fireplaces. And at the end of the first one, there were stairs leading to a second story.

"Sa-rah drink tea."

Again, there was no question. As the Indian girl moved away to the fireplace, Sarah was surprised to discover she wore no shoes. Obviously the girl was not unused to duties as a hostess, for she quickly poured the hot water over the tea strainer, then waited for it to steep. Not bothering to ask Sarah's preference, she removed the strainer and dropped two chunks of raw sugar into the cup.

"No milk," she said as she carried it back. "You sit."

Sarah eyed her warily, recalling all the awful tales of Indian atrocities carried in the London papers. And to her horror, the girl drew out a knife. Sarah's cup rattled nervously against the saucer, but she tried to appear calm. To her relief, the girl merely cut off a slice of some sort of bread and brought it to her.

"Thank you," Sarah managed politely.

For a long time they sat and stared at each other, Sarah in the stiff, high-backed wooden chair, the girl cross-legged on the floor. Had she not come so far, Sarah would have lost her nerve. As it was, she could not stand the silence after awhile.

"Can you speak English?" she asked finally.

"Men teach me."

"Where is Adam?"

"Jo-anh-ha send soldier for him."

"Did he name you?"

The girl shook her head. "Barclay call me Jo-anh-ha at school." She touched her breast again. "Indian name mean Woman Who Watches Water." She cocked her head and regarded Sarah soberly. "What Sa-rah mean?"

"I am told it means Princess."

There was an air of unreality to everything. To Sarah, it was inconceivable that she could be sitting across from her husband's mistress, making pitiful attempts at awkward conversation.

After several more minutes of strained silence, the Indian girl nodded toward the door. "Ad-dam come now."

It was as though everything stopped—her heart, her

mind, everything—as the door swung inward. Nothing could have prepared her for the stranger she faced.

"What the devil . . . ? *Sarah!*"

By the way he said it, she knew he was not pleased. She rose unsteadily, setting her rattling teacup aside. The girl Joanna darted past him, leaving them. He kicked the door shut behind her.

They stood, awkwardly taking stock of each other. There was little of the Adam she remembered in him. Gone was the scarlet uniform, the neatly tied dark blond hair, replaced by the worn buckskin shirt, leggings, and moccasins of an Indian. His hair, already bleached by the sun, streamed over his shoulders. And in open defiance of the officers' code, he wore a definite mustache.

To him, her elegant toilette was proof she'd changed. She looked far more the London belle than the Sarah Spender he'd once loved.

"Hello, Adam," she said finally, smiling uncertainly at the wild man before her.

"What are you doing here?"

"I came to join you."

A derisive snort escaped him. "Why? Did your London beau desert you? Or is one-third of my estate not enough?" he gibed. "You might as well go back, you know."

"I have no London beau."

All of the pain, all of the loneliness she'd caused him was like a bitter well inside. He wanted to wound, to hurt as he'd been hurt by her neglect. " 'Tis too late," he told her curtly. "I have found a new life here."

"Adam . . ." She reached out to him, touching his shoulder.

He flung himself away from her. "Do you think me such a fool that I do not know, Sarah? How many consoled you in my absence? Was it many—or but one?"

"It was but Dev, and—"

"Dev!" He spat out the word like it was a curse. "Did the two of you have no conscience?"

"Adam, I did not know! I thought—"

"All the lies! Aye—lies, Sarah! How long did my memories last for you? A month? Two?"

"Adam, 'twas not like that at all! Listen to me!"

"I married you, Sarah, thinking you were different from the other silly, shallow creatures! What a fool you made of me!"

"Will you listen to me?" she cried out.

"What happened—did Dev tire of you?"

"Will you *listen* to me?"

"No!"

She'd not traveled an ocean to be turned away before she could speak. She followed him across the room and caught at his elbow. He shook her off with such fury that she staggered. Angry tears welled in her eyes.

"You have no right to accuse me, Adam! How dare you think I have done as you have? 'Twas you who played me false, Adam Hastings! I cried myself to sleep whilst you lay with . . . with that savage!"

"Leave Joanna out of this!"

"I am your wife!"

"Meg wrote to me!"

"If she said I took a lover, she lied! Adam, look at me! Ask your father—your mother!" She bit her lower lip to stifle the sob that threatened a total end to her composure. "Adam, I beg of you—do not do to me what your father did to your mother," she whispered.

"Why don't you have me ask Dev?" he demanded sarcastically. "Or would he tell me a different tale?"

"I don't know what he would say. I can only tell you that he lied to me."

"And I suppose my offer to divorce you brought him to his senses?" He sneered. "He chose his career over you?"

"He offered to marry me."

"I don't believe you! Of all that can be said of Devin, he is not a fool!"

"He thought he could make me love him, Adam—and I almost did. I did not receive your letters, you know."

" 'Tis as well—they were but the maudlin meanderings of a fool," he muttered. "You behold before you a fool no longer, Sarah."

"I wrote to you also."

" 'Tis too late for lies!"

"Adam, I have come so far—I had to hear you tell me you love me no more. And if you can look at me and say it, I'll go." She turned and searched the bag Colonel Johnson had set inside the door, drawing out the sheaf of wrinkled papers. "All I ask is that you read what I wrote to you."

He had never wanted to believe in anything so much in his life, and yet he could not. "What did you do— write them after Dev changed his mind?" He swung around to face her. "You are too late, Sarah. My love for you died last winter."

"Adam—"

"You said you'd leave if I said it."

"I came here to make you understand!"

"You failed!"

She met his eyes bravely, her own swimming with tears. "I have loved you all my life, Adam, and so I shall until I die. Tempted though I was, I never played false with my wedding vows—not even when Dev lied to me—not even when he withheld your letters from me."

She was more beautiful than he remembered even, and he knew in his heart that he still wanted her. But he could not forget what she'd done to him. He tore away, walking to the safety of the fireplace. And when he turned back to her, he shook his head.

"Your own words mock you, Sarah. 'It was but Dev,' you said. You asked me to say I no longer love you, and I have done so. Now, take your letters and go."

Telling herself he *was* a stranger, that he was not the Adam she'd loved before, she gathered up the shreds of her dignity. Swallowing hard, she nodded.

"All right, I'll go. And I have no more need of the letters. I just wanted you to read them."

Outside, she stopped to lean against the porch for a moment. She felt a grief as great as if he'd died. It was over. She'd crossed the tossing seas for naught. There was nothing else to do but return to the Park and tell the earl she'd failed. At least she'd left her baggage on the boat for the return to New York. Without bothering to avail herself of Johnson's offer, she walked numbly back to the river, completely unaware of the appreciative gaze of every man she passed.

34

He was in the devil's own temper, and he knew it. Neither his men nor Joanna had dared speak with him after Sarah left. And now, as it grew dark outside, he shook his head at Joanna's offer of food, choosing instead to pour himself more of the half-empty bottle of rum.

He'd get over it—he'd thought he had before he'd seen her again—now he had but to put her from his mind once again. It would have been better if he'd missed her, if he'd been away when she'd come. But even as the rum dulled his mind, nothing seemed to dull the ache in his breast.

Damn her. Damn Devin. He'd really loved only two people in the world, and they had betrayed him. What had happened after he left? Had it been the loss of the babe? It didn't matter, he told himself. Neither of them had the right—she was his wife.

He had to stop thinking of her before he lost his mind. He started to reach for the bottle again. He meant to get as drunk as the night he'd last written to Sarah.

"No, Tecawrongati."

"I'll do as I damn well please, Joanna!"

"No."

"Who appointed you my keeper, anyway?"

"I post letter she bring back."

"Thank you very much," he muttered sarcastically. "You want a wampum belt for the service?" He looked down at her feet. "And for God's sake, put on some shoes!"

"Feet hurt in shoes."

"I don't care."

Instead of getting her shoes, she picked up the letters she'd gathered from where he'd scattered them on the floor in his anger. She placed them on the table in front of him.

"I told you to burn them!"

"Woman come far to bring." Seating herself opposite him, she picked one up. "O'Don-nell teach to read."

"O'Donnell teaches too damn much."

Unperturbed, she held up a page, reading aloud from the top: " '22 Jan-u-ar-y. Dear—' " She faltered briefly and half-turned the page for a better angle. " '—Hus-band.' "

He reached angrily to pull it away, and it tore in his hand. As he looked down, he saw the first words: "It has been so long since last I saw you, and I have tried to be patient, knowing how it must be with you." No, she could never have known how it had been. "But words cannot express my anxiety when I hear nothing, my love." How very like him she sounded. Drawn against his will, his eyes traveled down the page, reading of her loneliness.

Had she gone back and written it more recently than the date it bore? Somehow, the words betrayed a yearning that made him want to believe. When he looked up, Joanna was watching him solemnly.

"I still think you were misnamed," he grumbled under his breath. "You ought to have been called Woman Who Meddles."

"You want others?" she asked innocently.

"No."

"Afraid, Tecawrongati?"

Why now of all times did she choose to call him that? Man Who Dares or Man Who Defies—he was not quite certain of which it meant. Did she think to challenge him? He rose and walked to where the cooking fire burned beneath a kettle.

But words cannot express my anxiety when I hear noth-

ing, my love. Damn her! He'd written as often as he could. *It was but Dev.* She condemned herself with those very words. But then she turned around and denied it. *If she said I took a lover, she lied.* And how very affecting she was! *I beg of you—do not do to me what your father did to your mother!* It was by no means the same—his father thought he'd driven his wife into the arms of another man.

A sharp rap sounded on the door. He didn't turn around as Joanna answered it. He was in no mood to be convivial with anyone. As he listened to William Johnson speak to Joanna, he felt his cup of gall was full.

"You find me ill-suited to company, sir."

Johnson's eyes traveled to the bottle on the table, and he sighed. "So she took exception to Joanna, eh? I considered telling her differently, but I thought it ought to come from you."

"We did not discuss the matter," Adam answered coldly.

Johnson sat down and poured himself a glass. "Damned fine-looking female—had Abercromby's staff nearly tongue-tied."

"Did you never meet a female you did not admire, William?"

"Not many. Egad, where'd you get this?"

" 'Tis general issue."

"Ain't fit for a gentleman to drink." Just then, Johnson looked down and spied the letters. "Quite a collection, I'd say."

"Aye."

"Thought you'd be happier—your Sarah came a long way to see you." Drawing deeply of the rum, he leaned back to look at Adam. "But then Thompson saw her take the boat back to New York."

Joanna spoke up then, addressing the colonel in Iroquois dialect, speaking at length. As abruptly as he'd arrived, he rose to leave. His glass tipped over, spilling onto a sheet of paper, running the ink.

"Damn! Sorry, Captain—didn't mean to do that."

Joanna hurried to mop up the mess, blotting at the wet papers, spreading them out to dry. And Adam, not wanting anyone else to see what Sarah had written, moved hastily to cover them. His eyes caught the words "all my love," dissolving before his eyes. And suddenly he had to save them. He took a cloth from Joanna and began blotting carefully.

"Your servant, Adam. Joanna," Johnson murmured. "Mrs. Hastings told Thompson she returns to England as early as Tuesday next. More's the pity."

After the colonel left, Joanna took her fringed shawl, draping it decorously over her shoulders. Adam looked up from where he still separated pages.

"Where are you going?"

"See O'Don-nell."

"You and O'Donnell see far too much of each other, you know. One of these days, he's going to give you more than English lessons."

He managed to save all but two pieces of paper. Then, drawing the oil lamp nearer, he arranged them in order by dates, separating them into two sets. And much as Sarah had done more than a month before, he read them like questions and answers, beginning with the earliest.

How very alike they were, his and hers. At first, they were filled with shared memories, with hopes. And gradually the tone changed to fewer memories and more questions. Then finally there was the recrimination, the disaffection born of unanswered longing. He went back and read the earlier ones again, reliving the memories.

As brief as the marriage had been, it was difficult to forget the intensity of the passion between them. It had been as scales falling from his eyes that day he'd offered for her, seeing her suddenly not as a childhood friend but rather as a lover. And what a lover she had been. Closing his eyes, he could see again the exquisite pleasure he gave her written on her face. He could see her auburn hair spilling over the straw, and almost feel her body moving beneath his. She'd been so unlike the other women he'd known, loving freely, wholeheartedly, with a desire that matched his own.

And then the fire had died in his absence—or had it? He read again her later letters, feeling the desperate isolation she felt, and he heard her say again, *Tempted though I was, I never played false with my wedding*

*vows—not even when Dev lied to me, not even when he
withheld your letters from me.* Had "It was but Dev"
been no more than a poor choice of words?

She'd said she'd loved him all her life. And as he stared
down at her letters, he knew it for the truth. Very carefully he folded them, one by one, and slid them into the
bag where he kept his orders.

Moving restlessly to where the untended pot still boiled
away at the hearth, he realized that Joanna had merely
left him alone to read. He dipped a spoon into her stew,
feeling suddenly hungry. Striding to the front door of the
Dutchman's house, he discovered her sitting on the porch,
her shawl pulled around her.

"Where's O'Donnell?"

"Sha-won leave with Bur-ton."

"Thank you, Joanna."

"You hungry?" Then, trying out one of O'Donnell's
favorite words, she added, "I am fameeshed."

"Aye."

"You leave tonight?"

"In the morning. I have to get permission of Abercromby first."

She nodded. "And Jo-anh-ha fix coat."

"She may not want you here."

"Tell her I take care her too."

"And if she objects?" he asked gently.

A slow smile curved her lips and warmed her dark
eyes. "Then Jo-anh-ha marry O'Don-nell and Ad-dam
buy dress."

35

Sarah sat in her hotel room, staring dispiritedly at the trunks she'd brought with her. In them lay some of the loveliest gowns she'd ever seen, gowns she'd hoped Adam would admire. But now she was returning to England, and he'd seen but one of them. And obviously it had not had the desired effect. He'd scarce looked at it, in fact.

For four days she'd had naught to do but wait for the ship to sail, and all the while her thoughts had been haunted by things said and unsaid. Why had she not stood her ground in Albany? Why had she not made him understand? And each time she relived the humiliation, she wished she'd not come.

The whole meeting had not gone as she'd planned, and on reflection, it took on an air of utter unreality. She'd made such a fool of herself—she'd even allowed his Indian mistress to serve her tea! And there was so little of the Adam she knew in the hard, rough man she'd seen in Albany.

A great sense of loss stole over her whenever she thought of the letters she'd given him. It had been foolish to think he'd read them, and she bitterly regretted her rashness. Before, she could at least savor the better ones; now she had nothing.

"Mistress Hastings?"

They'd come for her trunks. She rose and straightened the full skirt of her dark green traveling dress over her petticoats. She'd forgone her hoops, thinking them but a nuisance in the narrow passages below a ship's deck. And even that reminded her of the day she'd shed her panniers on the way to the Park, the day she'd left Spender's Hill to marry him. How long—how long would her heart hold her mind hostage with such memories? It was time to put them behind her before she went mad.

Resolutely she walked to the door and wrenched it open. "My trunks are ready, and—" She blinked, too stunned to speak.

His scarlet uniform seemed to fill the door. Her eyes traveled upward, taking in the deep blue lapels, the rows of gold buttons and lace, the gorget that hung over his stock. His face was clean-shaven now, and his officer's wig set correctly on his head. In his hand he carried his braid-trimmed ramillie. He looked as though he'd prepared himself for a royal presentation.

His smile twisted crookedly, lighting his deep blue eyes. "Sarah, I am come to ask you to stay," he told her quietly.

She backed away numbly, and he followed her inside. His eyes traveled over the pile of boxes and luggage. "And 'twould seem I am almost too late." He reached beneath his coat and drew out a large canvas-wrapped packet, handing it to her. "If you cannot bring yourself to forgive me, I pray you will keep these."

It was his letters to her. She turned them over in her hands, seeing once again the bold, straight script. "Thank you," was all she could manage to say.

"And I hope you will understand that I have kept yours." His eyes searched her face, hoping for some sign she'd stay. "Though they are but lately read, they mean everything to me."

A painful lump formed in her throat and her eyes itched with unshed tears. "I . . ." It seemed impossible that he could be there before her.

"Sarah, you humbled yourself to me in Albany—would you have me at your feet?" he asked. "I'd do so gladly, you know."

"No," she choked.

"I have two weeks' leave, and I'd have you spend it with me." He dropped his hat on the floor and moved closer. "I lied to you, Sarah—I love you still."

Her lower lip trembled; then she flung herself against his chest. "Oh, Adam!"

His arms closed around her, holding her tightly as her whole body shuddered against him. For a time, he stood quietly, his cheek against her hair, letting her cry until he could stand it no longer.

"Don't, love—I cannot bear it," he whispered above her ear. "Just let me make up to you what we lost—'tis all I ask."

She clung to him, pressing her face against the hard-finished wool of his coat, feeling the gold braid and buttons against her face. He was there in the flesh and he loved her still.

Finally he lifted a hand to her chin, forcing it up. She sniffled self-consciously and tried to smile through her tears, but his face blurred before her eyes as he bent his head to hers. And it was as though the year of separation and the bitterness disappeared, consumed by the fire.

He kissed her mouth, her earlobe, her neck, eagerly, hungrily, eliciting an answering passion that made her forget all else. His hands smoothed her gown against her back, sliding downward to hold her hips to his.

"I hate corsets and stomachers," he whispered, his breath rushing hotly against her ear.

"I'll get out of it," she murmured, pulling him once again to her lips. Her free hand found the long row of buttons along his vest. "There are far too many of these, you know," she added breathlessly.

His hand caught hers, pulling her after him toward the unmade bed. They undressed each other with a clumsiness born of eagerness, reveling as each layer fell away until she stood before him in naught but her undershift. Then, her eyes on his, she lifted it slowly and deliberately, pulling it over her head.

His breath caught as the shift dropped onto the floor at her feet and she stepped again into his embrace. "Oh, Sarah, it has been so long—I know not if I can make it last," he groaned.

"If you cannot, I am patient enough to wait."

But even as she spoke, her body gave lie to her words, pressing hungrily against his, tantalizing him with her bare flesh. He lifted her to the bed and followed her down as she settled into the feather mattress. His hands moved over her, exploring her, and all the while he kissed her mouth, her throat, and her breasts until she thought she could not stand it. Her hands worked ceaselessly, caressing his shoulders and back, pulling him down to her.

When his hand slid lower, she stopped him, gasping, "There is no need."

" 'Twill not last long," he warned.

"Long enough."

Her arms twined around his neck as he possessed her body. She moaned, then began to move beneath him, her eyes closed in concentration, her tongue wetting her lips as her breath came in gasps. And she was as he remembered her, passionate and giving, yet demanding in return. They were no longer in a small hotel room, but rather back in the straw at Spender's Hill.

The fire raged between them, consuming quickly, leaving embers. He collapsed above her, whispering, "God, Sarah, but I love you."

She held him happily, savoring his strength, the weight of his body over hers. "I told you it was long enough," she murmured softly.

He eased over to let her breathe, and lay, his head against her breast, for a long time. Her fingers caressed the thick hair that streamed now, mingling with hers on her shoulder. For a time, she thought he dozed.

"You know, I despaired of ever knowing this again," he said finally.

"Even with Woman Who Does Whatever?" she asked.

"Watches Water. And—"

"No." She moved her hand over his lips. "I should not have said that—I don't want to know."

But since she'd asked, he would not be stilled. "Sarah, Joanna cooks and mends and tends to me, but never this— never this." He nibbled at her fingertips playfully. "Only once was I tempted, and then she had the greater sense."

"But she loves you."

"I suspect, my dear, that she loves a boy named Sean O'Donnell."

"Oh."

"I owe her my life, you know. I'd not send her away unless you wish it." He turned his head into her breast and his tongue moved over her nipple, making her squirm.

"I see." A wave of desire washed over her, and the problem of the Indian girl seemed suddenly remote. "I don't care—just love me again, Adam."

"I mean to—slowly."

Sarah blushed furiously beneath the stares of the curious when they came down to dine. "Do you think they heard us?" she asked anxiously, clinging to his arm.

"If they did not, they were deaf."

"Oh."

He found the proprietor and booked the room for ten days, and as he signed his name, the fellow looked up quickly, noting his uniform. "You him as nearly took that French bastard Reynaud?"

"Actually, he nearly took me."

Sarah remembered the puckered scar and shivered, knowing that had it been lower, she'd have lost him forever. Her hand tightened on his arm.

"Ain't the way we heard it, sir—heard ye rowed right into his camp."

"Folly on my part," Adam demurred, embarrassed by the way everyone watched him with renewed interest.

"Just the same, how else was we to know the murderin' savages was a-comin' down wi'out ye? They'd a been nigh to here." He turned the book around, shaking his head. "No charge fer the room—none a'tall."

"Thought he was a ranger," someone murmured behind them. "Fellow's a regular!"

"Let's get out of here," Adam told Sarah in a low undervoice. "I'd eat somewhere else."

Outside, she tried to keep his pace. "Adam, to those people you are a hero," she protested.

"Aye, but I know myself for a bumbler, Sarah. I should have taken the bloody bastard. Instead, I risked my men and got myself shot."

"Devin said you received a royal commendation for it," she reminded him. Then, realizing it was the first time they'd mentioned his brother since Albany, she hastened to add, "Why did you not take the promotion, Adam?"

"Because 'twas undeserved."

"Loudoun did not seem to think so."

"How did you know that?"

"I saw some of the dispatches."

There was a pause as he digested that; then he said, "I'd speak no more of Dev, Sarah—not at all."

And she wondered if he still thought she'd betrayed him with Audley. She could not let the matter drop quite like that.

"Adam, when I said 'twas only Dev, I did not mean I'd played you false. I only meant I thought I could turn to him for comfort."

His jaw worked visibly, and he shook his head. "It was not until I read your letters that I knew what he did to you—and to me. And I cannot forgive him that."

"He loved me, I think."

"He was my brother, Sarah. And I said I'd not speak of him again."

"All right." But as angered and hurt as she herself had been, she'd thought she understood how he'd come to do it. Nonetheless, she held her tongue. Looking up at her handsome husband, she managed to smile. " 'Tis over, in any event."

"Aye."

He took her to an inn overlooking the river, and there they enjoyed an excellent repast of duckling stuffed with chestnuts, pork pasties, early peas, and jelly tarts, all washed down with the host's best wine. The sun set, casting rosy hues over the river; then the twinkling lanterns of boats sparkled like hundreds of stars shimmering across the water.

There was so much to say and so little need to say it, and yet neither could refrain from asking about the lonely year just past. Adam leaned back in his chair, watching her as she watched the water, feeling an intense pride that she was his.

"You know," he mused aloud, "I was used to think

you quite lovely, but I was mistaken—'tis beautiful you are become, Sarah.''

She appeared to consider the compliment, then smiled, shaking her head. ''No. I am the same Sarah underneath the fine clothes, I fear. Despite what you see, I'd still run barefoot through the wet grass at Spender's Hill if I could.'' A slight dimple at the corner of her mouth deepened and her amber eyes gleamed. ''And beneath this elegant facade, surely you must have discovered I have not changed at all.''

He lifted his glass to that. ''Not at all.''

''And you?''

''What do you think?''

''At Albany I thought you'd become little more than a savage. You did not look at all like the Adam Hastings I knew.''

''And now?''

''Well, I suspect you are changed more than I.''

''I suppose there is truth to that, Sarah,'' he admitted. ''Life here is not much like it was in England.''

''And you like it—or so you wrote.''

''Aye.'' He leaned forward to refill her glass. ''Here 'tis far less important from whence I have come. There are fewer to care that I am Westerfield's younger son. Oh, Loudoun still worries over it, I know. But when I am crawling over the wilderness with my musket on my back, my men are more concerned whether I can lead them back alive.''

''Is it as bad as the papers make it sound—the Indians, I mean?''

''The scalps, you mean? 'Tis ugly and cruel and violent sometimes, but there is more to the situation than that.'' He sat back, staring almost absently over the water. ''You know, there are some things I could never speak of—of men lost in ways I'd not remember,'' he answered slowly. ''But beyond that . . . well, the Iroquois are a fascinating people . . . they have laws that bind amongst them as much as ours.''

''Joanna is Iroquois?''

He nodded. ''Onandaga—one of the Six Nations.''

Then, knowing he'd still not satisfied her curiosity, he sighed. "I told you 'tis different over here."

"Tell me how you came to have her—I'd know that at least."

"I was carried to an Onandaga village after Reynaud shot me, and because I had to send my men to warn Rogers and the others, she tended me. She is daughter to a subchieftain, and their girls make their own choices." He smiled wryly as he recalled Woman Who Watches the Water's determination. "She had been at Barclay's school, but was returned to her village when she contracted some illness. Her brief sojourn amongst us, however, gave her a passion for the white man's ways. She decided to marry me so that she could become like William Johnson's Molly Brant. It took a great deal of fortitude to convince her I was already wedded, you know."

"But you prevailed, of course," she said sweetly.

"I prevailed, but 'twas not without moments of doubt—particularly after I'd not heard from you in months, and then Meg implied that you were the toast of London's beaux."

"I was in mourning!"

"Were you, now? I'd heard you were quite the political hostess."

"Because I thought I was helping you! D—I was convinced that if Pitt were in control of the war, it would end quickly. Besides, I did not go about . . . We . . . I merely presided over dinners and blistered a few ears with my opinions."

"And enjoyed not a moment of it, I suppose."

A slow smile curved her mouth. "Well, I cannot deny I was quite a success. Indeed, I even attracted an admirer or two."

"Aye," he muttered dryly. "And I was up to my pockets in snow."

"Ah, but we both served in different ways, I expect," she responded blithely. "After all, King George finally named Mr. Pitt."

"Somehow I suspect your service was a trifle more pleasant than mine." He swirled the ruby liquid around in his glass, then sipped it. "You are become a bit of a baggage, Mrs. Hastings," he chided her with a grin.

"I always was—'twas what you liked about me."

"Aye." Then his mood sobered. "I almost didn't come after you, you know. 'Twas a gamble to leave those letters with me."

"So I thought later. I was desolate that I should never have them or you again."

"It was Joanna. I'd told her to burn them, but she wouldn't. She was determined that I read them, and when I wouldn't, she tried to read them aloud to me."

"And you let her?" Somehow the thought that another woman had read her pleas was lowering.

"Well, she does not read well yet—just enough to make me know that I didn't want to share them with anyone else."

"I suppose she was curious," she offered.

"No, she knew what she was doing. You see, my love, 'twas she who posted my last two letters to you. I'd thrown them away." He set down his glass and covered her hands with his. "Joanna may be an Indian, but she is female also—and I suspect that like most members of your sex, she is a matchmaker at heart. That—and if he'd ever ask her, she'd leave my quarters for O'Donnell's. 'Twas her way of taking care of me."

"I see," she murmured faintly, disconcerted by the warmth in his eyes.

"Do you? I'd have no more misunderstanding between us."

It was then that she decided to broach something that had bothered her for months. "If I must owe Joanna, then you should acknowledge a debt to your father, Adam."

His hands, which had been caressing hers, grew still, then moved away. "Joanna had the easier task, I think."

"Adam, 'twas he who convinced me to come. I was sure all was lost, but he told me to put it to the touch one last time. 'Do not let pride and ignorance lose him to you, gel,' he said to me. He did not want either of us to suffer as he has done."

"His suffering is of his own making."

"Can you not forgive? Adam, the reason he wanted me to stay at the Park was so you would come home again. 'Tell the boy it ain't just you and Dev and Em as has a care for him,' he asked." It was her turn to lean across the table to him. "Adam, when I was afraid, he told me the two biggest fools there were he and I."

"He believed I was not his."

"You believed I loved another—as he believed of your mother."

" 'Tis not the same."

"The pain is, I think. Adam, if you would but write to him—he grows old and lonely."

"Let my brother keep him company."

"Adam—"

"Nay. Let him write to me." His eyes met hers once again. "I'd not quarrel with you over Joanna or Devin or Papa, my love. If the truth be told, I'd very much rather rediscover the Sarah who would run barefoot through the grass."

The look in his eyes sent a thrill coursing through her body. "Find the grass," she said softly, "and I'll do it."

36

Sarah had always considered the time she and Adam had spent in London to have been the best of their marriage, but those few May days in New York were far sweeter. By day they walked lazily along the river's bank, watching the ships or shopping the market stalls, enjoying the quiet company. And by night they rediscovered each other's bodies eagerly, hungrily, as though they could somehow make up for the time they had lost.

And Sarah found that whether Adam chose to acknowledge it or not, he was a hero to many. As word spread through their hotel, people nudged each other, murmuring, " 'Tis Adam Hastings, the ranger who almost took that fiend Reynaud." Some of the bolder ones came up to him, admiring him openly, much as the hotel proprietor had done. While Robert Rogers' exploits had earned that intrepid ranger everyone's respect, there seemed to be plenty left over for Adam and the others who risked their lives in the wilderness. Although always civil and usually gracious, he found it difficult to accept their approbation, shunning places where he feared recognition.

After that first day, Adam dispensed again with the hated wig, storing it in a box. And sometimes, when the days were warm, he left off the regulation vest and gorget also, teasing Sarah that they were too difficult to get out of. When she chided him, reminding him of how magnificent he'd looked when he came for her, he grinned, admitting that he'd done it to impress her. Yet, everywhere they went, people turned their heads to watch them, the handsome soldier in his scarlet coat, his lovely wife in her elegant London gowns.

The day before they were to return to Albany, he hired a cart and horse from a stable and drove her into the countryside, telling her she'd see how pretty it was outside the city. At first, she was concerned they might encounter Indians, but he assured her that most were to be found further up the Hudson River, usually beyond Albany. And then they were the friendly ones.

The weather was warm, requiring but a light shawl over the shoulders of her deep blue gown. This time, because it would be their last day alone, she'd dressed herself unusually well, taking special care to wear her best tucked stomacher with its rows of small satin bows. She'd even worn moderate panniers to show her ruffle-trimmed skirt to advantage.

" 'Tis lovely you are today, Sarah," he murmured, smiling.

"One fine dress deserves another, do you not think?" she asked, her eyes on the sunlit trees.

" 'Twill be a while before you see me thus again," he admitted. "Tomorrow I shall be as you saw in Albany."

She wrinkled her nose in distaste. "I thought you appeared the savage there. Can you not go back to your regiment?"

"I never actually left it—I am but on assignment until the ranger ranks are full. But I must admit that I find it more useful to encounter the foe in the forests dressed as they are. Red coats, my dear, make deuced fine targets."

"What will you do—when we go back, I mean?" It was a question she'd dreaded to ask the whole time they'd been together.

"Well, Loudoun plans a campaign against Louisburg— against all advice, I might add. 'Tis why he remains at Halifax and leaves Abercromby to his own devices here."

"We go to Halifax then?"

"Nay. The ranger base is at Fort Edward, but 'tis scarce a suitable place for you. Our part sits on an island in the river—'tis wet in summer and mosquitoes are thick. Fort William Henry is not much better, but Johnson thinks Eyre and Munro better soldiers than Webb, and there are more troops there already."

The awful thought came to her then that they would be separated again. "Adam, I'd go where you go."

He shook his head. "By summer's end, there will be nearly three thousand men at William Henry, and possibly less than half that at Edward. Besides, I will be neither place much of the time."

It was as though he'd dashed cold water in her face. "But if the troops are there—"

"I will be part of a scout northward. Loudoun wishes intelligence should the French move northeast to reinforce Louisburg with their Indian allies."

"But if everyone advises against this place, why does Loudoun choose it?"

"Who knows? 'Tis but a maggot in his brain, I think, for everything we have seen indicates the war ought to be fought in the west. If we do not stop the French there, we shall be but a few colonies clinging to the sea."

She could not hide her disappointment. "Then I shall be alone."

"There are wives at William Henry, Sarah."

"Why do you have to go? Why can you not rejoin your regiment?" she demanded almost angrily. "I did not journey thousands of miles across the ocean in a rocking ship to be left again."

"I did not know you were coming when I agreed," he responded reasonably. "I had to beg Abercromby for this leave."

"But why must it be *you?*"

"Because I speak French better than Rogers or any of the New Hampshiremen—because I can pretend to be a *coureur de bois* as I did before."

"When you were shot? Adam, what if you are captured? Surely you can avoid this. Your father—"

"I am more than Westerfield's son, Sarah. I am a soldier—as I was when you wedded me."

She dropped her eyes and looked away. "But what if you do not come back to me?" she asked, giving voice to her worst fear.

He reined in and turned to her. "Believe me, I shall do my *damnedest* to live." With his free hand he lifted her chin, and his eyes searched her face. "I don't want to die, Sarah. I want to live—with you. And when summer's done, when this year's campaign is over, my duty is finished."

"Is it? Or will you want to stay in this place?" she cried. "Will I be forever watching you leave to fight the French—or some savage Indians somewhere I cannot even name?"

"We'll go wherever you wish," he answered quietly.

"England?"

"I'd rather fancied myself a landholder here, but if 'tis what you want, then England it is." He lifted her chin higher. "Sarah, my life is your life also."

"I'd rather live at Spender's Hill."

It meant he would have to approach his father or his brother, something he was loath to do under the best of circumstances. He exhaled slowly, knowing he could not deny her this. He'd have to swallow his pride that far and do it.

"All right. I'll see if Papa will sell it to me."

"Adam, I think he would."

He released her and turned his attention back to the reins. "For your sake mayhap—not for mine."

"Adam, you wrong him. He—"

"Would you quarrel with me on a lovely spring day, Mrs. Hastings?" he asked, smiling crookedly. "Or would you make better memories than we have had this year past?"

She sighed. "I'd not quarrel, but—"

"Good. I've a place to take you where the trees are tall and the grass thick enough to tickle your toes when you run in it. 'Tis so quiet that all you can hear are the birds and the water rushing through a brook alongside."

She looked back to the hamper behind them. "A place to eat, I trust."

"To eat, to drink—and to love. Who knows—I might run barefoot in the grass also."

His voice was low, soft, and more than a little seductive. Her gaze dropped to where he rested the reins against his thigh, and she was conscious once again of how strong his hands were.

"And I'll show you how the Iroquois make a bed of nettles and boughs on the ground," he continued conversationally.

She closed her eyes to hide what his nearness did to her. "That sounds dashed uncomfortable," she murmured, not wanting to appear to give in too easily.

" 'Tis why I begged a carriage rug at the stable." His arm slid around her shoulder, pulling her close. "And for once you will not have to worry who hears us. You can make all the noise you want."

"Adam!"

His boyish grin spread, crinkling the fine sun lines at the corners of his eyes. "Aye. In fact," he added wickedly, "I brought both nuncheon *and* supper."

"And if I prefer perhaps a more sedate entertainment?"

"The choice is yours." The hand that held her arm slid over it lightly, sending a shiver through her, and then he leaned closer, his breath warm against her ear. "Memories, Sarah—I'd give you memories you cannot share with your children, memories to make you blush when you are alone at night.''

"More of them?'' she asked weakly, turning her head into his shoulder.

"More of them. Definitely.''

But she was not going to capitulate entirely. "Will you come to visit me at William Henry?''

"If I have to scalp a dozen Indians to get there,'' he promised with a straight face. "Aye—and Reynaud also.''

The place he'd found was a small clearing bounded by a stream on one side and the forest on the other, and trees from both sides arched their branches heavenward, interlacing them like the cross-ribbed roof of a Gothic cathedral, giving it an almost unreal serenity. He jumped down and unhitched the horse to lead it to the water.

" 'Twould seem it was a small portage once, but there is no sign anyone comes here now.''

"Are you quite certain?'' she asked, looking around her.

"Aye. When the grass grows in summer, it gets high and 'tis as a wilderness. I discovered it quite by accident last year—when I thought I should go mad between Loudoun and loneliness. Wilcox and I came hunting here.'' He tied the horse to the tree and came back. "You can take off your shoes whenever you like.''

"Later, I think.'' She turned her attention to the basket in the back of the cart, lifting it.

"Let me get that.''

"Fiddle. As if I am some sort of London miss. You may place the rug.''

He carried it to the edge of the clearing and unrolled it, then lay down, propping himself with an elbow to watch her as she unpacked the food. She moved so gracefully, her full skirts swinging as she walked. There was nothing unpleasing about her, not even the faint sprinkling of freckles across her nose. The filtered sun dappled her hair with red.

"What did they pack for us?''

She looked up impishly. "Nothing you'd like—salt pork, beans, and berries, I think.''

"Surely not. I get more than enough of that.''

"Aye, and a jug of stout."

"Ugh! Sarah, you're bamming me—I know it."

"Actually, poor Mr. Thompson has outdone himself," she admitted. " 'Tis cold fowl, bread and jelly, oranges, and an assortment of tarts—and some sort of pasty, I think. Oh, and two bottles of wine. Do you think the water is cold enough to cool it?"

"Aye, probably, but I assure you I can drink it as it is—and I should hate to lose it."

She carried the open basket to him then and sat, her skirts billowing around her. Spreading out a cloth over the carriage rug, she began removing the food.

"I hope you do not mind if we eat first," she told him, "else my poor stomach will growl—and think how *very* unromantic that would be."

"The practical Sarah Hastings."

"I try to be." She pushed two tin cups toward him. "You may pour."

They ate slowly, leisurely, in no hurry now, enjoying the peaceful stillness of being alone with naught but the sound of an occasional bird call and the cool rush of the water. When she finished, she leaned back, propping her head dreamily against a tree. And for a long time they just drowsed, drinking in the beauty and serenity of the place, enjoying a sense of well-being.

" 'Tis quite lovely here—I thank you for discovering it to me," she said finally.

"The pleasure is all mine, Mrs. Hastings."

She cocked her head slightly, and her amber eyes were almost smoky. "Not quite all yours, I think," she murmured. Then, before he could reach out to her, she scampered up awkwardly, hampered by her panniers. Turning away from him, she lifted her skirts and untied the whalebone cage at her waist, letting it drop.

His breath caught, and he felt a surge of desire, but when she looked back at him, it was to say, "Do not be letting me lose them this time." Freed, she slipped off her shoes and wriggled her stockinged toes in the soft grass. "Mmmmmmm . . . I have longed to do this ever since I left Spender's Hill."

"Sarah—"

Her hands went to the thick curls piled atop her head. As she pulled the pins, her hair tumbled in wavy disarray over her shoulders. She tossed her head and pushed the auburn mass back from her face.

He felt his mouth go almost too dry for speech, but still she did not come to him. Instead, she lifted her skirts above her ankles, teasing him.

"No, Adam—you'll have to catch me first."

As she watched warily, he lurched to his feet. " 'Tis not fair—you ate and drank less than I," he protested, grinning.

"And you are wearing far less."

He looked down to where he'd forgone his vest. "Too much still, I think." Slowly, his eyes on her, he removed his coat, tossing it onto the carriage rug.

While he was so occupied, she rolled down her stockings and threw them on top of her panniers. Then, much as she'd done as a small hoyden, she half-crouched, waiting for him to move. With mischief in her eyes, she asked huskily, "Do you remember Catch Me If You Can?"

"Aye." His grin was lopsided. "And the prize if I win?"

"Whatever you want."

"Aren't you afraid of ruining your gown?"

"No. Turn around that I may count."

It seemed a long time before she began, and as each second crawled back, he felt his body grow tenser. Finally, she began slowly, "One." There was a whoosh of cloth that sent a shiver of excitement through him. "Two." Again there was a long pause. "Three." And finally, "Four!"

When he spun around, she was standing there in her shift, and her corset and gown were on the ground beside her. Her smile broadened. "Catch me if you dare, Adam."

It took him but seconds to discard his shoes and stockings also, and then he stood, gauging the distance between them. He feinted one way, and as she dodged, he went the other. But she was as quick as she'd been as a child, dancing away like a wood nymph just out of his grasp. Her throaty laughter carried through the clearing.

He chased her until they were both breathless. "If I lose?" he gasped.

"I do with you what I will."

He turned and walked back to the blanket, dropping down to lie there. "I surrender, then—torture me, fair Diana."

She came back to stand over him, her hair tangled wildly, her chest heaving beneath her thin shift. "And if I am not ready to accept your defeat?" she challenged.

His hand snaked out, catching her ankle, toppling her over him. "Then I win."

" 'Tis most unfair!" she protested, wriggling as his lips sought hers. "As an officer and a gentlemmmmmmmm—"

He rolled over her over, pinning her down, and kissed her thoroughly. She ceased struggling and twined her arms around his neck. And when at last he moved his mouth to her ear, he whispered, "The rules differ in America, Sarah." His hands slid over her body to find the hem of her shift.

She responded eagerly to his touch, her body flooding with heat as the thin cloth crept upward. His mouth seemed to be everywhere—her ears, her neck, her throat, her breasts, the hollow of her stomach even. She closed her eyes and moved beneath him, tantalizing his body with hers, moaning with the urgency she felt, then shuddering when at last he entered her. There was nothing else—nothing but the ceaseless rocking ecstasy between them. She writhed and cried with abandon, clutching and raking at his back, holding him, demanding more, until he took her there; then, slowly, as ease came in undulating waves, she fell slack beneath him.

It was a long time before either of them moved or spoke, but finally he murmured huskily against her ear, "We forgot the bed of nettles." Her arms tightened around his neck. "We didn't need it," she whispered back.

37

Adam had left in June, accompanied at first by some fifty rangers, with orders to divide up and form small scouting parties. And once again he'd chosen to take the same ones, explaining that they knew each other's habits. To Sarah's discomfiture, he'd also taken Joanna. The Onandagas were wavering in their English support, and it was felt that should they become hostile, her presence would be useful.

After a sojourn at Albany, where she passed several weeks in the agreeable company of Abercromby's officers' wives, Sarah set out for Fort William Henry with only half her trunks. The other women at Albany persuaded her to commission several muslin gowns, telling her that she'd have little use for silks and taffetas at the wilderness stockade.

The journey to Fort William Henry from Albany was an arduous one for an English girl from Spender's Hill. Passage was bought with a carter carrying barrels of salted pork, and that meant she traveled as he did—by bateau a dozen miles to Half Moon, a small place just above the mouth of the Mohawk River, then by ox-drawn wagon overland to Stillwater, another twelve miles north. There barrels and passenger were transferred to scows for another dozen miles upriver to Saratoga. Everything seemed to be in twelves, Sarah reflected tiredly, except the leg by wagon again between Saratoga and Fort Edward, which was an unlucky thirteen. The carters were used to it—they supplied some twenty thousand men out of Albany. The amounts required were staggering to

Sarah; her carter told her they carried nearly six thousand barrels of meat and bread on the three-week journey once each month.

They rested at Ford Edward while a quantity of the supplies was unloaded there, and she had the opportunity to see the conditions under which soldiers and rangers lived. She was not impressed. In fact, the filth and disease astounded her, for it seemed that hundreds of the inhabitants suffered fevers and dysentery from open privies and damp river air. She devoutly hoped that William Henry was better.

By ox cart to the head of Lake George, it was, of course, *another* twelve miles beyond Fort Edward, and those twelve miles were the worst. Deep ruts marked the cartage road, making for a slow, bone-jarring ride. It took four grueling days to get there.

By the time she arrived in the early-July heat, she felt very much like the handkerchief of a weeping woman. And she was bitterly disappointed, wondering how Adam could ever have thought to send her to such a place. As one carter explained to her, there were about twenty-five hundred men there, five hundred of whom were sick, while the rest were merely "poorly." "Bury five to eight a day, they do. Putrid and yellow fevers," he'd added by way of explanation. "Aye—and smallpox."

She stood there wrinkling her nose against a stench greater than that at Fort Edward. And it was no wonder it stunk so—the privies, kitchens, graveyard, and slaughtering pens were mixed together without order or consideration for sanitation. Had she not had to follow the same route back, she'd have returned to Albany.

Her arrival caused considerable interest. Until she was officially welcomed, she felt like an exhibit at a country fair. Common soldiers, many of them in dirty and unidentifiable uniforms, leered, while grubby children felt of her dress in awe. And it was a plain one, something she'd not dare to wear in London.

"Mrs. Hastings, I presume?"

She turned around, thankful to find someone in the correct uniform of a lieutenant colonel in the regular British Army.

"Yes."

"George Monro. Your servant, Mrs. Hastings." He turned, gesturing around him. "My apologies—'tis not what you are used to, I am sure."

"No. No, 'tis not."

"We are an outpost merely, and not an old one at that. You behold mostly colonial troops from Connecticut here, and some regulars, of course."

"I see," she murmured faintly. "And women?"

"The usual laundresses and nurses, wives, and . . . Yes, well, of course there are females, though not many ladies, I am afraid." He stepped back, nodding toward a low building nearby. "I have ordered tea for you."

She started to say she needed to freshen herself first, but then was afraid to discover they had not the means for that. She nodded. "Thank you, sir."

While she sat primly in what served as his parlor and kitchen, drinking her tea from an elegant china cup, she dared to broach the matter of her own quarters. "I do not suppose," she managed slowly, "that you have anything for officers' wives, do you?"

"Most of them share rooms with their husbands, Mrs. Hastings, but as we were apprised of your coming, Mrs. Burks has aired out Lieutenant Martin's quarters for you."

She must have looked startled, for he hastened to add, "Lieutenant Martin perished last week."

"Nothing contagious, I hope."

He favored her with a wry smile and shook his head. "We shall hope not, in any event. He was, rather unfortunately, captured by the Indians."

Her teacup stopped in midair.

"We believe he came upon a scouting party, for he and those with him were waylaid on routine training maneuvers. Nothing more serious than that."

His attitude astonished her. "Nothing more . . . ? I should think Lieutenant Martin thought it serious, sir."

"Aye, poor devil."

"Has my husband been apprised of this?" she demanded rather tersely.

"Captain Hastings? No . . . no—shouldn't think so, anyway. By now I expect he is on his way to Halifax."

"Halifax!"

"General Loudoun's express orders. He wishes a report before we attempt Louisburg."

Her heart sank.

"You will wish to become acquainted with some of the officers' wives," he continued smoothly. "Daresay Mrs. Burks will tend to that for you. And we do have card games to pass the evenings more agreeably amongst us."

After all she had seen, her quarters were better than she'd dared to expect. She had a room in a log house, the interior of which was plastered and whitewashed, and she had a narrow bed, a small table, two chairs, a cruzie lamp, and a fireplace equipped with a spider, a hanging pot, and a kettle. She checked the mattress for vermin and was pleased to discover none. But as she surveyed the late lieutenant's bed with a slight shudder, she could not help thinking he was fortunate he'd not had to share it with a wife. The thought that came to mind was positively indecent.

Outside, she could hear the incessant chopping of wood, and going to the window, she discovered an inordinate amount of activity in back of the fort. Perhaps seven or eight hundred yards away, on higher ground, men were adding to some sort of barricade. To protect it, small artillery pieces had been drawn up and set like sentinels.

Her attention was claimed by loud knocking, and she turned to find Mrs. Burks directing soldiers carrying her trunks. Not that she would need much in them, she reflected bitterly, for rags would do here.

Had Adam known what this godforsaken place was like? Surely not. But then, he'd grown used to Fort Edward, so perhaps he'd not considered what a shock it would be to her.

Once everyone left her alone, she undressed, relishing the feel of the air, however hot and damp it might be, against her bare skin. Then, pouring water from the pitcher into the bowl, she took a rag and began to wash her body as best she could. Later she'd ask if there were a tub to be had.

Refreshed and in a clean gown sans petticoats, she found her writing supplies and sat to write. At first she was tempted to complain bitterly of the place, but then she thought of Adam. While she slept in poor Lieutenant Martin's bed, he would be lying upon the ground. And while she ate the vegetables she'd seen growing in a plot between Lieutenant Colonel Monro's quarters and her own, he'd be chewing on hard biscuits and either dried venison or salt pork. No, she had not the right to complain. What had he said? "You knew I was a soldier when you wedded me."

For all she knew, in times of war, they all lived in hellholes like this. She dipped her pen and began to write.

My dearest one,

I am safely arrived at William Henry, and have been given a room which lately belonged to an officer murdered by the Indians. There is much sickness here, but I am well.

Monro has been most gracious to me, and I have partaken of tea with him today. I am given to understand there shall be card parties for our entertainment, and I mean to write your father of it. Somehow, I think the notion of my playing whist in the wilderness will amuse him.

I am lonely, of course, but my memories sustain me. When I think I cannot stand it, I close my eyes and see you running barefoot in the grass.

She paused, wondering if perhaps she ought to give him her other news, then decided to wait. This time, she'd raise no hopes beyond hers. Besides, there was no use giving him any other cause for worry. Instead, she went on:

The small malaise of which I wrote in Albany has passed. The carters were most kind to me, stopping so often that we lost a full day, I am told. Other than that

and the awful cart, the journey was an interesting one.
I think, dear heart, that I much prefer the waterways.

Monro tells me you will be in Halifax to confer with
Lord Loudoun soon. I pray for your safe journey and
your return to me. Until then, I am your anxious wife.

She finished it and sealed it into an envelope, ready to
give to Monro for enclosure with his messages to Loudoun. There were so many other, far more maudlin things
she'd wanted to say, but one never knew who might be
reading one's mail, and she'd say nothing to unduly embarrass either of them—unlike Adam.

His last letter to her had drawn forth such memories
that she'd burned at reading it. Oh, his references were
meaningless to others, she hoped, but he had such a way
of expressing little things they'd done together. "Next
time I shall promise you the nettles," he'd written, which
must have intrigued the scout who'd carried it. Not to
mention "When again we play Catch Me If You Can, I
shall let you ride."

When she was done, she laid the envelope aside and
sat on the narrow bed. She'd lie down awhile and relive
her memories, she thought. And hope that wherever he
was, Adam was safe.

38

They were all there—Rogers and his rangers, General
Loudoun, and most of the senior staff—poised to sail
for the French fortress at Louisburg. It was expected that
Montcalm would be massing every soldier, marine, and

Indian ally he could muster to defend Nova Scotia. Then the disquieting news came.

Major General Daniel Webb, commanding officer at Fort Edward, dispatched word that "two-thirds of Colonel Parker's detachment of three companies either killed or captured in an ambush on the lake," adding, "The French are certainly coming and will probably attack William Henry first." He'd ended with, "I beg you, send up the militia without delay."

The dispatch arrived on 5 August, bringing the first word that French General Montcalm was mounting a campaign of his own. Loudoun was certain that the French were in a more defensive mood, and the move into the Champlain Valley was but a diversionary ploy.

Back home at Fort Johnson, William Johnson, however, was taking Webb's appeal quite seriously. He sent word that he'd gathered an army of eight hundred colonial militia, Mohawks, and Mohegans, and they were marching in full war paint for Fort Edward to join Webb in the defense of Fort William Henry.

Regardless of whether Webb's alarm was justified, Adam was worried: his wife was there, he told Loudoun. Faced with the general's insistence that it was all a ruse on the part of the French, Adam for the first time in his military career considered insubordination.

Having argued the better part of the day with Loudoun and his staff, he was crossing the parade area to his quarters, his mind in turmoil.

"Adam!"

He stopped still, then deliberately went on, ignoring his brother's call. About halfway across, Devin caught up to him.

"Look, I know you do not wish to speak with me, but I have come all the way from London, and—"

"Nay."

Adam jammed his hands in his coat pocket and continued walking silently. When Devin reached out to touch his shoulder, he shook him off. Undaunted, his brother fell into step beside him. "Do you think it easy for me to come? Do you think 'tis not hard to admit one's error?"

Adam merely hunched his shoulders and ignored him.

"I loved her—'tis all I can say for excuse—and after she left, I nearly went mad, you know. But then I knew I had to come, to tell you the fault was not hers, to beg you to take her back." When Adam merely increased his step, Devin caught at his sleeve. "*Will* you listen to me? I'd know she is well—that all is as well as can be. I'd have her forgiveness, and yours."

Adam spun around, swinging at the same time, catching him fully on the jaw. Devin staggered and fell backward.

"Damme if it ain't a mill!" someone shouted.

Devin scrambled to his feet, wiping the blood from his chin with the back of his hand. "All I ask—"

He got no further. Adam's blow doubled him over. Holding his stomach, Devin tried again. "I came to tell you—" This time, his brother's fist snapped his head back, putting him on the ground again.

Adam stood over him, his fists clenched, while a crowd gathered. "I don't want your lies, Dev!" he shouted angrily. He looked at those around him, muttering, " 'Tis over," and started to leave.

Devin caught him from behind, tackling him, and they both hit the dirt together, rolling and flailing. Robert Rogers, a small, wiry man, did his best to separate them, pulling Adam off. As Adam got to his feet, Devin punched him hard, knocking the wind out of him.

Panting, he gasped, "Think I cannot . . . take . . . you still?"

Throwing Rogers off, Adam crouched, circling him. "I know you cannot—you are not up to my weight anymore." He jabbed, forcing an opening; then his fist crashed into Devin's face. Though his brother's head turned and he staggered, he stayed on his feet.

"Why'd you do it, Dev?" Adam gibed. "Papa wasn't enough? You wanted my wife also?" He hit him again, before his brother could answer. "You would have left me nothing."

The battle was joined, and it was a bloody one, with first one man down, then the other. The crowd took sides quickly, most choosing the ranger captain, but some ready to see him brought down. Sean O'Donnell started betting on the outcome, offering odds to anyone willing to wager on the elegantly dressed swell. Surprisingly, he had some takers. Waving his fist of money, he shouted Adam on.

"Come on, your honor—you ain't letting a fancy fellow take you! Hit him! Aye, again!"

They slugged and wrestled and fought their way across the parade ground, giving and taking blows until their hands swelled and bled, and still it did not stop. Burton started to intervene at one point when it looked like Adam might stay down, but three men jumped on his shoulders, holding him back.

"Gor! They's killin' one another!" somebody exclaimed in the crowd. "Get him, Captain!"

When they reached the barrels of supplies that had been unloaded but minutes before, Adam threw Devin into a heavy keg with such force that it rolled. It looked like the fight was over.

"Had . . . enough?" Adam panted.

"Nay," Devin gasped.

"Don't . . . make me . . . kill you, Dev." When his brother did not answer, he turned again, this time to stagger away.

"I'm not . . . done . . . yet."

With an effort, Devin pushed the barrel, catching Adam in the back of the legs. He fell forward, his face in the muddy grass, and before he could rise, Devin was on his back.

"Will . . . you . . . listen?"

"Nay!"

Adam rolled over, turning the tables; then, holding his brother down, he punched him several times. This time, Burton and Rogers both managed to catch his arms.

"Captain, you're killin' him!"

Devin's face was almost unrecognizable. His eyes were swelling shut, his nose bleeding profusely, and there were cuts and bruises all over both cheeks. He looked up at Adam through slits.

"What'd you do . . . that . . . for?"

"It . . . made me . . . feel good," Adam gasped, gulping for air.

Devin tried to get his breath and wipe away the blood while Adam wiped his own face on the sleeve of his deerskin coat. He couldn't tell whose blood was all over him. Satisfied that it was over, Burton and Rogers released him. He collapsed to the ground and sat across from Devin.

"Just came to tell you it wasn't Sarah's fault." Devin spat blood on the ground. "Didn't want you to turn her away."

"How very . . . affecting," Adam managed.

"Love you both, you know."

"Nay."

"Aye."

" 'Tis over."

Thinking he meant Sarah, Devin struggled to sit up. "Nay, she did nothing. Adam, I—"

"Somebody clean him up." Adam reached to pull himself up by Burton's leg. "I don't want to see him."

"Some mill that was," O'Donnell told Devin as he tried to stand him. "I thought I'd lost my blunt. Didn't think a man like your honor'd last above two blows."

At that moment, one of Loudoun's aides-de-camp came outside, drawn by the shouting. He saw Adam and he barely recognized Devin for a gentleman. Jerking his head toward two regulars in the crowd, he nodded toward Adam.

"Arrest that man!"

" 'Tis Adam Hastings, sir!"

The colonel looked at Adam, taking in his bloodied buckskins contemptuously. "I said arrest the bloody savage!" he roared.

Devin pulled his torn coat about his shoulders and tried to stand alone. "I am Devin Hastings, Viscount Audley."

At first the officer was reluctant to believe him, but he knew enough to know Audley was connected to the paymaster of the forces. And by the looks of it, the coat had been an expensive one.

"My apologies, my lord," he offered stiffly. "The miscreant shall, of course, be punished."

Devin's mouth hurt as he grimaced. "He's my

brother.'' He wiped his nose again with the sleeve of his fine linen shirt. ''And 'twas not without provocation.''

Everyone stared. Ignoring them, Adam walked slowly to his quarters. He ought to have felt better, but he didn't.

A second, more urgent plea from Webb came on the heels of the first, reaching Loudoun three days after the first one. And with problems that he'd been encountering with the Louisburg venture, Loudoun wavered, telling Abercromby to send whatever troops and militia could be found to reinforce Forts Edward and William Henry. On 9 August he allowed Adam to leave, bearing the orders.

As Adam, Joanna, and his men packed provisions for the long journey, word spread that a large army of Indians, reported to number six thousand strong, from tribes as far west as the Ohio Valley, had poured down the Champlain Valley, possibly accompanied by as many as eight thousand French and Canadian regulars. And while no one was yet certain whether the assault was aimed at the west valley or toward the English settlements at Schenectady and Albany, if it were Albany, Forts William Henry and Edward lay between.

Even if he could commandeer a fishing boat to float them across to Maine, Adam knew he was going to be too late. And every time he could spare a thought, he prayed silently and fervently that Monro and Webb would hold the French at bay.

It had been selfishness on his part to send Sarah to William Henry, but he'd believed her safe enough, and he'd thought perhaps he could see her more often there. Now there was not a minute that passed that he did not curse himself, not a minute that he had to waste.

They moved as quickly and as unencumbered as possible, leaving at first light. Devin met them at the boat. He looked awful, even worse than Adam, and he walked as though every muscle ached.

''I heard. I'm sorry. I'd help,'' he said simply.

There was no time for bitter recrimination now. Adam nodded curtly. ''So am I—and you cannot.''

''I'd go.''

''Nay.''

"I am begging you."

"Nay. Even if I'd take you, you could not keep up. Good-bye, Dev. We've got to cross to St. John from Port Royal, then down to Maine. It'll be a hell of a walk."

They set out, walking at a steady pace, maintaining as good a rhythm as they could, given the terrain. After nearly an hour, O'Donnell happened to look back. "Gor! The bloody fool follows us, yer honor!"

"He'll stop."

But after more than two miles were passed, Burton caught up with Adam. "He's still there, sir."

Tired, stiff, sore, and worried sick, Adam felt his patience snap. He stopped, unshouldering the musket he carried, and before Joanna and his stunned men, he half-cocked it, slid open the pan while tearing a paper cartridge with his teeth, primed it, rammed the ball, the remaining powder, and the paper up the barrel.

"Stand aside."

"Yer honor!" O'Donnell gasped.

Adam fired, hitting a branch next to Devin, who dropped to the ground and rolled.

"Thank God yer honor missed!"

"I meant to."

He turned on his heel, threw the gun back on his shoulder, and went on. He had a good fortnight and more of forced march, and he knew it, so he had not the time to deal with Devin. By late afternoon they'd reached the Bay of Fundy. He stopped and leaned against his musket, every muscle of his battered body crying out. Burton brought him a cup of water.

"Do we camp here, sir?"

"Nay, we look for a boat."

"Sir, the sun—"

"Stays up late up here," he finished for Burton tersely.

"Ad-dam right," Joanna spoke up for the first time in hours. "No stop now."

"Beggin' yer honor's pardon, sir, but he's still a-comin'," O'Donnell marveled as Devin staggered into the clearing and collapsed.

"Told you . . . I could keep . . . up," he gasped.

His stockings were rent, his knee breeches soiled, and

his shoes gone. Joanna reached into her pack and drew out a pouch of bark balm, then moved to kneel over him. ''Man walk no further.''

Under Adam's orders, Ben Dixon went upcoast to a small fishing village, where he haggled boat passage from hostile Acadians who remained after the British ban. They were, he insisted, French scouts who reported on General Loudoun's troop movement. Having a hatred of the British, the outlaw fishermen agreed to take them across. The half-breed spoke the Pigden French of the Indians to convince them. When he returned with two of them, Adam addressed him in French, but the others were careful not to speak at all.

As they were about to board, Devin roused from where he'd fallen asleep on the ground. He struggled to stand, and Joanna had to help him.

''Beggin' yer honor's honor, but now what d' ye want to do wi' him?'' O'Donnell whispered, shaking his head. ''Yer cannot leave 'im here.''

Adam looked to where Devin, his face white and drawn beneath the bruises, appealed mutely. He knew that it was unlikely his brother could make it back to Halifax alone, and he knew the bitterness of the Acadians toward the British could be fatal if his identity were discovered. Nodding, he muttered low, ''Throw him in the boat, and tell him to spout whatever French he remembers.''

39

Sarah stared grimly at the paper before her, uncertain that her husband would ever read it. There were no messengers coming or going now—not since carters who'd attempted to leave were ambushed, and those who'd escaped returned to tell a grisly tale of death and tortured comrades. Then Monro had sent frantic messages to General Webb at Ford Edward, receiving first an ambiguous reply, then later none. And now it would seem the French had cut off the road to Fort Edward, leaving them no escape at all.

She poised her pen, composing her thoughts, then wrote:

Dearest Adam,

Despite the rumors that the French greatly outnumber us, we shall not give up hope. It is still possible that Webb is coming at this very time, but Monro does not seem to think 'tis so.

The enemy within is nearly as dreadful as that which sits outside, for daily there are those who succumb to smallpox and the bloody flux. And how are they to recover? In the event of a siege of any length, we shall have to ration food.

The war drums have beat all night, and 'tis said there are as many Indians as French opposing us. And between the constant drumbeats and the sound of muskets firing on our patrol boats, there is little sleep to be had. The men in the outside stockade return fire, hoping to slow the positioning of the cannon.

General Montcalm sent an envoy demanding we surrender this afternoon, but as our defenses have not yet been breached, Monro refuses. He has sent one last plea to Webb, which we have prayed will reach Fort Edward on the morrow.

As for myself, I am well, dearest heart, and I am trusting in God to reunite me safely with you. If it be not his will, then I must still be content with what I have had. Your love for me has been the sustenance of my life, the greatest joy of my existence. And for that, I humbly thank you.

She stopped, wondering if she ought to tell him of the other, then decided against it. If she perished, why should he mourn doubly? Instead, she waited for the ink to dry, then sealed her letter. She could not post it, but perhaps it would be found and delivered later. Or she'd give it to George Monro. In any event, she felt better for having written it.

General Webb had sixteen hundred soldiers at Fort Edward. Surely to God he would send them. But even then, would it be enough? Those few scouts who'd made it back told of a huge besieging army, half of which were screaming, painted Indians.

She laid her letter aside, unable to deny her fears. She was terrified—and so was everyone else. She'd overheard Mrs. Burks say that Monro had not surrendered because he feared Montcalm would be either incapable of or unwilling to control the savages. And, the Burks woman had added darkly, everyone knew the fate that awaited them.

Macabre tales gleaned from gossips and news accounts came to mind, tales of torture, mutilation, slow deaths too horrible to contemplate, and even cannibalism. And that was if one were killed. Others carried stories of females forced into the degradation of being used by the savages, carried off as slaves and concubines, sold and passed from one buck to another. It did not bear thinking about, and yet such thoughts crowded the mind of every person there.

Sarah tried to keep her sanity by remembering Adam, telling herself that she'd been so very fortunate thus far in her life, for had she not loved and been loved as few others? Had she not been granted more than most females, those poor creatures bartered on the marriage mart?

She sat there, trying to blot out the sound of the war drums, then finally made up her mind to do what she could to help. There was too much suffering for one to sit and wait. There were too many sick and dying in overflowing hospital tents. Resolutely she rose, determined to at least ease somebody's pain whilst she could.

The stench from the slaughteryard and the privies no longer gagged her as she walked between them. They had merely become a fact of life to be endured.

When she entered one of the tents, the post's lone surgeon, Miles Whitworth, looked up from where he crossed a dead soldier's hands over his breast. "The pox claims another," he muttered. " 'Tis the fourth this day." Then, seeing who she was, he shook his head. "Ought not to be here, Mistress Hastings."

"What difference is there? A fever is preferable to an Indian's knife, is it not?"

"Still, 'tis smallpox, mistress. If you would help, 'tis best to look to the others." He waved vaguely toward one of the other tents. "There's wounded from the patrols—can't catch shot, you know." Then, straightening up, he looked at her closely. "Thing is, don't know if 'tis meet for you to be doing anything. I got no time to revive you."

"I assure you I am not queasy in the least, sir."

Those were words she regretted, for as she entered the other tent with him, she was greeted with the moans and whimpers of men crowded together, their filthy bedding shared. And in the early-August heat, blood and excrement combined with putrifying wounds to make her gag.

"Told you how it was," Whitworth murmured unsympathetically. "Ain't tea with the commandant as you are used to."

Across the tent, hovering in the sweltering duskiness, was a lone nurse. And by the looks of it, she was ministering emotional rather than physical care. The doctor followed Sarah's gaze and nodded.

"Kidd. Poor bastard."

It was then that she saw that the man's head had been horribly mutilated: from one eyebrow upward, there was no skin—and no hair.

"Left for dead. Pierson found him—poor bastard crawled back."

She did not have to ask. He'd been scalped. Covering her mouth, she lunged for the tent flap, then stood outside, retching. When she was done, she went back.

"Not enough for you?" he asked brutally.

"I cannot simply sit and wait to die," she answered.

He looked at her sharply, then relented, nodding. "Aye. Well, there is not much to be done for most—a change of dressing here and there, a drink when they thirst, food for those who can still eat—and company. Aye," he sighed. "Like most of us, they fear to die alone."

"Where would you have me, then?"

He shrugged. "The choice is yours, I fear."

A soldier nearby cried out, then sobbed, lost in some terrified dream. The surgeon shook his head. "Laudanum, but it eases also, and I'd not withhold it."

"What happened?"

"What happened to all of them?'Tis either balls or knives or tomahawks—the result is the same." But he walked between the crush of pallets to stand at the boy's feet. "In his case, 'twas a ball—shattered his arm."

She looked to where the sheet flattened against his shoulder and knew he'd lost the limb. "I see. Well, then I shall sit with him, I think."

As the evening wore on, she found herself holding the boy's one hand, wiping his sweaty forehead as he cried out against demons she could not see. And as the tent grew darker, she sat there amongst them, rising from time to time to give this one or that a drink, but always returning to the boy with one arm. Finally, thinking to ease him, she began singing softly, first a lullaby, then an old Scottish air, and then every song she had ever known. And when she grew hoarse, one of the others turned over, begging for his favorite hymn.

The French cannon began firing on Saturday and continued for three days without respite. Candles and lamps burned all night Monday inside the fort as Monro met with his officers. Webb was not coming now, and they knew it. And Montcalm's guns were taking their toll on the timber walls, both at the fort itself and on the barricades beyond.

As dawn broke and the damage could be surveyed, it was obvious that William Henry could not survive. At seven o'clock Wednesday morning, August 10, 1757, they ran up the white flag. Then, under a French escort, Colonel Young was sent to propose the articles of capitulation to Montcalm.

When he returned, he reported that the French general

was most courteous, accepting all of Monro's conditions: they would be allowed to leave William Henry with honors of war, officers were to keep their baggage, and a detachment of French troops would escort them to Fort Edward. And in his presence, Montcalm had summoned more than forty tribal chiefs to witness and agree to the articles. And they had.

A collective sigh of relief went through the embattled fort. The first French troops moved in to occupy the fort itself about noon, allowing the English another day to gather their possessions. And Sarah, like everyone else, collected what she could, leaving behind her trunks in favor of one of her more comfortable muslin dresses and her best shawl.

And while she waited, she wrote again to Adam, expressing her relief that it was over.

Dearest Adam,

Words cannot express my happiness that we have survived without great loss of life. It has been terrible enough to see the suffering of those who have been wounded on patrol and whilst they held their defensive posts. But it is over.

And the Marquis de Montcalm came in person this afternoon to assure us of his care. It was a very good thing, for the Indians move about under the watchful eyes of the French, taking whatever should gain their fancy. Poor Mrs. Burks had to give one of them her petticoat when he noted the satin bows on the ruffle. It was quite her most prized thing.

As for myself, I have been kept in Monro's office, and a French guard has been posted over me. Colonel Young mentioned to Montcalm that my papa-in-law is an English earl, so their officers give me the deference due a lady.

I have seen the *coureurs de bois* and in comparison you look a complete gentleman. 'Tis difficult to tell them from the savages themselves, as they are as naked and painted as the Indians they lead. Your Reynaud was pointed out to me by Young, and I must say he appears quite fierce. Everyone fears him—even the French.

They tell us to destroy all brandy and rum, but I see no evidence of anyone doing so. Alas, I must go, for they are gathering our belongings for the trip tomorrow to Fort Edward.

She hastily stuffed her writing supplies into one cloth bag, taking care not to wad the paper. She would write again from Fort Edward. Until then, she did not intend to sleep—not when painted Indians kept coming to the windows. It was bad enough knowing that Reynaud knew who she was. Aye, that foolish Burks woman, when he would have entered Monro's quarters, had blurted out, "There's Captain Hastings' wife in there!" And she'd seen him stop, arrested, and heard him spit out the word "Bourget!"

But it did not matter, she told herself. She was, after all, under the protection of Montcalm's soldiers.

They filed out of the fort, to gather in the encampment behind the barricades, each person carrying whatever prized possessions he or she could save. Behind them, the Indians and *coureurs de bois* poured into the abandoned fort, screaming and yelling, taking anything that gained their fancy, without interference from anyone now.

The wounded and sick had been left inside, with French assurances that they would be sent to Fort Edward when wagons could be provided. Their dependents remained with them.

And there, behind the barricades, Sarah and the others heard the shrieks and pitiful screams as the Indians, upon finding little rum, fell upon the infirmary tents. One of the French priests who'd come into the barricade with them rushed back in an attempt to stop the carnage. He was too late. He returned, visibly shaken and covered with blood, carrying a crying baby he'd bought from an Abnaki about to kill it. Sarah, who understood French better than the others, heard him tell one of his countrymen he'd had to scalp a dead soldier himself, then trade the awful trophy for the babe. She bowed her head, knowing her one-armed soldier could not have survived.

Now French assurances seemed less comforting as they

waited through the night for dawn. They huddled together, twenty-two hundred men and perhaps one hundred women and children, praying and crying. And the French priest went amongst them, giving what comfort he could. The baby he'd saved squalled uncontrollably until finally one of the women gave it suck.

Montcalm came, trying to pacify both them and the Indians, rebuking those who'd broken his peace. A Canadian officer, called the General of the Indians, was charged with the safety of the English. He and Reynaud promptly quarreled, but Sarah could not understand what they said. Reynaud, she observed curiously, seldom spoke French, choosing instead the strangely rhythmic Indian dialect. But it was all of a piece, she supposed, for he did not seem to be a white man in anything but hair color anyway. And even his head had been shaved, leaving only a scalp lock in the center, from which hung a collection of multicolored beads. In the August heat, he was nearly naked, eschewing clothing in favor of a breechclout and moccasins. But almost every inch of bared skin was smeared with paint—circles and stripes and zigzags of color. At his waist hung a belt from which dripped several fresh scalps. The blood ran in rivulets down his legs.

So this was the man who'd shot her husband, who'd left the scar she'd caressed. She shuddered every time she looked at him, wondering what could have made a presumably civilized man do what he did. As he spoke with de la Corne, another *coureur,* he gestured with blood-stained hands. She could not understand how God could let a monster like that live. It was no wonder Adam had so bitterly regretted not capturing him.

Finally they were lined up for the march to Fort Edward, and with their escort of French soldiers, they slowly filed out from behind the barricade onto the rutted Lyman road. The Canadian militia moved out about one hundred yards in front of them, and French regulars brought up the rear.

It was like running some awful gauntlet, with Indians crowding in at the sides, snatching anything they wanted from the English. Sarah had a tortoiseshell comb pulled from her hair by a foul-smelling savage, and was thankful that was all he took. The woman behind her, who struggled to keep a gold necklace, was tomahawked on the spot.

Then an Abnaki chieftain began an ear-piercing cry that carried above the frightened whimpers of the women and children, and it was as though it were a signal. At the back of the column, Indians swarmed over the New Hampshiremen, hacking at them. The English prisoners dissolved in disorder, fleeing wildly, some into the forests, with Indians in pursuit.

"In the name of God," Montcalm shouted above the din, "if you must kill, kill me! Don't harm the English under my protection!"

The French, hearing the massacre in the back, abandoned the front, rushing back to stop the carnage. And as they ran past, Sarah screamed for help. A frightfully painted warrior, the one who'd taken her comb, snatched her by the hair, his knife upraised. Then, as the women around her pushed frantically to get away, Sarah thought her time to die had come. She kicked frantically, clawing at his upraised arm. He caught her at the waist, and, knife still in hand, carried her toward the trees.

She flailed and shouted, to no avail, then sank her teeth into his bear-greased skin. He dumped her on the ground and raised the knife again. This time, another stopped him, holding his wrist, speaking sharply. They exchanged angry words; then her captor jerked her up, pulling her deeper into the woods. Tree branches struck her, cutting her face, as he walked rapidly. She stumbled and struggled, dragged after him. From time to time he jerked her arm again, forcing her to scramble to keep her balance. Finally, as the sounds of the massacre behind them faded, she fell to her knees.

He said something she could not understand, but it was not friendly. "Go ahead—kill me!" she spat at him. "I'd rather die now than later!"

He sheathed his knife and slung her over his shoulder before weaving between the trees. Her hair caught, tangling in low branches, and still he walked. The macabre thought that it would give him less to hang at his belt went through her mind.

There was a crunching of branches behind them as someone walked rapidly, gaining on them. And for a moment, she dared to hope they were being pursued. Her hope was dashed immediately when she heard more of the strange dialect yelled out. Her captor turned around, his arm over her legs possessively.

From the sound of it, it was a hostile encounter. Reynaud emerged from the timber, and in his hands he carried several fresh scalps. He flung them at the feet of the man who held her. They exchanged angry words. Reynaud loosened his belt, from which perhaps a dozen grisly human trophies dangled, adding it to the others. Her captor shook his head and started off. She grabbed his scalp lock and pulled hard. For her effort, she was rewarded with a hard blow to her back.

Again Reynaud barked out something, and this time she was dumped unceremoniously, falling headfirst over his shoulder. Her head struck a tree trunk, and she thought she'd surely broken her neck. The *coureur* again threw his belt and scalps at the other man's feet. This time he added a beaded bracelet he wore, flinging it.

There were more angry words. Her captor bent to grasp her arm, and as he did, Reynaud's knife sank between his shoulder blades. The Indian's face wore a look of surprise; then his eyes grew vacant. As he fell, his blood spattered on Sarah's skirt.

Reminding herself that the Frenchman was, after all, born a Christian, she nonetheless shook violently. But she tried not to show her fear of him. Surely he'd been sent by Montcalm to save her.

"Thank you."

He withdrew his knife. Then, lifting her erstwhile captor's head by his scalp lock, pulling it back, he carved the scalp from his head, much as one would skin an animal. Wordlessly he added it to the others, tying them together by the hair. She couldn't help herself then—she leaned into a tree and was heartily sick, retching until there was nothing more. When he straightened up, she swallowed, trying to regain her dignity before this savage man.

"He wanted too much for you," he told her in accented English.

"My husband's family will pay a suitable ransom," she promised quickly. "Aye—if you will but take me back to Montcalm, I shall see you are paid."

He laughed harshly. "I want Bourget." When she did not appear to comprehend, he added clearly and distinctly, "Adam Hastings."

"But—"

"No man lies to Reynaud and lives."

"But he's not here. He's—"

"With Loudoun?" He shrugged. "No matter—he will come." His white teeth flashed, an odd contrast to his painted face. "Either way, Reynaud gets himself fine English lady—*non?*"

"I'd rather die."

A glint of humor flashed through his eyes. "You fling yourself from the parapet, eh? *Non*—I do not think so, *madame.*" He wiped his bloody knife on the grass before sheathing it. "Come, we go where we may be found."

She passed her tongue over suddenly dry lips. "Montcalm—"

"Montcalm is a gentleman and a fool! I'd have you walk, *madame,* but if you won't, I'll carry you—most unpleasantly." His eyes traveled over her bloodstained gown. "The dress would have to go."

She considered running, but it was as though he knew her thoughts. He shook his head. "You would get lost—unless you found one of my Abnaki—or a Huron perhaps."

"Adam won't come after me," she tried desperately.

"He will."

She was beaten and she knew it. But for the time being, she was alive. And that ought to count for something. Besides, she could cling to the hope that Adam would bring enough men to take Etienne Reynaud. Her chin came up.

"Very well, sir—I shall walk."

40

Rather than taking Sarah to Montreal with the with-drawing French Army, Reynaud headed westward until he was sure everyone had passed. Then he cut back toward Carillon, and Sarah dared to think he meant to take her there.

The first day had been the worst, for she'd not known what to expect of him. Every time they'd paused to rest, she'd feared he meant to ravish her—or worse. And that first night, when he'd curtly announced they'd sleep, she tried not to show her fear of him. But he'd made a small fire to ward off the insects, telling her to sit next to the smoke. Then he'd disappeared for what seemed an eternity. And in the distance, she'd heard a musket shot.

When he returned, he carried a dead muskrat, dropping it at her feet. His war paint was gone, and his scalp lock was wet, but the breechclout was still bloody. She looked at the dead animal.

His white teeth flashed again as his mouth twisted into a semblance of a smile. "English ladies do not cook?"

"Not that."

"Here there is no use for a woman who is merely pretty, *madame.*"

Her skin crawled as he said it, but she'd not give him the satisfaction of cowing her. "You will not kill me, I think."

He appeared to consider her dispassionately then, and she tried not to flinch as his eyes traveled over her dirty, stained dress. She was cut and bruised and tired unto death, but she managed to meet his gaze when it returned to her face.

"*Madame,* I could take you now, then leave your flesh for carrion."

"You forget the influence of my husband's father. There would be a protest that Vaudreuil could not ignore. There are yet rules of war between civilized nations, I think."

"Vaudreuil! Bah! The governor robs me!" He leaned closer, menacing her. "And do not think your rules of war apply here, *madame.*"

"I think I am worth more to you alive than dead."

"How much?"

Sarah mentally calculated a figure she thought might intrigue him. "My husband's family is wealthy, *monsieur*— I ought to be worth at least a thousand pounds to them." When he did not appear impressed, she added, "Mayhap more—when 'tis known I carry my husband's heir."

His hand closed over her throat, forcing her head backward, and for a moment she thought he meant to strangle her then and there. His face was but inches from hers and his expression was far from amorous.

"You lie! You think to cheat Reynaud with lies to save your hair!"

" 'Tis why I have had the sickness!" she gasped.

"Does Hastings know?"

"Aye," she lied.

He released her then, a look of triumph on his hard face. "Then he has two reasons to come."

"Aye."

He dropped to his haunches and began skinning the muskrat. She sank to the ground and leaned her head against a tree trunk. She was in the hands of a madman. The less she said to him, the less she chanced provoking his violent temper.

It was not until he had the muskrat gutted and spitted that he spoke again. "When your husband has been punished, *madame,* I will take you to Montreal and demand a ransom for you. And if Vaudreuil thinks to cheat me or to keep the money for himself, then Reynaud has himself a fine English lady—*non?*" He appeared amused by the notion. "The *seigneurs* content themselves with wives of wealth—why should not Reynaud?"

His eyes flicked over her again, more speculatively now, and once again she knew fear. "But you are scarce fat enough to warm my bones in winter—I'd have to leave you in Montreal." He set the spit over the fire, then sat, his legs crossed as Joanna's had been. "Still, 'tis a man's ability to display useless, expensive things that makes him envied."

"With a thousand pounds, sir, you could display anything you wanted."

He digested that slowly, savoring it, and she could see he was intrigued. "I could have a house and servants," he mused. "Two thousand pounds—one for you and one for the babe you carry—in English silver. French *livres* are nearly worthless here."

"My babe would be Westerfield's only grandson," she murmured, hoping to persuade him.

"Aye." He looked at her sharply. "And, *madame*, if it is proved you have lied to me, if there is no babe, I will kill you."

She felt tremendous relief wash over her. She'd given him a good enough reason to keep her alive. "There is definitely a babe."

Sarah's feet were so sore that she could scarce walk, and she had to discard her shoes because of the swelling, and yet he did not stop. Twigs, rocks, and exposed tree roots cut at her soles until she could only hobble after him through brush and over the high, hilly terrain. Cursing in a mixture of French and Indian dialect, he would pick her up impatiently each time she stumbled, then push her ahead of him, deeper into the thick forest.

It was hot. The August sun steamed them, and still he walked relentlessly as she stumbled and swatted at the mosquitoes that seemed to swarm over her. Finally she dropped and could not get up again. She looked up at him with eyes that betrayed her pain and fatigue.

"Kill me and be done," she said finally.

"English females!" he spat at her.

"I doubt your French ladies could do better," she retorted.

"We'll camp—'tis not far," he muttered, reaching for her arm. When he saw that she could not rise, he cursed again, but this time he lifted her, shouldering her weight. She sagged against him. Disgusted, he threw her over his shoulder much as the Indian had done. "Three thousand."

She hung over his back, smelling his strong sweat, knowing that her gown stank also, and wondered how he could stand it. But at least he was not encumbered with a dress and petticoats—at least he was far cooler than she was.

He threw her down on a riverbank, where she lay facedown, clinging to the cool grass and mud, heedless of how she must look. He stood over her, staring down at her. Then, without a word, he moved away to the river, where he waded in, cooling himself. When he came back, his cupped hands held water.

"Drink."

With an effort, she raised her body and drank gratefully, falling forward again when she was done. He rolled her over with his foot and knelt to remove her damp petticoats from her hot legs. The thought crossed her mind dimly that she was going to be ravished, and she no longer cared. Suddenly he lifted her, standing her up, supporting her; then he unlaced her gown, murmuring he was glad she did not wear a corset. He pulled the dress over her head as she fought feebly.

And then he threw her into the river. She hit with a splash, her filthy undershift billowing out, and went under. The water was cold. She came up thrashing wildly, then went under again. Panicked, she tried to disentangle herself from her shift, but she was choking as the water filled her mouth. She was drowning—he was drowning her.

He caught her from behind, lifting her head out of the water, but she fought frantically, flailing with her arms and legs, until his arm cut off her breath. He hauled her to shore and heaved her halfway onto the bank. Turning her over, he hit her back, and she vomited.

"You were supposed to swim!" he shouted.

"I cannot."

He pulled her head away from the mess she'd made, yanking her by the hair. He rolled her over again, and she knew the shift did not cover her. He stood up and reached for his knife. She must have looked frightened, for he shook his head.

"*Non,*" he said curtly. He walked to where her dress lay and, picking it up, cut at the hem, making a place to tear. Revived somewhat, she watched him pull off two large squares from her skirt and fold them. Abruptly he disappeared into the woods, returning in a short while with what appeared to be chunks of bark. Sitting cross-legged at her feet, he put them into his mouth and chewed, spitting the mess into his hands. He continued spitting until he had a palm filled with saliva and crushed bark. Then he applied the mess to her cracked and bleeding soles, rubbing it over them. He finished by taking the folded pieces of her skirt and tying them around her feet.

"Thank you," she managed gratefully.

"As you said, *madame*, you are worth too much to die."

After that, he moved more slowly, stopping to rest more often until at last they reached Carillon. She could only stare hopefully at the timbered stockade when she saw it, but he shook his head. "I dare not take you in there, *madame*. 'Tis too much risk."

"But—" She looked down at her nearly unrecognizable shift, thinking how much she wished for a bath, a comb, and clean clothes.

"I will return with supplies."

It was then that she realized he meant to leave her alone. It had been bad enough listening to the sounds of wolves and stepping over snakes, but to be alone with them—it did not bear thinking about.

"A fire surely—"

"*Non.*" He stood and listened intently, then carefully pursed his lips, imitating a bird. The woods grew strangely silent, and then there was an answering call. Satisfied, he looked down at her. "We were late."

They waited there for more than an hour as the sun rose higher in the sky. Finally, four Abnaki warriors, their war paint gone now, emerged from a thicket of trees. They spoke at length, taking turns showing their scalp belts, apparently bragging to each other. One moved to Sarah, eyeing her curiously, walking around where she sat.

Reynaud's voice barked sharply, and the fellow jumped back. Then it seemed that they all laughed. Sarah crossed her arms over her chest.

To her consternation, Reynaud prepared to leave. "Nay! I'd not stay . . . with them," she managed to say. "Please, I beg you will take me with you."

"That you may seek to escape?" he gibed. He shook his head. "They will not bother you, *madame*—they are Christians. And I have told them you are mine."

"Christians! They have massacred innocents!"

"Ah, but they were on the warpath then." He whirled around and said something to one of them.

The buck immediately nodded, drawing out a rosary from amongst the scalps that hung at his belt. Brandishing it, he began to chant, counting off the beads as he went. Reynaud deliberately made the sign of the cross over Sarah's face, telling her, "I am showing them you are Catholic—don't deny it."

After he left, she sat uncomfortably watching the Indians who watched her. Her mosquito bites itched miserably despite Reynaud's bark balm, and she scratched openly, telling herself that they were savages and could not mind. To her utter horror, the one who'd had the rosary came over to her, and while she sat as still as stone, too afraid to breathe, he touched the bites on her bared arm. He drew a pouch from around his neck and opened it. His dirty fingers dipped inside, drawing out a greasy substance, which he smeared over the itchy bumps.

She not only did not understand a word he said, she did not understand much of anything anymore. It made no sense to her that an Indian who called himself a Christian could torture and kill, and even less that the same savage could minister to her.

When he was done, he handed her his rosary. She knew not whether he wanted her to join him in praying prayers she did not know, or whether it was a gesture of comfort and he meant her to pray alone. Apparently it was the latter, for he returned to his fellows, leaving her there. From time to time he looked back at her.

She bent her head over the beads, lifting them one by one. She was not a Catholic, so she said the Lord's Prayer over each, murmuring softly under her breath. Oddly enough, the rote saying of the prayer was comforting. And she began making up her own prayers then for the smaller beads. *Please, dear God, deliver me. I pray you will keep my husband safe. I pray you will not let Reynaud kill him.*

Once, when she looked up, the Indian who'd given her the rosary nodded his approval. If she survived, these would be tales to tell the child she carried, tales too fantastic to be believed.

Reynaud returned at nightfall, carrying a heavy pack on his back. As he unrolled the blanket around it, he withdrew a cotton skirt and shirt, giving them to her. "Frenchwomen find these more useful here," he told her.

She actually felt a surge of gratitude for this madman. "Thank you."

He snorted derisively. "Make no mistake, *madame*, were it not for my desire for revenge on your husband—and the money—you'd already be dead." He stopped to say something to the others, then turned back to her. "I have sent word to Fort Edward that I have you."

She licked her lips uncomfortably. "For the ransom?"

"For your husband."

"And if he does not come?"

"He'll come. We go downshore to wait."

"Mayhap he will bring soldiers," she murmured hopefully.

"*Non.* Your General Webb will say he has none to spare. *Non.* He'll have to come for you alone."

"You cannot know that."

"The rangers, *madame*, are still with General Loudoun in Halifax." He appeared impressed with his own reasoning. "But your husband will come."

"Why do you care so much?"

"I told you—he lied to me. This time, *madame*, he will not keep his hair. This time Etienne Reynaud takes his soul."

41

They'd reached Fort Western in Maine after an unbelievably difficult trip that had taken them nine days over land and sea, through rugged, untamed country to the navigable head of the Kennebec River. Exhausted, Adam and his party had to stop there for two days. It was Devin, whose spirit, if not his body, wanted to go on.

"Nay, you have not seen the rest of it," Adam demurred. " 'Tis rougher from here to there."

But while they bathed and soaked their sore feet, word came into the fort by breathless courier that William Henry had fallen. And Fort Western's commanding officer, knowing that Adam was based at Ford Edward, allowed him to read that General Webb had surrendered on 10 August and there had been an ensuing massacre. Initial estimates indicated from four to six hundred killed and another three hundred missing and presumed either dead or on their way to Canada. Others had been escorted to Fort Edward by the French.

There was, of course, no way to know what had happened to Sarah—whether she'd been one of the fortunate survivors. Adam grimly handed the dispatch to his brother, and watched him whiten as he read.

"Is there no quicker way?" Devin demanded angrily.

"We can sail to Boston, debark there, and cut across

south of the Green Mountains by horse to the Hudson.
Even then 'twill take eight days at best.''

"It took us too long to get here."

"Aye."

"The other way?"

"Over the mountains."

"How long?"

Adam turned to Joanna, who'd been listening silently.
She shook her head. "Hills too big—move too slow."

"Passages?"

"No."

"Does she know?" Devin asked curiously.

"Her people are part of a great league, and they trade
with or dominate other tribes. Aye, she knows."

"Then 'tis Boston, isn't it? Well, at least we shall rest
sore feet."

They'd reached a tacit understanding between them,
and if they were not particularly friendly, they were polite. No mention had been made by either of them about
the missing letters, but the rift still existed beneath a
facade of civility. Only Joanna knew, and she said nothing.

It had been strained those first days, days when the
battered Devin lay in a heap in the fishing boat, mum-
bling out his pain in French, days when he'd dropped and
Burton had had to pick him up. But their growing anxiety
over Sarah had gradually shifted their animosity inward.

Devin had made the journey out of guilt, out of a need
to atone, but Adam, in the back of his mind, felt as
though Dev merely wished to see Sarah again. By mutual
consent, they did not speak of her except in terms of
general worry.

On 20 August, exactly nine days after the massacre at
William Henry, Adam and his party landed in Boston
amid rumors that twenty thousand Indians and fifteen
thousand French were on their way to Albany, and the
next targets would be New York and Philadelphia. Upper
New York was supposedly in a panic, with General Webb
giving orders that deserters afraid to fight the Indians
would be shot on sight. And several had been.

Not knowing truth from fact, they did not tarry in Boston any longer than it took for Devin to purchase eight horses. The greatest problem seemed to be making a banker there believe the tattered and frayed gentleman was indeed Viscount Audley.

Only Cook and Kirk complained, and then not too loudly. The rest of them pushed themselves for Adam's sake. Joanna reverted to her Indian ways and she and Ben Dixon fell to disputing the shortest route. In the end, he deferred to her. Iroquois women, Adam explained to Devin, had a great deal more influence than English ones.

They reached Albany to discover that the hordes of Indians and French had been but rumor, after all. Montcalm had withdrawn again to the north, being unable to proceed further for lack of supplies. The Indians had melted into the forests, presumably to return home to their council fires from Canada to Detroit.

If there was a macabre side to the tales of horror coming out of the awful massacre at William Henry, it was that one of the western tribes, angered at having been stopped from killing the English prisoners, had turned instead to the graveyard for their grisly trophies. They'd scalped corpses of those who'd died of smallpox. And there was not an Englishman to be found who did not hope they died of it.

William Johnson was down from Fort Johnson, his disgust of General Webb written on his face.

"He had fourteen hundred men, sir!" he told Adam. "Aye, and I brought him eight hundred more! But would he move? Would he relieve those poor bastards at William Henry? Nay, but he would not!"

"I'd heard you went to him," Adam said, grinning at the story he'd been told.

"Aye, I went. And took the Mohawks and Mohegans from Canajoharie—as well as what militia I could gather. He had to wait, he said! I could not even shame him into it!" Johnson's face grew red as he recalled the scene. "I told him my Mohawks had had word of Montcalm's movements from the Sault St. Louis Indians, but he discounted it. He said he did not wish to expose his troops! And my people saw no reason to fight if the English general would not—can you blame them for it?"

"No. I heard you challenged him by throwing down the gauntlet."

"The gauntlet!" Johnson snorted. "Aye, that and everything else. I swore by my halberd and tomahawk that we should prevail! I challenged him with my shirt and my leggings also—but d' you think he heeded me? Nay!"

Adam had already heard the story from Johnson's detractors in Boston, who'd told of his undressing piece by piece, throwing his clothing at Webb's feet. And his Indians had done likewise, leaving the general with a room filled with tomahawks and clothing.

"And so he failed."

"Aye, but by the dispatches you'd not know it—they read as though he was the bravest fellow on earth! Well, the Mohawks think him a woman!"

"Aye, and so do I." Abruptly Adam's manner changed. "I do not suppose the French have prepared a list of prisoners yet?"

"The ones taken to Montreal? Nay, but we expect it shortly. Most of those that lived have made it to Fort Edward, and the stories they have carried are not—"

"I know what stories they carry! I want to know how many made the trip to Montreal."

"Aye—your wife was there. I'd forgotten," Johnson murmured, shaking his head. "I wish I knew—I honest to God wish I knew. I have heard that some who were taken by the Indians have been taken to Canada—that Vaudreuil ransoms them. But"—Johnson sighed heavily—"until we have heard from the French, I'd discount it. It could well be much as the rumor of thirty-five thousand headed to Albany, you know."

"I know."

Devin, who'd been seated in a chair, his eyes closed from the fatigue of the trip, spoke up. "Is there a list of the prisoners who returned to Fort Edward?"

"They still straggle in. Some have hidden in the woods for a fortnight, waiting to be certain Montcalm's savages are gone. Nichus tells me some have found their way into his villages."

There was no need to ask further. If Johnson had

known, he would have told him what happened to Sarah.
He rose to leave.

"I thank you for what you tried to do, William."

Johnson looked past him to Devin. "I pray you will
carry the truth back to the War Office, my lord."

"I shall."

Later, when they were alone, Devin asked Adam,
"Does this mean you think she is taken?"

"I know not," Adam admitted wearily. "I only know
I've got to press on to Fort Edward and see if she is there.
I blame myself, you know," he said for the first time.
" 'Twas for my cursed convenience I sent her there. I
thought I could visit her more easily than in Albany. I
sent her to a hellhole, maybe to die, Dev."

At Fort Edward, it was all Adam could do to maintain
the slightest civility toward General Webb, who spent the
first five minutes justifying his inaction. Finally Devin
cut in impatiently.

"Be that as it may, sir, our paramount consideration
just now is Mistress Hastings. Is there any word?"

"Nay. I have inquired, of course, and . . ." Webb hesitated, uncertain whether to report such news to a man
with reputed ties to Pitt. "Well," he said finally, " 'twas
hurly-burly for a while, and naught can be known for
certain, but—"

"Out with it, man!" Adam snapped. " 'Tis not time
for shilly-shally now—is there word or not?"

"Aye and nay. 'Tis reported she was abducted by a
buck in war paint, but it cannot be certain. We have sent
patrols out since, and there's been no sign."

It was a confirmation of Adam's worst fear, one that
he'd not wanted to consider from the first. Devin saw him
stiffen, then sit as still as though he were stone.

"I'll not believe it," Devin said firmly. "Adam, I'll
not believe it until I see her body."

The eyes that Adam turned on him were haunted.
"Nay, Dev," he said softly. "Most of the time you cannot recognize those who die in their hands."

"I am sorry, Captain," General Webb murmured.

"Sorry! *Sorry?* You bloody craven bastard! You tell me

my wife may have been abducted by savages—when you were too weak to go to her aid—and you have the temerity to say you are *sorry?*"

"I shall discount that as your grief, Captain," Webb responded stiffly.

"Come on, Adam." Devin rose and placed a restraining hand on his brother's shoulder. "It is not over until we find her." His fingers closed, squeezing. "Come on."

"Oh, there are some letters, Captain. They were entrusted to Lieutenant Colonel Monro." Then, almost as an afterthought he added, "I am told that many of our people were taken to Canada by their Indian captors in hopes of their being paid for them. Perhaps your wife's value could not be overlooked."

"She could scarce tell a savage that," Adam retorted. "She would not speak the language."

Devin had to drag him out of Webb's office. "I don't like the bastard either, but if you are in stocks, you cannot look, can you?"

Adam shook him off. "If aught's happened to her, I cannot forgive him—or myself."

"You did not get your letters," his brother remembered suddenly. "Wait here, and I'll go back for them."

"Captain Hastings!"

Adam turned around to recognize one of the junior officers who'd been sent from Edward to William Henry.

"Hay."

"Aye."

"Were you there?"

There was no need to ask where. A cloud passed over Hay's face. "Aye. One of the sons of bitches was about to slit my throat when Montcalm himself stopped him." For proof, he cocked his head, showing an ugly and still-healing gash at his Adam's apple. "It was a bad business, Captain."

"Did you see my wife?"

Hay shook his head. "Everything happened too quickly—everybody was too intent on staying alive to worry about anyone else. They were slaughtering anything—babes, children, the sick."

"I know."

"Oh, one thing, though." Hay hesitated. "Bad time to bother you with nonsense, I know. And that damned bloody son of a bitch Reynaud—I wish you'd got him, Captain, I do." He squinted his eyes into the glare of the August sun. "Arrogant bastard. I saw him kill Captain Burke myself."

"What about Reynaud?" Adam asked tiredly, interrupting him.

"Didn't Webb give you his message?"

"Nay."

"Guess he must've forgotten—or thought it unimportant just now. Saw it come in myself."

"What?"

"Said to tell you that Madame Bourget is well."

It was as though Adam's blood had turned to ice. A cold chill stole over him, and his stomach knotted.

"You all right, Captain?"

"Aye," Adam answered hollowly.

Devin returned, Sarah's two letters in his hand, and stopped still at the expression on his brother's face. "I say—you look as though you'd seen a ghost."

"Etienne Reynaud has Sarah, Dev."

It was a trap and they all knew it. Only Devin did not realize the significance of Reynaud's message. He shook his head, unable to understand the consternation that spread among Joanna and the small band of rangers.

"Can you not just take it as what he says? That she is well and safe?"

"Nay, when he called her Monsieur Bourget's wife, 'tis a taunt meant for me," Adam replied.

"But why would he care? You are but one man out of many," Devin protested.

"I don't know." Adam ran his fingers tiredly through his hair, trying to think. "Mayhap 'tis because I deceived him—mayhap 'tis because I escaped. Who knows what Reynaud thinks? The man's mad. I have seen him, Dev. He's mad."

"And mayhap the word you sent to Albany cost him with his superiors," Burton offered.

"Send to Araghi, Tecawrongati," Joanna advised.

"Reynaud with Abnaki—Abnaki enemy to Onandaga. Jo-anh-ha tell Kanendeyah, he tell Araghi."

"If he finds himself outnumbered, he'll kill her." It was an almost dispassionate statement, but even as Adam said it, he knew it for the truth.

"He kill her when you come," Joanna decided. "She worth no more then."

The discussion went on far into the night, with Devin saying little. It was argued that they knew not where to find Reynaud, that he could be anywhere, and that Sarah might already be dead—that Reynaud's words might merely be a ruse to draw Adam out. Joanna was adamant: the Onandagas would help. If Adam were too late to save Sarah, they would at least punish Reynaud. She would not be unavenged. Besides, some of the scalps that hung at Reynaud's belt belonged to her people.

O'Donnell sided with her, saying the more who looked, the more likely they'd be to find the *coureur*. And what if Reynaud lay ready to ambush them? A few Onandagas would give them strength in numbers. Ben Dixon agreed, arguing that they could use one Indian's knowledge of another if Reynaud had his Abnaki with him.

Abruptly Joanna terminated the argument. Standing, she pointed to the belt at Adam's waist. "I carry to Kanendeyah."

He shook his head. " 'Tis but a plain knife belt."

Her gaze traveled around the room, looking for something of value, then settled on Lord Audley's shoe buckles. "Them."

"What the deuce . . . ?"

Then she appeared to consider his embroidered waist-coat. "That."

"Gifts," Adam muttered tersely. "She wants your shoes and vest."

"What? What the devil for?"

O'Donnell's face broke into a grin. "Gifts for Araghi."

"Wampum."

Adam shook his head. "We have no beads."

"She wants to give my waistcoat and shoes to a savage?" Devin demanded incredulously. But as he could see that they all waited expectantly, he stood to take them off. "If I live through this, Pitt will never believe the tale."

Joanna went from man to man, collecting anything she considered to be of value, until she had Adam's knife belt; O'Donnell's religious medal; Burton's grudgingly given tobacco pouch; Kirk's magnifying glass with which he read his small Bible at night; Cook's prized watch fob—the watch he kept, saying a savage could not tell time anyway; and Ben Dixon's linen spatterguards, which he never wore. When she was done, she sat down and removed the beads she wore, adding them to the pile.

"Jo-anh-ha carry war belt to Araghi," she announced simply.

Her skirts swished, an odd contrast to her bare feet, as she left the room. O'Donnell looked uneasy, then finally blurted out, " 'Tis too far, Captain."

"She knows the way."

When Joanna returned, her full petticoats and corsets were gone, as was her printed muslin gown. Devin stared at her, for her thick black hair hung straight over her bare breasts, and her deerskin skirt came just past her knees, meeting leggings that ended in worn moccasins on her feet. She tied the gifts she'd gathered into a fringed shawl.

"Meet . . ." She hesitated, looking at Adam questioningly. "Where we meet?"

"Lake George—where William Henry was burned."

She nodded. Turning to O'Donnell, she spoke in her own dialect. He reddened, then answered her haltingly in kind. A wide grin split Ben Dixon's face until she said something sharp to him. Hoisting the shawl over her bare shoulder, she made a small bobbing curtsy to them and was gone.

"God go with you, Joanna," Adam murmured under his breath.

42

"T is Reynaud, all right," Ben Dixon announced breathlessly, returning with his news.

"And Sarah . . . and my wife?" Adam asked anxiously.

"She is there—as are four Abnaki. Beyond that, I saw no others."

"Was she . . . ? I mean, did it appear as though he's harmed her?" He found it difficult to put his worst fears into words.

"She looked well, Captain. She ate with the others."

" 'Tis as though he wanted you to discover him," O'Donnell murmured.

"Aye."

It was dark, and the fog rose mistily over the lake's surface, giving it an eerie, unreal appearance. The night sounds of frogs and crickets and katydids echoed from the marshy shores. The scene was both beautiful and forbidding, but every man was too tense to note it.

"Well, what do we wait for?" Devin asked finally.

Ben Dixon's black eyes glittered in the darkness, reminding Adam's brother that he too was little more than a savage. "We wait for Woman Who Watches the Water to come," the half-breed told him.

"That could be days—they could be gone then."

Dixon looked up into the misty sky, listening. "Nay."

Burton, who had little liking for any Indian beyond Joanna, nonetheless paid him heed. "You think the Onandagas will be here by the morrow?"

"They are here."

"But I thought you said—"

"I said we wait for her to appear to us."

Devin hunched against a tree, feeling the damp night air in his bones. It wasn't cold, just damp. And he was tired, so tired he never thought to be rested again. His feet were callused inside his moccasins, and he was far dirtier than he'd ever been in his life. If his valet could see him now, he'd swoon, and when he revived, he'd give notice.

It was another world out here, a world he could not understand—a savage, beautiful place where social niceties simply did not exist. Here, rather than worrying about the next races at Newmarket or the cut of one's coat, one was more concerned with the means of one's dying. Life was far cheaper in the wilderness than in the bowels of London's slums. Men spoke almost dispassionately about how the Indians scalped and tortured, how they sometimes boiled and ate the flesh of their enemies.

Even the brother he'd rediscovered had been changed by it. Adam was harder, harsher, and more inclined to risk his life than Devin could have imagined. He shifted uncomfortably against the tree bark, thinking he too had changed in the short while he'd been here. Different things were important to him. The body he would take back to London would be far harder, the mind more attuned to different values. Throughout the punishing treks, he'd seen how one man's loyalty to another carried him through, how it bound him beyond the shallow friendships he knew.

And above all, this awful, awesome experience had been a catharsis, purging him of his unholy love for Sarah. Oh, he still loved her—he always would. But never again would he place such a cheap value on his brother's love for her. As he watched the terrible, impossible things Adam had endured for her sake, he was filled with an intense admiration, a pride in him. His father had been wrong: Adam was the better man.

He came out of his reverie with a start as Adam and the others reached for their muskets. His brother leaned closer, his expression grim.

"You may have to shoot a man, Dev—and before you think you can't, think how hard 'tis to die slowly."

Nodding, Devin slid open the pan to prime his gun. "I can do it."

"And do not try to reload if we are overrun. Use your bayonet."

They sat, silently alert, each man's thoughts his own. And through the mists came the sound of oars cutting into the water, softly, leisurely almost, and yet with a rhythm that distinguished it from an occasional fish breaking the surface.

Ben Dixon fixed his knife to the end of his musket, ready for a close encounter. Sean O'Donnell primed and wadded his musket, then took out his rosary. Despite the darkness, Devin could see his lips move. Thomas Kirk lifted his head heavenward for a moment, then returned his attention to his gun. Only Burton seemed strangely detached, sitting there with his musket across his knees, his knife blade flashing in his hand. Cook crouched like a lion ready to spring.

The first dugout came ashore about fifty yards north of them, followed by several more. They butted submerged logs, making a swooshing sound as the water swirled around them; then men debarked in silence.

Adam put his musket on full cock even as a shadowy figure moved up the shore. "Tecawrongati?" someone asked low.

Devin raised his gun to shoot, but Ben Dixon pushed it down. "That's not the girl," Devin hissed.

The figure took shape—a tall Indian. Adam stepped forward. "Kanendeyah."

He wore Devin's waistcoat above his breechclout and Adam's belt at his waist. His face was painted. "Your enemy is my enemy, Tecawrongati. I took your war belt."

"Where is Joanna?" O'Donnell asked.

"Jo-anh-ha watch Reynaud across water." Kanendeyah turned as other Indians joined him. "I bring eight warriors from Araghi. Raydewahti would have Reynaud's scalp for his belt and eat Reynaud's heart."

"Surely—" Devin opened his mouth and closed it quickly as a squat, ugly Indian stepped forward.

The Onandaga spoke to Adam in a rush of syllables, gesturing as he spoke. O'Donnell, who'd been trying to follow what he said, leaned closer to Devin, whispering, "He seeks vengeance for his cousin's mother—I think."

"I don't know how you would know," Devin muttered dryly.

"I am learning the language of Joanna."

"Where did the other one learn to speak English?"

"Barclay. He's a Christian Indian."

"Tell him that he can have any of them but Reynaud," Adam ordered Kanendeyah. "Reynaud is mine."

They spoke in council without the customary fire, until it was decided to attempt surprising Reynaud and his Abnaki whilst they slept. Then Ben Dixon and one of the Onandagas disappeared into one of the dugout canoes.

"Try to sleep until they come back," Adam advised Devin.

But none of them slept; the tension was too great. Adam fidgeted and moved restlessly between the shore and their dark camp. Cook and Kirk and Burton spoke low, whilst O'Donnell wrote in his diary, his head bent beneath a cover to shelter his candle. The seven Indians sat apart, painting each other's faces in the darkness. Devin killed mosquitoes and cursed under his breath. But the underlying thought was that it was too easy, too obvious—surely they must be falling into Reynaud's trap. And if they were, it was possible that none of them would walk away.

And yet to a man the rangers had volunteered when Adam had received Webb's permission to look for his wife. Not that Webb could have denied him—not when the general knew that most of the men at Fort Edward blamed him for the massacre. Adam had initially asked only for Ben Dixon, but the others who'd been with him for so long refused to stay behind, saying they wanted to go.

To them, Devin was their vulnerability—no one wanted to take responsibility for a man who had influence in the paymaster's office—and no one wanted to be placed in a position of having to rely on a London gentleman. They'd very much have preferred that Adam had left him behind.

Cook had gone so far as to suggest that Devin ought to remain with the boats. And Devin knew what they thought of him. He sat, silently listening to the others talk.

"Ain't ye about got that girl bought?" Burton asked Kirk. "Seems to me she's coming dear t' ye."

"I sent the last money yesterday," Kirk admitted. "Going home to Catty when this is done."

"Ain't no woman worth six months of a man's pay," Cook decided. "None of 'em."

"Jacob worked seven years for Rachel, and when he got her sister instead, he worked another seven," the Scot reminded him.

"Oeeee! This Catty must be some figure of a female!"

"She is." Abruptly Kirk left them and moved to sit beside Devin. Taking out his knife, he honed it for what must have been the tenth time. "You ever see fighting, my lord? Action in Europe?"

"Nay."

"It ain't hard—kill before you are killed. Don't wait to see if you ought to do it—he ain't going to think twice about you."

"I'll try to remember that."

Kirk threw the knife into a nearby tree, where it stood at attention, its blade buried more than an inch. Rising, he retrieved it to examine the edge.

"You got to, my lord."

"What d' ye write, Sean?" Burton asked, looking to the boy.

"Words."

Twigs crackled on the forest floor behind them, sending every man scrambling for his musket. Then they relaxed. It was Woman Who Watches the Water. O'Donnell put his paper away and moved to make her a place.

"You saw Ben?"

"He come."

"Did you see Reynaud?" Adam asked, coming back from the shore.

She nodded.

"But only four Abnaki?"

She nodded again.

''Do you think there are more of them in the woods?''

''I think Fox wait for you. Other Abnaki gone with . . .'' she searched for a word, turning to Sean, then remembered it. ''Abnaki take prisoners.''

Raydewahti said something to her, speaking rapidly, and she responded, shaking her head. Burton looked at O'Donnell, mouthing the words ''What did he say?''

''He wanted to know if she would boil Reynaud for him.''

''And what did she say?'' Cook asked, curious now.

''She said she was a Christian—he'll have to cook him himself.'' O'Donnell turned to Devin, grinning. ''Sometimes they think it gives them power to eat their enemies.''

''And you would let him?'' Devin asked incredulously.

''I do not care what he has done, he is still a man.''

''Nay.'' It was Adam who spoke then. ''Tell him that we have need of Reynaud. Reynaud is mine—he'll have to take one of the others.''

Somewhere out in the darkness, a wolf gave its lonely cry. And shortly thereafter it was answered. Joanna looked at Kanendeyah, then at Adam.

''Dixon call.''

It was the signal that he and one Onandaga had positioned themselves about Reynaud's camp, where, if the need arose, they could cut off the Frenchman's escape.

''Do you think he knows how many come?'' Devin whispered to the boy.

It was Joanna who answered. ''He not know Onandaga here,'' she insisted. ''He have fire.''

The orders were issued tersely: Joanna and the Indians would take to their canoes, paddling toward Reynaud's camp, and at dawn's first light they would destroy his boats. When they were on fire, Kanendeyah would give the war cry, signaling Adam and the rangers to rush the camp.

Adam opened his pack and drew out two grenades, handing them to Joanna. He spoke slowly and distinctly, then waited for O'Donnell to repeat as best he could in the Onandaga language. Kanendeyah then repeated the instructions back to him in English to make certain all understood.

"If something goes wrong, if we are overpowered and taken prisoner, I want you to light this"—he pointed to the fuse that came out of the ball—"and throw it behind them. It will make much noise, and you can attack. Use both if you have to. Can you do it?"

Joanna tested the weight of one in her hand and shook her head. "Kanendeyah."

"All right. I don't care who throws them, but they must be thrown carefully." Again he spoke slowly and distinctly. "They will blow everything into pieces—everything."

The ranger party was to follow the shoreline on foot to Reynaud's portage, relying on the Indians to surprise and divert the *coureur*. Adam handed his last grenade to Burton, who was the biggest and therefore able to lob it the furthest.

"Ben and I and Kirk will proceed to within a few yards of the camp whilst 'tis still dark and wait for the sun to rise. We will circle around and come in from the north side. You will set off the grenade some twenty yards south when you hear Kanendeyah's war cry. Then we rush the camp, hoping they shoot in the wrong direction."

"Where would you have me?" Devin wanted to know.

There was a pregnant pause as Adam considered his brother. So much had not been said between them, not since the day they'd fought, and yet they'd shared the hardships of the trail. A crooked smile turned down a corner of Adam's mouth.

"Papa ought to have one of us come home to him whole, don't you think?"

"Aye, but I cannot stand and wait. Let me have the grenade. Burton will be of more use overpowering them."

It was a risk, and they both knew it—as did Joanna. There was a reason grenadiers were the elite corps: mistakes killed.

"This is not bowls, Dev."

"I know."

"Do you really think you can do it?"

"Aye."

Adam exhaled slowly, then nodded to Burton. "Give him the grenade. Dev, you've got to keep it dry."

"I will."

"And for God's sake, throw it when the fuse is lit— don't wait until it burns too low. And if it does not go off, don't go after it."

"Eeeeeeeeee-neeeeeeeee-yaaaaaahhhhhhhh!"

The penetrating cry cut through the rosy mists, echoing over the water until it died, and then it was repeated, joined by seven others with bloodcurdling intensity.

Devin knelt, sparking his flint, holding it close to the treated wick, watching it sputter with an almost morbid fascination. It caught, hissing as the flame licked downward. He stood and heaved it with all his might in the direction Adam had indicated.

A lone Abnaki sentry raised his musket, aiming toward where it fell, but never fired. Ben Dixon's knife flashed, there was a surprised gurgle, and the Indian toppled, his lifeblood spreading in a pool beneath his face.

The others came awake in an instant, thinking they'd been discovered by a war party. Naked, they grasped their knives and tomahawks, and crouched ready to spring. Sarah scrambled in terror for the woods, but before she reached them, the grenade exploded, sending shrapnel into the trees and raining smoke and hot metal.

She screamed, then stumbled the other way. Devin, seeing her, gave up his cover to run after her. An Abnaki raised his tomahawk to throw, but Kirk's knife caught him cleanly in the back. The surprised Indian fell facedown into the ashes of last night's fire.

"Oh, thank God you are come!" Sarah choked, forgetting all that had passed between her and Adam's brother before. "Adam?"

"Over there."

The remaining two Abnaki sprinted for the boats, only to discover they were afire in the water, and Onandagas were coming ashore. Turning back, they tried to run for the woods. Cook raised his musket, firing, but he missed. One of the Indians caught him just below the breastbone, bringing up the knife with deadly accuracy. "God, Captain—they got Cook!" O'Donnell yelled.

Joanna, seeing Cook fall, forgot her instructions. She lit one of the grenades and threw it toward a fleeing Indian. The Abnaki lost his arm in the explosion, and the squat Onandaga moved in for the kill.

The smoke from the gunpowder was overpowering. Coughing, Reynaud fought his way through the smoke, lunging for Sarah. Devin, who'd never fought a battle in his life, found himself facing the *coureur*. He moved between Reynaud and Sarah, his musket poised to fire.

"Reynaud!" Adam shouted.

The Frenchman whirled, snarling and throwing his tomahawk at the same time. Adam ducked, and the sharpened ax whirred past his ear so closely that he felt it. Reynaud, his eyes glittering strangely, drew his knife and circled Adam. Devin pulled the trigger, but the ball went wide.

"Before I go, I take you with me, English!" the *coureur* taunted, brandishing the blade.

"Kill me, and Raydewahti eats your heart, Etienne. Surrender, and I'll take you back with me," Adam offered.

For answer, Reynaud lunged. The knife blade sliced through Adam's sleeve. O'Donnell started toward them, but Kanendeyah blocked his way.

"Tecawrongati's medicine is good."

"You cannot let them fight!" Sarah cried, turning to Devin, clutching at his arms. "Stop them! Devin, stop them!"

"Stay out of it, Dev!"

Devin pulled Sarah back, trying to hold her while she struggled frantically. "I cannot, Sarah—I cannot."

"He'll kill Adam—he'll kill him, Dev."

"Mayhap not."

Adam crouched, holding his knife low, taunting in turn. "I don't think you can take me, Etienne. You don't have a dozen Indians to protect you now," he said softly.

"I have eaten the hearts of better men!" Reynaud spat back.

"You cannot leave here alive if I die."

"I should have killed the woman," the Frenchman admitted, moving warily, looking for an opening.

"But you didn't—and now 'tis too late." Adam lifted his knife slightly, as though he beckoned with it. "Come, 'tis now or not at all."

The encounter had not played out as Reynaud had planned. In his madness, he'd thought it would be only the Englishmen who'd come for Sarah Hastings. He'd not counted on Indians as blood-hungry as he. He'd not thought any still loyal to England.

The *coureur*'s thoughts could be seen in his face, and Adam pressed his advantage. "Which is it to be, *monsieur?* You take me, they kill you. I'd not care for the odds either way."

Reynaud knew it was the truth, but he also knew that if he surrendered, Adam would have to fight his Onandagas to keep him alive. That perverse thought appealed to him more than anything. And if he got back to Fort Edward, he would be treated as a prisoner of war, possibly to be ransomed. Besides, there was always the chance that one of his Abnaki had escaped to Carillon, and his countrymen would not want him to tell what he knew. Either way, Adam Hastings would have to fight to keep him.

His knife flashed in his palm; then he held it out hilt-first. And his white teeth contrasted with his dark skin as he smiled. "Now, English, I leave it to you to see me safely to Fort Edward." His eyes mocked Adam. "If you can."

But it was Sean O'Donnell who took his knife. Adam had already turned to Sarah, holding out his arms to her. Devin let her go, and she threw herself into her husband's embrace, crying and laughing at the same time. Words of relief tumbled out.

"I knew you'd come—I knew it. He thought you'd come alone again, or just with rangers. But I prayed, Adam . . . I *prayed*, and . . . Oh, God, Adam, but I am glad 'tis over!"

"Shhhhh. 'Tis done now," he murmured, folding her against him. "Gad, Sarah, but I had such a fright—I thought I'd lost you again." His hands moved over her back, smoothing the rough blouse she wore. "Never again, love—never again will I leave you." He laid his cheek against her hair, whispering, "I'll send to Loudoun asking to be relieved."

It was over quickly, the whole assault lasting perhaps ten minutes. And there were three Abnaki dead and one escaped. Kirk moved to tie Reynaud's hands behind his back, and his eyes were streaming tears. "Cook's dead, sir—one of the bloody savages got 'im." As he looped the thongs around the Frenchman's wrists, he gave his hand a brutal twist. "I hope they hang this bloody bastard."

Adam slid his arm to Sarah's shoulder, turning around to see Ben Dixon closing his fallen comrade's eyes, and he felt a painful tightening in his own chest. For a moment he considered executing Reynaud, but then reason prevailed. His own eyes burning with unshed tears, he shook his head.

"Nay, he knows too much. I'd send him to Abercromby."

"It makes no difference, English!" Reynaud spat at him hatefully. "You can take Reynaud, but you have lost. We took Oswego and William Henry—the Six Nations will fight for the craven English no more! Not even Warraghiyagey can make them fight for women!"

"Sean, put a rag in his mouth," Adam ordered curtly. "He babbles too much. Burton!"

"Aye, sir!"

"Order the woods searched! I'd not have any live to carry the tale."

"Aye, sir!"

But even as he gave the order, Raydewahti returned, bearing a proof it was already done. He dropped the scalp lock when he saw Reynaud's hands behind his back. Drawing his knife, he leapt over one of the bodies at the *coureur.* Thrusting Sarah away, Adam caught him before he could plunge the blade into the prisoner, and he and Burton held him back.

An argument broke out between the Onandagas, with Kanendeyah and Joanna gesturing and speaking vehemently to the ugly little man. The other Indians joined in, some on one side, some on the other. Finally they apparently reached an agreement of sorts, for Raydewahti still grumbled, but Joanna told Adam, "Let him go, Tecawrongati."

After Adam released him, the squat man proceeded to carry his bloody trophy away. "He is unhappy that his cousin is not avenged," Kanendeyah explained. "He'd wanted to carry proof home to the mother."

"Tell him . . ." Adam was so tired he could scarce stand now, his body giving in to the awful tension he'd felt for so long. He passed a weary hand over his eyes, seeing the mists take on a rosy hue. "Tell him that I will send a wampum belt to him for the service he's done me this day."

The message was conveyed, but still there was much discontent, and it was spreading. O'Donnell, who'd been listening carefully, leaned to whisper, "Captain, they say they are eight and we are six."

Joanna spoke to them again, her voice rising like a fishwife's. When she was done, she moved to stand with Adam. Kanendeyah hesitated, then followed her. Slowly, three of the others came also. Shouting epithets, four collected their scalps and hurriedly left the camp.

"What do we do now, Captain?" Burton wanted to know. "What if they come back to get him?"

"We bury Mr. Cook and try to sleep until 'tis dark again. Then we move as quickly as we can back to Fort Edward. Hopefully, we get him there before anyone from Carillon knows he is taken."

Joanna met Sarah's eyes. "We come for Tecawrongati wife," she said simply.

She left briefly, and going to the dugout canoe she'd come in, drew out her English blanket. Walking up to Sean O'Donnell, she held it out to him. His face reddened, but he nodded. Joanna faced Adam.

"Ad-dam buy Jo-anh-ha bride dress."

His arm still tightly around Sarah's shoulders, Adam nodded. "After today, I'd buy you anything you asked. Woman Who Watches the Water watches well."

A smile broke across the girl's face. "Tecawrongati not named wrong"—she looked at O'Donnell again, as was her habit when she searched for a word—"neither," she finished triumphantly.

43

Etienne Reynaud lay facing the sleeping rangers, his expression intent. Slowly, his face not betraying the pain he felt, his hands worked loose the leather thongs that bound him; then he relaxed and waited, biding his time until someone made the mistake of coming too close. Of the eleven other people still left in camp, two stood sentinel, one by the water, the other facing the woods.

Hours passed and still he waited. Burton shook Ben Dixon awake, and they exchanged places, the half-breed moving to his post. Adam rolled over at the sound, and eased his numb arm from beneath Sarah's head. As dirty and unkempt as she was, she was still lovely to him. He looked to Reynaud, who feigned sleep; then he relaxed.

It was over, and over easily. He was the most fortunate of men, for he had his wife safely in his arms again. And when he got back to Fort Edward, he was going to consider his duty done. Sarah had endured too much to have to bid farewell to him again. His eyes traveled to the thick woods, and he felt a pang of regret. He'd lived too long in them, he supposed, for he'd grown to love the rugged beauty of this land, and for some time now he'd wanted to stay. But he'd not ask it of Sarah—not after this. She deserved the life of an English lady.

The sun reached its zenith overhead, and the woods were alive with the hum of cicadas competing with Burton's snores. And for the first time in weeks, Adam Hastings felt good: he'd proved himself, and was no longer merely Westerfield's younger son. He'd led men who gave their loyalty based on a man's worth rather than rank or name. And above all, he had the love of Sarah Spender. Nay, he had nothing left to prove.

Rising carefully so he would not wake her, he left Sarah to relieve himself in the woods. And as he passed, he did not note the flicker of Etienne Reynaud's eyelids.

Reynaud waited until he was out of earshot, then spoke low. "I'd have water."

Joanna rolled to her knees, reaching for the knife she kept in her leggings. "Fox not need water," she said contemptuously. "Fox drink later."

"I thirst."

She shook her head.

"A cup is all I ask."

She said something insulting in her own tongue, and lay down again. The Onandagas grunted and turned their backs on him. For a moment he considered lunging for a weapon, but he knew he had not a chance that way. What he had to have was a hostage.

Devin, awakened by the sounds, rose and stretched, his bones aching from the damp ground. He was filthy and covered with insect bites because he'd not wanted to use the nasty stuff the others wore. And his week's growth of dark beard itched like the very devil. He scratched at his leg beneath his breeches, thinking perhaps he ought to bathe. Bending over, he retrieved the knife Adam had given him. It would be a poor substitute for a razor, but he could no longer stand the beard.

"A drink, *monsieur*," Reynaud asked hopefully.

Joanna shook her head. "Let him suffer."

Devin shrugged. "There seems to be little enough harm." He moved to where he kept his cup, then poured from his water bottle.

Reynaud had wanted the woman, but an English lord unused to fighting was perhaps as good. He struggled to sit, his hands still behind him, holding the leather thongs in place. And as Devin came closer, cup in hand, Reynaud's whole body was tautly poised, ready to move.

He had to be quick, to take the Englishman before any could come to his aid.

He sprang, knocking the cup from Devin's hand and sliding his arm around Devin's neck, choking him. Joanna was there in an instant, but she stopped in her tracks. Devin's face was darkening.

"Get back," Reynaud snarled, reaching around to take Devin's knife. He eased his hold, bringing the knife to rest at the Englishman's throat. "Call for aid and he dies."

For the briefest moment Devin considered struggling, but knew one slip could well be his last. Reynaud stepped backward, pulling Devin with him.

"The canoe."

They were all awake now, but it was too late. Sarah, white-faced, scrambled to her feet. "Nay! Adam! He has Dev! *Monsieur*, I beg of you—'tis Lord Audley you take!"

"Non." His grin was unpleasant. "Not this time, *madame.*"

One of the Onandagas moved forward, his own knife flashing in the sun, menacing Reynaud as though he were considering rushing him. For answer, the Frenchman pressed his blade beneath Devin's chin. A trickle of blood flowed and disappeared into his shirt. Kanendeyah looked to Joanna and she shook her head. He barked an order to the other Indian, who fell back silently.

Adam came out of the woods to the sight of Reynaud holding his brother, and fear gripped his insides. Gloating, the *coureur* shouted at him, "We are not done yet, Bourget! Tell them if they move, he dies!"

"He's worth more alive, Etienne!" he shouted back.

"Reynaud is not such a fool twice, *monsieur!*" He moved sideways, murmuring against Devin's ear, "The boat—walk to the canoe."

"Turn him loose and we'll not pursue!" Adam called out.

"Non!"

"I'll ransom him at Carillon!"

"Non!"

"One thousand pounds, Etienne!"

Reynaud shook his head.

"Vaudreuil will have your head if he is harmed!"

"Vaudreuil does not rule Reynaud! But we waste time. Tell them to move away from the canoes! And throw away the weapons!"

There was no question that Reynaud would not hesitate to kill Devin Hastings, and they all knew it. But they knew also that as soon as he had no use for him, the *coureur* would do it anyway. And if he got him to an Abnaki village first, the English lord would die slowly.

Nonetheless, Adam moved back, throwing down his knife and signaling the rest to do the same. Sarah watched mutely as Reynaud pushed Devin toward the shore, always keeping his prisoner's body between them.

It was Joanna who spoke first. "We can follow."

"Nay."

"Adam . . ." The appeal in Sarah's eyes was unmistakable.

"Burton . . ." He spoke under his breath to the big man as he moved between him and Reynaud, obscuring the Frenchman's line of vision. "Give me your musket. When I tell you, pass it to me."

"Captain—"

"Just do it. Yours is closest."

Reynaud and Devin had reached the boat portage, and the *coureur* said something to Devin that none of them could hear. Devin stepped forward toward the canoe, Reynaud's arm still over his shoulder, the knife at his chest.

"Now, Burton—for God's sake, *now!*"

" 'Tis primed, Captain," the big man told him, thrusting it at him. "But you cannot—"

The *coureur*'s hand came up, and the knife flashed.

"*Adieu,* Bourget!"

In that moment Devin jerked forward, and Adam fired. Devin and Reynaud hit the water together, turning over the canoe between them. Adam dropped the gun and ran for the water with two Indians on his heels. Blood spread over the surface, and Adam feared the source.

"It took you bloody long enough," his brother sputtered, surfacing. "The bastard said he'd slit my throat before your eyes. I tried to jump."

Relief washing over him, Adam waded in to reach for Devin. His arms closed around him, enveloping him in a bear hug, and tears flowed freely.

"Papa would never forgive me if anything happened to you, Dev."

"Gor! You got 'im clean, Captain!" O'Donnell breathed in awe.

Joanna turned to Sarah proudly. "Tecawrongati named right—no?" Then, realizing the other woman did not understand, she explained, "Tecawrongati—He Who Dares."

Reynaud lay facedown in the water, blood pouring from a wound over his ear. "You might have missed him, you know," Devin told him, grinning.

"I had to try." Adam nodded to Kanendeyah. "Take his scalp to Raydewahti and tell him I have avenged his cousin."

They came out of the water arm in arm, their clothes soaked and streaked with Etienne Reynaud's blood. Sarah was on the sloping shore waiting, her love showing on her face. Adam broke away, slogging through the marshy mud to reach her.

"Is he . . . ?"

"Aye. 'Tis over, Sarah," he murmured, wrapping wet arms around her, holding her close. " 'Tis time to go home, love. To England—if you wish it."

And Devin, despite the pain he still felt when he saw them together, managed to smile at her. "Can you still find it in your heart to call your first son Devin?"

Much of the bitterness she felt toward him dissolved as she met her husband's eyes. "Aye. I think I can, Dev. You may stand godfather in February."

For a moment her news escaped Adam. Then he stared, stunned.

"Aye." She smiled mistily at him. "And I do not think we have to worry about this one, do you? If he can survive all that has befallen me, he ought to be a sturdy little fellow."

44

Albany, New York: September 27, 1757

The room was dark save for the single candle on the table where he wrote. Behind him, Sarah slept deeply in the postered bed, her tangled hair spreading over his pillow. Every time he looked at her, he felt that his cup truly did runneth over. He had so much now: Sarah, Devin, the coming babe. Somehow it did not seem right for a man to be so happy, and yet he was.

There remained but one thing to make his life complete. He reread the words he'd so carefully written, knowing that as imperfect as they were, they came from his heart.

Dear Papa,

By the time this reaches your hand, Devin will have already given you news of us in person. He left yesterday from here, and with good winds and fair weather, he should be in England ere All Saints' Day.

Do not let Dev make you believe me a hero, for I am not. He owes his skin as much to his jump as to my musket. But I shall let him tell you of the awful adventure we shared, though I counsel you to consider that his view of it is decidedly prejudiced by his love for me.

He dipped the pen and went on.

Sarah is well, far better than you could imagine after what she has suffered. But the physicians here advise against travel until after she is safely delivered of either Devin Charles or Mary Emma.

There, he'd said that much at least. But somehow that did not go far enough. He took a deep breath, then added:

There are so many things I'd say to you, Papa, so many words I'd call back if I could. For my sake and yours, I'd begin anew with you. Perhaps 'tis the notion that I may have a son, or perhaps 'tis Sarah, but I'd have us be the family that we can be rather than the strangers we are.

He stopped again, rereading it, thinking how terribly inadequate it was, how terribly maudlin. But love was so very difficult to express, particularly to one's father.

We shall return to England next summer. I'd once hoped to stay here, for I find the land magnificent and the people to my liking. But Sarah, I think, longs for England. I'd buy Spender's Hill for her, sir, and refurbish it as it ought to be.

I pray you will convey my regards to Mama, and to Meg and Chatwick also. Aye, and tell Devin I shall call him to book for his fulsome praise. Abercromby will not allow me to refuse my promotion, though I have made it plain I do not intend to stay beyond my tour of duty here.

Last, I ask your blessing, Papa.

Adam Hastings,
Major, Thirty-fifth Foot

He'd been so intent on composing what he could only count a woefully inadequate letter to his father, that he'd not heard Sarah rise and come up behind him. It was not until she leaned forward to read and her hair brushed against him that he knew she was there. His hand came up to clasp hers against his shoulder.

"I finally wrote to him."

" 'Twas time."

"Aye. 'Tis the first time, you know."

"But not the last, I think."

He leaned back, resting his head against her still-flat stomach, savoring the faint scent of lavender on the nightrail she wore. "You've given me much—more than I ever deserved," he said quietly.

She stood very still, her eyes on the pages before him. "You've made one mistake, Adam," she murmured above his shoulder. "I don't want you to buy Spender's Hill." Then, as he twisted his head to look up at her, she smiled. "Aye. I'd visit England and the Park, but I'd not stay there."

"But—"

"I'd rear my son where 'tis what he does rather than to whom he is born that matters," she said softly, paraphrasing what he'd once written to her. "Oh, and I'd have you give your papa my love also."

Before he could answer her, she leaned closer, sliding her hands into his thick hair, massaging his scalp the way he liked.

"Aye, Sarah—'tis the second-best feeling I know."

"For the first you will have to come back to bed."

About the Author

Anita Mills lives in Kansas City, Missouri, with her husband, four children, sister, and seven cats in a restored turn of the century house. A former English and history teacher, she has turned a lifelong passion for both into a writing career.

PASSION RIDES THE PAST

☐ **SAN ANTONIO by Sara Orwig.** In America's turbulent old West, Luke Danby, a tough lawman, vowed to exact revenge upon the vicious bandit who had raided a wagon train years ago and murdered his mother. But his plans turned to dust when Luke met his enemy's beautiful daughter Catalina . . .
(401158—$4.50)

☐ **THE GATHERING OF THE WINDS by June Lund Shiplett.** Texas in the 1830s where three passionately determined women sought love's fiery fulfillment— Teffin Dante, who was helplessly drawn to the forbidden man, Blythe Kolter, who lost her innocence in the arms of a lover she could neither resist nor trust, and Catalina de Leon, who could not stop her body from responding to the man she wanted to hate. Three women . . . three burning paths of desire. . . .
(157117—$4.50)

☐ **SONG OF THE BAYOU by Elinor Lynley.** Beautiful Susannah fell in love with the bold, handsome planter who was her father's enemy. But their forbidden love kindled into wildfire passion in the sultry Cajun nights.
(401980—$4.95)

☐ **TO LOVE A ROGUE by Valerie Sherwood.** Raile Cameron, a renegade gun-runner, lovingly rescues the sensuous and charming Lorraine London from indentured servitude in Revolutionary America. Lorraine fights his wild and teasing embraces, as they sail the stormy Caribbean seas, until finally she surrenders to fiery passion.
(401778—$4.95)

☐ **WINDS OF BETRAYAL by June Lund Shiplett.** She was caught between two passionate men—and her own wild desire. Beautiful Lizette Kolter deeply loves her husband Bain Kolter, but the strong and virile free-booter, Sancho de Cordoba, seeks revenge on Bain by making her his prisoner of love. She was one man's lawful wife, but another's lawless desire.
(150376—$3.95)

**Buy them at your local
bookstore or use coupon
on next page for ordering.**